ARTURO ENRIQUEZ AT VANTAGE POINT VISUAL STUDIOS, INC.

BENJAMIN ALIRE SÁENZ is the author of *In Perfect Light* and *The House of Forgetting*, as well as several children's books. He won the American Book Award for his collection of poems *Calendar of Dust*. A former priest, Sáenz teaches creative writing at the University of Texas at El Paso.

Praise for
CARRY ME LIKE WATER

"Sentimental and ferocious, upsetting and tender, firmly magic-realist yet utterly modern. . . . Sáenz is a writer with greatness in him."
— LUIS URREA, *San Diego Union-Tribune*

"Sáenz is wonderful, at times magnificent."
— *Baltimore Sun*

"A powerful and poetic novel. . . . Demonstrates a perceptive novelist's knowledge of those deeper, interior rhythms that somehow propel us, at times in beauty and at times in tortured patterns, across the surface of the earth."
— *Albuquerque Journal*

"*Carry Me Like Water* is indeed a lovely first novel, rich in its sense of place and people. Benjamin Alire Sáenz has a fine talent."
— LARRY MCMURTRY, author of *Terms of Endearment*

"*Carry Me Like Water* is full of love, loathing, and a cacophony of characters which people the spiritual airwaves from El Paso to California. Certainly a new perspective in the Chicano novel."
— RUDOLFO ANAYA, author of *Bless Me, Ultima*

"Benjamin Sáenz has created, with his first novel, a work of unique and endearing quality. The characters and conflicts appear as in no other book I've read. There is a well-wrought and compelling ferment of pain and pathos, the familiar with the supernatural, the poetic with plot."
— LUIS J. RODRIGUEZ,
author of *Always Running* and *Music of the Mill*

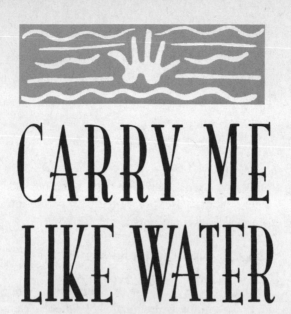

CARRY ME LIKE WATER

A Novel

BENJAMIN ALIRE SÁENZ

An Imprint of HarperCollins*Publishers*

Patricia, eres la lluvia en mi desierto.

I give you this book—every word—for you.

Quotations from Karen Fiser's poetry are from *Words Like Fate and Pain*. Copyright © 1992 by Karen Fiser. Reprinted with permission of Zoland Books, Inc., Cambridge, Massachusetts.

This book was originally published in 1995 by Hyperion Books.

HarperCollins books may be purchased for educational, business, or sales promotional use. For information, please write: Special Markets Department, HarperCollins Publishers, 10 East 53rd Street, New York, NY 10022.

First HarperPerennial edition published 1996.

First Rayo edition published 2005.

Designed by Gloria Adelson/Lulu Graphics

ISBN 10: 0-06-083133-2
ISBN 13: 978-0-06-083133-2

05 06 07 08 09 RRD 10 9 8 7 6 5 4 3 2 1

ACKNOWLEDGMENTS

Teachers come in all forms and I have had many teachers who have taught me to accept my sorrows when they came my way and to look for ways to articulate hope whenever possible. This book could not have been written without my association with people who taught me that despair is absolutely unacceptable: Karen Fiser, Larry Schmidt, Denise Levertov, the late Arturo Islas (who saw me through the genesis of this book, but did not live to see it to completion), Barbara DuMond and Virginia Navarro (who always believed), Ricardo Aguilar, Teresa Melendez, The Lannan Foundation, Scott Michaelson, Bobby and Lee Byrd, The Before Columbus Foundation, Mary Helen Clarke, Denise Chávez, and Daniel Murphy.

I owe a debt of gratitude to Alison Deming, a gifted writer and friend, who urged me to send my manuscript to her agent. Jennie McDonald is one of the finest professionals I have ever had the pleasure of working with. A fine editor in her own right, she is literate, intelligent, and possesses a relentless sense of humor.

Yvonne Murphy at Hyperion was an astute and enthusiastic editor. Her faith in this book made its publication possible. At every step she was supportive and respectful of my work without losing her critical acumen.

And to Patricia Macias—the woman with whom I share my home, my life, my body, my mind, and my heart—I give my deepest thanks. She saw me through this book, and still she is smiling. Amor, te adoro. Eres un milagro.

Finally, I would like to express my gratitude to my parents, my brothers and sisters, and the people of El Paso/Juárez—my people.

We divide time into years. We divide years into seasons. We have different names for every river, a different name for every ocean on the earth. But the river does not know that we have named it ''river''—it does not know that it is separate from the waters that call ''Come.'' Come. The river has flowed a thousand years. It is spring, and the river is spilling with the newness of winter's melted snow, each season flowing into each season. River, I have been gone a long time. I am returning to your waters. River, I've come back. River, I'm afraid. Carry me like water.

ONE DAY THEY WOKE AND FOUND THEIR LIVES HAD CHANGED

WHEN DIEGO WOKE from his uneasy sleep he was lost and sad and far away from himself. It was as if he was always fighting to belong to his body, to himself, to the city he lived in. Always he woke wondering where he was, his body hurting. Naked, he felt himself trembling as though he were a tree whose leaves were being torn away by a wind that had no respect for anything that was green and growing, anything weaker than itself. His limbs felt bare and raw—exposed. In the winter, he shook from the cold; in the summer, from the heat. He took one hand and grabbed the other to make it stop shaking. He wanted to yell, scream, clear his lungs of everything that had settled inside him. When he woke, he always had the feeling he had taken into his lungs a million grains of sand—had swallowed all of the desert's dust in one night, dust that cut into him like tiny pieces of crushed glass. His lungs and throat felt dry as ashes. He was drought itself. He was dust.

Diego wanted to wake and see a morning made of more than gray, colorless shadows that stood motionless and large before a dawn that was dark despite the rising sun. He wanted to wake to a good and perfect sun that would lift all the gray and dirt from the air. *He wanted to wake*. Instead, he remained in his noiseless trap of a body, caught in the endless repetitions that were his life. He always woke before the light entered the room. It was always the same, always black: black as his coffee, black as his eyes, black as his hair and the dreams he tried to keep himself from remembering. He stared at his hands, his legs, his feet. He stared at himself until he remembered where he was: in this room, this room where he slept but which would never be his. He felt himself to be always on the edge of homelessness. He could not talk. He could not hear. But in the morning that was all he ever thought of doing.

 2

She is in a church. She thinks, "I do not know this place; I have never been here before." Her gaze moves from one statue to another, each statue as unfamiliar as the one before. She focuses on the stained glass windows, and notices that the room is lit with a sun that is either setting or rising. She has lost her sense of time, her sense of direction, her sense of place. Looking for something familiar, she finds herself staring at a statue of some kind of virgin whose heart is pierced with a sword. Her blood looks real; her skin looks real, is real. She looks into the face of the suffering virgin that has come to life and recognizes the face. "Mama," she whispers. "Mama!" She moves toward the woman and reaches out to comfort her, to touch her. But she cannot touch: She finds she has no hands; she has no body. She does not exist. A sense of panic fills her. She is lost. Perhaps, she thinks to herself, she is dead. Her panic is real, her love for the woman is real. She sees. She knows that she sees. But where is my body? She begins to weep. She thinks she will weep forever. But then, she hears a man's voice, deep, masculine, strong and steady. "You are more than your body," the man says. "Do not weep for your body." She looks up. The man—blond and strong—as beautiful a man as she has ever seen, smiles at her. She loves him and knows if she could regain her body her heart would bleed like the virgin's, but she knows, too, that she does not need a body to love him. Still, she wants to touch him. She gazes into his eyes and finds a pain not unlike the virgin's.

5

She searches his thoughts for his name, but when she is close to finding it, the man disappears. She begins to weep again. She wants to hug herself, but there is nothing to hug. "I will weep forever, I will, I will, I will . . ."

Lizzie woke, startled and tired from her dream. "I will, I will," she kept repeating. I will what? she wondered. She felt sad and disturbed, but she could not remember her dream. She felt a stranger to her body, and somehow it was useless and heavy, a burden. She pressed her fingers against her temples and tried to make herself remember her dream. The harder she tried to remember, the more frustrated she became. She sat up on her bed and stood on the firm floor. "It's just a damn dream," she yelled. "What's a dream?" She wondered why she was yelling.

 **3**

HELEN STOOD in front of the gas stove and watched the pasta as it danced around in the boiling water. The golden drops of olive oil swirled around like fish darting in a pond. She was mesmerized by the common occurrence—the physical fact—as if she was seeing something new and rare, as if she was observing some kind of miracle. She combed her hair out of her face and smelled her hands. Garlic. She sliced a lemon sitting in the fruit bowl, squeezed the juice into her palm, and rubbed it into her hands as if it were lotion. She liked the tingling, slightly burning sensation on her skin. She put her hands over the steam of boiling pasta, and smelled her hands again. Lately, she had taken to smelling herself—but not only herself—everything. It seemed that the world smelled so close, so intimate, so green like a freshly cut lawn or freshly picked cilantro. She breathed in the steam coming from the boiling water and held it in her lungs. She looked down at her large belly, and touched it. She ran her hand over the smooth, well-worn cotton fabric that pressed against her stomach as if she were rubbing a crystal ball, as if that ball were telling her the future would be as good and as warm as the evening sun that was filling her house with light.

She whispered to her baby, only half-aware she was speaking: "Does baby like pasta?" she asked. "Daddy loves it; Mama loves it; does baby love it, too?" She smiled as she rubbed herself. Her friend Elizabeth had told her she would never have a firm stomach again. "I never had one to begin with." She laughed softly, then slowly her laughter filled the air until there were more echoes of her voice in the room than there were rays of light. She stood glowing in the kitchen. She felt like one of the haloed madonnas in the paintings she'd seen in her husband's art books—well-framed, well-kept, protected from all harm. So this is joy, she thought, so this is what it's like. And though she knew this rush of pure adrenaline would melt as fast as snow on the desert, she felt complete and happy. When the sharp feeling passed, she did not feel sad and disappointed. She felt as if she had just had sex with Eddie, his warmth still inside her. She bit into the pasta. "Perfect," she said. Just as she walked over to the sink to rinse the strands of thin pasta, she heard her husband walk through the front door. He stood in the doorway to the kitchen and stared at her. He did not say anything, but she saw the look on his face. Neither of them spoke. She looked at him and tilted her head: She became a camera photographing his face, swallowing him into her lens. She was drawn in by his fair skin, dark hazel eyes, the slight wrinkles around his eyes, his thick dark hair he could never tame. She knew everything about his face, every detail, how it was warm and soft when he laughed, how it could look like unbreakable glass when he was distant or sad, almost turning his eyes to blue, or how his mouth stretched to distortion when he was silent and angry. She could read every change of mood. "Te adoro," she wanted to say, but she could not bring herself to speak to him in that language. She looked up at him from where she was standing. He said nothing. They studied each other for a few moments. "Pasta," he finally said. "Pasta," she repeated. *So this is joy.*

 **4**

On Second Street, in El Segundo barrio, someone spray-painted the back wall of a convenience store and turned it into a political statement: LA POLICIA ASESINA A CHICANOS. Another sign, near Sacred Heart Church, read: MUERTE A LA MIGRA. No one ever attempted to erase those pieces of graffiti. They had been there for as long as Diego could remember. He thought of them as landmarks, murals, voices of the people who lived there. The spontaneous letters on the wall were as solid as his hands, full of a brash humor that bordered on violence; loud, bright, but weak like the light of a waning moon. For all their energy those words on the wall were harmless—they went unread by the people they were aimed at. Written in Spanish, they could not be read by the gringo.

Diego read the signs every day as he walked home from work in the evening. The harsh sun did not seem to dull the fluorescent letters on the walls. He read them, all of them, even the ones with obscure messages he couldn't understand. Sometimes the signs did not seem to him to be written in Spanish at all, but in a private language to which he had no access. He knew that behind the scrawled hieroglyphics there were worlds that he could not picture in his head. But some of the writings were clean and simple messages proclaiming perfect meanings. He smiled at the ones that promised undying love between people he would never know: MONICA Y RUBEN

9

FOREVER. He wondered about the people who were bold enough to write public messages of love or daring enough to proclaim their political manifestos to a world that did not read, a world that did not acknowledge that the senders of the messages existed, breathed, lived—and hated. He smiled—laughed about these writers—and on his more cynical days he thought them all to be exhibitionists.

He had never known his father, and he was no longer curious about him. When he was young he had asked his mother about him, and all she said was that he had died. He had never believed her, but it didn't matter since he would always be out of his reach—a man banished from his world for reasons he could not guess. His mother died when he was nineteen, though he did not remember anything about her death. But he did not want to dig deep into himself for that memory. Though he was only vaguely aware of it, he wanted to keep a part of who he was hidden from himself.

He no longer remembered what his sister looked like. She was five years older than he, and was alive somewhere, but he did not know the name of the city where she was now living. He had not seen her since their mother's funeral, and neither one of them had made any effort to make contact. "What for?" he thought. He knew she didn't like to see him. He had always seen in her eyes a need to run, as if somehow just the sight of him placed her in a prison where she could not escape. He was her jailer and keeper without even wanting to be. Perhaps, Diego thought, she was tired of being his voice. Perhaps she felt that because he could not speak that it was *she* who was obliged to be his lips, his voice. Or maybe she no longer wanted to be anybody's sister—especially his. Diego had never understood her feelings. She had never spoken to him about what she felt, but he knew they shared an anger, and a common beginning—a beginning that mattered, *that had to matter*. But it was useless to think of bonds and beginnings because she had left him. *Goddamnit, she had left him.* Well then, Diego was glad of it, glad because he was free of her stupidity. He remembered vaguely how once he had written her a note and flung it in her face: "I am not a vegetable. I'm your brother." She had ripped up the note in front of him. He had written about her in his journal, and all he had written was: "She was lost listening to the sound of her own voice.

She was too proud of having one." After that, he'd stopped keeping a journal. He burned it.

He no longer lived in El Segundo barrio. He had moved to the other side of downtown, to a place called Sunset Heights. It overlooked Juárez and the tall buildings of El Paso. Sunset Heights: He had liked the name when he first moved in. It was poetic, he thought, but after ten years of living here, the place had lost its poetry—if it had ever had any. He had heard there was a tunnel from Juárez that went under the river and into one of the houses in the neighborhood. The tunnel was supposed to have been used to smuggle guns, money, and ammunition into Mexico during the revolution. Diego had tried to find the tunnel when he first moved here, but he had stopped looking for it. He did not believe the tunnel had ever existed, and he could not remember why he had ever wanted to find it.

Sunset Heights was now nothing more than a once-fancy neighborhood with a false name, a place whose fame had faded. Most of the buildings still had the markings of wealth, but the façades resembled aging gravestones whose details had long since been erased by time and the wind and the rain. The rich had built their homes here at the turn of the century, but their money had been taken to other neighborhoods farther away from the traffic of downtown, farther away from the river, farther away from the illegal comings and goings of the border. All that was left were the rotting skeletons that had long since been turned into apartments like the one he lived in. The handcrafted, carved wood was buried beneath layer upon layer of cheap enamel. Diego often tried to reshape the houses in his mind. He thought of sanding off the cheap paint—freeing the wood. But it was too much work to sand it off. And like the wood, the inhabitants of Sunset Heights had been covered with too many layers of cheap paint. At least the rich could not take the view of the Juárez mountains with them. Often he felt as if the mountains had eyes and ears and lips. They heard everything. He wrote in his journal that if the mountains had legs they would run from the things they witnessed. But they *did not* have legs, so for now, the mountains were his. Unlike his sister, they would not abandon him.

The part of Upson Street where he lived faced the freeway and

11

the remodeled train station that was newly equipped with automatic chimes. The new chimes rang out on Sundays and holidays—he read people's lips at the place where he worked, lips talking about the new chimes. What was that to him who could not hear? And anyway, the station was still empty. It would become a restaurant or a clothes boutique, and it would be emptier than before.

But always the Juárez mountains were there with houses going right up to the point where they grew too steep. Always they were there to give him comfort. He imagined they held him close—closer than his mother had held him when he was a little boy. At night, the lights from the houses looked like vigil lights surrounding a darkened altar. He had read somewhere that the Empress Carlota's jewels were buried there. Maximilian had given them to her as a sign of enduring fidelity. Diego suspected Maximilian had not been the kind of man capable of being faithful to anyone but himself. He had read all about Maximilian and about Mexico, but he liked the legends he read on people's lips better than the things he read in the books of the library. He liked to think about the legend and he dreamed of going into the mountains to find them. "Imagine me finding all those jewels—diamonds, gold, silver, eagles made of emeralds and rubies—every color in the world locked in a chest, imagine how they would look, how they would glitter, how they would feel in my hands." The thoughts occupied him, but they passed—they were just thoughts that swept like clouds across the desert all summer long without dropping any rain. "I'll never own Carlota's jewels. I'll never even go looking for them." He knew the mountains were dangerous. He remembered his mother had warned him that the foothills were filled with thieves. "They'll kill you," she had admonished, "they're poor, they're hungry, and they're mean. They have nothing better to do than sit around all day and sharpen their knives." He had explored all of Juárez, but he had never explored the mountains because his mother's voice had kept him afraid. And even if he knew where to go looking for the jewels, he would find himself with a knife in his back. Still, he thought, returning again to his fantasy, it wasn't a bad way to die. He would die holding the jewels in his hands, the smell of Carlota all around him, the smell of her madness. So what if someone stuck a knife in him? No one would ever find his body. His funeral would be cheap.

Every day he crossed downtown—every day he followed the same steps, the usual journey into El Segundo barrio. He worked at a place called Vicky's Bar, a bright blue square building which was not really a bar and not really a restaurant. It wasn't much of anything. It was small and sat on a corner—and once it had been a house. After that it had been a bakery. It had been many other things after that; it had had many lives. The building had been so many things that no one remembered who had built it, why they had built it. It was a plain, worn-out ugly building; it should have been abandoned, should have been left to rot in the heat. Diego wondered why people insisted on resurrecting what should have been left for dead. His boss had painted the building a bright blue: "To match the color of the sky," he said. "It looks cheap," Diego thought. The paint drew attention to the sadness of the building—it wore the paint in the same way an old woman wore a tight dress: There was something sad and embarrassing about it. "It's a happy color," his boss's wife had told him once. People will want to walk in here, and have fun." He had stared at her handwritten note for a long time. He had nodded and written "yes" below her handwriting. But Diego could not imagine anyone having fun in this dark and over–air-conditioned hellhole. Happy people didn't walk into Vicky's. Every morning, when he walked through the doors, he could smell all of the building's former lives mixed with cigarette smoke, pine cleaner, and stale beer. The smells were thick and rancid, and they only served to darken the already dull lighting.

He was the cook, janitor, waiter—the only full-time worker. He got paid three dollars an hour—cash—and he was happy to make that much since the money paid for his one-room apartment, and the food was free. But he had never liked crossing the downtown area at five in the morning. It was no more than a thirty-minute walk, but the journey frightened him, and not even the rosary in his pocket, which he fingered as he walked, could lift the fear that fell over him. Walking through El Paso at that hour was like walking through an ancient, empty church, a church he often dreamed about. The church was so large that the more he walked toward

13

the altar, the farther away it got—and in the dream he never reached the front of the church, but he could not turn back because the entrance had disappeared behind him. He woke from the dream knowing he had been swallowed up by a God who was not good. He knew there was a good God somewhere—but *that* God was not in his dream; that God did not visit the place where he worked; that God did not comfort him in the night. At five o'clock in the morning the streets of El Paso were like the endless rows of pews in that church. As he walked through the streets, he tried to shut out the dream because he knew the dream was real and he was living it in those awful sunless moments. But even when he was successful in chasing the dream away, it was only replaced by the feeling that he was being followed by shadows who were as noiseless as he was. It was an odd feeling—almost evil—and he had come to the conclusion that dark, empty streets were paths that the spirits reserved for themselves, and who reluctantly gave up their territories to the living—the living who were too arrogant to believe in anything but themselves.

He arrived at his job around five-thirty and prepared all the food for the coming day. He cooked the beans, the meat for the tacos, the red chile, the rice, and the soup. The special of the day was always the same: red enchiladas with rice and beans. Nothing ever happened at work. He didn't like to think about his job very much because he knew his thoughts would change nothing.

Some of the people who came in to eat seemed nice enough. Others weren't nice at all and he read their lips as they complained about the food and the prices, the weather and their wives, their jobs and this city. There were days when he wanted to throw all the plates of food at every person who walked in. Other days he felt as though he might break in half or cry, and the floor beneath him did not feel hard but soft, so soft that it seemed unable to support his thoughts, his steps, his weight. On those days he walked carefully as if he were walking on leaves he was afraid of crushing. On those days his boss would stare at him and shake his head. Diego would smile at him, and his boss would walk away.

He needed more sun, he thought. Once, he considered asking his boss to install a window in the kitchen, but he knew the answer would be "no," so sometimes he pretended there were rays of light where he worked. In his mind he worked on a painting. He pictured his hands with a brush in them, and colors as deep as the Juárez mountains in the evening. The canvas was as big as a wall, and the canvas was full of nothing but soft green grass, full of the dawn, full of a light that emanated from a sun that would not burn his skin.

 5

Helen softly squeezed an avocado marked with an or-ganic label at the Whole Foods Market. An older woman stared at her and smiled. "You know my daughter's pregnant, too," she said. "After three miscarriages, she finally had a boy. And now, she's about to have her second." Helen had heard a hundred little confessions everywhere she went since the day she started showing. At first she had hated the fact that complete strangers would walk up to her and editorialize about morning sickness, about cravings, about miscarriages, about the night they knew they conceived, about the names they might label their forthcoming progeny, the pluses and minuses of knowing a child's sex before birth, remedies for swollen feet, and the best positions to sleep in after the sixth month. But now she enjoyed the small kindnesses, the unthreatening intimacies, the quiet words that made her feel cared for, made her feel like an indispensable part of the world that suddenly appeared to be inexplicably kind. As she waited in line at the checkout, she turned over a bottle of wine in her hand. She imagined how it would taste. It had been almost seven months since she touched any alcohol or drank any caffeine. *Her baby was going to be perfect.* But the feeling that she'd like to sit alone and enjoy a glass of wine entered her and took control of her body. The urge to drink wine was solid as a stone hitting her in the stomach. She pictured herself in her back-yard, at ease, sipping on a glass of wine in the late afternoon, the sun reflecting in her eyes, reflecting off the glass. She felt the wine on her tongue, and swallowed the cool, rich, red, silky liquid. The taste of the wine was so real it held her motionless—then let her go like a strong hand loosening its grasp. She found herself standing in an aisle of the grocery store.

The sack girl asked her if she needed help lifting the groceries into her car. "No," she said—then changed her mind. "Yes, that would be very helpful." Another sacker, walking in the opposite direction, spoke to the young girl who was pushing Helen's basket. "¡Que muchachita tan linda!" he said. "Te quiero." He said it half seriously, half in jest. Helen pretended not to hear, and, for an instant—perhaps for only a second—her face filled with an over-powering shame, a shame she could not hide even from herself, a shame that was as much a part of her as the color of her eyes, or the thickness of her hair, or the soft lilt in her voice, a shame that was part of a memory larger than the baby in her body, louder than her laughter, a shame that could never deliberately be remembered or recalled but could never be forgotten, a shame she kept success-fully hidden most of her waking moments, a shame that kept re-turning to her like a boomerang or a bad penny or a bad dream. In that instant, that shame rose to her face and she felt the entire world could see it, could see the ugliness of her life, could see she did not deserve a husband or a baby or the house she lived in. She wanted to cover herself and be protected; she wanted to weep because she felt she would never be an adult, never be a grown-up woman because she would always be a little girl whom someone had hurt. And then the look was gone. Nobody in the store noticed. The look that deformed her face was too fleeting, was over almost as soon as it had arrived. She took a deep breath and steadied herself. She took several deep breaths—controlled her body—she kept it from shaking. "It's just the pregnancy," she told herself, "it's just the baby."

The young girl noticed her look of discomfort. "He didn't mean anything by it," she said, "he was just messing around. He's a little forward, but he's nice. You speak Spanish?" Helen forced a smile and shook her head. "Oh, then you must be Italian."

"Yes," she said, "I'm Italian."

After lunch, Helen stepped out of her house on Emerson Street, and wandered slowly through her English garden. She bent down with a little difficulty and smelled her lavender bush, then the mint growing next to it. She snapped off a leaf from the mint and bit into it. She liked the way the taste exploded in her mouth. The late spring afternoon was too perfect to drive a car. She decided to walk. The northern California breeze was typically light, and the blooming tulip trees swayed softly in the breeze. The wind here was never cruel, never too hot, never threatening—not like El Paso's. She hated thinking about the place of her birth, but lately that god-damned city had been visiting her like a craving for chocolates. She tired to push the desert from her thoughts. She looked at the green all around her, and took a deep breath. For the first time in five years, the Bay Area had not had a drought. The winter rains had come day after day after day, and now that they were gone everything in Palo Alto was bright green, flowers growing like weeds.

She walked down Emerson a few blocks and took a right on University. She walked into a small bookstore. She had no idea what she was doing in this unfamiliar place. It was Eddie who liked books, not she, and Helen realized she had never been in a bookstore without him. He's rubbing off on me, she thought. She walked around looking for nothing in particular and found herself standing before the poetry section. She stared at the names of the poets, and read out the titles she found interesting. *The Only Dangerous Thing*, *Oblique Prayers*, *Diving into the Wreck*, *Letters to an Imaginary Friend*. She picked up a small book whose title she could not see from the binding and touched the printed letters with her fingers: *Words Like Fate and Pain*. It was a strange and sad and hopeless title. She wondered about the woman who wrote the book, wondered what it was like to write something, and then allow strangers to read her secrets. Maybe it was a kind of freedom. Or maybe it was just another form of imprisonment. She had no desire to read the book, but she found herself opening it, she found herself staring at the words, she found herself reading:

> For you there was no conscious departure,
> no hurried packing for exile.
> You are here, anyway, in your own
> minor archipelago of pain.
>
> Do what every exile does. Tell stories.
> Smuggle messages across the border.
> Remember things back there
> as simpler than they were.

She did not want to think about the words on the page. She knew she could not bring herself to read anymore, but for some reason she reread the words before shutting the book and placed it back on the shelf. She quickly stepped out of the bookstore. She looked around as if she were afraid someone had seen her in the bookstore. She felt stupid for feeling paranoid. She laughed to herself: "It's a bookstore—not a sex shop." She looked at her watch and walked toward the bakery/coffee shop where she was meeting Elizabeth. She thought of the poem as she walked, and was sorry she had not bought the book. And yet she did not want to buy it. She was sure it would be sad; she was sure it would make her remember.

As she crossed the street and slowly made her way toward the coffee shop on the corner of University and Waverly, she shook her head at all the stores that crowded around her. Every other storefront was a restaurant. "You'd think all we do around here is go out to eat. Maybe it's true. Maybe we're just a bunch of pigs." She remembered how one morning she and Eddie had gone running very early in the morning, and how they had run past a shop window that someone had spray-painted: RENOUNCE YOUR WEALTH RICH SWINE. She had said nothing, but her husband had laughed. "Good for them," he said. "Things are too neat around here." "Maybe *we are* swine," she said softly, though she did not really believe it, *did not* believe it. She had lived in Palo Alto for five years now. In the beginning she had loved this peaceful, well-to-do town. It was clean, idyllic; the weather was perfect. She had never lived in a place like this, and living here had made her feel safe. She and her husband often jogged through the university. Watching the students ride their bikes to class made her feel as if she had become a part of America. She felt silly thinking it, but she thought it anyway. She never told her husband these things. If she had, she would have had to explain more than she wanted him to know. But lately, the material comfort she was living in had begun to make her feel uneasy. The house meant less to her than she thought it would mean. Nothing she had or wore or owned meant as much to her as she thought it would— except for Eddie. Eddie was everything. Her friend Elizabeth was raised here; she had moved to San Francisco because, she claimed, "the City's not so goddamned white." "What's wrong with white?" Helen had asked. Elizabeth had laughed, kissed her on the cheek, and said, "Never mind." Helen had hated the condescending tone. If Elizabeth knew how I'd been raised, she had thought at the time, then she'd be ashamed of herself for speaking to me in that tone of voice. But hadn't she led Elizabeth into thinking she was whiter and more sheltered than she actually was? Hadn't she made Elizabeth believe she was born in the same kind of environment? As she walked past the Burger King, a man asked her for some change. She did not look into his face as she handed him a dollar. "Hope your baby's bew-tee-ful," he said. She turned around and smiled at him. "He will be," she said, then turned around and kept walking. "He will be beautiful," she said to herself, "he'll be perfect." She'd had a dream. She knew it would be a boy—a perfect, smart, happy, handsome boy. She ran back and gave the man another dollar. This time, she made sure she looked into his eyes. She walked away from him slowly. She hugged herself as she arrived at the coffee shop.

There was a short line at the coffee counter. She looked around at the casually well-dressed clientele. "Everything here's so studied," she muttered to herself. She felt a sharp and sudden loathing for this town, this place she had made hers but would never really belong to her. She saw no sign of her friend. She ordered a cappuccino for Elizabeth, and a cup of decaf for herself. She found an outside table, and placed Elizabeth's cup of coffee opposite her own seat. As she took a sip from her cup, she felt the baby moving inside her. She touched her stomach, and tried to enjoy the baby's dance in her womb. It hurt—but just a little. The first of a thousand little hurts. "Motherhood hurts—los hijos calan." She winced at the thought of her mother's voice. I don't want her here—not today. Please not today.

"Well, don't we look stunning?"

Helen looked up and laughed. "Yes, we do, don't we? It's the extra passenger. Does wonders for your complexion."

"You really are radiant. How can you stand it?" Elizabeth bent down and kissed Helen on the cheek. She sat down and played with the cup of coffee in front of her. "What do I owe you for the coffee?"

"Don't be silly, Elizabeth, it's on my husband."

"Ahh yes, the husband. How's the husband?"

"He's as gorgeous as ever. We've fallen back in love with each other—didn't I tell you?"

"I never knew you were out of love."

"Well, not exactly out of love—just, you know, seven-year itch kind of thing."

"No, I don't know. My longest relationship has been two years—my men have shorter attention spans than Eddie. On the other hand, my relationships never last long enough to get boring."

"I didn't say we were bored."

"Isn't that what the seven-year itch is—boredom?"

"No. I think it's just that we were getting a little too used to each other. You know, taking each other for granted. But suddenly, it's as intense as ever—emotionally, I mean."

"How long's all this emotional intensity going to last?"

"I know that tone, Elizabeth Edwards. Don't be so cynical."

"My first boyfriend, who never tired of telling me he loved me, broke up with me because I wouldn't have sex with him—then told half the school I gave him a blow job. My first real serious boyfriend left me for another man. My second real serious boyfriend was more passionate about cocaine than he was about me. My first husband—not one year into the marriage—had a heart attack in the arms of another woman, and my current beefcake is a sex addict. He asked me last night if I was interested in three-way sex. I didn't ask him if he had another woman in mind, another man, a dog, a horse, or a snake. I know this is 1992, Helen, and God knows I'm anything but moralistic about what happens between consenting adults—but Jesus H. Christ, I just want something that resembles sanity. So Helen, I'm not cynical—though God knows I've a right to be—I'm just asking a question."

Helen shook with laughter. "I've forgotten your question."

"I asked, 'How long will this love nest of yours last?' "

"Does it matter? We're happy. As soon as we become parents, we'll forget about love and each other and obsess about the kid."

"Just try and be nice to each other, will you? Look at my parents—every one of their children is all screwed up—and all because they forgot they were married to each other."

"Every one of their children, Lizzie? There's only two of you."

"And we're both basket cases."

"Oh, you brother's fine—he's nice."

"I think he's a transvestite."

"How do you know that? Did he tell you?"

"Of course he didn't tell me. Transvestites don't make confessions to members of their families."

"So what makes you think he's a transvestite?"

"I found a silk dress in his closet."

"What were you doing in his closet?"

"Never mind."

"You know, it could be his girlfriend's."

"His girlfriend dresses like June Cleaver—not the silk-dress type."

Helen laughed. "I wish you still lived across the street. I miss you, Lizzie, when are you moving back?"

"This dump? Never. I grew up in a Protestant suburb of Chicago called Libertyville. No one could recover from that, Helen, no one—everyone there is as screwed up as they are white. And then my dad gets this job in what we now call Silicon Valley. Silicon Valley!—shit, that's worse than Libertyville. When I was in high school my father used to take me to the Hoover Tower and when we'd get up to the top, we'd look out at the Stanford campus, and he'd tell me, 'This is your school, baby—it's all yours.' When I didn't get in, he blamed the 'chinks' and the 'blacks' for using up my assigned place in the select school of his choice. It didn't seem to matter to him that I had nothing but C's and D's—and I was stoned out of mind when I took the SAT . . ." As she continued talking, Helen watched her friend intently and smiled to herself. It didn't matter in the least to Lizzie that Helen was intimately familiar with every detail of the story she was telling. But Helen didn't mind: Lizzie's voice was warm and intense and comforting, the sound of a woman who was real, who enjoyed being alive, enjoyed having a voice, and understood the great pleasure of using it. Helen envied her spontaneity—Helen who was cautious, Helen who was often conspicuously quiet.

The light pink in Lizzie's short fingernails flew around in the air, and her long, cheap, flamboyant earrings dangled like chimes in the wind as she emphasized the point she was making. ". . . of course, my parents have never really gotten over my attitudes. Well, I've never gotten over theirs. Did I ever tell you about the time I asked my mother if she'd ever had oral sex with my father? She really lost it."

Helen smiled. "Yes, you told me. But what did you expect? Did you expect her to tell you about her sex life? Give the old girl a break."

"You always take her side."

"That's not true. Why are you always expecting your mother to be someone she's not? You know her; you know her borders, her limitations—what you can and can't say. Why do you expect her to change just for you?"

"Well, that's what's so wrong with this pop stand of a town—it has too many lines you can't cross. Everyone's busy writing their stupid scripts and reading them as if they were the truth. You know, Helen, sometimes people have to depart from the roles their parents hand them. It's so sickening to watch all the energy people exert in this place to look and be *sooo* sophisticated, but once you get inside their houses you might as well be living in a small town in Texas. It's all for nothing, Helen."

"And San Francisco's better?"

"Yes, it's better."

"There aren't any snobs in San Francisco?"

"Oh, there are plenty of snobs. If we made them illegal, they'd start speakeasies." She laughed. "But in the City—in the City at least everybody's all mixed up with everybody else. Here, in this small town for the overly paid, everybody believes in recycling, everybody drinks expensive coffee, everybody buys organic vegetables and chicken breasts from free-range chickens. But all the Blacks and Latinos who work behind the counters live in the next town. I don't want any part of it."

"You *are* a part of it, Lizzie."

Elizabeth sipped her coffee, and rearranged one of her earrings. "Yes, I'm a part of it. In some goddamned way we're all a part of it. But it's not OK, Helen. Don't you think there ought to be a revolution in this country?" She pushed her hair back. She laughed at herself. "I'm being ridiculous." She reached over and grabbed Helen's hand. "It's the smoking," she said, and then added, *"but there ought to be a revolution."*

"The smoking?"

"Yeah, the smoking. I quit—cold turkey. It's been three weeks. Can you believe it?"

"Oh, Lizzie, that's great."

" 'Oh, Lizzie, that's great?' That's it?"

"Well, I could have said it's about damn time."

"No, that's my father's line—he of the pack-a-day habit."

"Do you miss it?"

"Do I miss it? Are you nuts? Of course I miss it. I'm completely crazed. Oh, Helen, I can't tell you how much I miss my little lovers. They're so much more comforting than men."

"But I bet you feel better."

"No. I feel worse. I *will say* that my sex addict lover tells me I smell much better. He also says I'm better in bed since I quit."

"And are you?"

"I suppose so. It's all that rage—he likes angry sex. Anyway, I feel as though any minute I'm going to start up again."

"I stopped three or four times before it finally took."

Elizabeth stared at her friend with a look of amazement. She ran one of her fingernails against her teeth. "I've known you for five years, and you never told me you smoked?"

"I never had a reason to tell you."

"I talk about smoking constantly—"

"Incessantly."

"Incessantly—and you never told me you smoked! You snake in the grass."

Helen smiled and placed her hand over her cup of coffee. "I keep secrets."

"How many secrets do you keep?"

Helen kept a steady smile. "Oh, I don't want to talk about this, Lizzie. Let's not. It was a long time ago. I have a different life now. And it's this one that counts." She looked at her watch. "Listen, are you free for dinner?"

"I thought you'd never ask."

"Eddie will flip when he sees you."

"Yes, your husband loves to be entertained."

"He loves you, Lizzie. He adores you."

"Well, I like him, too," Lizzie admitted, "I just wish he didn't look and live like such a Republican. My father likes him, you know—that's not a good sign."

Helen shook her head and grinned. "Well, Eddie may dress like a Republican, but he makes love like an anarchist."

"Well, it sounds as if—"

"Shut up, Lizzie, and help me up."

"Oh, Mama's getting pushy. Are you going to be a pushy mama?"

Helen put her hands out as Lizzie took hold of her and tugged her up. They both grunted, then broke out laughing. They held on to each other as they walked down the street. Helen wanted to lean into Lizzie and cry and never stop crying. She wanted to learn to let everything out like Elizabeth—all of Lizzie's words were beautiful balloons floating up into the air, higher and higher. But not hers—she felt too heavy and too self-conscious about the life she'd constructed out of nothing more than words that had no reference to truth. Every word had to be the right word. She was no longer able to enjoy her own speech. She felt obese and ugly and awkward. She wanted to be light, full of grace. It's this pregnancy, she thought. I'm falling apart. As they turned on Emerson to walk toward her house, Helen hesitated. "Wait," she said as she turned around, "I want to buy a book."

Helen rushed into the bookstore, and a few minutes later she held a book in her hands.

"I didn't know you read poetry."

"I don't, but, well, I just, I don't know. I just got this urge to buy this book. It doesn't make sense, does it? Cravings. Pregnant women get cravings."

"For poetry?"

"It beats the hell out of anchovies."

 **6**

OFTEN, DIEGO WONDERED what it would be like to be dead. Probably, he thought, it couldn't be very much different from Vicky's kitchen. He had decided a long time ago that he didn't like the idea of being alive. When he was twenty, he had begun a suicide note. He was serious about it, and he meant to kill himself as soon as he finished the letter. He worked on his letter almost every day. He told himself he'd end his life when the letter was perfect.

During the week he woke up at three-thirty. He shook—he always shook. It was as if his blood was too heavy for his veins to carry, too heavy because it had picked up the litany of loneliness that made up the hours of his life. So he shook. And after the shaking stopped, he made coffee. Waking up in his room was like waking up in Vicky's kitchen. He sat at the window looking at the outlines of the downtown buildings and the soundless freeway that was almost empty of traffic. The cars moved so quickly when he saw them pass and he wondered about the sound of moving tires on the pavement.

He had constructed a desk out of a few wooden boards and some bricks he'd stolen from a torn-down building. That was all downtown seemed to be: torn-down buildings replaced by new buildings that would also be torn down. He drank coffee and read the newspaper from the day before, the newspaper his boss gave him as he went home every day. He enjoyed reading the news a day late.

He put down the newspaper and took out his suicide note, which he kept displayed on the corner of the desk next to a stack of books he'd checked out from the public library. He looked it over carefully, trying to think of changes he might make. It went that way every morning. He added, changed sentences around, scratched out entire paragraphs, and sometimes reinserted them in different places. He scratched his head and drank his coffee, lost in his thoughts. Somehow, he felt there had to be a way of saying everything he had ever wanted to say—everything he had ever thought. He had read a book on how to write, but it did not seem to have helped him very much. He read the letter slowly to himself:

"To whom it may concern . . ." That part bothered him, but he couldn't think of what else to say. If it was addressed to someone other than the person who found his body, then there was the real chance they would not even bother reading it. He hoped the landlord wouldn't be the person to find his body. He hated the thought of Mr. Arteago standing over his dead body like an unholy angel sneering down at him—and worse—he hated to think that he would read his letter. He wanted to write "To whom it may concern (except Mr. Arteago)" but he knew his landlord was just the kind of man to read it anyway, so it was a useless addition. He shook his head knowing there was no way out of his dilemma and continued reading:

"Death is easy. It was life that was so damn hard . . ." He wasn't sure about that part either, not because it wasn't true but because it was so true that everybody already knew it. Why was it necessary to state the obvious? People might not like it and never read the rest of the letter. He scratched it out with pencil. Maybe he could find a better way of saying the same thing. He made a note to himself to go to the library and check out a book of quotes or something like that. Maybe he could find an appropriate quote as a kind of epigraph to his letter. It would be a nice touch. He continued reading: "I always hated that I was born deaf. I think my mother always hated it, too. She never learned sign language. I don't think she wanted to learn, or she didn't have time—I don't know. I think

28

sometimes that she never wanted to hear what I had to say. She knew when I was hungry or thirsty or tired; she knew when I was happy or upset; she knew the easy things, but that's all she knew. Maybe she didn't think I had real thoughts. Maybe she thought things were different for the deaf. I don't know. Maybe she figured because I talked with my hands she could guess everything about me from the outside. She was like everyone else I ever met: always smiling at me and hoping I would somehow go away. Where the hell was I supposed to go?

"I guess it doesn't matter much. I know she loved me as much as she could. And she loved me better than anyone who has ever known me . . ." Maybe I should add something here, he thought. He took a drink from his cup of coffee, shook his head, and took down a few notes on the margins of the paper. ". . . Now, I just go to work in a place where there will never be any signs of the sun and I come back home. I watch people talk; I read their lips and they say things like, 'I need to get out of his hellhole of a town. I hate this city—it's fucking dead.' I saw this lady once, dressed real nice with lots of jewelry, like the Empress Carlota's, and she was telling her friend that life was a piece of shit; 'My husband, he buys me rings and necklaces and clothes, and he takes me out once a year like a moveable, decorated Christmas tree.' I think she wanted to cry—but she didn't. The look on her face wasn't angry. She was mostly sad, I think. Sad. And the people I see at work, they look like they're in a war or something. They don't even have enough energy to raise the flag of surrender. They all took tired. Maybe it's me who's tired—that's what my friend Luz says. She says everyone looks tired to me because *I'm* tired. I wrote out on my pad: "Your eyes would be tired too, Luz, if you always had to stare at people's lips to see what they were saying." She told me to stop being angry. "You're not the only one who has to look at those faces," she said. Maybe she's right, but goddamnit, I can't help being angry. I can't stop myself. Besides, Luz is as angry as I am.

"Most people don't know I can read lips. It's a secret I like to keep. Why should I tell them? I just pretend I don't understand, so they write things down for me. When we have to write things down, we're all equal. The people who come into the restaurant always tell me I have real nice handwriting—but I read their lips and they say things. And I don't care for what they have to say. Well, it's their world—but they don't have hearts. Luz says I'm too nice to people on the outside and too hard on them on the inside. But one thing I do know: The only way to find out if some people have hearts is to cut them open and take a look because I sure as hell can't tell by the way they act . . ." Right here Diego stopped and shook his head. Luz is right, he thought, I *am* too angry. It wasn't fair to be so hard on people. And what if someone found this letter when he was dead? Wouldn't they hate him for it? He laughed. But he'd be dead—he wouldn't feel a thing. He made a mental note and continued reading:

"The owner of the place where I work, a place called Vicky's Bar, he beats his wife. I've seen her bruises. She left him. She walked in one day and started throwing glasses and dishes and turning over tables all over the place. She had the strength of an earthquake. Talk about angry. 'You're lucky I don't cut your balls off and feed them to the pigeons at the park!' That's what she yelled. She yelled all kinds of other things. He laughed at her and told her all kinds of things. I couldn't read his lips very well, but I do remember he kept telling her she was crazy. But she wasn't crazy, not crazy at all. Anyone could see that. He called her a puta. Puta, puta, nothing but a whore. 'Not yours!' she said, 'not yours anymore.' And afterwards I had to clean up the mess.

The boss told his friends that if he ever saw her again he'd beat the shit out of her. He almost changed the name of the bar after that since he'd named it after her, but he figured he might lose some business, so he kept the name. The boss doesn't like his sons much, either. He says they're like their mother. He hired me instead of one of his sons because he said they would rob him blind. He called his sons a bunch of cabrones, and everything else he could think of—lazy, castrated thieves on top of everything else. 'And besides, the deaf guy's cheaper.' I saw him say that to his friend. Everybody's a target to hit with fists or words; everybody's toilet paper; everybody uses everybody. Everybody's mad at everybody—me included. Who wants to live in a world like this? I don't. Not me. What for?"

He finished reading the letter, and looked it over. He hadn't signed it yet. Today, it struck him he liked the ending very much, but he didn't much like the part about his mother. Why drag her back into the world by mentioning her in his letter? She had died her own death already. Why drag her through another funeral?

March 27, 1992

*Lizzie, you're just tired—I kept repeating that to myself all the way
home. But that last patient, that newly admitted patient, he was real.
And I know that being tired has nothing to do with anything. He just
stared at me with eyes as black as the grave, stared and stared and then
he took my hand and stared into my palm. I had never seen him before
and yet his hand felt safe and familiar. "You have a gift," he said. I
smiled at him: "Will my gift get me a raise?" "No," he said. He didn't
smile back. "It's not a commodity." He seemed so sane and deliberate in
his speech. It seemed impossible that such a body could speak with such
force. I've seen so many AIDS patients that their breaking bodies no longer
affect me—and yet I was surprised to feel afraid in his presence. I tried
to make a joke. "You're telling me I can't make money on my gift?
What about the free market? This is the nineties—Marxism is dead." He
laughed, but there was something cold and hard and ironic about the
sound of his laughter. It was as if he was laughing not from his heart
but from his memory. I felt a chill. The man kept talking, and it seemed
odd to me that the cynicism in his voice completely disappeared: "You
know, I used to be a Marxist—a real one. But now I've regressed back
into Catholicism. Did you know you were born a Catholic?" It occurred
to me that he had developed dementia. After I changed his IV, I asked*

his name. "Salvador," he said. "It's a lovely name," I said. "Your friends call you Sal?" "I don't have any friends," he said, "they're missing in action." He sounded as if he were already accustomed to being alone—his voice as lonely as his laugh. I started to walk out of the room, but he spoke again. "You don't believe, do you?" "Believe what?" I asked. "You don't believe you're Catholic," he said. "You have to believe." I lost my composure for no reason at all. I just wanted to leave the room. I wanted to run. "We're all Catholic," I said, "everyone who works at St. Mary's becomes a Catholic. All the nurses here are nuns." I laughed nervously, but as soon as the words were out of my mouth— the strangest thing—I could suddenly read his mind: "Check the records. Go ahead. Check the records. Mission Dolores. You know where it is. See for yourself." I had my back to him, but I could hear everything he said, and his voice was inside me—it was his voice, and it wasn't passing through the air—as immediate as someone touching me. "Stop it," I said. I think I almost yelled it. "It's not me who's doing it," he said, but he didn't actually say anything at all—I was reading every word in his mind again, but really it wasn't even sounds, the words, they had no sounds. I just knew what he was thinking. In that instant, I could read what he was thinking, just like watching a patient being cut open on the operating table for the first time. And then I read his great loneliness, his physical pain, the mourning he felt for his body, the regrets that covered his mind like the unintelligible chaos of graffiti on a wall. His grief was the heaviest thing I've ever felt. I don't know how he bore it, and I was ashamed of myself because I had always assumed I knew what they were going through, my patients. I thought I knew. I was ashamed.

It's a strange thing to be writing down, but I'm very certain I felt his voice inside me. It's something beyond words. Sometimes, the simplest physical facts become impossible to describe. I felt the sickness of his body— it was as real as my skin. I started to turn around. I wanted to comfort him. I wanted to confess my shame. I wanted him to be my priest. "Just go. Don't look back. You're the one—I'm sure of it." His words were in my mind, not on his lips—but it was his voice, his voice, though I'm not at all sure it was a voice at all. But the words were there. I ran out of the room as fast as I could.

As I drove to Palo Alto to meet Helen, I tried to shake his words from my mind. I felt violated—his words in my body. As I drank coffee with *her in the sun, I felt the fear lifting. She looked radiant sitting there, and I was in awe of her. She was so perfect. She's the most beautiful pregnant woman I've ever seen. She took everything away like magic. I laughed at myself. I knew what I had experienced in Salvador's room had not been real. I was so relieved to think I had imagined it all.*

But it was real. Something is happening. Someone is trying to speak to me, but I don't understand the language it speaks. When Helen placed my hand on her belly to feel the baby kick, I knew something was wrong. Someone was talking to me. I started to shake, and only the fact that Eddie called Helen to the kitchen saved me from looking like an idiot. I got up to use the bathroom, my knees almost buckling. My heart was pounding, and I could see Helen's baby while I was sitting down in the bathroom. He was strong and perfect, but he was surrounded by a sea of total quiet. The silence covered him like a funeral pall. It was like living in a coffin. And yet the baby was breathing and there was light everywhere, and there was no mourning. I don't know yet what that silence meant, but it was so real and overwhelming that I expected to be deaf when I walked back into the dining room. When Eddie asked me if I was all right, I wanted to weep at the sound of his voice. I'd never realized what a kind voice he had. And that same feeling came over me on the way home. I felt that silence again. I wondered if real speech could reach anyone as deeply as I was being reached at that moment. But I don't speak that language. I don't know what's happening. I wish I knew what was happening.

Elizabeth shut her journal, turned off the light, and stared out her window at the sky. She tried to remember the last time she had looked out into the night. She tried to imagine the stars. What she hated about living in San Francisco was the fact of too many lights. The night was never dark in the city—she could never see the stars. She walked around her living room. She realized how much of the room she could see with the light that poured in from the window. She felt as if the full moon were in the room. "Maybe I'm going crazy," she thought. "It's the goddamned cigarettes. I never should have quit. I haven't got it in me." It comforted her to think that all these strange occurrences were due to the fact that she'd quit smoking. Cause and effect, something she could measure. She walked to the kitchen, poured herself a glass of wine, and sat in the moonlight.

Sometime after she finished drinking her wine, she fell into a deep sleep. She woke up lying on the floor trying to shake off her dream, but on her way to work she remembered it. She was a little girl, and her mother was far away from her, and the maid who cared for her as a child was singing a song in her ear. It was a strange dream with no meaning, but something about it made her feel peaceful and happy. She had not thought of that maid in a long time. She had been from Mexico—must have been from Mexico since she spoke no English. She always smelled of soap and lilac, and she could have sworn that her smell was in the room when she woke from the dream. And then she remembered she'd smelled that same odor in Salvador's room. She was sure of it.

When she arrived at St. Mary's, Lizzie began her morning rounds. She slowly worked her way to Salvador's room. When she arrived at the door to room 709, she hesitated before entering. When she walked through the door, the room was empty. She stood in the room, almost numb, and sat down on the bed Salvador had occupied the day before. One of the patients who was taking a stroll on the floor called out to her. "You OK, Lizzie?"

She looked up and smiled weakly at the man who was standing at the door. "Just tired, Charlie," she said.

"You been out with that man again?"

She smiled and forced herself to rise from the bed. "Charlie," she asked, "you know anything about the guy they brought in yesterday?"

"Good-lookin' Latino guy?"

She nodded.

"He bought the farm." He looked for a moment as if he might cry, then smirked at her. "He's pickin' tomatoes on that farm of his."

Lizzie showed no expression at all, then smiled. "You'll never be anything more than an Iowa farm boy, Charlie."

"It's not such a bad thing to be."

"No, it isn't." She combed his hair with her fingers. This good man—he will die, too, she thought. *If he can keep himself from crying—then I can, too.* "It's pretty quiet around here. Let me wash your hair."

"Only if you promise to dye it red."

"I'd advise against red," she laughed. "I tried it once and it attracted nothing but perverts."

"Dye it, dye it!" he screamed. "Please dye it!"

Around ten o'clock Lizzie took her break and called Marsha, who worked the graveyard shift. She knew she wouldn't have gone to bed yet. If anyone knew anything about Salvador, it would be her. She made everything on the ward her business—it was her biggest flaw as a nurse, but it was also her virtue. She heard Marsha's raspy voice on the other end of the telephone.

"How's the single life?"

"Lizzie! Haven't seen you in ten million years. Haven't seen anybody, really. You on break?"

"Yeah, and dying for a cigarette."

"You'll get through."

"Yeah," Lizzie nodded, then fell silent. She was trying to think of how to phrase her question. She felt stupid, inadequate. She thought of hanging up the receiver. She heard Marsha's voice step into an awkward silence:

"You calling me about the guy in room 709?"

"How'd you know?"

"Well, I'm sure you didn't call me to find out about the single life. Besides, he told me you'd call. The guy's psychic—or *was* psychic. And don't lecture me. I know you don't believe in all that stuff, but I do. Still, it's pretty weird. He said he'd done his duty—that his life wasn't a complete waste. He went into the night calm and peaceful like, Lizzie, you know?"

" 'Went into the night?' Is that your new expression for dying?"

"What do you think of it?"

"I hate it. It sounds like a bad line in a poem. Why don't you just say he died?"

"I'm sick and tired of the word 'died.' I hate that word, Lizzie."

"I know," she whispered.

They were both silent for a moment.

"What did he mean by having done his duty?"

"He didn't say, Lizzie. I was in the room when he stopped breathing. For some reason I just knew he was going to die even though he didn't appear to be as sick as some of the other guys. It's strange. How do we know these things? Anyway, you know how I am—if they're dying, I hang around, especially if there's no family. I hate when they die alone. Promise me you won't let me die alone, Elizabeth."

"Don't be silly, Marsha, the whole world will be there."

"Just make sure my ex-husband is far, far away."

"I won't let him near—I swear I won't. But tell me the truth—you'd be hurt if he didn't show, wouldn't you?"

Marsha laughed, then abruptly stopped. "Oh, Lizzie, we've been doing this for too long. Some days I just can't take it anymore. This guy, he, well, this Salvador—he got to me. There was something about him. Scary—but not scary. Anyway, he mentioned you. He said something about a gift, how he'd given you a gift. He said he would have known you anywhere. I don't know what the hell he was talking about."

Elizabeth was quiet on her end of the phone.

"Lizzie?"

"He said I had a gift. I didn't know what he was talking about either."

"And he didn't say anything else?"

"No. Nothing. He said I had a gift. I made some dumb joke, changed his IV bag, and left. This morning, I walk into his room and he's gone. End of story." Elizabeth paused. "Did he say anything else?"

"He said he'd only used the gift to get what he wanted. He said you wouldn't do that. And he told me his last name—he said you'd want to know."

"Why would I want to know?"

"He said it was important. Aguila. His last name was Aguila. Does that mean anything to you?"

"It means eagle. Is that all he said?"

"Yeah, that's all."

"Nothing else?"

"What's this about, Lizzie?"

"I wish I knew."

"Well, you want to know something really weird? When I was doing his charts, and the paperwork, I noticed his birthday. *Lizzie, you and he have the same birthday.* Same day, same year. What do you make of that?"

"Nothing."

"Nothing?"

"Well, there's several hundred of us—maybe a thousand of us—born on that day in that year. So what?"

"Yeah you're probably right. Still it's pretty strange, huh?"

"Yeah, pretty strange."

When Lizzie arrived home after work, she had a message from her lover on her answering machine. As she heard his voice on the tape, she felt as if she had swallowed a rock that had settle permanently in her stomach. She wanted to rid herself of the foreign object in her body. He was too desperately in love with sex, but not quite as in love with anything or anyone else. She had given him a book for his birthday. He later confessed to her that he never read books: "I don't even read magazines." She wanted him to disappear. She popped her knuckles. "I am so sick and tired of men with bigger penises than brains, bigger penises than hearts. And why is it always our job to end it? Jesus Horatio Christ." She picked up the receiver and dialed his number. He wasn't home, so she spoke into his machine. "Listen, Conrad, I can't—can't go out with you tonight—" She paused. "As a matter of fact, I can't go out tomorrow night either." She paused again and took a deep breath. "Look, I just got to do this, *I just got to.* You know something, Conrad, I think it's time to call it a day. I know you think we've just started exploring the possibilities between us, but I really can't go out with you anymore. Last night, the fat lady sang. I'll send you a year's supply of condoms as a consolation prize. Don't call, Conrad. Please don't call. I'm changing my number."

As soon as she put down the receiver, she felt herself filling up with a sense of regret as if she were an empty jug being filled up with toxic waste. She was ashamed of herself. She burst into tears.

"Why the hell am I crying?—I can't bear this man, can't bear myself when I'm with him." She should have had the guts to speak to Conrad directly. She felt guilty, felt that she'd exposed herself to what she really was: a spineless bitch. She laughed to herself. "Ahhh, the guilt, Lizzie. Maybe Salvador was right—maybe I am Catholic." She laughed and bit her thumbnail. She laughed again, then picked up the phone. She dialed Conrad's number, and spoke into the machine again. "Listen, Conrad, I just did a really shitty thing. It isn't that I'm changing my mind or anything like that. I really meant what I said, but I should have had the decency to talk to you in person—not on a stupid machine. Damnit. Listen, I'm not really changing my number. Call me. We'll talk." She felt better about herself as she hung up the phone. "You're not a bad woman, Lizzie, you're really not. Repeat that a hundred times."

She fought the urge to run to the corner store to buy a pack of cigarettes. The worst thing about living in the Mission District was that there was a Mom and Pop grocery store on every block— and damnit, they all sold cigarettes. "Damnit," she kept repeating, "damnit, damnit, damnit." She walked around her apartment as if she were lost, as if she had never seen the space where she lived. She kept hearing Salvador's voice in her head. She wanted to scream, turn herself upside down and shake herself until his voice emptied out of her. But somehow the scream was caught between her lungs and her throat. She couldn't rub away the pain in the back of her head. She walked into the bathroom, turned on the faucet in the bathtub, and kept her hand beneath the running water until she felt it growing warmer and warmer. When it was hot, she placed the rubber plug in the drain and slowly started taking off her clothes. She felt odd and numb, and as she stripped off her underwear, she became excited and afraid. She looked at the hot, clean water in her tub, and wondered what it would be like to drown and enter into that dark and unknown kingdom of the dead. Perhaps death was simply a word that stood for a place that was too beautiful and too perfect, and therefore unimaginable in the small and cynical minds of the living. Perhaps death was nothing-ness, but why was nothingness something to be afraid of? She hesi-tated. If she stepped into the clean and hot and seductive water, she knew she would not rise out of it the same woman; she would be different forever; she would never see the same things because something would change, something more essential than the color of her eyes or skin, more essential than her sex. Everything, *everything* would be different, and she could not stop it, and she knew she had lost control of everything in her life. She was trembling like the first time a man had touched her breast, afraid and yet wanting, wanting to be touched everywhere and wanting to touch back. She could hardly wait for her body to lose itself in the hot water because she needed to feel surrounded by it so desperately—to be protected. From what, she wondered. From whom?

She moved toward the water. As soon as she immersed herself she felt as if she were floating out of herself. Her eyes closed, and when she opened them she found herself floating in the air, looking down at her body in the bathtub. She was weightless; was free of her history, had no anxieties about her future with or without men; she had become an intimate part of the air and the light and the steam. She felt as if she had become a pure and simple prayer, so pure and so simple that she had actually regained her original innocence. She stared at her body in the bathtub. How strange it was to be outside of it, to see it, watch it, examine it. She floated down toward that strange and foreign and abused and hated body lying in a bathtub. That's me, she thought, then laughed and floated away from the motionless shell that always had to be cleaned because it was always getting dirty in the world. She was indifferent toward that material thing—neither attracted to it nor repelled by it. It was nothing more than a wordless stone, a monument to a dead, nameless stranger. She willed herself to float over her apartment and found she was free to move anywhere by simply manipulating her mind—though she was not sure she had a mind. She was no longer ruled by the physical world, by the rules that governed it. She was free of the poverty of her body. When she thought right, she moved right; when she thought left, she moved left; she thought "out the window" and found herself floating into the night. "I am going into the night and I am not afraid. I am beyond all fear. I have become the night itself." She thought of Conrad and found herself moving toward his apartment. The trip took no more than a few seconds, and entering his apartment, she immediately sensed where he was. She discovered he wasn't alone. She did not recognize the woman who was making love to him. She watched them and smiled. She felt no anger, no sense of betrayal. She watched them enjoy each other, the two bodies rubbing against each other, the searching hands, their skin moist with sweat. She laughed and half-expected the couple making love on the bed to hear her, but her voice was beyond their hearing. What a strange thing to have a body, she thought, what a strange thing to need one. After this, would she want one?

As she watched the pair of lovers on the bed, her thoughts left them. They were entitled to their privacy—they could keep it, she thought. She thought of Salvador taking her palm: "Check the records—Mission Dolores. You know . . ." As soon as she thought the words, she was out of the room floating toward the mission. The rectory was closed. Everything was dark. She would have to wait until tomorrow—and then she laughed at herself, realizing the boundaries, the rules, the way she did everything had changed. She could do anything she wanted. A locked door could not keep her out. "How to find the records? What kind of records?" Miraculously, she found dozens of old leather books neatly lined up on a bookshelf. Each book was labeled with a year. She had no body, no hands, no fingers. She half-remembered a dream where she could not touch because she had no hands—touch whom? Had it been a dream? She focused on the books. How could she look through the books? She concentrated on the book labeled with the year of her birth. The book came down from the shelf and opened because she willed it to open; the pages turned because she willed them to turn. The names of the baptized, the godparents, the parents were all listed. If she had been born on August 10, 1955, then she could have been baptized anytime after that. She looked not for her own name, but for Salvador's, as if her own name did not matter. She found it easily. Everything was so easy. The body meant work. Now she was free of it. Jesus Salvador Aguila was listed as having been baptized on August 22. His date of birth was listed as August 10. She stared at the next entry: Maria de Lourdes Aguila, also baptized on August 22, date of birth also August 10. The parents were not listed for either child, but the name of the godparents appeared: Juan and Gloria Silva. There were no other baptisms recorded on that date. She thought of Salvador as he touched her palm. She remembered how familiar his hand had felt, and she suddenly became acutely aware that she had no palm, no body. She wanted, inexplicably, to clothe herself in her own skin again.

She willed the book back on the shelf. She wanted to leave, to rest. She was tired, and had become afraid, and she felt the need to get back. She was outside again, and as she hovered over the church, she imagined what the inside looked like, and she had the odd feeling that she had been in that church somewhere, perhaps in a dream, but the dream frightened her, and she did not want to think of what she had seen there, so she willed herself to move away from the church as quickly as possible. As she floated through the sky, she felt again as if she were a part of everything in the world that was not human. It was good to be a part of the sky.

In her apartment again, Lizzie stared at the body in the bathtub. She no longer felt indifference toward that shell of fragile bone and skin. She felt a great and sad love for it. She went near the body, and wanted to touch it. She willed to be a part of it again. She opened her eyes. She touched herself. She felt her wet hands wrinkled from soaking in the water. She rubbed them against her wet skin, shivered, and stared at herself. She felt heavy as she picked herself out of the tub. As she dried herself, Lizzie smelled soap and lilac. The maid in her childhood felt close, and she half-expected to hear Salvador's voice reverberating through her body. "What's happening to me? My God, what's happening to me?"

 **8**

On weekends Diego slept late but always managed to wake in time to watch the sun come out. No Vicky's on weekends, no dark kitchens, no smell of pine cleaner, no boss's face to make him feel unworthy of breathing the air. On Saturdays, his body didn't tremble as much; his inner earthquakes let his body rest.

He sat at his desk, which he had placed directly in front of his only window. He drank a second cup of coffee, letting the familiar bitterness seep into him as he watched the sun cast its light, creating pink and purple shadows on the Juárez mountains. He thought of Carlota's jewels. He could almost see them sparkling in his hands, feel their hard surfaces almost melting against the touches of his fingers, see his own reflection in them. He dressed himself in a hurry, not caring or even noticing his body or his clothes. He did not take the time to smell himself and did not worry whether he needed a bath. He started walking toward the river—just like he did every Saturday. The walks toward the river were rituals he attended to as if he were an old priest saying Mass, an old priest who was no longer conscious of the sacredness or necessity of the act. Somehow the ritual simply helped to keep him alive.

The river on Saturdays was better than San Jacinto Plaza that sat in the center of downtown. He did not like San Jacinto Plaza anymore. He had liked it as a boy, but back then it had a fountain with alligators in it—alligators whom he had feared and loved. They did not belong and yet they were there. He felt close to those alligators as if they were personal pets. One Saturday night some drunk soldiers from Fort Bliss had managed to slip into the fountain and slit the throats of the sleeping alligators. After that, the park was never the same. And anyway, there were too many pigeons who did more shitting than flying and too many people asking him for cigarettes and money. He was tired of giving his cigarettes away to people he didn't know—and there was no money to give them.

At the edge of Sunset Heights, Diego passed the steps that went nowhere. He supposed that the houses the steps led to had burned down. He pictured the fires in his mind, the flames lighting up the night like a huge candle with a crooked, wild wick. He wondered if anyone had died inside the burning houses. The people, perhaps not wanting to return to the memories, decided not to rebuild their houses and left the ruins, forgotten, at the top of the steps. They sat there, abandoned and noticed only by children and people who had nothing to do but explore. Diego climbed to the top of one set of steps and walked through the ruins. The bricks were so soft that they broke beneath him as he stepped. Weeds were growing everywhere. Some things can grow anywhere, he thought, even without rain. He saw crumpled rubbers where teenaged lovers had left them after sex. He tried to picture their awkward passions. Once he had caught a couple having sex here. He kicked the bricks beneath him and walked back down the stairs. For some reason, Diego could not pass by the steps that went nowhere without climbing them. It was another one of his rituals. Something in him half-expected to be surprised by something up there, but nothing was ever different, except that time when he'd seen the couple with no clothes. When he first moved to Sunset Heights, he had hoped someone would grow a garden where the houses used to be, but now he thought it had been a stupid, romantic idea. The only thing that had a right to grow here, he thought, were the weeds that needed no caring, that needed no rain. Now, he felt the steps should always lead to nothing.

He walked slowly toward the Santa Fe Bridge enjoying what was left of the cool. He passed the bright red warehouse where he bought his clothes for thirty-five cents a pound. He stood at the very top of the bridge where the American and Mexican flags flew next to each other. The wind wasn't blowing today, but on some days the winds twisted the flags in every direction and they almost touched for a second in midair—they almost touched like dancers who reached endlessly for each other, dancers who knew they would never couple.

He looked down at the Rio Grande that looked impressive only on a map. The river was old and lazy. It was neither deep nor blue nor beautiful nor wide. It did not reflect the sky or the clouds—and if it reflected anything at all, it reflected the color of the mojados who had learned to cross it faster and safer than the cars that drove across the bridge. The muddy river was now completely tame, and whatever bed it made for itself, the part of it that ran through the cities of Juárez and El Paso had now been replaced by a bed of smooth, hard, gray cement. The river was poor like the people, Diego thought, and though there was nothing beautiful to see in its waters, he liked coming here to visit it. Something about the river made him feel as though he belonged.

He looked for Luz, who often came here on Saturdays. Like him, she was addicted to the river. She loved it even as she laughed at it, even as she spit at its poverty, at its insignificance. She was too tired to clean houses six days a week, so on Saturdays, she rested and came to watch the river and speak to it. Diego caught sight of her as she sat next to an old man who had a porcelain bowl placed in front of him. He watched as she pulled out two quarters and placed it in the old man's bowl. She said something to him and laughed. He laughed with her. Diego could watch her for hours, the way she carried herself, the way she made people seem so important. He knew she must have been very beautiful when she was younger—and even now she had the kind of face that made people want to stare. Luz looked up and saw him. She waved him to come closer. When he was next to her, she looked up at him from where she was sitting on the concrete walkway. She pressed her palm on the concrete next to her and patted it. Diego recognized it as an invitation for him to sit next to her. "¿Cómo estás, Dieguito?"

Diego smiled and shrugged his shoulders.

"How long have you been standing there watching me? I don't like to be watched. My first boyfriend used to follow me around—and watch. I hated that. It made me feel—I don't know. I just didn't like it."

"I don't follow you around, you know?" Diego wrote.

She nodded. "Sometimes, the past comes back just when you think it's disappeared. Nothing ever disappears. I think we shrink when we get old because the years become so heavy—they don't go away, they just twist us, bend us over until we can't walk anymore."

Diego nodded. He was afraid she would cry. He never knew what to do when people cried.

She placed her hand on his cheek. He thought of his mother.

She pulled her hand away and looked toward the immigration booths where border guards stopped people and asked their nationalities. "Well," she said firmly, "they're still trying to keep us out, aren't they, my Diego?" She spoke English to him, and she always spoke clearly so Diego could read her lips—she never turned her back to him. She learned to read Diego's handwriting as he wrote on his pad, so she could respond immediately to what he was saying. Diego never minded that she looked over his shoulder when he wrote. He knew she was not a patient person, not the kind of person to wait for things to come to her—not even his notes. And besides, Diego liked that Luz was not afraid to get near enough to touch him.

Diego took out his pad and wrote: "Why do you always speak to me in English? I know Spanish just like you. I had a teacher who taught me to read in Spanish, I used to go to her house after school. She taught me to read books in Spanish. It took me a long time. I spent three summers in her house—every day. She was old and patient and good. She died. Speak to me in Spanish. I worked hard, Luz."

Luz stared at his pad and grinned. "Yes, you're very intelligent," she said, "but I'm a U.S. citizen ¿que no?" Yes, Diego thought, that's true. She *was* a U.S. citizen. He remembered how the first time they met she had told him she had decided to live in Juárez because it was cheaper, and he remembered smiling when she referred to herself as an expatriate.

"So what if you *are* a U.S. citizen," Diego wrote, "Spanish is your first language. Why don't you speak to me in your first language?"

Luz pointed her lips at him: "Because you can't make fun of my accent and you can't tell if I pronounce something the wrong way. Besides, I like to speak English—I just don't want the gringos to know it."

Diego smiled at her and wrote: "Why don't you want gringos to know you like to speak English?" He wrote quickly and clearly. Luz leaned over his shoulder as he wrote and watched the clean words appear on the white paper.

"Because," she said, "they already think English is better. Don't you know that? They think English is the only language in the world. I hate that, Dieguito, I really hate that. I don't want gringos to ever suspect I enjoy their language. No, I want to enjoy English in my own private way. I don't have to yell about it. And, anyway, Spanish is the superior language."

"Actually," Diego wrote, "American Sign Language is the superior language."

She nodded, but her nod was polite—without conviction—and Diego did not mistake her gesture as a sign of agreement. She didn't believe what he had just written. She never did. "So Dieguito, when do you think they're going to stop all this nonsense about borders?"

He shook his head and wrote: "About the time the river freezes over, which will be about the same time my boss gives me a raise."

Luz laughed. "Look at that river. It's dirty and small. They've taken all the fight out of it. I bet it was strong and beautiful once." She laughed. "Strong and beautiful once—like me." Sometimes, even Luz could not hide the sorrow she held within her like the root of a cactus held water. This is not what she had planned—this is not what she had wanted. Her mother had told her that her looks would save her from a common life—but her looks had not saved her from anything.

Diego watched her as she spoke of the river, her face sad and distant because she was not only speaking of the river, but of her own life, a life where more weeds had grown than flowers, a life with few choices, a life of too many regrets.

". . . Oh, Diego I wish for so many things." She stopped speaking and shook herself as if she were an old rug full of dust. "That poor goddamned river. You know, mi amor, I wish I understood why I loved it. It's not a line on a map, you know. And it isn't a border. You call this poor excuse for a river a border? Ha!"

He wanted to tell her not to be sad. But she always picked herself up. "Keep fighting, Luz, just keep—"

She looked at him and smiled. She stared at his pad.

"I've heard they might build a wall," he wrote.

"You're deaf—you couldn't have heard a damn thing."

"Don't be so literal, Luz."

"I just like to argue with you, amor. And you shouldn't be listening to talk about walls."

"But I read about a 'Tortilla Curtain.' "

"Tortilla Curtain my brown ass, Dieguito. The gringos like to talk. If they built a wall, they couldn't chase us down anymore. They'd have to find a new sport."

"You should never never underestimate la migra. If they want a wall someday, they'll build it."

She looked at Diego's pad and laughed. "You're damn smart, my Diego. Maybe you're right. But if the time ever comes, we'll just have to fight them."

"With what?"

"With out bodies, with our voices, with our prayers."

Diego smiled at her and nodded. "You're crazy if you think anyone's ever going to listen to our prayers."

"We'll make them listen. And you're right, I'm crazy—damn crazy. So what? All the sane people I know are bores, do you hear me, Diego? My mother told me never to trust a sane man. 'Get rid of those kinds of men,' she said, 'they're not good for nothing—not even sex.' She said that sanity was like happiness: Nobody knew what it was."

"Your mother sounds like she read Hemingway," he wrote.

She threw her head up and cackled. "No, she never read that stupid American. You're the only one I know who has time to read that stuff, Dieguito. You and your library. You should stop all that bullshit, Dieguito. Books aren't good for you. What the hell do they teach you? I'll tell you what they teach you: they teach you to want things you can't have . . ." Diego smiled to himself as she spoke. He knew she herself had her own small library in her house. Sometimes she was all show. ". . . No, Dieguito, books aren't good for you. Stick to work on your suicide letter. Are you almost finished?"

"I'm thinking of throwing out the part about my mother." She watched his hands glide across the paper.

"No, no, no, Diego, you got it all wrong. No seas pendejo, leave your mother in. She deserves some credit, you know? The women always get left out. Do we need to grow dicks to get a good part in people's stories?"

"It's not a story, Luz, it's a letter."

"It's all the same thing, Diego, trust me. Give your mother her due. She gave you life, no?"

"I don't think she'd like what I wrote about her. It's not the kind of credit she would have wanted."

"Very neat handwriting," she said, "very bold—like a true American." She clapped her hands and laughed. When she'd finished laughing she wrinkled her forehead and looked at Diego seriously. "Look, about your mother, well forget your mother, Diego. Stop your worrying. Why are you worried about what your mother will think? Dios la tenga en paz, but she's dead." She crossed herself and though her lips did not move, it seemed to Diego that she was smiling. "Ay, Dieguito! You don't know by now that mothers aren't perfect? You feel sad for yourself because your mother wasn't a copy of some idea you got in your head? You think there's a perfect mother out there who behaves like the Virgin Mary? Not even the Virgin acted like men think she acted. You think you were cheated because your mother was human? You're like my sons, you really are, my Diego. Well, you're a man—you can't help it—and once you discover that your mothers had sex in order to have you, then you turn around and look at us like we're all whores. ¡Pendejos! Forgive your mother for whatever she did, Dieguito, forgive her— and leave her in your letter. It's the way you feel, so just leave everything the way it is."

Diego nodded, and wondered who taught her to see things so clearly. It was not a gift he had been born with.

"So when are you going to finish the letter, my Diego?"

"When they move the Statue of Liberty to the Rio Grande." He smiled at her.

"Well," she nodded, "then you have some time. Have you thought about how you're going to end it?"

"The letter or my life?"

"*Your life*, not the letter. To hell with the letter."

He nodded and wrote: "Maybe I'll throw myself off this bridge."

She let out a cackle. Diego stared at her face and could tell she was laughing hard—even for her. "Pendejo. You have an American sense of humor. You think you'd die from jumping off this bridge? I'll tell you, Dieguito, they have real bridges in California, but this bridge here ain't shit—it isn't high enough for suicide."

"I don't intend to break my neck," he wrote, "I intend to drown."

"Diego, you think you'd drown in this river? Nothing could drown down there. You don't even have to be Jesus Christ to walk across it. You might as well drown in your bathtub. And besides that, the Border Patrol would save your brown ass. Those green uniforms would be all over the river saving your worthless life from drowning even though they don't give a devalued peso for your soul. They'd save you just so the whole damned city could see what good Joes they are, and there you'd be, making them look like heroes. And believe me, my Diego, with your luck you'd wind up breaking all your fingers and wouldn't even be able to write. What would you do then?"

Diego smiled at her. "Maybe. But I'd be dead by the time the migra found me. I'd drown before they could reach me and make it look like they hadn't tried hard enough to save me. It's worth a try." He was writing faster than usual. "I might even make the newspaper and get my letter published or something. And besides, it would make an interesting grave—the river—don't you think?" His hand moved across the note pad, smoothly, evenly, each letter, perfect.

"It's already a grave." She threw her head up and laughed.

Diego smiled. He wondered to himself if she really believed all of the things she said. Maybe she just wanted to believe them. Diego loved watching her lips and reading what she had to say, but it made him sad because he felt people would always find a way of stepping on each other. Nothing would ever change. But he needed Luz, and he needed to read her lips, and he was glad she liked to fight.

They watched the people coming and going. Luz ate her home-made bread and pointed at a woman swimming across the river. "Swim!" she yelled. "Look at her, Dieguito, an Olympic star! Swim!" she yelled. "Swim before the migra comes back from their goddamned coffee break!" Diego clapped his hands. Luz gave him a kiss on the cheek.

At noon, he left her there watching the river people. He laughed to himself as he thought about how she loved people who had no respect for borders. "Bring your letter with you the next time you come," she yelled. Diego nodded. He thought she was beautiful, beautiful because she refused to be beaten, refused to be humble, refused to say *yes* when she meant *no*.

He took a last look at her. From a distance she looked like a broken old woman. He looked down at the river and wondered what it sounded like. Sometimes, he wanted to hear the river speak his name, speak it, and then spell it out one letter at a time. Most of the time, he could imagine what things sounded like, but the river was silent. So very silent.

 **9**

Joaquin's breathing was heavy and thick as he slept on the couch, his black hair shining in the light of the late morning sun. Jacob thought it was a sad and tired sun that fought vainly to break through the San Francisco fog. He stared out the window. The fog had finally begun to burn away, but Jacob knew it would return. He looked away from the window and stared at Joaquin; he tried to picture his lover's dreams as he sat and watched him from the dining room table. He wanted Joaquin's breathing to go on and on and never stop. "Can't it stay like this—perfect and warm and quiet?" He put down the newspaper he'd been trying to read for the last half hour. "Have to stop talking to myself. Gonna make myself crazy. Just be normal." He laughed at himself. Nothing in his life had been normal yet he could not exile that word from his vocabulary. He looked at his watch, then looked at the mess around him. "Damn!" The house looked like a college dorm room, clothes everywhere. "Have to pick up this dump, have to go to the grocery store—maybe Joaquin will be up for a movie or a night out at a quiet restaurant—no, it's better that he rest—but . . ." Everything in their lives had become maybe: "Maybe we'll make it to that party, maybe we'll have people over for dinner, maybe we'll sleep an entire night, maybe we'll have a good day, a peaceful day, an entire day when we don't think of our bodies and all the things that are going wrong with them." They were no longer in control of their lives, no longer able to utter simple nos or yeses to the questions they were asked. But it was getting harder and harder for Jake to exist in that doorway, that uneasy, liminal place of permanent maybes, the floor constantly shifting under him as if the house had been built on an endless moving walkway that provided no place to exit. He rolled up the newspaper in his fists. Tighter and tighter and tighter. At least Joaquin doesn't cry anymore, he thought. He made himself believe his rage had subsided—at least the rage in his stomach, in his throat, the rage that coated every goddamned word that came out of him with a film that disgusted even him and everyone around him—that rage—that rage had left him. At least that part was over. Everything was calmer. He wanted to believe the rest would be easier than what they had been through already, wanted to believe that the rest of their pain would be purely physical, as if there was such a thing as purely physical pain.

He wanted to hold on to all the good things he'd ever had—and yet even now there were days he simply wanted to let go. If he could let go, then he could walk into the place of eternal nos—no light, no breath, no body, no Joaquin, and no maybes.

He watched his lover sleep. He smiled. He wanted to whisper something that would make Joaquin feel better; he wanted to hold him in his arms. He wanted to be his father, his mother, his brother, a great being whose only purpose was to protect. He had felt the same way toward his younger brother—but he had been unsuccessful in protecting him just as he was incapable of protecting the man who'd shared the only part of his life that was good. As he watched Joaquin, thoughts of his little brother came to him. His open palm clinched into a fist—a reflex. He wondered if it was sheer coincidence that his lover was his younger brother's exact age. He had always asked himself if he wasn't trying to obsessively recover his younger brother through every lover he'd ever had—all of them having his brother's features: dark, thick hair with boyish good looks. All of them, every damn one of them, had seemed a little sad and far away—until they smiled. But when they smiled it was as if they had never come near to anything in life that resembled sadness. They had all been hopelessly scarred to the point of self-destruction or melodrama, just as he had been predictably unable to cope with their confusion. He wondered if he and all of his lovers were helplessly sick, wondered if there was a cure for any of them— even Joaquin had not cured him. But Joaquin had brought calm into his life, and had taught him to bear himself. It was something. It was something. So now he had Joaquin and the memory of his brother, but he did not think of that memory as something intangible. For him, the past was something solid and hard and tangible as flesh. His younger brother consistently stepped into his house— unannounced—like an old friend who always showed up at the worst possible moment but was somehow welcome just the same.

His brother had been born when he was eleven, and he remembered his mother telling him it was his job to protect him. He remembered holding him. The first time he had held that strange and fragile being in his arms, he had understood what love was, what it meant, and he had understood for the first time that he was capable of something more than fear. He had never felt any warmth for his parents: they were not the sort of people who inspired tenderness, not the sort of people who required affection from the people around them—not even their sons. Those two beings who had fathered and mothered him had always kept him at a distance, and his brother was the only warm thing that had ever entered his house. It had been over twenty years since he'd seen him, and as he watched Joaquin get sicker and sicker, he thought of his brother more and more. He knew he would never see him again and he couldn't help mourning that fact, though he did not want to mourn. At times his self-pity was stronger even than his anger. *I should have looked for him. I should have looked*—he kept his picture in the living room, and he often stared at it. His brother's seven-year-old face smiled into the room. The photograph had become a kind of holy card, an amulet, Jacob's most precious possession. He all but lit candles to it.

Lately, he had begun to regret that he had not attended his parents' funeral. If he'd gone, he could have spit on their graves; if he'd gone, he could have danced around the polite high church Episcopalian crowd, spewing all the family secrets; *if he'd gone, he would have seen his brother*. At the time, he hadn't thought of his brother, hadn't thought of anything. He had gone completely insane, completely unconscious. His body had taken control because his mind had left—left, perhaps, because it could not handle the weight of a life it was supposed to rule, and unable to rule it, had opted for the painlessness of chaos. When he heard the news of his parents' death, he felt a surge of exhilaration, a kind of orgasm that left a smell and an aftertaste of having made love to someone repulsive and detestable and irredeemably ugly. That smell was still a part of his own body—and sometimes he could still detect its faint odor. He suddenly felt free of the people who had brought him into the world and raised him. The only thing that prevented him from yelling out his joy was the rage of having been born their son. Sometimes, he could hear their voices in the words he spoke.

He remembered reading about their deaths in the newspaper: HEIRESS KILLS SLEEPING HUSBAND, KILLS SELF. He could still picture the headlines; they had become a part of him just as that ink had become a part of that newspaper. He drank for days, weeks, months. He had no memory of how he had survived. It was as if he had died and been raised back to life. An old friend had found him lying on the street, an old friend who, by chance and in a moment of compassion, looked down at his blank and anonymous body and had miraculously seen a man with a name and commanded him back to the fields where people worked and played and laughed. After his mind had come back, he had locked his parents in the part of him that could not make words, the part of him that no one was allowed to see or touch—except Joaquin. Joaquin had touched every part of him—even the part where he kept his parents. When Joaquin died, he knew that his final days or weeks or months would be heavy and inconsolable and his days would be without light. Maybe he would take to the bottle again and walk out into a cold and barren field that was far away from everyone and praise it for its solitary existence—and cut himself until he bled rivers.

Joaquin opened his eyes and stared blankly around the room. He sat up slowly.

Jacob smiled at him. "Tired?"

"Not as tired as yesterday. I had a dream." There was still sleep in his voice.

"You wanna talk about it?" he whispered.

"I don't remember exactly. Someone was chasing me."

"Jesse Helms."

Joaquin laughed. "No—someone I knew." He thought a moment, and Jacob could see he was trying to piece his dream together. He shook his head. "I can't remember. It doesn't matter, does it, Jake?"

"No. It doesn't matter."

Joaquin stretched his arms and grunted. "How come you let me sleep on the couch?"

"You were tired. I didn't have the heart to move you."

"I'd have rather slept with you."

"Who wouldn't?" Jacob smiled. "Take your medicine."

Joaquin shook his head. "Jake—I can't—not today."

"Joaquin—don't. We've been through this a thousand times."

"That shit is poison. I'll die of it."

"I can't take this today. Let's not do this—I can't—" He covered his ears with his palms.

Joaquin sat a moment and watched him. He walked over to the cabinet, showed his medicines to his lover, smiled, and took his daily dose. "Ummmmm. That was gooooood. Sabrosisimo. Are you happy now, gringo?"

Jacob kept himself from smiling. He crossed his arms and locked his hands under his armpits. Joaquin walked up and stood behind the chair where he was sitting. He kissed the top of his head. "I know you're dying to laugh."

"Am not."

"Are too."

"Am not."

"How old are we?"

"Nine. We're nine."

"Nine, Jake? Nine? I couldn't get it up when I was nine. Can't we at least be sixteen?"

Jacob smiled. "Late bloomer, huh?"

"Well, I made up for lost time when I reached sixteen."

"OK. We're sixteen."

Joaquin kissed him on the top of the head again. "I'm going to hop in the shower." He walked out of the room and down the hall. Jake stared at the couch where Joaquin had slept. He remembered the first time he saw him, just standing there by himself like a beautiful silk shirt hanging over an empty chair. He had wanted to reach out and touch. He had seen him many times before he had spoken to him. He had taken it for granted that Joaquin had noticed him, too—noticed him because everyone noticed him—at least noticed his looks, his body, his masculine presence. But if Joaquin had taken note of him, that fact was not detectable in his face. He'd asked him if he could buy him a drink.

"No, gringo," he said, "I don't want a drink."

Jacob had immediately noticed his voice—a voice that was calm, comfortable, and free of any discernable rage. "You don't drink? Or you don't like gringos?"

"Oh, I drink."

"But not with gringos?"

"They're too used to being liked—they expect it."

"Not all of us are that superior."

"No—*but you are.*"

When he'd said that, something had shot through him, and he had wanted to strike out at him—to bust his jaw—to put a mark on his dark and perfect face.

"I can practically taste your hate, gringo."

"I have a name, godamnit!"

"So do I," he'd said quietly. "My name is Joaquin." He'd walked away. As Jake sat there remembering, all the confusing feelings came back, as if he had stepped back into the past. "You arrogant sonofabitch!" That's what he'd yelled at him. Joaquin hadn't even bothered to turn around and acknowledge his presence. He remembered how he'd just sat there and gotten drunk and picked some guy up and took him home—and forgot him almost as soon as their sex was finished.

A week later, he had seen Joaquin sitting on a park bench, drinking a cup of coffee from a Styrofoam cup and smoking a cigarette. He pretended to himself that all he wanted to do was hit the sonofabitch. He walked by him, and pretended not to notice he was sitting there. "Hey, gringo," Joaquin said, "want to get laid?"

"What's the difference between now and the other night?" he'd muttered.

"The difference is that I need the money."

He'd walked away without answering. Joaquin had run after him, smiled at him, and laughed, "Gringo, how come you let people push your buttons?" He remembered grabbing him by the collar: "My name is Jake—you got that?"

Joaquin had simply smiled, unafraid of the physical strength of the man that had him by the collar. Jake had grabbed him by the arm and pulled him home. He remembered undressing him, he remembered everything about the first time he'd held Joaquin's body, and how he had wanted to be violent, but wound up touching him softly as if he were a rare and fragile thing. "How old are you?" Joaquin had asked him. "I'm thirty," Jake said. "How old are you?" "Nineteen." After a few weeks of endless sex and endless talk, Joaquin disappeared back into the city. After two months, Jacob had given up looking for him; he swore to himself that if Joaquin ever showed up on his doorstep again he'd kick his ass all the way back to Mexico. About six months later, Joaquin knocked at his door.

"Where the fuck have you been?" Jake said. He was more hurt than angry—but no matter how much he tried, his hurt always came out as anger.

"My mother was sick," he said. "I went back to Mexico to see her." Joaquin swallowed hard and looked down at the floor. "I had to bury her," he whispered. He sat down on the stairway outside his house. When Jacob had reached out to touch him, he began to shake and say things as if he might die if he did not say them. Jake was not sure Joaquin was aware of the words that were coming out of his mouth: "As long as she was alive, Mexico was still mine—somehow it was still mine. Now, it's not mine, but here is not mine either. So where do I go, gringo? Cuando uno está perdido ¿dónde se va? I used to send her money. Soy huérfano ¿sabes? Soy huérfano." Jake had not understood what the word *huérfano* meant, but he understood that the word carried a weight and a sadness that he had also carried, and he understood that Joaquin was lost, and when he began to cry, he held him, and the young man in his arms howled as if he were nothing more than an animal, an alien being who, despite losing his capacity for speech, had not lost his capacity to feel pain. Jacob had carried him inside as if he were a baby, and when at last Joaquin had been able to speak, all he was able to say was: "Gringo, don't hurt me."

They had been together for twelve years and Jake no longer knew what it was about Joaquin that had made him such a necessary part of his life—whether it was his lover's body, his intelligence, his sense of humor, his awful pride. When they had met, he was still something of a boy—and he had remained something of a boy. He had never stopped attending Mass on Sundays, had refused to give God over to the straights and the gringos and the Protestants because he said, "They don't own him—he is not theirs." Jacob had never understood that side of him. Once, while watching his lover nurse a dying friend, it occurred to him that the man he had fallen in love with was good, was decent. He had never consciously thought about "good" until then, and since becoming aware of it, he began wondering about himself. He didn't think of himself as being good. He understood pain and he understood pleasure, and he had decided that his life, whatever else it was or meant, was dedicated to the avoidance of pain, and the pursuit of pleasure. But as he sat in his house staring at the couch where Joaquin had slept all night, he realized he loved this man, and his love was no longer the mere pursuit of pleasure. He sat there remembering, remembering everything. It was good to have a memory. "J, I want to go first. Let me be the first to go."

La Jolla, California. 1968

Jacob walked through the door of the living room and hung up his red letter jacket in the entryway closet. He ran upstairs and dumped out his duffel bag, his dirty football jersey and cleats falling on the floor. He lay down on his bed. He focused on his body. He was proud of it; he'd worked hard to sculpt a body that was perfect, and sometimes he could hardly believe it belonged to him. He rubbed his chest with his palm and reached for one of the magazines he kept under his mattress. He was surprised when he felt nothing there. He jumped out of the bed and lifted up the mattress. "Not there! Oh, shit! Oh shit!"

He lay shaking in his bed the rest of the afternoon until it was time for him to go down to dinner. He relaxed a little when he remembered his parents were having company. If his parents had found his magazines, they would not bring up the issue in front of guests. He would excuse himself, and go out for the evening—and think of what to say, what to say?—but what was there to be said? The magazines, full of pictures of nude men, said everything simply and plainly. Maybe Esperanza had found them when she changed the sheets to his bed, maybe she had thrown them away without mentioning it to his parents. Maybe it would be all right. But he knew Esperanza would not have touched anything that did not belong to her.

He made sure he went downstairs after the guests had arrived. His mother and father acted the same way they always acted when they had guests—they pretended to be fun and interesting and kind people. The only time his mother and father touched each other was when they had guests in the house. When they were alone, they either did not acknowledge each other or they argued. He found it odd that they became such strong allies whenever he challenged either one of them. They always jumped to each other's defense. Jacob had decided that being married was like being in a club—and that he was a threat to that club—or, at least, that was the way his parents treated him.

He recognized the two couples who were his parents' guests. He greeted them warmly. He smiled and glanced over at his parents. They smiled at him. "Where's Jon-Jon?" he asked.

"Your brother's sick," his mother said. "They called me from school, so I sent the car. When he got home, the poor thing was burning up."

"Maybe I should go up and see him," Jacob said. He started toward the hallway. His mother stopped him.

"He's sleeping, dear. He really needs to rest. Maybe you should wait until tomorrow." She looked over at one of her friends. "He's a very devoted brother."

"Yes," his father nodded.

He didn't like the tone in his parents' voices.

He was sorry Jon-Jon was not at dinner. Without him, the evening seemed endless. He tried to shut out the voices of the people who were sitting at the table. Something in the way they sat and ate and spoke betrayed the fact that they believed in only one thing: that the world belonged to them—that they were entitled to it, entitled to use it, to poison it, to dominate it. Their codes were easy to read. He knew he would not live his life like them, and as he sat there he was grateful he was gay—that separated him, set him apart, made him different from them. Their lives made him sick. Already he had inherited his parents' contempt without even knowing it.

As soon as dessert was brought out, Jacob asked to be excused. When his father allowed him to leave, he went directly to Jon-Jon's room. He sat on his brother's bed and turned on the lamp. He felt his brother's forehead, then held one of his hands. Jon-Jon opened his eyes and smiled at his brother. "Hi, Jake," he whispered.

"Are you gonna be OK, Sport?"

"Yeah," he said, "I'm just tired."

"You don't have to talk—I just wanted to sit with you a while, that's all." Jacob placed his hand on his cheek. "I think you need to take another aspirin," he said. He got up, took an aspirin from the medicine cabinet and made his brother drink it down with the orange juice that sat on the bookcase next to his bed. "Who brought you the orange juice?" he asked.

"Esperanza. Do you like her, Jake?"

"Yeah, she's nice.

"I like her, too."

"I bet she's a nice mother."

Jacob nodded. Nicer than ours, he wanted to say.

They sat in the quiet for what seemed to Jacob a long time. When he thought his brother was asleep again, he started to get up off the edge of the bed where he had been sitting.

His brother tugged him back with his voice. "Jake . . ."

Jake waited for his brother to continue—but he didn't. "Did you need something, Jon-Jon?"

His brother was silent for a while as if he were considering his words. "Jake, you think we could go and live with Esperanza? Do you think she'd let us live with her?"

"Why do you wanna live with Esperanza, Sport?"

Again, he paused and finally spoke. "Did Dad ever—I mean—did Dad—did Dad ever touch you?"

Jacob didn't need an explanation. He felt his heart begin pumping *hard, adrenaline running through him like an arroyo in the desert after a thunderstorm. For an instant, he held the image of himself in front of his father—he was killing him with his bare fists. That bastard, that sonofabitch. Outwardly, he remained calm. His parents had taught him a great deal about pretending. He kept himself from trembling. He sat back down on the bed, and took his brother's hand and held it tight. "Have you told anybody?" Jake asked.*

"I'm scared, Jake."

"Don't be scared, Jon-Jon. Don't be scared. I'll protect you. I promise. Go to sleep, Sport—I'll stay here till you're asleep. Everything's gonna be fine. I promise—everything's gonna be fine." When his brother fell asleep, he tiptoed out of the room. He heard his father's laugh downstairs. They were in the study—he could tell. They always had drinks in the study. The sound of his father's laugh made him crazy, he felt as if he were nothing more than anger—an anger so pure it made him feel perfect. Then suddenly, his whole body trembled, and he could see his hands shaking in front of him. He grabbed his left wrist with his right hand as if that would stop the shaking, but the shaking was coming from a place far away from his hands. He found himself in front of the study. The French doors were open. His mother noticed him standing there. "Why, Jacob, you look white as a sheet—are you coming down with something, too?"

Jacob stared at his mother.

"Jacob?" she asked again.

He could not make himself speak.

"Jacob," his father said, "your mother asked you a question?"

And then he heard himself say it: "If you ever touch my brother again, I'll kill you. He's a boy, he's a boy, don't you know he's just a boy? I swear if you ever touch him again, I'll cut your balls off and stuff them down your throat." He clenched his fists, and placed them in front of him as if he were in the ring. He began dancing around the study as if he were a boxer. "Pederast," he yelled. "Pederast! I looked it up in the dictionary when I was nine. You're a goddamned monster, Dad."

His father's face turned white—as if his son had drained him of his blood.

His mother jumped to his father's defense. "Have you gone crazy, Jacob? After all we've done—and then you turn around and accuse your father of—you're a monstrous ingrate." She began to cry and shake.

It was at that moment that something snapped in his body, and he no longer felt any loyalty to the people who stood before him, people who not only posed as his parents, but who posed as human beings. It was the way she had said "monstrous"—like an actress performing a role for an audience that could no longer sit quiet until the end of the play because the performance was insultingly unconvincing. He was free of them and their rules. He had walked down the stairs and into the study like a mindless robot, but suddenly, on hearing his mother's voice, he had acquired a consciousness, and felt whole, felt he could control himself and everyone in that room. All of the fear that had surrounded his entire life disappeared completely. All this time he had been taught to pretend they were a family—but they were not a family, and he was no longer their possession. They were not honorable people and he would no longer pretend to honor them. They couldn't hurt him. They couldn't touch him. He would take Jon-Jon with him. He liked that he had an audience—he would expose his parents to their guests. "Mama, when I was ten, I told you what Dad was doing. You slapped me—and then slapped me again. You told me to shut up, you called me a liar. I'll take that slap with me to the grave." He looked at his father. "When I grew big enough to defend myself, you stopped coming into my room, you sonofabitch." He looked around at his father's guests. "I wonder what you people are like with your children?"

"Shut up!" his father said. He felt his father's hand across his cheek. He fell backward. Only the wall kept him from falling to the floor. He and his father stared at each other. "Why don't you just admit that you're the one who's the pervert," his father said. "We found all your magazines underneath your mattress. It's disgusting."

"At least they're pictures of men, Dad—not little boys."

His father took a step toward his son.

"One more step, Dad—just one more step. I'll kill you—I swear I will."

His father stood perfectly still.

"I'm leaving tonight—and I'm taking Jon-Jon with me."

His mother stepped between them. She stood so close to Jacob that her face appeared disfigured, distorted, her breath beating him down. She started to speak. The two couples in the room moved toward the door.

"Don't leave, now," Jacob said. "Why don't you stay and see the real

Marsh family in action.'' The guests paid no attention to him as they hurried out of the room.

"You're going to pay for this little episode,'' his mother said. Her voice was as cold as it had always been, and though he had never lived in a place where ice and snow were common, he felt he had been frozen by the shadow of his mother's body. "Go ahead and leave—but you can forget about taking your brother. If you ever come near him, I'll have you arrested for kidnapping. You'll never see him again.'' There was something absolute in her voice—but Jacob refused to let her see his panic. "I'll find a way,'' he yelled, "I'll find a way to steal him from you. He's mine! He's mine!''

"I want you out in half an hour. You can take your clothes, and anything else that's in your room—and that's all. You're eighteen—you're of age. Your father and I never want to see you again. If you ever try to see your brother, you'll regret it.''

Jacob stared long and hard into his mother's face. He knew what she was like, knew she was capable of doing a great deal of damage. She knew enough people in power to get anything she wanted. He had seen her in action. He had no way of fighting her. He wondered which of his two parents was more deformed.

"Can I say good-bye to him?''

"No,'' she said, "we can take care of everything.''

"Just like you always have,'' he said softly. He said nothing else. He walked to his room, packed the things he wanted, and stuffed them into his biggest suitcase. His parents stood at the door making sure he did not disturb his brother. They walked him down the stairs. No one said a word. When Jacob opened the front door, he turned around and faced his parents. He looked straight at his mother. "There's one thing I've always wanted to do, Mom.'' He stared directly into her face, then slapped her across the face. She fell backward onto the floor. His father leapt at him. He wrestled him off, grabbed him by the collar and threw a punch at his face. When he drew his fist back, his father's face was bleeding. "If I ever see you again, I'll kill you,'' he said. He slammed the door behind him. As he walked down the street, he wondered where he would go.

The cops caught up with him in less than ten minutes.

 **10**

THE SUN COVERED the city in a film of dust and sweat. Diego walked to the corner of Fifth and Oregon to watch Crazy Eddie preach. He wasn't at his usual corner; it seemed unnatural to see the corner empty of Eddie's waving arms. I'll come back later, Diego thought. He walked up and down the streets, looking into the windows of stores filled with cheap clothing and people turning garments over in their hands. He imagined them thinking about the prices, trying to reach a decision about a certain article of clothing. Was it the right thing for the right price? Was the shirt really needed? Children were playing and running, and their faces were contorted in laughter. Some were crying. Mothers were chasing some of them, and Diego smiled at the awkward movements of women in heels chasing their agile offspring. Something about children trying to escape the grasp of adults made him want to laugh.

He walked along and was happy among the crowds of people even though he didn't know them. He did not have to know them to feel a part of them. Across the street, he caught sight of someone he thought he recognized. The woman stopped, spoke to herself, then crossed in the middle of the street without bothering to see if any cars were coming. A car slammed on its brakes and honked, the driver hanging out the window and cursing her. But she did not stop to acknowledge the upset driver nor his vehicle that had just come close to running her down.

There's that crazy gringa, Diego thought to himself, but it was an affectionate thought. Her skin was so pale his eyes hurt to look at her, and her blue eyes looked like a little girl's. She talked to herself all the time—just like Diego, only Mary did it aloud. She wore piles and piles of clothing that were in various stages of decomposition and she smelled of pigeon shit, but she was nice most of the time, and she usually had the time to talk to Diego. But there were other times when she didn't even recognize him—it all depended on what kind of day she was having. When she was having a good day, she remembered everything, remembered Diego and that he was deaf; when she was having a bad day, she remembered nothing, not even her own name. On those days she walked the streets and talked to herself like a drunk who had not seen a sober day in years. But when she was good she'd run up to Diego, hug him, and smile with a set of dentures she said she'd stolen from a nursing home. She always reminded Diego that she was the Virgin Mary, and that he should be good to her because of it. Luz hated her for her blasphemy, and would not go anywhere near her. "I'll kill her if I get too close to her," she said, "She believes her own damned lies. And it's all an act, anyway. Only men are stupid enough to pay any attention to her." Diego had tried to convince her that whatever Mary was, she was not a liar. "Maybe she's a little crazy," Diego tried to explain, but Luz wouldn't listen. "If you want to hang around garbage that's your business, Diego, but remember she's going to bring you trouble—and if you begin to smell like her just remember that garbage likes to spread its smell around." Diego was sorry Luz felt that way, but he knew he would never change her mind, so he avoided mentioning Mary's name in her presence.

There was something very beautiful about Mary's face, sensitive, verging on innocence—and yet it was very hard as if her very face had taken the brunt of the hits and slaps that her days of living had given her—the price for breathing. Something about her absorbed something of the air. She shines, Diego thought, like a puddle of water shining in the sun after a rainstorm.

Mary considered herself one of a long line of successors to the original Virgin. Each generation had its particular reincarnation, and she had been chosen from before her birth. "In a former life," she once told Diego, "I weren't no virgin, but this time around I've hit the jackpot. I came back," she smiled, "because there's entirely too much sinning going on. Gets worse and worse. Seems like we'd learn, but we don't, so I'm back to remind the earth. I'm just here to remind, that's all." Diego understood her logic—it was her way of connecting herself to the world, her way of belonging, her way of placing herself in the universe. She wasn't so crazy, he thought.

He watched her cross the street, and as she looked his way she flashed him a smile. She was having a good day: She remembered. She flipped him a finger and smiled. She ran up to him carrying a bag of clothes and hugged him.

"Hey Juan, how you be?"

Diego nodded.

"Well, you look real good, honey, like a pig in shit. Ain't you somethin'—and ain't it nice today? Ain't it nice?"

Diego nodded and pointed at the noonday sun.

"Yeah, sugar, shinin' like Liz Taylor's eyes."

Diego took out his pad and wrote: "Better than Liz Taylor's eyes. That sun's shining like Carlota's jewels."

She read the pad much slower than Luz. "Well honey, I don't know nothin' about that lady's jewels, but if you say so, Juan, then it must be so."

He laughed.

"I like it when you laugh, Juan, makes you look like James Dean with them dimples and all. I mean it—such a handsome man. How come you ain't married or nothin'? You like my outfit? I saw myself in the window this morning and I swear I looked to be the spittin' image of Miss Kitty."

Diego nodded, though he had no idea who Miss Kitty was.

She broke out laughing and suddenly grew serious. She wrinkled her nose and fought back the tears that seemed to come from nowhere. "Juan, oh, Juan honey, just makes me so sad. You know, Johnny, there just ain't figurin' people out. Some bastard man just told me I was an awful, wicked woman. Not in so many words, but I saw it, I saw it in his face. He treated me so bad like I was some cheap tramp. If I was a weak woman I'd have cried—I'd have burst into tears and bawled my eyes out—I'd have burst into tears like the second flood. But not me, honey, I ain't weak; I didn't cry. That bastard man, I tried to tell him, Juan, but he ain't like you, no sir, he weren't sweet and kind, and he weren't no believer. I tried to tell him about me, about how I was the Virgin Mary and how Gabriel came to me and all, and I described his halo as bright as the sun on the water and his wings as strong as twenty eagles. But some people, sugar, they just don't want to hear the truth— too hard to hear, I guess—just don't want to. That awful man, may God strike him, that awful, awful, man. He looked at me like I was vile and evil and crazy. I could see it all in his eyes—you can see everything in people's eyes, Johnny, I swear you can. And I could see in his eyes that he felt I was an abomination. Scared me so, those lies I saw in his eyes. I told him it was all there in the Bible, description of me and all." Taking a deep breath, she put her scarred hands on her chest.

Diego stared at her hands and looked back at her pale, quivering lips. Her lips were easy to read. Some lips were almost impossible, but Mary's were easy. Luz said it was because she was a goddamned actress. "She knows damn well you'd sit and listen to everything she has to say. She's crazy, but she's not stupid."

Mary took her hands off her chest and touched Diego on the shoulder. "Do you know what that damned man did? He threw me a quarter—that's right—a quarter! And I says to him, 'You gonna toss the Virgin Mary a quarter? A quarter? You'd think a well-dressed Christian man like yourself would give the Virgin at least a dollar—maybe two.' So he picked up his quarter and put it back in his pocket, and before I let that man get away I told him I knew for sure my son didn't die for his sins, no way, no how. I picked myself up and walked away—yes, Juan, that's just what I did." Diego tried not to laugh and looked at her sympathetically, but despite himself he smiled crookedly.

"Oh that smile, Johnny! Takes my breath away."

Diego wrote on his pad: "I'm sorry about how that man treated you, Mary, I really am, but what did you expect? He's a man, isn't he?''

Mary read what Diego had written and went into a fit of laughter. "If more men were like you and my son, my Johnny, I might enjoy this damn fool world, yes sir, I would. Look, honey, if you see that man, you kick his ass for Mary. But ain't it a nice day? Ain't it though?" She kissed him on the cheek and straightened out her clothes. "But really got to run, honey." She looked at her watch admiring it. "See my new watch?" She put her wrist in Diego's face. "Ain't it nice?" Diego took a good look at it and nodded even though he wouldn't know a good watch from a cheap one. "Sometime I'll tell you all about this watch, Johnny, it's got a story. It was a present, a gift—from a man—can you believe that, honey, a gift from a real man! A real good looker, too. He thought I was gonna give up being a virgin for a watch. No sir, not Mary, no way. The Virgin ain't lookin' for no suitors. I just took the watch and marched myself down the street, and I didn't look back neither." She picked up her bag and walked away swiftly as if she had some-where very important to go. Diego watched her. In the sun with all those clothes, she looked like a flag. Even her walk made her clothes seem as if they were being blown by a soft wind that made Diego think she had wings.

As Mary walked down the street, a woman threw a dirty look her way almost as though she was tossing a penny in her path. It might as well have been a bullet, she thought. "Mary, why does it hurt? Why does it still hurt?" For no reason at all, she thought of the way her mother-in-law had always looked at her—always throwing her out of her house with her eyes, her exiling stares. She wondered why the past still haunted her. Her husband had left her years ago, had taken her children with him. It was no good to think of them. It was better when she had no memory, and she cursed this day for her temporary sanity. She chased away the memory of her husband like she would chase a cockroach out of a clean kitchen. She thought, instead, of Diego. "The kindest man I know." She detested days like these, abhorred them, hated being so lucid, hated remembering she had a history on the earth, hated these moments when she appeared ridiculous even to herself. She touched her face with her thin bony fingers. "I am the Virgin. I am the Virgin. I am ... Mary just don't cry—don't—this will pass, will pass. Memories are of the devil. God, take it away, take it, take it. This moment will pass. You won't remember a thing, Mary, you won't remember . . .''

The thought crossed Diego's mind that Mary was one of the only gringas he knew—her and the nurse at La Fe Clinic. He thought for a minute, and it entered his mind that maybe Mary might be just the right person to receive his suicide letter. He thought about it again and decided it wasn't such a good idea since Mary might not be right on the day he killed himself. Maybe the nurse or maybe Luz would be better choices, but Luz was his editor. He would have to give it more thought. He liked the idea of addressing his letter to the nurse, since she wasn't as crazy as Mary and she seemed to be very understanding. She touched people, and Diego knew that her voice had to be as soft as her hands. She would read his letter and understand. Diego thought about the nurse; he pictured her and imagined her smell. She smelled like the inside of a church. He laughed at himself, and his thoughts returned to Mary. He wondered where she lived, where she slept, where she ate. His boss had kicked her out of Vicky's more than once. He said she wasn't very different from most gringas: all of them were crazy, and all of them claimed to be virgins.

He walked toward La Fe Clinic to see if Tencha was selling fruit. She had set up shop in front of the clinic since it was situated right in the middle of the Alamito projects. It had been a shrewd business move on her part, and a profitable one. Everyone who came in and out of the clinic stopped to buy fruit from her.

As Diego approached the clinic, he could see Tencha talking to some of her customers. He let them talk as he reached into Tencha's shopping cart that she had stolen from a nearby grocery store. He picked up a mango to see if it was ripe. Tencha watched him and shook her head as if to say that he had not picked a very good one. She picked up a better one and handed it to him. "Mira, m'ijo, compra ésta, te aseguro que está madura." He nodded and handed her twenty cents. He had no idea what she'd said though she appeared to be yelling. People did that. She smiled at him and continued her conversation with her friends. He smiled back.

He walked toward the Bowie Bakery, which was a fifteen-minute walk. He took the shortest route through the barrio, the projects, and the pink and lavender houses. It was a good time to walk through this neighborhood—mornings and early afternoons were safe. The night wasn't so good—the gangs were out then, and there were lots of them. He only knew the gangs' names through the graffiti on the walls. Mostly, the gangs were unknown presences to him: He knew they existed, but his life was so separate from theirs that they did not seem real to him. He knew a couple of the guys from the T-Birds whom he had met once at La Fe Clinic when they were waiting to be patched up after one of their fights. One of them had a finger cut off, and Diego remembered that he had not appeared to be in very much pain. They hid their pain well, Diego thought, and who knows, maybe it hadn't hurt as much as he imagined. He knew the gang members didn't like him, but a kid in the barrio had once handed him a note telling him not to worry because he had heard the big guys say it was bad luck to beat up on a deaf guy. They left him alone. As long as he walked the streets during the day, he wasn't afraid of running into any trouble with the gangs; their lives were lived by night.

The line at the bakery was long—it was always long. The Bowie Bakery, named after the high school in El Segundo barrio, was one of the most famous places in the barrio, and even people who lived in other parts of the city came here to buy their baked goods. It wasn't unusual to see many gringos standing in line alongside the people who lived here. He saw the people speak to one another as they waited in line. A lady was telling a young woman that her mother was at the county hospital. He couldn't read her lips well, so he missed out on the name of her illness, but he knew by the expression on her face that it was serious. Probably cancer, he thought. Cancer seemed to be everywhere, and Diego had a theory that people were getting cancer simply from being alive, from breathing in everybody else's anger.

He waited for his turn in line, and unlike most people, Diego enjoyed the wait. He was happy to be a part of the line and he liked imagining the sounds of the people's voices. Their voices, he thought, must be the same color as their skins: they speak in brown. He pointed to two apple empanadas, two fingers for two of them. The guy behind the counter knew him; he was a regular at Vicky's. "¿Dos empanadas de manzana? Sí, señor. Thirty-five cents!" Diego could see he was yelling, the veins popping out from his neck as he shouted. The man yelled again, repeating what he had just said, and then wrote "35¢" on a pad and showed it to Diego. He yelled again: "¡Treinta y cinco centavos!" Diego wanted to yell back: "I can't hear you any better because you're yelling, you idiot!" He smiled at the man and gave him thirty-five cents. "Thank you," he yelled, "y vuelva." Diego nodded. When he walked out he flipped him one of Mary's fingers. No one noticed.

He walked down to the Mexican Consulate on San Antonio Street and began eating one of his empanadas. He sat on the steps and watched the traffic moving at a Saturday pace—slow and steady—cars with drivers who seemed almost not to be aware they were actually driving. He noticed the Border Patrol vans moving up and down the street, the men in the front seats noticing everyone on foot, staring at them, watching for signs of foreignness like scientists looking for that virus that did not belong in the healthy body. Some of the vans were half-full; some were almost empty. The passengers stared at him or the sky, stared out at everything outside of the van, their eyes like hands ready to grab at anything. Every time Diego saw those men staring out at him from the inside of a green van, he wanted to do something, hit someone, set them free—and yet, it was all so useless, and even his own feelings seemed useless to him—not worth anything at all. Maybe, he thought, I've been having too many conversations with Luz.

Another van passed him slowly, looking him over. He waved at the uniformed man behind the wheel and whispered quietly to himself: "Hello, you bastards." He smiled, and cursed them, and it made him feel happy that they did not know why he was smiling. The green uniforms smiled back at him. He wasn't afraid of them anymore. For the longest time he had lived in fear of them, always wanting to run when he saw them approach him, and then one day it happened: They picked him up. It had happened at San Jacinto Plaza, and after the whole incident had passed he'd wondered why he had ever been afraid. They were nothing, Diego thought, nothing. Luz was right about them. They were even stupider than his sister: They couldn't even figure out he was deaf. They thought he was just another Mexican who couldn't speak English. He had even signed things to them, and had tried to pull his pad out from his coat, but they grabbed him as if he was reaching for a gun or something. He toured the city with them, and when they'd filled the van with people who looked just like him, they'd driven them all to the bridge. At the time, he had enjoyed the ride since it was slower and cheaper than the city buses. He had had a good time driving around the streets of El Paso.

They asked him questions at the immigration office at the border, and finally he convinced them to let him write something down: "My name is Juan Diego Ramírez. You know, like the guy who discovered Our Lady of Guadalupe, and I want to see a lawyer." The two officers had looked at each other with questions all over their faces. One of them asked him if he was a U.S. citizen. Diego had nodded and written: "Why didn't you ask me that before you decided to give me a free ride around the town?" One of the guys laughed and told him to beat it. "And try and stay off the streets." What did he mean? Why the hell should he stay off the streets? "No," he had written to Luz, "the streets are mine." Luz had agreed. "Damn right," she'd said, "they think everyone can afford a car."

Now he was less afraid. Luz had said that the border patrolmen were just a bunch of pendejos who had reached their highest station in life. "Some day somebody is going to write a story about them," she said, "and they're going to let the whole world know what a bunch of assholes they are." But nobody will ever write that story, Diego thought, never write it because El Paso was too far away from all the places in the world that people liked to read about. Nobody would ever want to read a book about the border and the migra— it would all be too strange, too foreign, too dull and hot, too poor and desolate to be considered exotic. People liked exotic, Diego thought.

He finished his second empanada. He played with the mango in his hands tossing it from one hand to the other. He would save the mango and eat it for dinner. He walked slowly toward home on San Antonio Street. He found himself standing outside the county jail, a tall, gray, concrete building with tiny windows. It was supposed to be escape proof, and as far as Diego was concerned, it was. Luz had brought him here once and pointed at it saying: "This is a giant dick, my Diego, that's exactly what it is: a giant dick they use to screw the Mexicans." He didn't know what to think about that. Sometimes she said things because she was as much an actress as Mary, but he appreciated the logic behind her words. He once told Luz that Mary and she were very much alike in the way they thought. She had gotten so angry that she shook him by the collar and threatened to hang him up by his balls on the flagpole at the bridge: "The American flagpole," she had yelled, "as a warning to other assholes." He had apologized and she had forgiven him.

Outside the jail, he saw mothers and children and old people gathered around the benches as if it were a park. Some were eating lunch and drinking soft drinks. Some were waving toward the windows as if they were waving at soldiers in a parade. Every day, there were people gathered here, happy and waving at windows and making signs—and behind those windows stood husbands, fathers, brothers, uncles. Their tongues were useless, here. All they had to speak with were their arms and hands. Diego felt close to them. He loved to watch them. A girl asked her mother which window was her father's. The mother answered: "Over there, the one at the very top. He can see everything. Right now, he can see you." She smiled at her daughter and took her up in her arms. Diego walked over to them and handed them his mango. The little girl laughed. He walked away reluctantly wondering why they weren't angry or sad or ashamed.

LIZZIE STOOD at the entrance to the rectory of Mission Dolores. She looked around nervously and stared at the outside of the church. For some reason, looking at it made her nervous. She pulled her eyes from it, wondering at her strange attraction to that building—it was as if she carried a memory of it around in her. But it was not possible that she remembered her own baptism. A chill ran down her spine. She looked away from the church, rang the bell, and walked in just as the sign instructed. A dark-haired woman in her late fifties with a friendly voice was sitting behind the desk. She asked Lizzie if she had an appointment with one of the priests.

"No," she said, opening her mouth to say something more—but stopped.

The secretary watched her for a moment. "Would you like to make an appointment—or are you here to pay for a Mass?"

Elizabeth paused for a moment, "Well," she said, "neither. You see—well—I'm looking for some information." She had carefully planned out the encounter, but now she felt stupid for playing this childish game. She was too old to be playing hide-and-seek, but this was the only way of making sure that her visit last night had been real. It was as if she were here to spy on herself. She was no longer sure of anything. "You see," she continued, "I'm a nurse at St. Mary's, and one of our patients died yesterday. He mentioned he'd been baptized at Mission Dolores Church. For some reason, it seemed like an important thing to him. I don't know if it's true or not—sometimes it's the dementia. Anyway, if he *was* baptized here, I want to give a gift to the church in his name." She paused. "He was a special patient. I wanted to do something." Her palms were sweating. She felt her story was a little precious, but when she had come up with this plan, she had figured if money was involved, the church would not ask too many questions. She despised herself for her cynicism. She was certain the secretary would discover her lie, but she had decided that telling the truth was not an alternative. "I'm a little nervous," she said. "I've never been this close to a Catholic church."

The secretary smiled. "There's really nothing to be nervous about." Her voice was warm, deep, a slight Mexican accent mixed with a heavier southern drawl. "I know how you feel, though. I once went to a wedding in a Baptist church. I was so nervous, you'd have thought I was the bride."

Lizzie laughed not so much because she thought her joke was funny but because the laughter helped her relax. She was desperate for a cigarette.

"It's very nice of you to want to do something in your friend's name." The woman's smile was warm and strong like a cup of coffee on a cool morning. "I love your earrings—beautiful." She turned off her electric typewriter and gave Lizzie her full attention. "I'm sure that if he was baptized here, we'll have a record. The only problem is that our system is a little bit, well, outdated. One of the younger priests wants to computerize the whole system, but the pastor won't allow it. The old priest has this idea that's it's holier to write things out with your own hand than to write something out on a screen. And, me, well, I don't take sides. I do what I'm told. Anyway, all of our records are kept in books—handwritten. There's no way I can look up your friend's record without knowing the year he was baptized—that's how we do it here—by the year. It's a simple system but it works."

Lizzie listened, already knowing what she would say. She paused a moment. "Well, according to his records at the hospital, he was born on—well—I have it written down." She opened her purse, unfolded a piece of paper, and read the date. "He was born on August tenth. Does that help?" She felt as though the secretary could see right through her bad acting.

The secretary smiled. "Do you have a year?"

"Oh yes—of course." She stared at the paper. Nineteen fifty-five."

"I'm sure we'll be able to come up with something." She looked at Lizzie as if she were waiting for something.

"Yes?" Lizzie asked.

"His name. I'll need his name."

Elizabeth broke out laughing. "I guess I expected you to have telepathy."

"Empathy, yes. Telepathy, no. I haven't learned that one yet."

"I have," she said. Lizzie was immediately sorry she'd spoken.

"What?"

"Nothing. It was just a joke." She smiled to herself. "His name's Salvador Aguila," she said.

"Aguila? What an unusual last name. Are you sure it isn't Aguilar?"

"No. It's Aguila—I'm sure of it."

"Very unusual," she repeated, "But it should make things easier. At least he's not a Garcia or a Gonzalez—we have thousands of those. One moment. Let me just look this up in our records. I'll be right back—it shouldn't take too long, but you never know."

"I have time," Lizzie said matter-of-factly.

The woman walked through a door and down a hallway. She carried herself with grace, with a sense of certainty. Lizzie was sure this woman did not simply "do as she was told." She sat in the room already familiar with its smell. It had smelled the same way last night, had smelled of book mold, and old wax, and old furniture. She thought there was something very soothing about this place. She felt tired and wanted to rest here for a long time.

She expected to wait for a while, but the woman appeared almost immediately, holding two big leather books in her hand. "See," she said, "if he was born in August of 1955, he was either baptized later that same year or very early in 1956—sometimes people wait a while for a relative to come into town or something. Take me, for instance: My godmother had to travel from Mexico City to San

Antonio in order to be present at my baptism. She was sick when I was born. By the time she recovered and made the journey, I was already eight months old. Of course, back then, she made part of the journey in a horse-drawn carriage. You know, when I went to her funeral, I just hopped on a plane. I sometimes think we don't live on the same earth as our ancestors." As she talked, she opened the book labeled "1955." "Let's see, we'll begin just after August tenth." Something in her hoped this woman would confirm what she'd found the night before—then she would know that last night's travels had not been a dream; then she would know that she had actually left her body and floated through the night like a holy specter; then she would know that her life would never again be ordinary, that she had left the legacy of the dull suburbs behind for good; then she would know she was sane, she would know she was gifted—gifted by that man whose voice ran through her like a cool wind. Salvador. She half-whispered his name. But the other half of her wanted her to find no names, no Salvador Aguila, no Maria de Lourdes Aguila, nothing. Half of her wanted this to be nothing more than a vivid dream born out of the sickness of being raised upper middle class. She sat there in the waiting room amid the familiar smell of dust wanting the smell not to be familiar. "Ahh," the woman said, "here we go. Jesus Salvador Aguila, baptized August twenty-second, nineteen fifty-five, by a Padre Diego Landa. It's him—I'm sure—date of birth, August tenth." She looked up at Lizzie. "That wasn't so hard, was it?" She looked down at the book again. "Did you know he was a twin?"

"A twin?"

"Yes, a twin. I'm sure of it. There's another listing on the same day: Maria de Lourdes Aguila, born on the same day, and baptized by the same godparents. The parents' names don't appear."

"Is that unusual?"

She nodded. "See." She lifted the book and showed the place in each entry that listed both the parents and godparents. "It used to be that parents often did not attend their own children's baptism. I know that sounds strange, but in the old days, the parents stayed home to prepare a big feast. Even so, their names always appeared in the record."

"Why do you suppose the parents' names don't appear?"

"I don't know. There must have been some special circumstances—otherwise the priest would have never allowed it."

"Are you sure the two are twins?"

"Two children born on the same day, baptized by the same couple on the same day, neither one listing the parents. Yes, I'm sure they were twins. You have a better explanation?"

Lizzie smiled at the woman. "It sounds reasonable."

"Did the sister go and visit him?"

Lizzie shook her head, then changed her mind. "Well, yes, she visited him once—but only once." She wanted to move away from the subject of the sister. "Anyway, I'd very much like to give a gift in his name." She reached into her purse and pulled out a pen and her checkbook. She wrote out a check for two hundred dollars, and handed it to the woman. She started for the door. As her hand touched the knob, she turned around and asked, "You wouldn't happen to know if he's having his funeral Mass here, would you?"

"No," she said, "there's nothing scheduled that I know of."

"Is it possible one of the priests forgot to tell you?"

She laughed. "It's possible. Anything's possible." She laughed again, "But I practically run this place."

Lizzie smiled. "Good for you," she said. "Thank you so much. You've been very helpful." She closed the door behind her softly.

As she walked down the steps, she heard the woman call her name. She looked up at her. "If I hear anything about his funeral, I'll call you. I'll take your name and number from the check—would that be all right?"

Lizzie smiled and nodded. "Thank you," she said again. "You're very kind." As she got into her car, she noticed the church. She wondered what it looked like on the inside. She sat in her car for a long time fighting the urge to go inside. She did not know why she was afraid. She turned the key to the ignition and slowly drove away.

"What brings you to Palo Alto in the middle of the day?" The old woman reached out and embraced her daughter. "You look a little tired." She took Lizzie by the hand and dragged her into the kitchen. "I just now put on a fresh pot of coffee. Your timing is perfect." She poured them both some coffee. "So, did you escape from the City to spend the day with Helen?"

"Actually, Mom, I took the day off because I've been working too hard—and I needed a rest. And I needed to talk—" She paused and shook her head. "God, I wish I had a cigarette."

"It'll pass, Lizzie."

"No it won't!" she yelled. "Sorry, I didn't mean to yell."

"What is it, Lizzie? What's wrong?"

"I don't know where to start."

"I'm your mother, Lizzie, just talk—but don't yell. I hate it when you yell. I'm not up for a fight today."

"Oh, Mom, I've been telling you everything I wanted all my life— and that's been the cause of all our fights. I'm constantly pissing you off about everything."

"A mother's supposed to frown at her child for saying 'piss' in front of her. Don't you know that, Lizzie? That sounds stupid, doesn't it? *It is stupid*." She reached over and touched her daughter's earrings. "Where did you get these earrings? They're lovely."

"I thought you'd find them a little overstated."

"Everything you wear is overstated, Elizabeth—but that doesn't mean I don't like what you wear. You're outrageous, overstated, and stunning."

"Mama, how come you're being so nice today? Your timing is awful."

"Elizabeth, you have an interesting memory. Why is it that you only remember our disagreements and never remember how well we usually get along? I don't understand you."

"Do we get along, Mama?"

"We both like to fight—so what?"

Elizabeth smiled, then looked down at the floor.

"Elizabeth, what? Talk to me."

"Mom, I came here to fight with you—to have a real good fight— and as soon as you open the door, you're so damned nice to me that I could just throw up."

"Sometimes I could just slap you, Lizzie."

"That's more like it, Mother."

The old woman shook her head. Elizabeth reached for her hand. They looked at each other for a long time. "Mom, I'm going to ask you a question—and I want you to tell me the truth."

Her mother sensed the urgency in her voice. She became afraid, braced her body, felt her heart pounding faster and faster. She knew what the question would be—did not know why she knew but she knew—and wondered if, after all this, she was about to lose the young woman who sat in front of her. She let go of Elizabeth's hand. "Ask me anything you want, Elizabeth. Anything."

Elizabeth sensed the resignation in her mother's voice. She took a deep breath, sipped her coffee, and whispered her question: "Am I adopted?"

Her mother heard the question and sat perfectly still as if she were absorbing every word into the deepest part of herself. The old woman refused to simply nod. She wanted to answer her daughter's question in words. It had been a hard question to ask—and she wanted to answer it. Somehow, she knew this day would come, and she refused to make herself the center of the moment, refused to play a helpless old woman begging for sympathy. She forced herself to speak. "Yes," she paused for a moment and searched her daughter's face. "Lizzie, you're adopted. It was wrong of us not to tell you—but sometimes you're so deep in a lie that the truth becomes impossible." She stopped herself from saying any more, and waited for her daughter to speak.

Elizabeth combed her hair back and looked straight at her mother. She studied her for a moment, her graying, thinning hair, the lines on her face, her hands beginning to twist from an arthritis that punished her body day after day. She looked at the woman she had known as her mother for all of her life. It wasn't true that she didn't feel cheated—but she knew she could never hate her, could only love her despite the fact they had never agreed on anything. It occurred to her that she was glad to love the old woman standing in front of her. She was almost surprised by what she felt. She could ask her anything, now. She could trust herself. "Mama, what was my name before you named me Elizabeth Edwards?"

"If you know you were adopted, then you must know what your name was."

"I want to hear it from you, Mama. I want to hear you say my name."

The old woman nodded. "Maria de Lourdes," she whispered, "Maria de Lourdes Aguila. It's a lovely name. I wanted to keep it. Your father wouldn't hear of it."

"And what happened to my brother?"

"So you know about him, too. He was adopted by someone else."

"Do you know their names?"

"Juan and Gloria Silva. He used to work for us. He was the gardener. They took your brother."

"Didn't you want him?"

"To tell you the truth I wanted him more than I wanted you. I was so in love with him."

"Why did you take me instead of him?"

"Elizabeth, I don't want to . . ." She reached for her daughter's hand. Her lips quivered. She bit them to keep them still. "I'm so ashamed." She let go of her daughter's hand. She walked away from the kitchen table and looked out the window. She turned toward her daughter and gave her a crooked smile. She decided just to say it, to say it and get it over with, be free of it. Elizabeth waited patiently for her mother to speak. "Your father didn't want your brother because he looked too Mexican—plain and simple. I don't know how else to put it." She cleared her throat. "I don't have to explain your father to you, do I, Elizabeth? He could ignore the fact that your mother was a Mexican maid because you didn't look like her. Funny, how selective our biases are. Look at your skin, Elizabeth. Your mother called you Blanca when you were born because you were so white. I wanted to call you that, too. But your brother could have never passed—it's as simple and as ugly as that. Your mother left you both with me, and I had to find a home for your brother. She asked me to have you baptized—it was all she asked. So the Silvas had you baptized along with your brother. Your father never knew. He would never have allowed it. You know, Lizzie, when I was younger, I was an arrogant woman. *I let your father break me.* I begged him to let me keep your brother. *I begged him.*

82

He said he'd let that baby die before he let him live in his house. I've been punishing your father for his refusal ever since. I hate him—but that's not new to you, is it?"

"Why don't you leave him?"

"Let's not talk about me right now. There's nothing pressing about my feelings toward your father. Never mind your father and me." She wanted her daughter to say something—anything at all.

"I think I resent you for staying with him, Mama." She unhooked one of her earrings, and clenched it in her fist. She tossed it in the air and let it fall to the ground. She stared at it. "I met my brother, Mama. I met him before he died. Yesterday, he died of AIDS at St. Mary's." She thought of the gift he had given her. "Mama, was there something unusual about my mother?"

"What do you mean?"

"Was there something special about her?"

The old woman nodded. "She used to tell me things about myself. She used to take my palm and read it. She said I would have arthritis when I was older. She told me my marriage would always be unhappy. She said my husband was infertile, and that I must never believe that I was barren. She said I would live a long time, and that I would die a peaceful death. She died less than a year after you and your brother were born. She wrote to me and told me she had always known she would die young. That's why she'd given you up. Apparently, she died of some kind of cancer. Your mother was a seer. Is her daughter a seer, too?"

Elizabeth nodded.

"I hope she's not afraid of it."

"Mama, *I am afraid*."

"Learn not to be. Don't be afraid of your blood."

"Blood?" She shook her head. "Am I my blood?" She looked confused. "Do you know anything about my father?"

"Only that he was killed just after you were conceived. Your mother never said how. And I know his name—his name was Jaime."

"I don't know what to do now, Mama. I don't know if I can face Sam again. I never liked him. He never felt like my father. But what will that mean?"

"It will mean you can hate him freely."

"I meant, what will it mean *for you*?"

"Don't worry—please don't worry. He made me promise I'd never tell you about your background. I had no right to make that promise. He had no right to ask me to keep it. Do what you have to do." She tasted her coffee. "It's cold," she said. "Is there anything else, Lizzie?" Her voice was soft.

"Well, one thing, Mama. How is it, if I was born in Chicago, that I was baptized in a church in San Francisco?"

"*You weren't born in Chicago*. You were born here. We moved to Libertyville right after we adopted you. Your father had a business in Chicago—so we moved—he didn't trust me to keep you away from your brother. The Silvas stopped writing me after a few years. I think your father had something to do with that. I'm sure he paid them off." She looked at her watch. "Listen, your fath—I mean he'll be home soon. He's taking the afternoon off. You'd better go—unless you want to see him."

"No."

"Then go."

Elizabeth hesitated. "But—" She stopped, then started again. "Don't you want to know how I found out?"

"I think I already know."

"You know?"

The old woman smiled and nodded. "Wait here," she said. She left the room for a moment. It didn't take her long to return with an old letter in her hand. "I received this letter before she died." She opened it carefully and began reading. "The boy has a strong gift. Nothing will come of it in his life. I had a dream. My son was pale and dying. He'll die young like me. He was holding his sister's palm—and giving her his gift. I had the dream many times . . ." Her mother stopped reading. She handed her the letter. "Take it."

Lizzie didn't look at the letter. She folded it, and held it in her hand. She looked at the old woman sitting in front of her. "You believe?"

"Sometimes it's not hard to believe."

Lizzie unfolded the letter and stared at her mother's handwriting. "My mother could write English?"

"Why shouldn't she? She was a very literate woman. She was educated by nuns."

"Was she born rich?"

"Very. Somewhere along the line she divorced her family."

"But why?"

"She never said. Your mother kept a lot of secrets. I suspect it had something to do with her politics." She looked up at the kitchen clock. "You'd better go, honey. He'll be here any minute."

Elizabeth placed her hand on her mother's face. "I'm sorry I've been such a pain in the ass all these years. I should've been nicer. Mama, I just didn't—"

"Shhh," her mother said. "We do what we can with what we know." She held her daughter as tight as she could, then let her go. "Don't come back. Don't ever come back, Maria de Lourdes. There's nothing here for you."

"What about you?"

"You'll hear from me."

Elizabeth nodded. There were no words left inside her. When she reached for the woman she had known as "mother," she heard her voice inside her just as she had heard Salvador when he had given her his gift. Only this time the voice was soft and at peace. The voice she was hearing was simple, and said only that she was loved, that she was deeply loved. She could say nothing. She kissed the old woman on the forehead and embraced her. "Come with me," she whispered. The old woman shook her head. Elizabeth turned and walked toward the door. She heard the old woman's voice in her body as she left the house. "Her name was Rosario—your mother's name was Rosario."

When the old woman shut the door, she noticed her daughter's earring lying on the floor. She clutched it in her hand and put it in a place where only she could find it, in the place where she had kept Rosario's letter.

On her way back to San Francisco, Elizabeth decided to take the highway along the ocean. She stopped in Pescadero and bought a sandwich. She drove to the beach and peacefully ate her lunch. The homemade bread was fresh—it was soft and good against her teeth and tongue. The breeze was cold, and she shivered as she hugged herself. She concentrated on the feel of the sand on her feet. It was a simple fact: sand on the feet. It was good to have a body, she thought. But she also thought it was good to know she was more than a body, more than something physical.

She wondered if she could leap out of her body at will. She closed her eyes and imagined herself leaping into the air. She opened her eyes and looked down at her body lying on the beach. Oh this is good, she thought, this is good. She floated through the salt air and thought of what her mother had said: "Don't be afraid of the gift." She thought of the house she had grown up in and remembered she'd always felt a stranger there. Now she knew. She thought of her mother, the father she had never known, the brother who had found her and passed down this strange identity. She was new. She repeated her name until the strange word she was uttering became a part of the wind: Maria de Lourdes, Maria de Lourdes, Maria de Lourdes. From where she was floating, her body was no more than a speck in the sand, just another grain. She willed herself to go back. She reached out for her body and entered herself again. She opened her eyes and laughed at the sight of the water.

12

EDDIE PLACED HIS HEAD on Helen's stomach as they lay next to each other in bed. The full moon softly lit the room; the breeze flowed in through the open window and Eddie shivered. Helen combed her fingers through his hair. "Cold?"

"A little."

They were quiet for a long time listening to the breeze, a cricket, and each other's breathing.

"A cricket is supposed to bring good luck," Eddie said.

"Uh-huh," Helen said lazily.

"I don't feel sleepy." Eddie's voice was quiet as the breeze.

"I'm not either."

"Wanna talk?"

"Something in particular?"

"Not really."

"How was work today?"

"Oh, let's not talk about work."

"That bad, huh?"

"Not really. I like work—it's just fine. It's even fun—can you believe it? I just wish I could take some time off right now."

"Well, you have a month after the baby comes."

"I want a month *before* the baby—just me and you. We could

stay home, and we could talk all day long—and I could spoil you. And we could get to know things."

"Things?"

"About each other."

"Don't we know what we need to know already?"

He said nothing.

"Eddie? You falling asleep?"

"I was just thinking."

"Tell me."

He sat up in the bed and hugged his bare knees as he faced his wife in the dark. "Remember the deal we made, Helen?" He waited for her to say something, but she remained quiet. "Helen?"

"I'm listening."

"Well, I don't think it's such a good idea anymore."

Helen looked directly at the ceiling. "We promised, Eddie."

"It was a game, Helen. It was just a silly game."

"And it was your idea, Eddie. You said, 'Let's not talk about our pasts—let's never talk about them.' "

"I didn't know then that we were going to get married. He rubbed his face with his palms. "We have pasts, Helen—they don't go away, you know? I think I want to tell you."

"That means I have to tell you, too, Eddie." He understood his wife's tone perfectly.

"It's time, Helen." He tried to hide his desperation. "We're going to have a baby. I want you to know everything. Some of it's not very pretty. Don't you think you should know?"

"Damnit, Eddie, I don't give a damn about anything but the present."

"Carpe diem and all that shit, huh, Helen?"

"Yes, carpe diem, Eddie. I don't want to think about the past—not mine, not yours. It's not as if I lived this life of crime, as if I was a prostitute or a drug dealer or as if I killed anyone—or any of those things. And you either."

"How do you know?"

"Don't be funny. I know you weren't a criminal—or a rapist."

"That's not the point, honey."

"I'll tell you what the point is, Eddie: I left who and what I was behind *because it wasn't a life at all, not at all. It was shit; it was like being dead, Eddie.* And I'm alive now, damnit. I breathe and I laugh, and—look, if I told you all about it, it wouldn't even be that interesting. It hurts too damn—look, Eddie, I don't want—Eddie, I don't care about what you used to be. I don't care how good or how bad it was—it's over. The past is just a dream—even if it had been a good dream—it was just a dream. There's nothing real about it." She reached for his hand and squeezed it. "This is all I want—just you and the baby." There was a stubborn note of finality in her voice.

Eddie squeezed her hand, and got back under the blankets. They said nothing else as they held on to each other in the cool night. Helen felt the warmth from Eddie's body as he pressed against her. She rubbed the palm of her hand on his back. "I love you, Eddie," she whispered. The breeze through the open window reminded her of something in her childhood. She fought the memory by playing a game: "A is for apple. B is for Boy. C is for calendar. D is for Diego"—the name just came rolling out as if it were natural. She didn't want to think about him, his deafness, her brother, the brother she'd abandoned, the brother she had run from, the brother who paid unwelcome visits and spoke to her as she walked down the street, as she washed dishes. Maybe he was dead—but she knew he was alive and living in El Paso. She wanted him to be dead— that would be easier. But he was alive and he was poor and he had no one. How could she have left him? She didn't want him in her room; she didn't want him in her head. She started over again. "A is for apple. B is for birth. C is for coffee, D is for deliberate, E is for my Eddie . . ." She listened to her letters, and her husband's familiar breathing as she fell asleep.

How long can we keep it back? Eddie thought. We can't stop it. It's coming. For both of us.

A full moon, round and desolate, hung in the night sky like a dead man at the end of a rope. Eddie ran his race, the leaves of the trees slapping his skin as he moved. Shadows danced around him like fighters in a ring. He ran, eluding them, but he knew he would not win the race, but he ran not knowing what else to do. He looked at the moon as if it were a god who might intercede; Eddie tossed it a prayer. Please! Please!

He kept running. Behind him, footsteps pounded the ground like fists, the earth about to break. Pain cut through his lungs as if they were being scraped raw by the razor-blade air. He rubbed his chest and kept running; his legs tightened; he pushed himself toward the light of a house in the distance: Have to reach that light, have to reach. The footsteps grew closer.

The man's breath was at the back of his neck—hot, sour, stale. Eddie screamed, no one to hear him but the moon. The man grabbed him, spun him around, breathed in his face, threw him to the ground. As he slid, his pants tore and his knees went numb. He could smell his torn skin against the earth—just a boy. He could feel the hand ripping at his clothes. He was being crushed by the huge body. "No! Get off me! No!" His voice went hoarse. "No," he whispered. He felt the man's hand over his mouth rubbing him into silence. He felt like a limp armless doll. A sudden pain— a knife cutting him in half. The man smiled and kissed him on the cheek. He lay on the ground and looked up at the deaf moon who never heard his prayer—the deaf moon whose dull light kept the earth in darkness.

Eddie woke from his dream, lost and wincing from the cramps in his legs and stomach. He rubbed his calves, and wiped the sweat from his face. He felt his heart pounding as if it wanted to leap out of him, as if it were a knife tearing at his skin. He hugged his knees and looked out the window. He stared at Helen who was still asleep. The moonlight was kind to her, he thought. He rose from the bed and pulled the curtains shut, then lay back down and shook. "No, I hate—you—I hate—why are you back goddamnit?" For ten years that dream had come to him, that dream that had taken over his nights, his mornings, his life—for ten goddamned years. When Helen had come into his life, the dream had vanished. She had been the miracle that had sent it away, had sent away the shame, the guilt, the great sadness that was his childhood, the sadness that followed him to adulthood. He had seen something of the same look in her when he had first spoken to her. They had been mirrors of each other, had used each other as stumbling blocks to memories that could not be healed by willful amnesia. Helen was a woman, not a miracle. It was not her fault. Now the dream was back, and he knew he would not be able to run from the grief, the anger, and the remembering that came with it. He sat on the edge of the bed and wept silently. He kept himself from howling—not wanting to wake his wife.

At five-thirty in the morning, Eddie opened his eyes at the sound of the alarm. His hand reached over to switch off the annoying beep. He slowly eased himself up and sat at the edge of the bed and willed himself to wake. He was groggy and exhausted. He turned his head and saw Helen sleeping peacefully. He envied her. She could sleep through anything. She was not like him—her sleep was not easily disturbed. He had suffered from insomnia since his father had— since his father had started coming into his room—since he was seven. Now, his dream was back. It was as if his father was still disturbing him, preventing him from sleeping his entire life. The dead do not sleep, he thought, and they do not let the living sleep either.

He leaned over and kissed his wife. He lightly touched her belly. She moaned softly but continued sleeping. He wanted to climb inside her brain to find out how she saw the world, to find out what peace was like, to find out how it felt to love simply and easily.

As he stepped out of the shower and dried his skin, he felt as if he were still dirty. He covered himself quickly with his clothes. He watched the coffee pour down into the coffee maker. As the almost-black liquid streamed into the glass pot and the aroma filled the kitchen, he thought of his father. His father used to watch the pot of coffee boil on the stove every morning. He thought of his dream. "How could you have done it, Papa?" He was that little boy again. He saw that boy that lived in his head, became that boy, *him*, that boy with the wide-open eyes and a mouth that was sewed shut by a father's sickness. He wondered if he would ever stop being that disturbed child. He hated that disfigured, confused little boy, wanted to exorcise him, burn him into ashes, bury him in an earth that would never surrender him ever again to the open air. He had the urge to throw the glass pot of coffee against the wall. But the wall wasn't his father.

Then he had met Helen. A new life, he had thought. The impossible had happened: He had fallen in love, and the dream that haunted him had vanished. But as he sat there, he smelled his father's breath next to him, and felt his heavy body on top of him. "God damn you." He whispered it again and again. "God damn you."

He had the urge to call in sick, but remembered he had an important meeting. "An important meeting, an important meeting," he mumbled to himself, but it wasn't important—not to him—not to anybody. They were all just pretending. Every meeting was labeled important as if to mask their insignificance. He had lied to Helen. He hated his job, found it relentlessly boring, and he felt it was killing him. He thought of a newspaper article he read about a woman who was addicted to cutting herself with a razor blade. He had read it at work and he had not found it a strange thing. He wondered what it would be like to cut himself—every day, slowly— but he thought going to work every day was the next best thing to slicing himself with razor blades. He wanted to quit, but could not bring himself to live off his parents' money. It was dirty, their money; it was more than dirty—it was not money honestly earned. When he had asked Esperanza how much money she made, she had told him she made four dollars an hour—six days a week—no overtime no matter what. Four dollars an hour to keep his mother's house immaculate. A month after his parents' funeral he had written her a check for a hundred thousand dollars. She had refused to take it. "Please," he had begged her, "please take it." He had seen where she lived, had known that she cared not only for her own children, but for her mother and father who were old and had nothing and knew no English, who had lived poor and would die poor and would know nothing of the world except for the fact that it had made them work. He had gotten down on his knees and wept. "Please take it. Please. Esperanza, you have to take it." He refused to get off his knees. "You have to take it." She had held him in her arms as if he were a little boy, but he had refused to stop crying until she agreed to take the money. He felt forgiven when she took it. It was the only part of his parents' inheritance he'd ever spent.

He closed up his parents' huge house, their corrupted house, their protected house that could not protect them from themselves, from their own violence. He'd worked his way through college by waiting on tables and working at pizza joints. He had re-created himself in the image of the working class. He had been an activist throughout his college days, and almost none of his friends had been white— and if they were white, they were either gay or strictly blue-collar. He always remained the friendly outsider among his own friends, keeping himself at a distance. He never allowed himself intimate relationships, as if he was punishing himself, doing penance for the sin of being his father's son, never allowing himself to be touched, to be known, to be loved. Whatever he had suffered, he had never known material deprivation of any sort, and he carried the knowledge that his parents' money was his for the taking at any moment he chose. He knew his poverty was chosen—chosen, and therefore disingenuous. If he had been taught to believe that private lives were necessarily miserable, then he was also raised with a deep sense that the public world was created for him and for his kind. He was too sensitive, too damaged, and too honest to believe he could ever know what it was like to be a worker. His own struggles had never been theirs, and though he succeeded in hiding his privileged background, he could never hide it from himself. When he watched young men with a background similar to his, he wanted to spit in their faces. He could tell them by their clothes, their confidence, the way they walked on the street as if they already owned it, the way they talked to each other, the knowing way they condemned people with just a look because those people did not acknowledge their superiority. His own class grew up with a peculiar and odious sense of entitlement, and he could read his own easier than he could read the people he loved or admired. He was disgusted by them, and wondered why more of them were not murdered. But he knew that he could not hate them without also implicating himself. So he lived hating himself, hating his own people, and always knowing that he suffered from a very peculiar sense of self-loathing.

His father's lawyer had warned him to sell the house: "If you don't sell it, I'll take your inheritance." Eddie had simply switched lawyers—something the lawyer had not counted on. "I was your father's best friend," he yelled. "I was his friend." "Do you abuse your children, too?" He'd asked as he walked out the door. He didn't know why he wanted to keep the house.

As he sat and drank his coffee in the kitchen, he stared at the morning paper. The headline read: DROUGHT NOT OVER DESPITE RECORD RAINS. He didn't want to read about the weather. It suddenly occurred to him that he could go back to teaching high school—he had loved that job, and now he sat and wondered why he had left it. It wasn't respectable—"You teach high school?" Too many people had looked at him as though he were unfit for anything else, as if he had settled for a second-rate profession. Now, he had money—and it was his. He had earned it. "But I haven't earned it," he mumbled. "Janitors and teachers and waitresses and farmworkers—they earn their money." He was disgusted with himself. He was becoming like his parents—his house was even beginning to look like theirs. "I have to quit. I have to quit." He thought of the baby and Helen. What did they want? What did they need? He looked around his house. "They sure as shit don't need all this." He was tired of pretending he liked this house, that he liked his job, but he had led Helen to believe he was happy—perfectly happy. What would she say if he said he wanted out—not out of the marriage, but out of this life that led to nothing. His parents had lived for comfort. He laughed to himself when he thought of how they ended their lives. He was glad he hadn't been in the house when his mother decided to kill his father—then herself. "If I had been there, she'd have offed me, too." He remembered the lawyer reading the will. Everything went to him—nothing for his older brother. Well, a hundred dollars. A hundred fucking dollars—and millions, millions for the younger son who had learned to make himself mute, learned to dress up for them, smile for them, be nice to them, respect them. He was nothing more than their nigger. He was their possession, their property, their houseboy. "Take the money, Eddie, you earned it. You showed your father a good time." He still remembered the last time he'd seen his brother. He pictured him sometimes sitting at the edge of his bed looking at him with his deep serious eyes that didn't know how to be happy. He knew his parents had sent him away because he'd beat them up. He remembered his parents' bruises, and he had always wished he had been strong enough to inflict wounds on them. He loved his brother even more for having fought back. He'd beat them, beat them because he had escaped from their control. When his parents had died, he had looked for his brother—but he hadn't looked hard enough. "I should have hired a detective. I was too young and too stupid." He laughed. "Oh, so today is beat up on Eddie day, huh? Stop it, Eddie, stop it. Take the money, Eddie." He pushed his hair back, then pulled it with a closed fist. "Would I be such a bad man if I took the money? Would I be like my parents?" He shoved his parents away from his mind. He brought his fist down slowly on the table, then opened it. "If I find Jacob, he will save me, he will save me and Helen. We will be whole, we will all be whole."

When Helen woke from her deep sleep, she looked at the clock and saw that it was after ten. "Oh shit," she said. She forced herself up from the bed, and slowly made her way downstairs. She found a note from Eddie on the kitchen table:

> Sorry I didn't wake you, but you looked so peaceful. And besides, the baby needs you to rest. Call me after you get back from the doctor. I want to know what she has to say. Want to go to dinner tonight?
>
> Love you, Eddie

She held his note in her hands and shook her head at his handwriting. "Such terrible handwriting. I bet you got F's in penmanship." She was suddenly filled with a deep sense of regret. She knew nothing of her husband's childhood, nothing of his past. He was somebody's flesh and bone. He was somebody's blood. He had not created himself, had been a part of someone, a part of the world—and she knew nothing of that world, just as he knew nothing of hers. She was sorry about their stupidity, and today she had a sudden urge to know everything about him.

She stared blankly out the window. The sun was beating down on her garden, and she knew it would be a hot day. Hot days always reminded her of El Paso. Eddie didn't know where she was born, where she had lived until she had moved to California and met him. He didn't even know the name she was born with—the name she'd legally changed as if she could change herself by picking a new name. One magic day she erased Maria Elena Ramirez from the record and she became Helen Rosalie La Greca. She'd found the last name in a phone book. She invented a vague Italian family whom she had broken with. As she sat there, her legal name seemed to slide away and she felt an alliance to her birth name and her brother and her hometown—it wasn't love exactly—just an intimacy that could not be affected by legalities. She could not banish what she had been.

Tired; she couldn't fight the memory that popped into her mind as she looked out into her garden. Her mother was reaching for a peach that dangled from a tree. Her baby brother sat on the ground next to her. She had bruises on her face, her legs, her arms. "No era tu culpa, Mama, no eras culpable." She did not notice she was speaking in Spanish. "What am I going to tell Eddie?" she asked herself. "What am I going to say?" She had lived this invented life for so long that she was no longer absolutely clear about her identity. If she told him the truth, would it be the truth? Or would it be just another invention posing as the facts of her past? But there was something else, something she had been refusing to acknowledge. The suppression of her self had nothing to do with her husband. She had changed her identity before she had even met him. And Eddie wouldn't give a damn about her past, would not stop loving her because she had hidden her history from him. They had both done that, because it had been easier, because they were keeping something not from each other but from themselves. But it was no longer easier to pretend that they were not the products of a past that had formed and deformed them to a greater degree than either of them cared to put into words. They had played a game with each other, but if they didn't stop playing soon, the game would end badly—for both of them. It wasn't working anymore. Eddie was right. As she looked out into the morning light, she knew she could tell Eddie everything. "But, Helen, what are you going to tell yourself? How the fuck are you going to fix what you've done?" She shook her head in disgust as she heard herself use the word "fuck." It was not a word she liked to use. "How will I find him?" She whispered his name. *Diego*. His name was a people she could not run from. She wondered how the return to her brother was possible. Why wasn't Eddie enough? Eddie wasn't everything after all. Everything was impossible—everything was too much to ask. She remembered the last lines of the poem she had read in the bookstore:

> Remember things back then
> as simpler than they were.

She laughed and shook her head. She walked upstairs slowly to look for the book she had bought. She had hidden it in the bottom drawer of her desk. She had the urge to spend the day reading poems—to do something different. She opened the book and touched the letters of the poem she had read in the bookstore. "For you there are no conscious departures . . ." She repeated the words again and again as if she were sewing them into her skin.

She picked up the phone; her husband's secretary greeted her in that perfect telephone voice of hers. She heard herself ask for her husband, felt the stones washing around in her stomach, then heard his voice. She tried to speak but the words were stuck in her throat. She forced out the word that was her husband's name: "Eddie." "Eddie," she said, "can you take me to the doctor's this afternoon?"

"What's wrong, honey? Is it time?"

"Yes, Eddie, it's time—but not for the baby."

"What?"

"Nothing, Eddie, I just want you to take me to the doctor's office. Then I want you to take me to the ocean and hold my hand as we walk on the beach. And then I want to tell you stories about my previous lives."

Her husband was quiet on the other end. "Yes," he said, but he was whispering, "I'll be there after lunch." She did not know what to think of the quiet in his voice. "Helen," he said, but before he could finish his sentence, she interrupted him.

"My name isn't Helen," she said. She paused, and tried to control her trembling. "My name is Maria Elena—Maria Elena Ramirez." She felt the tears roll down her face as she heard herself say her name. She had not heard it in so long that the sound of it was louder than she had imagined. It was a big name, large, heavy, bigger than anything she had ever carried—heavier than her baby. And yet, saying it, she felt a kind of freedom as if she had just given birth.

Eddie was silent as if he were listening to her tears. "Well," he finally said, "Helen isn't such a long way from Elena. It wasn't such a big lie." He laughed into the phone. "Maria Elena," he said, then repeated it. "Maria Elena. It's a very beautiful name."

She nodded, "And, Eddie, I was born in the desert, and I was poor, and I had nothing, and I wasn't raised in a suburb, and I'm not Italian—"

"Shhh," he whispered, "no fair. No more letting out secrets till I get home." His voice was soothing, and she felt calmer. "Just remember, honey, you can't do all the talking. I have stories, too."

"Yes," she said, "tell me a story. Just hurry, Eddie, just hurry and come home."

 **13**

Luz's hand reached out, lit the newly bought candle, and placed it on her altar. She touched the feet of each of her saints, and crossed herself. She kissed the feet of the crucifix, warm against her lips, warm from the heat of the desert that penetrated the entire house. She completed her ritual worship with a sense of duty—a sense that was, for her, a natural act. Her prayers were neither overly pious nor overly self-conscious. She prayed. It was what she did, what she had always done—even when she had denounced the European God. But she had remolded his face into something that looked like her world, like her people. She touched the silver milagro shaped like a human heart. It was hot to the touch. Everything in her small house was hot and she felt its heat deep within her. In all the years she had lived in this desert, the heat had never bothered Luz; her body was a part of it. But now that she was edging toward sixty, her body was no longer strong enough to absorb the harshness of the desert. With age, her body was divorcing itself from the land.

She smiled at the cheap reproduction of San Martín Caballero and thought of her mother who had given it to her when she had first married. San Martín, a gentleman in rich attire on a horse, was handing a fine red robe to a naked beggar. As an adolescent she had pointed at the picture and complained to her mother that the rich man should have given much more than a robe to the poor man. He should have given him his horse—even his house. "The rich don't give away their houses," she had answered. "So why do we worship a rich man?" "Because he was kind—he didn't have to give him anything." "Kindness is not enough, Mama. The rich man has a name—but the beggar is nameless. We should be worshipping the beggar." Her mother had not hidden her displeasure: "Who are you to criticize the saints? And if you don't like the idea of a nameless beggar, then give him a name." In the end, she had left the beggar nameless. She still hated that picture, and only kept it because her mother had given it to her. She had never prayed to San Martín Caballero, had never wanted a thing from him, not a robe, not a peso. She looked away from the picture and stared at her statue of San Martín de Porres. She whispered a greeting. He had became her favorite saint—aside from the Virgin. She was in love with his black skin and his perfect posture. Her mother had told her he was the son of a Spanish don and a black slave, and she often wondered about his mother's life. Perhaps it was his mother who had been the saint, but the fact that she'd had a son *carnally conceived* disqualified her from veneration. Luz spoke to him as she often did. "Qué bueno que no saliste como tu papa. You're lucky you got your mother's blood—that's why you're a saint. Don't ever forget it." She nodded her head, kissed the tip of her fingers, and rubbed her kiss into San Martín's feet.

She fingered the frame around the picture of her two sons. She kept the only letter the youngest had sent years ago. They were both doing well in Mexico City, both of them married and successful. She kissed the picture. "I was not a good mother—but was I so bad?" She had spent too much time trying to find another man, had left them alone too often. She spoke to the picture. "But I loved you, con todo mi corazón, les di todo."

Cinco de mayo, 1954. El Paso

She stood over the stove making dinner, the baby asleep in a basket near the screen door that led to the alley. There was a hint of the coming summer heat in the breeze that blew softly into the warm kitchen. Her older son, three years old, played with wooden blocks worn with use next to his slumbering brother. She watched them as she turned over a tortilla on the comal. "Your Dad will be home soon." She had not seen him for two days. She fluctuated between worry and rage. She kept herself from falling into a panic, a panic that would make her insane. Who would care for her children? He had been gone for longer stretches at a time, yes, much longer. He had promised to be faithful, and perhaps he had been faithful, but it was not another woman that took him away from her. She had not counted on his drinking. As she turned over a tortilla, she wished he was addicted to women instead of to the bottle—a woman she could fight. I should leave him, she thought. A man looked at me today at the market—he looked at me with want. Twenty-one is not old, not too old. She shook her head. She put the stupid thoughts out of her head. She had allowed him too much power. It was too late for her. She would forgive him, forgive him for everything. He's a good man, she thought. When he's sober, he has no equal, the best. I married the very best. She made a vow to herself to stop nagging him about his drinking. I make it worse, she whispered, I make him stay away. When he comes back, I will make him want to stay. She bit her lip and whispered his name: "Ricardo, te estoy esperando." She pictured herself walking with him down the street, arm in arm, she in a flowered dress, he in a white shirt and khakis—the most beautiful couple in the barrio. She rolled out the last tortilla on the table, looked at her children, and noticed that a man was standing at the door. She held up the rolling pin like a bat.

"It's me," he said.

"You scared me. Pasale." Luz liked her brother-in-law. He had become overly anglicized in manner and speech, but he was kind and he loved her children. He stepped inside, picked up the boy playing with blocks, and kissed him on the forehead. She noticed a strange look of worry on his face.

"Antonio, what is it?"

He said nothing. He put the child back where he had been sitting and put a block in his small hand.

"Antonio?"

He tried to speak.

She grabbed him by the shoulders and shook him.

"It's Ricardo," he whispered.

"No," she said. Luz slapped him, already knowing the news, already denying it, already wanting to blame the messenger.

"They found him," he said.

She slapped him again.

He held her against his chest

"On the street," he whispered, "this morning."

She did not ask what had happened, she did not want to know. She held the picture of them together walking down the street, the spring breeze blowing softly against the skirt of her dress. She dug her face into the shoulder of her brother-in-law.

Years later, Luz tried to remember if she had cried or not. It was a long time before she could bring herself to touch her children—they looked too much like her Ricardo. She did allow herself to remember how much she had loved him, and she did not even let herself know that she looked for him in all the lovers she had ever taken.

Luz looked around her small house. She took off her shoes and felt the coolness of the cement floor. At least the cement was still cool—so long as she hid it from the sun. She stood before the curtains she'd made herself. She kept the house dark in the summer because the darkness softened the hard heat of the desert. Today, the darkness provided little relief from the heat. *Lluvia, San Martín, lluvia. We need the water.* As she flung the curtains open, the light flooded into the room. She opened the windows. She saw her surroundings clearly. For an instant she hated the poverty she struggled so hard to love, to embrace. Today, the sight of her house made her sad and sick, sad and sick as the brown river that pretended to be a border between Juárez and El Paso. She felt a vague rage rise from her stomach to her throat like an ugly word wanting to find its way into the air. Luz would not let the word out—she would not speak it. She felt calmer when she sat down in a rocking chair her mother had given her. She stared at her books on the opposite wall and shook her head.

She rested for a moment, then rose and turned on a small fan she kept on the kitchen table. She thought of moving to El Paso— she could move there anytime she wanted—it was her home, her country. Her mother had chosen her nationality for her. She had waited until she was about to deliver, then walked into a clinic. She had been born a U.S. citizen in an ambulance on the way to the county hospital. She wondered why she had to choose between Juárez and El Paso. Everyone had always expected her to choose. But she would not choose, *would never choose*. She had spent a lifetime not choosing. She could not relinquish her Juárez because her family had lived in this ragged city for generations; it was her blood, her history, her inheritance; but she could not relinquish El Paso because it was the piece of dirt her mother had bequeathed to her; it, too, was her blood; it, too, was her history. When she first began working as a maid, she had hated El Paso more than she thought she could hate anything, hated the gringas who hired her and gave her their leftover clothes, their leftover food, their leftover conversations. They thought she knew no English because she spoke to them only in Spanish, and it was a disgusting thrill to know everything they said when they thought she could not understand their North American words. They assumed she was illiterate because she worked with her body. She had more books in her house than any house she'd ever cleaned. When she laughed at Diego for reading too many books, she knew she was laughing at herself.

At times, she could have killed the women whose houses she cleaned for their arrogance, for their sense of superiority, their great pride in their whiteness, their nationality—but she hated their men even worse. One man promised her papers for a blow job. He had pulled her neck toward his crotch. She bit his hand. Her English appeared before him like Guadalupe had appeared to Diego at Tepayac. "I don't need no papers," she'd smiled. "I'm a citizen. And I have rabies so you better get a shot." Before she had quit, she informed his wife—in English—about her husband's advances. "Why should I believe you?" she'd shouted. "Because I'm a woman," she'd yelled back. She never went back. After that, she chose her employers with care though they always believed it was they who chose her. She hated El Paso because it wanted to be an all-American city, wanted to pretend to be the heart of a great country, but could never be anything but a city on the fringes of Gringoland because too many people like her inhabited it, worked

103

it, worshipped it, loved it until it disappeared into them. She had worked in El Paso all her life, had cleaned so many houses that her hands reeked of gringo dirt and gringo sweat and gringo shit. And yet she loved it—because she knew what everyone in Juárez knew, knew that El Paso belonged to them, belonged to the border, would never be like the rest of America because their faces were printed on its land as if it were a page in a book that could never be torn out by any known power, not by God, not by the Border Patrol, not by the president of either country, not by the purists who wanted to define Americans as something organic, as if they were indigenous plants. Luz laughed. El Paso was hers and she felt it like she felt the presence of the saints on her altar, and she would not relinquish it to any gringo—or any Chicana—who was not intelligent enough to acknowledge she was entitled to its poverty *and* its riches.

Luz felt sick, and she needed to know the sickness, heal it. She thought of Diego, his raw intelligence, and his sense of wonder. He carried a great sadness she could not lift, and yet she found it disturbing that he was such an innocent. He was too old to be an innocent—he had no right to be one. She stared again at the picture of her sons. She had done badly with them, had been too harsh. After the death of their father, she had lost something of her ability to love. But she would not do badly with Diego. He was the only man she'd ever met that was capable of any kind of faithfulness. She wanted—needed—to protect him. But today she knew her sickness would not go away. More than she wanted to protect him, she needed time to rest—not from work—but from this place that was her. She stared at San Martín and waited for an answer. Finally, she heard him speaking to her. She could hear him whispering *Chicago, Chicago, Chicago.* She waited for Carlos to come and visit. When he arrived, he said he would take her with him. *But I will be back, my Diego. I will be back to take care of you.*

14

JOAQUIN WALKED into the living room and shook his wet hair like a puppy. "Want breakfast?" he asked. "I'm starved." He threw himself on the couch, then rolled onto the floor.

"What's gotten into you?"

"Nothing—I'm just hungry, Jacob. It's as if I haven't eaten for months. I just want to eat and eat."

"A real appetite, J?"

"I don't want to be J—not today."

Jacob nodded. "Joaquin," he said. "Stay," he wanted to scream. "Stay with me forever."

"I haven't felt this good in months. The poison pills I take must be working—at least today anyway."

Jake smiled but said nothing.

"Wipe that I-told-you-so grin off your face. I hate it when you gloat."

Jacob laughed. "I'm right about the medicine—and you know it. I enjoy being right."

"Well, what the hell—it doesn't happen that often. You want breakfast?"

"I'll make it."

"You always make it, Jake. Let me do it."

Jacob nodded. "OK. Let's see—I'll take two eggs over easy, English muffins lightly toasted, a side of hash browns, and freshly squeezed orange juice."

Joaquin opened the refrigerator door. "We're fresh out of oranges, fresh out of English muffins, and the potatoes are growing roots. Better run to the store, gringo."

"Gringo hates grocery shopping. If Joaquin is feeling so great, why doesn't he go grocery shopping?"

"Joaquin doesn't want to waste the best day he's had in months on a trip to the store. Why don't we just go out?"

"There's an idea."

"I'm serious, Jake."

"Well, it sounds serious, anyway."

"I have to get out of this apartment. I'm gonna go crazy. I haven't been out for a couple of weeks. I feel like a dog in a kennel."

"What if you get overtired?"

"What if we stay home and get killed in an earthquake?"

Joaquin laughed, but Jake shook his head.

"C'mon, honey, let's go out."

"Honey?"

"I forgot you don't like to be called that too—too domestic, too feminine." He laughed. "Come on, Jacob Lesley—let's you and me go out."

"I don't want you to get sick, Joaquin."

"I have AIDS, Jacob, *I am sick!*"

Jake slammed his fist on the table. "Don't use that word. I hate that word—you know I hate it."

"I hate that word as much as you—but it's not the word that's killing us, Jake."

"You promised not to use that goddamned word." He shook his forefinger at his lover.

"It was a stupid promise. I'm dying, goddamnit—*but I'm not dying today*—today I'm going out, today I'm dressing up, today I'm going to enjoy being alive without being afraid." He waited for Jake to say something, but nothing came out of his lips. He watched as Jake sat there clenching his teeth trying to reel in the rage that often threatened to possess him completely. He waited, and when he felt the threat had passed, he spoke again: "You can't save me." He paused, considering what he would say next. "It's not your fault," that's what he wanted to say, "it's not your fault." Before he said anything else, Jacob interrupted him.

"If I can't keep you healthy—then what the hell can I do?"

"Take me to breakfast and a movie."

Jake rose from his chair and held him. "Why am I always fighting you?" he whispered.

"It's how you love."

"I hate the way I love."

"Don't hate it. Please don't hate it."

"Why are we whispering?"

"So no one will hear."

Jacob laughed. "No one's here but us."

Joaquin raised his voice and talked into his neck. "We could eat breakfast at some joint, take a walk around the city, go to an afternoon movie—maybe see some friends—what do you say, Jake?"

Jake kissed him on the forehead. "How about if you dry your hair first?"

Joaquin dug his head deep into Jake's chest. "OK," he said. "You know, I feel almost normal today."

"Then let's have an almost-normal day."

Julimes, Chihuahua. 1974

Joaquin watched passively as the men lowered his father into the grave. He moved his eyes from one mourner to the next wondering why anyone would feel sad at this event. Perhaps it was all a public performance, a ritual everyone needed to enact.

Even as he was being lowered to the ground, he saw his father's dark face, his smile, and he could almost smell the liquor on his breath. Once, he had refused to tell him where his mother had hidden a bottle of whiskey; his father had knocked him to the ground and he had only stopped beating him because his brother had taken the bottle from its hiding place and waved it in front of his face. "Mom will be mad," he'd told his brother. "You should have let him keep beating me." "He would have killed you," his brother had said. He stared at the men who had carried his

107

father's casket to the cemetery. He studied the priest as he handed his mother a crucifix and whispered something in her ear. He liked the priest's face; he liked the way he moved, the way he respected the ground. The priest was as old as his father, but stronger and kinder, and he had smile lines on his face. Joaquin had once asked him if he could be his father. "No," the priest had said, "we don't pick our parents. God gives us all a mother and a father." "Then God chose badly," he'd answered. He had expected the priest to get angry but the priest had smiled and put his rough hand on his face. "God doesn't choose badly, but people often do," he said. "Just remember that." After that conversation, the thought entered his head that his mother had chosen very badly. He stopped blaming God for her choice.

Two nights earlier, Joaquin's mother had told him that his father had been killed in an accident, but he knew his father had been shot in a fight—he had heard it from his friends, had heard his older brother talking, and had heard the talk in the streets of the village. A man had killed him because he was sleeping with his wife. His mother could not protect him from the voices of the village. Julimes was not a good place for secrets; Julimes knew every woman his father had bedded down, every man he had ever cheated; Julimes repeated the secrets of the fathers to the sons.

He stared at his mother's face, her long perfectly combed hair that was as black as her dress. Her eyes were red, and the tears fell slowly as if they were keeping time. He wondered if she had loved him—or if she was crying because she was relieved. But it was he who was relieved, he who was glad he no longer had to defend his father's reputation in the village, he who was glad he no longer had to pay him respect in his house as if he was some kind of god. His father had never spoken to him except to utter a command: It was Joaquin's job to keep his father's shoes shined, his job to bring in water, to gather wood, to run all his errands, his job to ask for credit at the village store. Joaquin had once gone out to hunt rabbits with his older brother and had accidentally found his father making love to a girl. His father had slowly dressed himself, then slapped them both with all his might. Joaquin had fallen to the ground. "That's to remind you to keep your mouths shut." His father had later given him some money. Joaquin had taken his father's bribe quietly. Now, as he took one last look at the old man's body, he was almost happy. He had been treated as if he were invisible, and now he would no longer have to pretend he was a ghost. As he watched his mother cry, he imagined she was crying because she was now as free as he was, free of her bad choice. He hoped she was not crying because she had loved him; he did not deserve her love or her tears. He reached for his mother's arm. *"Mama, no llores. Yo te protejo."* His mother had clutched him to herself and wept into his shoulder. He had vaguely hoped she would never let go of him.

Two weeks after his father's death, Joaquin's mother went begging for food in the village. The priest sent her home with beans and rice, and told her the streets were no place for a decent woman. A day later, he arrived with a job offer for José, Joaquin's older brother. The man who maintained the church grounds and cemetery was old and sick; he had gone to live with his daughter in Monterrey. José's salary at the church was small, but it was enough for them to live on. They had little, but they needed little. The priest was kind, and sometimes he brought José and Joaquin new clothes or brought his mother fabric to make sheets and skirts.

Joaquin spent his free time playing and hunting in the desert. He knew every arroyo, every path, every bush. He knew the best places to hunt rabbits, knew where the rattlesnake dens were located, knew where most of the people of the village hid things. Sometimes he dug the treasures up, and examined them—but it never occurred to him to take what did not belong to him.

Now that his father was dead, he felt that the desert had taken his place. The desert loved him, was good to him, gave him food, provided a place to run and play. He never thought of other places, never even imagined a world outside of this vast and desolate place. In his mind, he would be a boy forever and he would live with his mother and brother— and when they were in trouble the priest would help them. They would live like that forever—just him and his family and the priest and the desert. His mind was a simple place, and, for a time, there was nothing to disturb him.

One evening, he came home with three rabbits and handed them to his mother. She smiled at him. *"Mi hombrecito,"* she said, *"te adoro."* But she looked sad and Joaquin discovered his brother, José, was sick. He tossed and turned on the bed, and he was white and could not keep from moaning. She stayed up all night trying to keep the fever down, but in

109

the morning he was still on fire. "Go and get the priest," she told Joaquin.
He ran to the church and returned with the priest. When he entered their
house, he sat with his mother and they spoke. Joaquin did not listen to
what they were saying. José seemed to be far away and he wondered if
his brother would return from the place to where he had drifted. The
priest stayed. He took out his holy oils from his bag and rubbed them into
José's forehead, his hands, his chest, his feet. He spoke words over him,
and Joaquin and his mother answered the priest's prayers as they knelt
beside the bed next to the candles and the crucifix and his brother's sick
body. Joaquin could hear his mother begging God not to take him. "No
te lo lleves. Diosito Santo, no te lo lleves." When he stopped breathing,
his mother howled into the night like a wild animal caught in a trap.
She pounded on the priest's chest as he held her. Joaquin thought she
might cry until she, too, died.

Now, he was the only one left. He would have to take care of her.

A month after they buried José, Joaquin and his mother left for El
Paso. The priest had a sister who lived there, and he promised she would
take them in. One night in December they swam across the river with a
crowd of strangers.

The day had felt almost normal. They held hands during the
matinee—something they had not done since they first moved in
together. They had taken a walk after the movie, and they tried to
laugh about things, but nothing seemed funny or amusing. The sun
seemed hallow and fake, and the evening light in the apartment
was as dull as Joaquin's mood. The day was long, went on forever.
Joaquin waited for it to end, but as night fell, he could not sleep.
In bed, as he listened to Jake's breathing, he leaned into his chest.
He thought of his childhood sky, a sky as pure as anything he had
ever seen. For an instant he smelled the earthen floor of the house
where he was born. The smell of his lover's skin made him think
of rain in the desert. He wanted to go back there, to be buried there,
to lie in that ground forever. "But who is left there to remember
me?"

He thought of his father's death, the house where he had lived
with his brother and his mother, the arroyos where he learned to

dream of water. He remembered the crude crucifix that hung above the bed he shared with his brother. He remembered the old church where the kind priest said Mass for the people of his village and the odor of candle wax and incense and dry adobe made him believe for an instant that he was back in the place of his genesis. He wasn't sleepy or tired and he was happy to lie there holding on to the only human being left in the world who would mourn his passing. The thought occurred to him that he would never live to be forty. His hands would never feel Jake's skin again. He fought the sadness. Why should he be sad? He was sick of the world, sick of the way it lived and behaved, sick of the attitudes it fostered—rewarding those that least merited reward, sick of the way it treated those who wanted nothing more than to live simply, sick, sick at the fact that the world he knew had always made him feel like a freak because he had been born poor and Mexican and gay, sick of being hated, sick of his body's disease. What was there to be sad about? Why should he be sad to leave a physical world when it had exiled him from the very beginning. "Why do I want to live? Mama, tengo miedo. Mama." He shook in the darkness, and everything became so dark that he felt he had fallen into a hole where no light could ever enter. There would be nothing forever. It was as if he had died and he could no longer feel Jacob next to him. He was alone in the coffin dark. Then, Joaquin saw a dark-skinned woman surrounded by light coming toward him, closer and closer. She sat at the edge of the bed. "M'ijo, no tengas miedo." She touched his shoulder and whispered his name. "Joaquin, no llores." She spoke in the language of the desert—in a voice he had not heard in twelve years. He had whispered in her ear, "Mama, no tengas miedo." She had come back to return the gift. Her touch was as warm as he remembered it. She sat for a long time, and he was happy staring into her eyes and began thinking he had died and gone to a perfect place. Then she was gone. The room was again dimly lit with the lights of the city. He could feel Jacob's skin; he could hear his heart pounding and he was glad to be breathing, happy to have lived. He wanted to wake Jacob; he wanted to make love to him; he wanted to feel every part of him while he was still able to feel him. "Jacob, wake up," he whispered. "Please wake up."

 **15**

DIEGO WALKED BACK toward the corner of Fifth and Oregon. By now, Crazy Eddie should be preaching, he thought. From two blocks away he could see Crazy Eddie's hands flying in the air like pigeon's wings. As he moved closer he could see the Bible in his hand, he could see the words come from his lips, lips that resembled Mary's: "He has shown his might with his arm; he has scattered the proud in their conceit . . . The rich he has sent away empty." His eyes flashed like firecrackers and the veins in his neck popped out making him look as if he were about to explode. "Do you hear me?" he yelled as he pointed at the sky, "Do you hear? He speaks to us. He gives us his word."

The young cholos sitting across the street yelled things at him, and began throwing rocks. Diego caught sight of one of the boys' lips as he was saying: "We don't hear God, old man, all we hear is you. Shut up—shut the hell up!" The boys who sat next to him laughed.

But Eddie kept preaching. Diego turned to watch him as he lifted up his Bible: "Blessed be the Lord, the God of Israel for he has come to his people and set them free."

One of the cholos stepped up to him and began yelling in his face. Diego couldn't see everything the cholo was saying, but he was able to read, "Shut the fuck up before someone locks you up for good."

112

"And God will rescue me," Crazy Eddie yelled back.

"And who's gonna rescue us from you, old man? Who's gonna set us free from all the pinche locos?"

Eddie shook his head and kept reading from the Bible. "Every valley shall be filled, every mountain shall be leveled . . ."

The young men sitting on the street corner shared a cigarette and passed it between themselves. Diego watched to see if anything else was going to happen. "Why doesn't God level the migra or the fucking police?" one of them yelled. "Tell me why—tell me that!" The young man stared at Eddie and turned away from him. He said something to one of his friends, and for a long time they all sat there quietly. Diego stared at all of them: the five youths sharing a cigarette and sitting at last in silence, the people passing, and Crazy Eddie reading the Bible. He pulled out a dollar from his pocket and pulled at Eddie's sleeve. Eddie stopped his reading and stared at him. "Here," Diego wrote on his pad, "this is for you. I believe." Crazy Eddie smiled and put the dollar in his pocket. He took a deep breath and began preaching again.

Diego began walking toward Sunset Heights. The day had grown too hot—the morning had melted away. As Diego approached his house, he saw what looked like the figure of an old woman: a shadow with a dress draped over a form. The form was sitting on the steps to his apartment house. As he walked closer he thought the woman was the landlord's wife who often sunned herself—fully clothed—on the steps of the house. Moving closer, he realized the woman sitting on his steps was Luz. It was strange to see her sitting in front of his house since she had never once visited him in the few years that they had known each other, though she had always known exactly where he lived.

She saw Diego moving toward her; she waved her arms and appeared to yell something. Diego could see her Mayan lips move, but he was not close enough to guess what she had said. He motioned to her and pointed at his ear. She laughed—and as Diego moved up to where she was sitting he took out his pad and wrote: "So what brings you to my neighborhood? I thought you hated Sunset Heights."

"I never said I hated Sunset Heights. It's nice here, Diego." He smiled to himself; she did not seem to remember saying how much she detested this neighborhood. "And what do you mean 'what brings me here?' I'm waiting for you, pendejo—what else would I be doing sitting on your front steps?"

Diego laughed and wrote: "Twice in one day, Luz! I don't know if I can handle it!"

Luz smiled softly. "Twice in one day," she repeated. "Well, good friends can see each other as often as they like. Don't you agree, Dieguito?"

He nodded, but he knew Luz was not here simply to make small talk. There was something on her mind, something she wanted to talk about. "So," Diego wrote, "are you here to take me to a late lunch?"

Luz looked at his pad and laughed. "No lunches, Dieguito, not today." She stopped talking and was lost in her thoughts for a few moments. "Guess who I saw right after you left me at the bridge? Carlos. He says he's going to Chicago, says he has a place to live with some people he knows, and he says he has someone who's going to take him. He says maybe I should think about going with him."

"Well," Diego wrote, "are you thinking about going?" He stopped, then wrote: "What will you do in Chicago?"

"What the hell do I do here? I can be a maid anywhere, can't I?"

"It seems like you want to go."

She stared at Diego's handwriting. She was quiet. "Give me one of your cigarettes." Diego reached into his pocket, handed her one, put one in his own mouth, and lit both their cigarettes. Luz took a deep puff and exhaled the smoke slowly through her nose. "Ay, Dieguito, no sé. I just don't know. I'm tired of this city—I'm tired. I'm so damned tired I could lie down and die."

"I thought when you got tired you only got madder."

"God, Dieguito, you really are a pendejo. Do you believe everything I say?" She took another drag from her cigarette and said nothing. Both of them sat in the hot afternoon sun sweating and smoking their cigarettes. She grabbed Diego's arm: "Diego," she said slowly, "listen to me. Listen. There's nothing in El Paso for me.

My sons are gone, and neither of the bastards ever bother to write or send any money. Sometimes, I miss them—and I write to them, but nothing ever comes back. And you know something? They can go to hell along with everybody else. Malditos. Ungrateful pigs— that's what I raised, and goddamnit, I don't deserve to be treated like that. Diego, I want to go somewhere. Just somewhere, Dieguito."

Diego laughed and touched her arm. She brushed her fingers against his hand.

"What do you think I should do?" she asked.

"I think you should go," he wrote. "What the hell? If you don't like it you can always come back. El Paso's not going anywhere. What have you got to lose?"

She nodded. "And you, Diego? Why don't you come with us?"

"I can't."

"Why not?"

"I'd lose my job."

"Why don't you tell that son of a bitch you work for to go straight to hell? Tell him to shove Vicky's blue bar up his ass."

"What would I do in Chicago?"

"Same thing you do here—nothing."

"Well then, I think I'll stay." He printed his letters firmly, stubbornly.

"You're never going to get anywhere with that attitude, Diego."

"It's OK," he wrote, "as soon as I was old enough to know I was alive, I knew I would never be going too far."

Luz cackled. Diego could almost picture her laugh in the air. "You have a sense of humor, mi amor. Hold on to it."

"A sense of humor?" Diego wrote, "Not really, Luz. It's just that you laugh at everything."

"You're damn right, Diego. You learn to laugh at everything. People who cry are boring. There's nothing more boring than someone who's always crying." She flipped her cigarette to the ground and stepped on it. As Diego watched her, he felt the urge to tell her to stay. He wanted to yell at her: "Stay where you belong. Who will I talk to on Saturdays?" She looked at him. "You know, Diego, I'm getting old—but I'm going to laugh until the end. If I stop laughing they'll treat me like a cigarette butt."

Diego nodded. He put his pen on his pad and asked: "So, when are you leaving for Chicago?"

"Hell, I don't know. I have to think about it some more."

"If you decide to go, come and say good-bye to me at Vicky's."

She took his pad away and wrote: "What am I going to do about you, my Diego?" She looked straight into Diego's eyes and said, "If I'm not at the bridge next Saturday you'll know I've gone with Carlos to Chicago." She squeezed his hand. "Thanks for the cigarette, Diego." She rose from the steps slowly and walked down the street. She wrapped herself in a black shawl even though it was too hot to be wearing one. He wanted to grab her and keep her from going. He wanted to scream at her: "Goddamnit, don't go!" He wanted to hear himself yell it; he wanted to know what it was like to feel sounds coming out of himself, to feel the notes touch the insides of his throat like fingers.

THE HERON DIES
IN FLIGHT

"No more medicine, Jake. I can't do it anymore."

"You'll die."

"Then let me."

"I can't."

"When my body wanted to breathe, it breathed, when it was hungry, it ate—now it's hungry for other things. Let it go, let it die."

"You talk about your body as if it doesn't even belong to you anymore."

Joaquin bit his lower lip, then licked it, his mouth as dry as the soil he was raised in. "I know. But there's more, there's more than just the physical, there's more than—"

"More what? More shit?"

"Not more shit, Jake. I don't know—"

"Oh, you mean like heaven. Shit, J—"

"I didn't call it heaven."

"Oh, the great beyond?"

"Don't, Jake. You think there's nothing more to you than your body?"

"It's a great place to start."

"But is it a great place to end?"

"We don't have any options. That's where it starts—that's where it ends."

"There's more."

"No—"

"You don't know."

"What we—you and I—what we *know* will be gone. Our two bodies, they'll be gone. I don't care about anything else, J."

"It's just that you don't know anything else."

"Do you, Joaquin?"

He bit his lip again. He stared at Jake for a long time—then reached over and combed his blond hair with his trembling fingers. "I had a dream last night. It was dark and there was light around her and she kept saying, "No tengas miedo. Hijo de mi vida, no tengas miedo."

"Which means?"

"She was telling me not to be afraid."

"Who's the she?"

"My mother."

"It was a dream."

"She came for me."

"That's ridiculous. What do the dead need from the living? The dead have no lips, they have no voice. The dead don't speak, J— and even if they did, they'd only speak to each other. Let the dead care for each other—let the living do the same. And it's the living that matter. Take your medicine."

"That stuff is killing me, damnit. I know my body. I know what it's saying. I heard it tremble the first time I saw you in that bar, gringo, I heard it almost scream. I felt it turn into a fist when my mama died." His voice was beginning to sound like the desert. "I know my body. You have to help me die."

"I won't."

Joaquin leaned over and kissed his cheek. "Jacob Lesley Marsh, you don't have a choice."

Jake pushed him away. "The hell I don't." He started walking toward the door.

"When are you gonna start accepting what's happening to us?

Stupid gringo. Are you just gonna play hide-and-seek until it's time?"

"What's that supposed to mean?"

"Jacob, aren't you tired? Aren't you ever going to get tired of being angry? What's so great about being pissed off all the time?"

Jacob stared at him for a long time. "I don't always want to hear everything you have to say."

"I've heard that line before, Jake."

"No, I don't think you've ever heard it."

"Are we going to fight?"

"No, we're not going to fight." He slammed the door as he walked out of the apartment.

Joaquin stood at the door and laid himself down on the floor. He felt small and fragile and was afraid he'd break if he made a sudden move. "I'll be safer on the floor," he said, forgetting that Jake had just left. He stared at the ceiling and tried to think of a reason to keep fighting.

2

DIEGO THOUGHT ABOUT Luz all week. He felt her breath in his room, smelled it; he dreamed her face fading away like smoke. At night he would stare at his pad and spell "Chicago." C-H-I-C-A-G-O. It was a strange word and he thought the word looked Aztec, but he had gone to the public library and discovered that Chicago meant the place of bad smells. He wrote a note to himself: "Who wants to live in the place of bad smells?" He thought of sneaking over to the barrio to spray-paint a new sign on the walls: CHICAGO STINKS! VIVA JUÁREZ! He thought he might add: "Luz, don't go. Don't go, don't go, don't go." He almost ran to the door and down the stairs to buy the spray paint. He pictured himself spraying the letters on the wall; he could see his handwriting, large, angry. But he changed his mind because he felt he would be making a public beggar of himself. How would it look, him begging an older woman not to leave—how would it look?

Saturday morning he woke up, put on the coffee, and went to his desk and grabbed his suicide letter. He did not read it, but took it back to bed with him and held it. He tried not to think about Luz—she'll be at the bridge, she'll be there. He drank his coffee as dark and bitter as his room, and did not rise until the light of the morning shone through the window. He combed his hair in the mirror and looked at his face. He saw the lines coming out from under his skin, from somewhere deep within him. Soon my face will be a map, he thought, a map of crooked roads going nowhere like the steps. He read the newspaper from the day before. The printed words were all jumbled; he could make no sense of the sentences—they seemed to be knots on a string, knots he wanted to untie but somehow he felt his fingers were not gifted enough to undo them. He threw the newspaper down on the floor, lit a cigarette, and puffed on it furiously. He could feel the smoke in his throat and lungs. He puffed on his cigarette faster and faster as if he were trying to catch himself on fire. He lit one cigarette after another until his throat felt as though he had eaten ashes. He sat at his desk, took out a piece of paper and wrote: Luz, be at the bridge. Luz, be at the bridge. Be at the bridge.

At eight-thirty he thought it was time to take himself down to the river. He wanted to run all the way to the bridge, but he dressed himself slowly. He went up the steps that went nowhere, then back down. He walked through San Jacinto Plaza and noticed the Border Patrol eyeing him. Diego watched them watch him. He walked toward Sacred Heart Church making himself walk slowly, making himself count his own steps: one, two, fifty, one hundred. He walked into the church, dipped his hand into the holy water, and crossed himself. He lit a candle before the statue of St. Jude and whispered, "Luz, be at the bridge." He made the sign of the cross, kissed the feet of the statue, genuflected, and inched himself out of the church heading toward the river. As he reached the top of the bridge where the flags were being tossed by the hot wind, he stared down at the river of mud. Today it was browner than usual and it was running fast, almost angry. He turned away and faced the place where Luz always sat. He opened his eyes. She wasn't there. He walked up to the place where they first met, stared at the blank spot on the hard cement—and waited. He tried to concentrate on the people hanging around, the people walking toward El Paso, the people selling their goods. A small boy selling Chiclets came up to him; Diego handed him a quarter. He smiled at him, lit a cigarette, and waited. He knew she would not come.

At noon he walked back to Sacred Heart Church and blew out his candle. He kept going to the bridge every Saturday, and every

Saturday he stared at the river, closed his eyes, watched the people—and waited. He did this for a few weeks until one day he stopped going. He stopped working on his suicide letter. Winter in El Paso came early that year.

About the same time Luz left, Mary disappeared. Diego looked for her on the streets but he could not find her. Crazy Eddie and his boss were the only two people he saw regularly and neither wanted to take the time to talk to him. Sometimes he tried to get Tencha, the fruit lady, to talk to him. She was kind, a good woman, but Diego knew his presence made her feel guilty because she could talk and he couldn't. Some people were like that. She smiled a lot but she couldn't bring herself to have a conversation with him. Diego stopped writing on his pad. He left his suicide note on top of his desk but he never touched it. He was tired of trying to think of the right words.

One morning he tried to throw his letter out the window, but before he could make himself let go of all the pages as he held them in the air, he pulled them back inside his room. He wadded up the pages, wadded them up into balls, and threw them against the wall. He stared at the white balls on the floor, picked them up, and smoothed them out with his hands. He put them back on his desk.

Mr. Arteago had left for the winter and didn't turn on the heat. Diego's apartment was so cold that he was glad to be in Vicky's kitchen. One night it got so cold that Diego went out and bought a bottle of Jim Beam and got drunk. He jumped up and down on the floor and wished Mr. Arteago was home so it would drive him crazy. He lay there, took another drink, and laughed. He remembered Luz saying "People who cry are boring." He lay on the floor and laughed to himself all winter.

 **3**

"HI ," HE SAID quietly as he walked in the front door.

"Hi," she said.

Eddie and Helen looked at each other, then looked away, then stared at each other again. He wanted to kiss her. Maybe she didn't want to be kissed. We'll talk, Eddie said to himself. How to start? Open your lips and say—what? His mind had forgotten all the words. He felt as if language had abandoned him completely. There was nothing but chaos in the forgetting of all words—he panicked in that dark. He put his hands in his pocket as he stood in the entryway. He wanted to turn around and run. Instead, he locked his knees. Helen stood at the bottom of the stairs.

"I was just going to put on some coffee," she said, a stiffness in her voice as if she were being extra nice to a visitor she was obligated to care for.

He nodded.

She cleared her throat.

"I should change," he said, playing with his tie.

She nodded.

Eddie started to walk up the stairs.

Helen walked into the kitchen.

"It will never be right again. Maybe it was never right, maybe the fantasy's over. Maybe everything is over. Is it over, Helen? So

125

soon? Is it over?" Eddie ripped off his shirt and tie and tossed them impatiently against the wall. He put on a T-shirt. He let his dress pants fall to the floor. He stepped on them. "Maybe if we just make love it will be fine, everything will be—" He put on a pair of jeans. He looked in the closet for a pair of tennis shoes. He picked up an old pair, then threw them against the wall, almost hitting the window. She would know it was all his fault. He put on his sneakers in slow motion, looked in the mirror, combed his hair, walked down the stairs. He saw his wife sitting at the kitchen table. He stood in the doorway and took a deep breath. Eddie smiled nervously at the woman he married. "Was it her I married? Was it me? Were either of us there that day?"

Helen returned the smile. She seemed nervous to him—that was good, he thought. He wanted her to be as nervous as he was.

"It's like a first date," she said.

He nodded. "What did we do on our first date?"

"We went to a concert," she said.

"No, I mean what did we say?"

"You came to the door and said 'hi.' And then I said 'hi,' and then we didn't say anything. It was hard for us to talk. I remember."

He nodded. "What did we talk about?"

"Our parents."

He looked at her strangely.

"I was only kidding."

He nodded.

She played with her watch on her wrist. "My name's Maria Elena Ramirez," she said quietly, "and I was born and raised in El Paso." She paused. "That's in Texas."

"Yes," he nodded, "I know where it is—and it's a beautiful name."

"You said that to me on the phone."

"*It is a beautiful name,*" he repeated. "And my name's Jonathan Edward Marsh and I come from—" His voice cracked. He took a deep breath. "I come from La Jolla, California." Tears rolled down his face, he stopped, started again, then stopped. "And, uh, and my father had sex with me from the time I was seven until I was—"

126

His voice cracked again. He placed his hands over his eyes. "Fourteen," he said. "Until I was fourteen." He wrapped his hand tighter around his face.

He felt his wife pull his hand off his face. She opened his palm and kissed it. He felt her arms around him, her big belly rubbing against him. She rocked him gently. "Oh my Eddie," she whispered, "how could he have done that? To you—my Eddie? To you? Who could hurt you? My Eddie. Milagro, eres un milagro, mi amor." She felt free—to say words she had never allowed herself to utter in his presence. He wept into her shoulder. He could not control what his body was doing, it trembled, it did whatever it wanted. "And my mother let him." His voice was muffled and distant and distorted in the same way a mute distorted and made distant the sounds of a trumpet. "She let him." Maria Elena felt him tremble in her arms. She wanted his hurt to run through her blood like wind ran through the desert in the spring. She wanted his sadness— to keep it and then to let it blow through the air like a light and graceful kite and then show him, "You see? Do you see? Look, it's not as heavy as you thought." Maybe people could be happy, she thought, maybe it was possible. Maybe Eddie could be happy. Maybe she could be happy, too. She wanted to spell out the word and make sure it was a word, and make sure it had a meaning. "Corazón," she whispered. He wept on her shoulder for a long time, washing her shirt in the salt that sprang from his years of silence. "Tears are a funny thing," he said—and then stopped crying.

He shivered for a few moments, then took her by the arm and led her upstairs to his office. He took out three plain black notebooks from the shelf and handed them to her. "You can read these when you have time," he said. He pointed to the shelves. "There's a few more." His eyes were red, and his hair was wild and uncombed as if he had been walking in a strong wind. She sat down on a chair and opened one of the books; it was filled with pages and pages of Eddie's handwriting. She leafed through the book and stared at the dates. Each entry addressed to a man whose name her husband had never uttered in her presence. She looked up at him as he watched her. He looked fragile and hurt and afraid. She stared at the handwriting then looked up at her husband again. She looked at the man's name and was afraid to say it aloud. "Who's Jacob?" she asked. "Is he a former lov—"

"My brother," he said.

"Oh." She was ashamed of her accusation. He didn't seem to notice.

"Is he dead?"

"I'm not sure."

"What happened to him?"

"I don't know. My parents kicked him out of the house when I was seven. I never saw him again."

"And you loved him."

"Yes."

"And so you addressed your journals to him?"

"Yes—I addressed my journals to him."

"Did it help?"

"It helped."

"Do you know anything about him?"

"I know my parents had him arrested when he left the house."

"Why?"

"He beat them up. They deserved it."

She nodded.

"The night he left, I asked him if Dad had ever touched him. I didn't realize it at the time, but Dad had used him for—for the same thing. I think he wanted to protect me. I think he confronted my father—I'm not sure—but I think that's why he left. I think that's why he roughed them up. I don't know—maybe I'm making all this up. Do you remember when you told me you loved me?"

"Yes."

"And, I asked you: 'Are you certain?' "

"Yes, I remember."

"You thought it was a strange thing to ask. For me it was completely logical. I've never been certain about anything. Sometimes, I'm not sure I know the difference between what I've made up—about him, about me—and what really happened. Sometimes I think everything about me and my brother is a lie. I want to be certain. Anyway, he was eleven years older than me, and it was good that he left—good for him, anyway. Sometimes, I hated him for leaving me behind. But when I think about it—how could he have taken me with him? My parents would have never allowed it. It wasn't that they loved me—it was just that they needed to have control. He was just a kid. I used to ask our maid to help me find him—but she said she didn't know where to look. I asked my mother about him all the time, but never my father. My father told me never to say his name. One day my mother was drunk and I asked her about Jake. She told me that he was a homosexual. She sneered when she said it. I wanted to cut her open, but I just smiled at her as she sipped on her scotch. 'Your brother's a sick and violent animal,' she said without emotion. 'You're better off without him.' "

Eddie shook his head and looked at his wife. He wanted to ask what she saw. "Can we go to the beach?" he asked. "I need some air, I want—I want to feel the sand on my feet."

She smiled at him. "I need to see the doctor in half an hour. After that, you got yourself a date."

He nodded. "Is the blanket still in the car?"

She nodded. "We should take some sweaters. It's always cold there."

"It feels that way because you're from the desert."

"It isn't cold for you?"

"No—not really. Cold? Cold was the house I was raised in."

"Help me up." she said. She held his journals in one arm and held the other arm out. Eddie gently helped her up. "If this baby doesn't pop out soon, we'll need a crane to lift me out of chairs."

"Beautiful," he said.

"I don't feel beautiful."

"You should."

She placed her palm on her husband's cheek. "Never leave me."

"Never. What if you leave me?"

"Nunca."

"Nunca?"

"First Spanish lesson. Nunca. Never."

"Nunca," he said.

She combed his hair with her fingers. "What happened to them?" she asked.

"My parents? A week after my eighteenth birthday, my mother took a gun and shot my father—then shot herself. Nice, huh? The old girl just couldn't take it anymore. Did you know their house is still standing—my house really. I actually pay someone to live there. Well, actually, they live in what used to be the chauffeur's house."

"You were very rich?"

"Am rich."

"How rich?"

"Well, I haven't checked in a while. This guy handles everything. He gives a copy of everything to my lawyer."

"I didn't know you had a lawyer."

"You've met him."

"Where?"

"Company parties. He does some work for the company."

"So how much?"

"Thirty million dollars—something like that—well, no, a lot more—I can't know—I'm not that interested. And then there's the house. You want it?"

"Their house?" She grinned. "I have a house. Besides, I'd rather be homeless than to live in their house."

"Me too. Do you want the money?"

She was half-amused, half-disgusted by his question. "No," she said, "I don't want the money. I have enough."

"What am I going to do with it?"

"Do you have to solve it today?"

"No," he said.

"Good, then grab the sweaters and help me down the stairs."

"To the doctor's," he said, and kissed her halfway down the steps.

Eddie was sleeping in the waiting room when Maria Elena came out of the doctor's office. The receptionist smiled knowingly at her. "They fall asleep everywhere, don't they?"

Maria Elena smiled. "But they're so nice when they're asleep."

Eddie woke at the sound of her voice. He smiled lazily.

130

"We don't have to go to the beach," she said, "you look tired."

"No. I want to go. I want to look at the sea. Did you know that sometimes I dream that you and I go to the water's edge?"

"And what do we do there?"

"We're just there, that's all. And we're looking out at the water, standing at the place where the world ends."

"Do we want to jump in?"

"Maybe we do. I don't know."

As they drove toward one of the beaches near Pescadero, Maria Elena told Eddie what the doctor had said. "Perfect, Eddie, the doctor said *perfect*—just as I suspected. He says I'm healthy and the baby is perfectly healthy and that he doesn't anticipate any problems. He told me not to worry. I told him I wasn't worried one bit."

"You lied to him like that?"

"I didn't lie."

"The hell you didn't—you're worried as hell about this baby."

"Why shouldn't I be?"

"I didn't say you shouldn't be, but you should at least admit to your doctor that you're a little worried."

"Oh, there's nothing wrong with a little lie."

"One thing leads to another," he said.

When they arrived at the beach, already it was foggy and cool, nothing of the noonday's warmth left in the sky. They walked hand in hand saying nothing, both of them staring at their bare feet as they walked, both of them listening to the waters swaying back and forth on the earth, the two of them riding the sound like a swing. They felt each other's palms. "I have a brother, too," she said breaking the silence. Eddie liked the sound of her voice against the beating of the waves. He looked at her, and noticed the sea in the background framing her face.

"What's his name?" he asked.

"His name's Diego."

"Like the artist?"

"Yes. Well, actually my mother named him after the saint."

"What saint?"

"You ever heard of Our Lady of Guadalupe?"

Eddie nodded, "The Virgin."

"The story goes that she appeared to a poor Indian whose name was Juan Diego. My mother was very religious. She loved him."

"The saint or your brother?"

"Both."

"Do you believe?" He watched her eyes.

"In what?"

"Don't be funny—you know what I mean."

"I dunno. I guess I do. I can't help it really."

"So what happened to your brother?"

"I don't know. I left—abandoned him."

"Don't be so hard on yourself. I'm sure he can take care of himself."

"No, Eddie, you don't understand—he's deaf. He's kind of an innocent. I just left him. He was young when I left—around twenty—maybe younger. I can't remember his exact age right now. Isn't it funny—I worked so hard to forget that I'm actually forgetting. I didn't want to take care of him. I didn't want to be poor. I didn't want to be Mexican. I didn't want to live in El Paso my whole damned life and never go anywhere and never see anything and die there. I didn't want to sacrifice my life the way my mother did."

"Did you hate him?" He stared at her feet in the sand.

"Yes."

"Do you still?"

"No."

"Do you want to find him?"

"I don't know." She squeezed his hand. He stared at her face, her tangled hair. She resisted the urge to comb his hair—it was a useless gesture in the wind. She wondered why she didn't tell him the truth, why she didn't tell him that her brother was an obsession, a ghost who haunted her, stalked her. She knew she could never again be at peace if she didn't find the brother she had thrown away like a paper plate. She shrugged her shoulders. "I guess I don't know a lot of things, huh?"

"I have another question: Where in the hell did you find the name La Greca?"

She laughed. "In a phone book."

132

He smiled at her. "Is that the truth?"

She nodded.

He bent over laughing. "A phone book. A goddamned phone book." She thought he would laugh all afternoon. "Maria," he said, "Can I call you Maria?"

"Call me Nena," she said.

"Nena?"

"My mother called me Nena. It's a nickname."

"You speak a lot of Spanish?"

"It was my first language."

"Really?"

"Yes. My mother spoke to me only in Spanish—and my father spoke no English."

"Neither parent spoke English?"

"Mama's English was fine. But she loved me in Spanish."

"She loved you in Spanish? How do you love in Spanish?"

She smiled and looked into his eyes, then laughed. "I'll show you sometime."

They walked a long time without speaking. When they turned to walk back toward the car, Eddie led his wife to the edge of the water. They looked out at the waves. "What do you see?" Eddie asked.

"Desert," she said.

"Desert?"

"The water always reminds me of the desert. You can drown in the desert, you know?"

"I have a confession to make," he said.

"Another one?"

"I hate my job," he said.

"Quit," she said.

"And I hate Palo Alto."

"Good," she said. "We'll move. Lizzie will be thrilled."

"And what about Maria Elena?"

"Maria Elena doesn't care where she lives as long as she lives there with Jonathan Edward Marsh." They stood at the edge of the water for a long time, neither of them wanting to move. They both looked out at the ocean as if they were searching for some lost thing, as if they might find the faces of their brothers on the far horizon.

THE WINTER CAME and went. One Saturday in the early spring, Diego ran into Mary as he was walking down Stanton Street. It was she who had noticed him first. "Juan, honey!" she yelled, but since he had stopped looking for her, he did not notice her until she ran up to him, pulled his arm, and turned his face toward her. When he caught sight of her lips, he smiled and laughed. "Juan, darling," she said. He hugged her as if he was never going to let her go. She giggled like a little girl, and finally pulled herself away so he could see her lips. "Juan, sugar, ain't you somethin'. You missed Mary, did you?"

He nodded.

"Ain't you the nicest thing?"

He took out his pad and wrote, "Where were you?"

"They sent me away, Juan, put me in a place where they talked at me forever. Asked me questions 'bout everything I ever done, everything I ever thought. I never did let 'em know. I just looked at 'em and made things up. And that weren't the worst of it neither, no sir, Juan, but I don't want to think about it no more. I'm back now, Juan. It sure is good to see you, honey. Just lookin' at you makes me forget about that awful place. I'm back."

Diego smiled. "Would you like to have lunch with me?"

Mary laughed. "Oh, Juan, you're sweeter than my mama's pecan

134

pie. But really, I'm so busy." She played with her dishwater blond hair and combed it back as if she were in front of a mirror. "And look at me, Johnny, I'm a mess."

"But you still look better than me," he wrote. He winked at her.

"If I didn't know better," she said, looking at his pad, "I'd swear you was makin' a pass at me, honey."

He laughed. "It's an honest offer."

She grabbed his arm and looked at him. "If I wasn't so hungry, darlin', I'd be more difficult." She looked at her watch. "I suppose the rest of 'em can wait while Mary eats with a gentleman." She kept talking, telling him how good he looked as they walked. "Ever so much better than James Dean. Why, Juan, you look better than the sun in a blue sky after forty days of rain. Don't you know that, Johnny?"

Diego smiled at her and nodded.

She talked all the way to Sol's Barbecue. They sat at a table near the window, and Mary kept talking. She talked and talked for over an hour and ate at the same time. Diego couldn't make out half of what of what she was saying. Even *her* lips were impossible to read with Sol's barbecue hanging out of her mouth. He noticed she was pretty—he had never noticed that before, and he also noticed she didn't smell like pigeon shit anymore and that she didn't seem to be as crazy. Diego figured she would always be a little off, but she wasn't crazy like before. "And," she said—enunciating every word—"them people where I was at never did believe me about me bein' the Virgin. There was one man in there, Juan, I swear he was the craziest, meanest man I ever did meet. Said to me one day, 'I hear you think you're a virgin.' 'I'm not a virgin,' I says to him, 'I'm *the* Virgin.' 'That a fact?' he says. 'Indeed I am,' I says. 'Well,' he says to me, 'I can smell a virgin for ten miles, and you don't smell like no virgin I ever smelled.' And I says to him, 'That's because your nose ain't smart enough to smell the real thing, ya hear? Your nose couldn't tell a skunk from a mangy mutt. Your nose couldn't tell a cat from a possum.' That's what I tell 'em. But I'm boring you, ain't I, Juan? Me and all my stories—but one thing, Juan, one thing I tell you. I tell you 'cause I know you won't breathe a word: I ain't goin' back. I told 'em I'd be back, but it weren't true—I ain't never goin' back to that place. I live on the streets 'cause the Virgin ain't got no place to lay her head. S'posed to be that way."

Diego nodded all the way through Mary's story. He touched her hand, then pulled himself away. Even though he had never known very much about her and she liked to talk too much, he had missed her. The streets of El Paso had not seemed the same without her.

"Will you meet me on Saturdays and have lunch with me?" He showed her his pad.

Mary stared at him. She thought for a while. "No funny business?" she asked.

Diego shook his head.

"Well, I don't know, Juan," she said, playing with her hair. "God knows what he'll have me doin'. It's so hard to say."

"No funny business," he wrote, "and I promise I'll pay for the meals. A Virgin needs to eat good meals. And besides, maybe God wants you to spend some time converting an old sinner."

Mary laughed, pointing her head toward the ceiling. For an instant, she looked like Luz. "You silly thing, you ain't no sinner. You're an innocent. I swear you're so pure that the sun shines off your face. I swear it's true." She looked at her hands, rough and scarred, and stuck them out in front of her. "I do believe I could use a manicure." She put her hands against her face. "Juan, honey, I don't see how I can resist such a tempting offer, it comin' from a gentleman and all. We can meet here every Saturday if you like, but if we agree on it, and if you ever stand Mary up, then Mary's gonna be plenty upset. Mary won't forgive a man who leaves her lookin' like a fool."

Diego nodded. "I promise I'll never leave you waiting," he wrote.

She smiled, kissed him on the cheek, and stood up. "It's settled then, honey," she said. She winked at him and disappeared out the door, taking the crackers on the table with her.

Mary walked into her one-bedroom efficiency and smiled. She had more secondhand clothes than furniture: a bed, a table, a chair, and a closet full of dresses. She thought of Diego, his boyish handsome face, his shy smile, his straight white teeth. She wondered why some woman hadn't seduced him away from his virginity. She was sure he was a virgin. As far as she was concerned his deafness was more of an asset than a handicap. Most men were in love with their own voices. She wondered what he thought of her, did he like her, could there be something—she shook her head. She reached for her medicine, stared at the label, and took her dose. She was better since she'd been taking it. Maybe the doctor at the hospital where she'd been had been right. Maybe sanity was a better option than all the craziness she had been living the last five years. The medicine made her feel as if she had a center somewhere inside, a center with an intelligent heart. Maybe, if the pills worked—if they kept working—maybe she could get back her children. Maybe just see them and hold them, just for a short time. New Orleans was a long way from El Paso. Mary did not even remember how she had gotten here. "Maybe the pills, maybe the pills and Diego will save me." She looked around her room. It wasn't much, but it was better than the streets. "Maybe I'll find me a nice picture."

Diego stayed behind at the restaurant and ordered another cup of coffee. He wondered what Luz would say about his new relationship. He knew she would think he was a pendejo. He could almost see her lips saying: "That pinche gringa's gonna soak you for all the money you got. Isn't it just like a Mexican man to fall for a gringa." He smiled to himself as he drank his coffee.

He walked toward the Bowie Bakery like he did every Saturday by way of La Fe Clinic. As he reached the Alamito projects on St. Vrain, he noticed Tencha running in the middle of the street like a scared rabbit. She was waving her hands in the air like the flags on the river. Diego sensed she was in trouble, and ran toward her. She was yelling something and crying, and all the while her hands were waving. Diego grabbed her and shook her. "¡Lo mataron!" she screamed. Diego saw the words but didn't understand. He looked at her face. "¡Lo mataron!" she screamed again, pointing toward a dumpster. The green-eyed nurse from the clinic stepped out into the street and stared at them. Diego motioned her over for help as he dragged Tencha from the middle of the street. Tencha kept yelling and kicking and screaming, and Diego was happy he didn't have to listen to her screams. If they sounded anything like the expressions on her face, then he was sure the noises she was making were awful. As Tencha waved her arms, she caught his cheek with her elbow. The nurse grabbed her and tried to settle her down. Diego took a deep breath, and stared at the nurse who was trying to calm the crazed woman down. Luz would slap her, he thought. He remembered the dumpster Tencha had pointed at. He walked toward it and stared at a man's body lying on top of the garbage. He ran toward the nurse and pulled her away from Tencha. He tugged her toward the dumpster. "My God!" she said. He watched the nurse closely. She wanted to run, but didn't. She took a deep breath and reached her hand in the dumpster. She grabbed Diego's arm and spoke directly into his face: "I can't reach him. Can you help me get him out?" Diego nodded, hesitated, then jumped onto the dumpster. He climbed inside trying to ignore the stench of rotting food. He slowly and awkwardly lifted the man's body, and he was surprised that the body was still warm and not very heavy. Slowly, he and the green-eyed nurse managed to pull the body out without dropping it and lay it on the sidewalk.

"There's a pulse," she said.

Tencha stared at the body and screamed. Diego caught sight of her contorted face. Her scream must have been loud because suddenly the residents of the projects gathered as if someone had rung a bell calling them together. One of the ladies grabbed Tencha and tried to comfort her. She enjoyed hysterics, he thought. A group of men ran toward the clinic and came running with Dr. Dominguez.

Diego watched as the doctor knelt next to the nurse and the body. "Lots of blood," he said. "It's a wonder this guy's not dead. These guys are built pretty tough." He said something else, but Diego couldn't see his lips. He ripped the wounded man's shirt open and looked at the nurse. "Let's call an ambulance," he said.

Diego tugged at the nurse's arm and pointed to his lips and ear. The body moved his lips. He started to mumble, but Diego could

138

not make out his words. The nearly dead man tried to force himself to speak and lift his head.

"He said he doesn't want to go to no damn hospital. He says he doesn't want any cops." Carolyn spoke directly into Diego's face.

One of the younger men in the crowd pulled at Diego's shoulder. He spoke into Diego's face deliberately. "Hey, I know you—I've seen you around—can't talk, huh?"

Diego nodded.

"Listen, I know this guy, he's bad news, his name's Mundo, and he's always in deep shit. Tell 'em to call the cops."

Diego nodded. He took out his pad and wrote, "His name's Mundo." He showed the note to the nurse.

The nurse looked at the note and spoke to the man, "Mundo, you're going to be OK, but we've got to get you to a hospital."

He made a face and said something.

The nurse looked at the doctor, then at Diego. "He said 'No fuckin' hospitals.' "

For a while the doctor and the nurse looked at each other trying to decide what to do. "Let's get this guy inside the clinic," the doctor said finally, "I doubt if he'll die on us. Jesus Christ! These guys have nine lives. They're hard as hell to kill." He shook his head and laughed. He ran inside the clinic and came out with two men and a stretcher. They lifted Mundo and took him inside the clinic. Diego followed them in. The crowd stayed behind staring inside the dumpster.

The nurse took Tencha inside and tried to calm her down. Tencha was unable to control her wailing, and the nurse seemed to walk a fine line between patience and anger. She finally stopped crying, but after a few minutes of silence she began throwing her arms in the air and yelling. Diego kept his distance, afraid Tencha would hit him again. Finally, the nurse cradled her in her arms until she calmed down. One of the other ladies in the clinic came over to them.

"Can you take her home?" the nurse asked her.

The lady nodded. The two old women walked out of the clinic holding on to each other.

Diego looked up at the nurse as Tencha walked out the door. "She gets a little excited, doesn't she?" he wrote. He flashed her his note.

The nurse smiled. "She can't help it. You know, her son was killed in a fight a few years ago. She still hasn't gotten over it. Anyway, she's prone to theatrics—you should have seen her at her son's funeral. She threw herself on her son's casket and when one of her brothers tried to pull her off, she belted him a good one."

He pointed at his cheek where Tencha had hit him. "Some women are pretty heavy-handed."

She looked at his note and laughed. "Some of us are determined to leave our marks on the world—one way or another."

Diego laughed and nodded. "That's OK with me," he wrote, "so long as the marks aren't on *my* body."

She let out a strong laugh. "Hell," she said, "our bodies always take the worst of it."

"You're right," he wrote. "If the people around us don't kill us first, then time will take care of us sooner or later. Hell, look at my hair—it's already rotting. See all the white?"

She read the note and shook her head. "You're exaggerating. You're a long way from death."

Diego nodded. He smiled at her—but he thought she was wrong; he never thought of himself as being very far from death. "Do you think Mundo will be OK?"

"I'm sure he will be. Dr. Dominguez is a very good doctor." She pointed down the hall. "If he were that bad, if he were dying or something, he would have already called the ambulance. I'm sure he'll be fine. These gang members have nine lives." She looked at him carefully to make sure he understood.

Diego nodded and motioned her to sit next to him. She looked at him. "If you sit next to me," he wrote, "you can see what I write easier and we can almost have a normal conversation." He handed her the note.

She smiled as she read it. "Good idea," she said. She sat next to Diego and watched his hands as he wrote.

"Are you going to call the cops?"

"We're supposed to."

"But are you going to?"

"Probably not," she said.

"How come?"

"Well, if he's going to be OK, then what's the point? The poor guy's got enough troubles, don't you think? He's probably on probation and if we call someone he'll probably end up in jail. Jail won't do him any good—it's too late for that."

Diego stared at her lips and noticed the faint smell of perfume. "You seem to be pretty calm about all this."

"It's happened before," she said, "they're always stabbing each other. Only usually, we don't have to pick them out of the garbage."

"Do you like them?"

"The gang members, you mean? They're OK. I mean, they try to put the moves on me when I have them as patients, but it doesn't bother me much. I think I recognize Mundo, now that I think about it. He's a real ladies' man. Anyway, these guys aren't as creepy as they make themselves out to be, they're just a little confused. I mean, they're not smart like rich people—rich people don't kill each other—they kill other people. But these guys, they're always killing each other."

"What do you mean about rich people killing other people?"

"Nothing, never mind—I'm just talking."

"You think these guys will ever stop stabbing each other?"

She stared down at the pad. "I doubt it. They're not very different from anybody else—you ever watch the news?"

Diego shook his head. "I don't have a TV."

"It's just as well. All you see are governments warring with each other—all over the globe they're at war with each other. Governments are supposed to be civilized. They're supposed to know better."

"I guess so," Diego wrote, "I never thought about it very much."

"Well, maybe you're better off. It's better not to think about things you can't do anything about—gets you into trouble. Makes it hard to sleep." She noticed a pack of cigarettes in his shirt pocket. "Do you mind if I have one of your cigarettes?"

"You're supposed to know better," he wrote.

She smiled at him. He handed her a cigarette. She looked around, lit it, and inhaled deeply. "I shouldn't be doing this." She looked tired. "Why are you waiting for him?"

"I want to make sure he doesn't die."

The doctor came out of the room and down the hall. "I think we can handle it," he told her, "but I'll need your help, Carolyn." She put out her cigarette and followed him in. Diego sat and waited. He fell asleep in the chair. Sometime later he felt a hand on his shoulder. "He's going to be all right." The nurse asked him for another cigarette. "Maybe now I'll have enough time to smoke it." She lit the cigarette and dropped her shoulders. "He'll have a few more scars to show for it, but he's going to be fine."

Diego nodded.

"Do you know where he lives?"

"No. I don't even know *who* he is. Just his first name, that's all." He handed her the note.

She crumpled it up. "He won't tell us his full name, and he won't tell us where he lives. Stubborn as a mule."

"So what are you going to do?" He stopped and looked up at her, then wrote, "I like your name."

She nodded. "It was my grandmother's name, too." She took a puff from her cigarette, then put it out.

"Is she still alive?"

The nurse shook her head. "Dead like everyone else."

"Like everyone else?"

"Never mind," she said. She stretched her arms and yawned. "I've got to get home and get some sleep."

Diego looked at her.

"Well, Mundo can't stay here, that's for sure. This isn't a hospital. No one's here to take care of him, and he's going to have to stay in bed for a few days. I sure as hell can't leave him out on the street, and I sure as hell don't want to take him home. I've done that before—and I'll never do it again. If he doesn't give me some information about where we can take him, I'm going to threaten him with the cops."

Diego thought a minute. He nodded and a grin came to his face. "I just thought of something," he wrote.

"What?"

"He can come home with me. I mean, it's not a great place or anything like that, but it beats the hell out of a dumpster."

She looked over his shoulder and stared at his handwriting.

"That's very kind, she said, "but this guy's a badass. I don't imagine he'd be very easy to live with or take care of. What if he doesn't like you?"

"Who cares?"

"What if he makes your life miserable?"

"My life is already miserable."

She laughed. "He's going to be a pain in the ass."

"That's OK. I don't hear, remember? All I have to do is look away if he starts insulting me. And it doesn't look like he's in any shape to rip me up with a knife, does it? It's only for a couple of days and these guys aren't really so bad when they're away from their friends. I'm not afraid."

The nurse thought about Diego's suggestion. "Yes," she nodded. "I'll help you get him to your place."

JOAQUIN SAT in the dark apartment and waited for Jacob to come back home. He always left in anger; he always came back; Joaquin always waited.

"You didn't come home last night."

"You're lucky I came back at all."

"I don't feel lucky. Not right now."

"I didn't mean that. I'm an asshole sometimes, J. I wasn't with anyone."

"Doesn't matter if you were. Other people are not what's wrong with us."

"You gonna leave me, then, J?"

"I would if I could."

"Why can't you?"

"I can't. You're the one that's going to have to do all the leaving." He could hear a thousand conversations between them. He had been gone a long time now. But he always came back. *Come back.* He didn't want to turn on the lights. "I have to get used to living without them." He thought of Julimes, of his brother. He wondered what would have happened to him if his brother had lived, if his father and mother had not died. It was so useless to think about things that had long since passed, about people who had already died, and he tried to stop. "Maybe it's natural to think about the

144

dead," Joaquin whispered. He wondered why he was whispering. "The dead are alive!" he yelled. "The dead are alive." He coughed, then laughed. He wanted to think about the bodies who had returned to become a part of the earth because he was more a part of them now than he was a part of the room he was sitting in. He tried to picture his brother's face, then his mother's. It comforted him to think he would soon be a part of the communion of the dead.

He remembered the day he crossed the Río Bravo with his mother. He remembered his mother had felt something—but he had not felt it. To him, it had just been a river. Later, he had understood what the river meant. He remembered learning English, how it had been a game—how he had learned to recognize sounds and how the new arrangements that came from his mouth had become something meaningful. And yet in the deepest part of himself, he felt the sounds he was making to be meaningless. Languages meant so much to the people around him, but he had always been a little indifferent about the sounds of people's words. But his dreams were still in Spanish. Jacob had told him he'd always be a Mexican. "I'm not," he'd said, "I'm not a Mexican." "Well, you're not really an American," his lover had answered. "No, and who cares?" He had yelled back. Even now, he had no loyalty toward the place where he'd lived most of his life. It was a country, and in so far as it had deserts and trees and grasses, it was good, but he had never thought of himself as a citizen of any nation. He remembered telling Jacob that his body wasn't the possession of any goddamned country. Jacob had laughed. As he sat there he remembered the conversation, the condescension in Jacob's laugh. "Let's just drop it," he'd told him. "Are you mad, J?" Jacob had asked. "Don't be mad. Look, you were born in Mexico—you're Mexican. I was born in America. I'm American. It doesn't have to mean anything." Joaquin had nodded. After that, he'd stopped discussing certain things with his lover. Later, Jacob had asked him, "But you love America, don't you— don't you love living here?" He had nodded. He had lied. What he loved was the desert. And in his mind the desert did not belong to a nation. To belong to the desert was enough. If he loved America at all it was because it had given him Jacob who himself was as hot, as wordless, as quiet, and as untamable as the desert itself. Now that he was sick he wanted to go back—not to Mexico, but to the desert. He wanted to die there, there where he had first lived. But if he went back to that place, he would have to go without Jacob. Jacob's body would have to be enough desert for him to die in.

He felt sleepy, he wanted to lie down, but the bedroom seemed as far away as his body. He slowly pushed himself off the chair he was sitting in. He stared into the darkness of the room. He wondered if he had died. He touched his own arm. He thought it strange that his skin was still smooth. He didn't think it was an odd thing to be dying—he thought it a strange thing to be breathing. Everything he had done and felt and seen and touched had just been a dream— and he knew he was about to wake and find something completely unfamiliar. He felt tears running down his face, and found it odd and incongruent to find himself crying. Why was he crying when he felt nothing? He fell down on his knees, then crawled around the room as if he were searching for something. He was a baby again. He started yelling for his mother. "Mamá. Mamá." He started yelling for Jacob, but he didn't know he was yelling. No one came to him. He prostrated himself on the floor and wept. His mouth was dry. He wanted water. But he could not make himself rise. He fell asleep exhausted.

He was standing in the middle of the desert dressed like a groom, his pure white shirt so bright and perfect it seemed it had been cut from the sun. He watched himself as he undid his bow tie, tossing it on a cactus, the thorns shredding it as if it were nothing more than paper. He took off his socks, his shoes, the desert sand burning his feet. He tugged off his shirt as if it were an enemy killing him, the buttons flying into the sky. He ripped the shirt in half and wiped the sweat off his face. He saw that he was strong, his skin pulled tight around the muscles of his arms and back. He shone in the morning light and, for a moment, he was a god. He let his pants drop to the ground and stood naked, completely a part of the desert. He was not afraid of the burning around him. The desert was in flames and he walked through them, and his skin did not burn. Nothing could harm him. In the distance was a river, and he ran toward it, and the river was calling, "Come." And the river repeated his name.

"Joaquin." He kept running through the endless flames, and the river did not seem to be getting any closer. Suddenly, inexplicably, the river was in front of him. "Come." He looked back one last time to see Jacob fully clothed in the distance behind him. "Come back!" Jacob yelled. Joaquin looked into the cool waters of the river—and jumped.

Joaquin woke up and felt Jacob's arm around him. "You're burning up, J," he said. He wiped the sweat from his forehead. He rocked him in his arms. He froze for a moment when he realized Joaquin's breathing was heavier than his body. "Is it hard to breathe?"

Joaquin nodded. He took a deep breath. "I was having a dream, gringo," he whispered. "The desert was on fire. And there was this river—"

"Shhhhh—don't talk. Just don't talk. I've got to take you to a hospital."

"The river was so clear and blue—bluer than your eyes, Jacob. I could even see the fish and they were gold. And I was thirsty and the desert was on fire. And you were calling me but I couldn't go back so I just jumped."

"It was just a dream."

"I wish you believed in dreams."

"It doesn't matter."

"Do you remember the time you left me?"

"Shhh—we don't have to talk about that anymore."

"I waited and waited, and then I thought you'd never come back. I thought I'd never see you again. I wanted to die, did I tell you?"

"But I came back."

"Are you glad?"

"Yes."

"I'm tired, Jacob."

"Don't talk. You don't have to talk."

"I'm tried." Joaquin looked up at his lover. "You seem so far, Jake. Are you going away?"

"I have to get you to a doctor."

"Can't I just sleep here?"

Jacob kept rocking him in his arms. "Shhhh. Shhhh. I'll carry you."

"Like water?"

"What?"

"Like a river carries water."

"Yes—just like that."

"How serious is it, Tom?" He had long ceased calling his and Joaquin's doctor by his title. Tom seemed too young to be a doctor though he'd been one for twenty years, and Jake wondered how it was that a man who worked so many hours managed to look so rested and relaxed. He wanted to like him as he stood in the hallway of the hospital, not that he hated him anymore, just couldn't like him. *"It was only a kiss, Jake—a very small one." "Did you—" "Look, we're friends, and have never been more than that, and will never be more." "I don't believe you." "That's because you don't know how to have friends." "What the fuck does that mean, J?" "Look, we're just friends." "He had his arm around you." "I'm only going to say this one more time, gringo, Tom and I are friends. You don't get to pick my friends and I don't get to pick yours."* He looked at the way Tom was processing his simple question—he hated that about him sometimes—the way he was too careful, the way his sincerity took up all the space in the room. "How serious, Tom?"

"Well, it's serious."

"A vague answer to a vague question, Doctor." He combed his hair with his fingers, then pulled at the ends of his hair.

"Pulling your hair out, huh, Jake?"

"Why'd I have to pick a gay doctor with a sense of humor?"

"Good taste."

The doctor nodded. "You want to have a cup of coffee instead of standing here in a hospital hallway in the middle of the night?"

"Nothing's open."

"We can get some in the lounge. It's a friendly place—always open, always coffee. They're nice to visitors on this ward—didn't you know?"

"Yeah, I remember. The last time Joaquin got sick, they were redoing it—making it more user-friendly."

"It isn't an instrument."

"Isn't it?"

"It's just a room with a few couches. Let's have some coffee."

"I don't want to leave him."

"He'll be OK."

"What if he dies?"

"Not tonight."

"How the hell do you know?"

"I know." Tom walked toward the lounge. Jacob followed him down the hall toward the lounge near the nurses station. Jake noticed his walk—*tight, I wonder what Joaquin ever saw in him? Too asexual.* The hallway was quiet, and it seemed the whole world had gone away and left him with this man, this doctor. The lounge was dim. The carpet was soft and thick and Jake felt his feet sink into the fabric as if he was walking on mud. He read the plaque on the wall that read: IN MEMORIAM: NORMAN CAMPBELL ROBERTSON. There were magazines neatly arranged on a glass table and a bookshelf full of books. There was a refrigerator and a drip coffeemaker on a shelf next to a small sink. He stared at the plaque and sat down on a beige-and-turquoise couch that was comfortable enough to be in somebody's living room. "Very Santa Fe," he mumbled, then shook his head.

"Huh? Did you say something?"

"No, I was just making remarks about the decor."

Tom handed him a mug of coffee and sat on an overstuffed chair opposite the couch. "Where were we?"

"I asked if it was serious and you gave me the kind of answer they teach you in medical school."

Tom smiled, then sipped from his coffee.

"Nice set of teeth, Doc. I bet your parents paid a bundle for those."

"As a matter of fact I was born with this set of choppers. Are you flirting with me?"

"No. I'm not interested in white boys."

Tom laughed and shook his head.

They sat in the quiet for a long time, the sound of footsteps moving in the background like calm waves in an ocean. Jake stared at Tom for a while as if he were about to ask him something, but said nothing. Tom remembered the first time Jake had walked into his office. *"Just good old-fashioned gonorrhea. Are you allergic to penicillin?"* *"Nope."* *"Talkative, are you?"* *"Didn't come here to talk."* *"I suppose you didn't come here to talk about your sexual practices either?"* *"What's that mean?"* *"It means you should be careful."* *"I know about sexually transmitted diseases."* *"Firsthand, I'd say."* Tom had hated him then, hated him for his don't-give-a-shit demeanor, his superior sense of masculinity, the complete look of disdain he wore on his face as if it were a medal won in a war. He'd been this man's doctor for seventeen years, and he felt no nearer to knowing him as he sat there than he had the first time he'd walked into his office. He remembered the first time he'd met Joaquin, how they had connected instantly, how Jake had resented their friendship from the moment it began. *"I want your paws off my boyfriend, Tom."* Some people were not meant to be friends, he thought, and yet he had never stopped trying. He wanted to break the silence, but it was as hard as the ice of his Minnesota childhood. "How's the coffee?"

"It sucks."

The silence returned like the San Francisco fog. "It's OK to be afraid," he said finally.

"Thanks for your permission."

"It's OK to be afraid," he repeated, "but it's not OK to be an asshole."

Jake smiled. "I deserved that one."

Again, they sat in the quiet. A patient down the hall was moaning. Jake shivered. "Why are we sitting here?"

"We're sitting here because your lover has Pneumocystis carinii, and I happen to be your doctor and your friend."

"Joaquin's friend," Jake corrected.

Tom nodded. "Sorry. You know, it's a good thing I like you, Jake. Otherwise, I'd kick your ass from here to L.A."

Jacob laughed. "That'll be the day." He shook his head as if his hair was wet and he was attempting to dry it. He leaned back and looked up at the ceiling. "I don't think you do like me, Tom."

"Yeah?"

"Yeah." Jake sipped on his coffee. "This is really bad stuff." He looked at Tom. "How can you do this for a living?"

150

"I was born to it, I guess."

"I'd hate it."

"That's because you'd have to be nice to people. You'd have to touch them."

"You know what your problem is, Tom? You think life is a good thing."

"It is a good thing."

"Yeah?"

"It's not as disgusting as all that, Jake."

"Well, you and Rick are a pair, aren't you?"

"Don't start in on Rick, Jake. He's a decent man."

"Meaning he's a politically correct faggot."

Tom kept himself from wincing. He kept his voice steady without hiding his disgust at Jake's remark. "You have an interesting way of thinking about things, you know that, Jake? You're so fucking insulting sometimes."

"Are we taking off the gloves now that Joaquin's not here to play referee for us?"

"How come life's a boxing match for you?"

"I had a psychology class in college, too, Tom."

"Did you pass?"

Jacob stood up from the couch and glared at the doctor. "That's it—I'm outta here."

"Finish your coffee." Tom said calmly. "I don't want to fight. I'll change the subject. It's too late to be arguing with you, Jake. And it's useless."

"For both of us." Jake sat back down.

"Yeah, for both of us. Look, go home and get some rest. You look like hell."

"To you too, Doc."

Tom got up and put his mug in the sink. "I'll come by sometime before noon and check in on Joaquin. I need to check his vision. You'll be around?"

Jake nodded.

"Get some sleep, Jacob."

"Tom?"

"Yeah."

"Am I gonna lose him this time?"

Tom took his time with Jake's question "I don't know. Maybe we should . . ." He paused. "We should be ready for anything."

There was quiet again between them, but the sadness over Joaquin was shared, and so, for a moment, they did not feel so far away from each other.

Pneumocystis carinii, Pneumocystis carinii. Jacob kept repeating the Latin words like a prayer at matins. He spelled it out in ink over the headlines of the morning newspapers. He thought of the conversation he'd had the night before with Tom. He was a good doctor—the best—and he trusted him completely. Mister Clean, Mister Responsible, Mr. Spokesman for Safe Sex, good diets, and holistic health. If he had been born straight, he would have been unbearable—too many virtues for Jake's taste, too much of a social conscience in that morally superior Protestant way he had. "If I hear Dr. Gay Community Awareness say 'the common good' one more time tonight, I'm going to stuff my fist down his throat." He remembered saying that to Joaquin at a party one night. *"How come you think life is a boxing match?"* He looked out the window—the sky seemed as dark to him as Joaquin's black hair. He sipped on his morning coffee. He picked up the phone and called his office. He recognized Alice's raspy voice. "I won't be in till this afternoon."

"Are you OK?"

"Yeah. It's J. He's in the hospital again."

"Take the whole day—we can handle it. You got some time coming—take as much as you need. The ads keep coming in by themselves. The *Chronicle* will survive—just make sure you do the same."

"Thanks, Alice."

"Give J my love."

"Sure thing."

"And eat well, Jacob."

"Don't you have enough sons?"

She laughed as she hung up the phone. At least she has a heart, he thought. Thirty years of selling ads for the *Chronicle* and she still had a heart. Amazing. "I'd have killed somebody by now."

He got up from the kitchen table, pulled on his bathrobe, and stared at a blue patch of sky that was somehow visible through the fog. He watched as it disappeared. For some reason the sky reminded him of the summer he'd spent in Seattle. He didn't even remember how'd he'd gotten there—he'd just found himself in that strange and lonely land of rain, nineteen years old with no money and no place to go and no plan and no one to belong to—with no future and a past that only made him want to throw himself or somebody—anybody against a wall until all the bones that held the body together broke and cracked. Didn't somebody have to pay for what had happened to him? "I should have killed them." Even now, more than twenty years after he'd left his parents' house, he felt intimate and comfortable with that hate. "I should have killed them."

He remembered himself in Seattle that summer. As he had walked along the shore of Lake Washington, he remembered seeing a heron gliding over the water, its wings flapping, then spreading, the labor of its slow-moving wings dwarfing the sky. He remembered how it had flown up, up almost as if the white and lonely bird knew he was there and needed reminding that flight and movement and grace were possible in the physical world despite the limiting pull of gravity. For a reason he did not understand at the time, he felt the heron was freeing him, and that flight, common occurrence that it was, was anything but common. That flight was everything there was in the world, and everything seemed to depend upon the grace of that flight. He urged it to fly on, to fly as if the beating of its wings would save the world, would save him from all the cruelties that had been and were yet to be. He remembered the clarity of his voice as he shouted at the great white heron: "Fly, fly!" He had yelled and yelled until he had almost gone hoarse. He was so mesmerized by the flight that he had lost control of his voice, of his mind, of his body. It occurred to him that he had never bothered to watch birds in flight; he had been oblivious to them because nothing else had existed except his pain. He had not felt himself to be a part of the world, of the earth. He was a permanent and unnatural foreigner, and there could be no possible home for him. But he knew he would keep what he had just seen, he would put the scene in his brain as if it were a pocket where he could store a lucky penny.

Many years later, he had dreamed the flight of the heron and it had been so real that he expected to find himself at that same lake when he woke. Joaquin had asked him about his dream. "You were yelling, 'Fly, fly!' " "I don't remember," he'd said. He'd lied and had not felt bad about the lie. There were certain things that were only his and not even Joaquin could have them. He looked out the window at the slowly moving fog and thought of that nineteen-year-old boy wandering, lost. He was moved by the image of that wounded boy, and wondered how that boy had managed to survive the cities he had lived in, had managed to survive his own rages, his own flirtations with destruction. He loved that boy, now, loved him for what he had survived. On the way to the hospital, Jake wondered if it wasn't time to start thinking about letting go of Joaquin. "But how will I live without his eyes, his hands, his voice?" He saw a convenience store, found a parking spot, then ran in and bought a pack of cigarettes. He sat on the hood of his car surrounded by the gray morning, and smoked a cigarette. He held the smoke in his lungs as if it were Joaquin.

 **6**

ALL MUNDO REMEMBERED of his stabbing was the face of the sonofabitch who stuck a knife in him. He remembered thinking "I'll find you, I'll find you." He couldn't recall how the fight started, why it started, who had started it. He remembered the stench of rotting tomatoes as he fell into another world. He remembered thinking that Rosie would come and save him. He smelled her sweat as he fell into a deep sleep, her smell overpowering the smell of rot around him. When he woke, he half-expected her to be at his side— there, beside him again. She was not there—she had not come. As he slept in Diego's apartment, a part of him reached for the world of the dead. No longer having a sense of direction, he was lost, unaware of where he was. He stretched out on Diego's bed, shaking and mumbling to himself. He felt tired. He wanted to let go. He wanted to sleep forever, go to a place where there was no more fighting, no more pain. Maybe Rosie would be waiting for him in that place. He would make love to her there and she would hold him until there was nothing but peace.

Diego watched the young man lying on his bed but couldn't make out anything he was mumbling. He saw his lips move occasionally and his attempts at kicking off the blankets. Maybe he wasn't saying anything, Diego thought, maybe he was just moaning from the pain.

He had stitches over his left eye and a bruise on his cheekbone. He had bandages on his side where they'd stuck him with a knife. The nurse had promised to come by if they needed her. "He was lucky," she said, "the knife missed his vital organs. He'll live long enough to get himself into another fight."

Saturday night Diego slept on some blankets on the floor. Sunday, Mundo slept all day. Sunday night, his new roommate seemed on the verge of waking up. He kept opening and closing his eyes. Diego sat at his desk wondering whether or not he was going to be all right. He should have woken up by now, he thought. Maybe he should get Mr. Arteago to call the nurse for him.

Diego looked up and noticed Mundo staring at him.

Mundo did not recognize the man in the room with him. The thought occurred to him that maybe he had died and the man standing in front of him was God. He shook his head, his vision returning clearly. He laughed to himself. How could that man be God? In the first place, Mundo was certain he would never make it to heaven. In the second place, the man standing before him looked like a Chicano. God, a Chicano? He wanted to laugh at his own thoughts. His mother had given him too much religion as a little boy—it had made his head soft. He stared at the man who was looking at him curiously. "Where the fuck am I?" he asked.

Diego stared at him and started to write an answer on his pad.

"How come you don't answer—answer me, godamnit!"

Diego put down his pad and took out a large sheet of paper.

"Calm down, you're all right. I'm deaf so try not to speak so fast so I can read your lips. And save your voice—it won't help if you yell."

"Oh shit!" Mundo said. "I died and got stuck with a goddamned deaf man as my roommate." He lifted himself from where he was lying and sat up on the bed. He winced. He placed his feet on the floor and made circles with them.

Diego looked at him blankly. "If you don't look at me, then I won't be able to answer you." He lifted up the paper and showed it to him.

Mundo tried to laugh. "I'll be goddamned." He began laughing, trying to hold back. "I hate to fuckin' read, man. I don't even fuckin' read the *National Enquirer*."

Diego nodded. "If you don't read it, how do you know it exists?"

"My old lady reads it—it's the only thing she likes to read. You ever read it?"

"No," Diego wrote. "I like real newspapers."

Mundo saw a copy of the *El Paso Times* sitting on the floor. "You call that real?"

Diego shrugged his shoulders. "It's the best we got in this city."

"Better to have fuckin' nothing."

"Something is better than nothing," Diego wrote.

"That's bullshit, man."

Diego said nothing. They sat in an uncomfortable silence for a while. Finally Mundo said, "Hey, you read lips pretty good. It's a nice trick, man. Not bad for a deaf guy."

Diego smiled. "I got a good brain. It works real good."

"That's cool," Mundo nodded. He looked around the dark room. "How long have I been here? What's your name, man?"

"My name's Diego," he wrote.

"No shit? My old man's name was Diego. That sonofabitch took off—haven't seen him for a while. He just took off from the house one day. Just split." He kept moving his feet in circles. "So what day is it?"

"Sunday night."

He stared at the note. "Ah shit! Sunday night? I been sleepin' all that time?"

"You lost some blood."

Mundo laughed. "No shit. But I kept enough to stay alive, right? I got more blood than those pinches figured I had. So how come I wound up here with you?"

"The nurse from La Fe Clinic helped bring you here. It was that or call the cops."

"Which nurse?"

"The gringa with the green eyes."

"Yeah, I know which one. She's all right. She's a little tight sometimes, you know? But most of the time she's OK."

Diego nodded in agreement. "I like her—she's a good person."

"How'd I get to the clinic?"

"Tencha, who sells fruit in front of the clinic, saw you in one of the dumpsters. You almost gave her a nervous breakdown."

"What the fuck's a dumpster?"

Diego looked at him. He thought a minute and wrote, "You know, one of those big things where everybody throws the trash."

"Those fuckin' bastards!"

"If you get too excited, I won't be able to read your lips." He held up the paper.

"I can't fuckin' help it," he yelled. He clenched his teeth and mumbled something.

"When you clench your teeth, I can't make out what you're trying to say."

Mundo nodded. "Hijos de sus chingadas madres. When I find those motherfuckers, I'm gonna castrate each one of them. Those sons of bitches threw me in a trash can!" He coughed and winced from the pain in his side.

"Got any booze? Algo fuerte."

Diego nodded, got up, and walked toward the closet. He took out a bottle and two glasses and poured them both a drink. He handed Mundo one of the glasses.

Mundo took a big gulp. "What is this shit?"

Diego stared at the gold in his glass. "Cognac," he wrote.

Mundo looked at the unfamiliar word, "Cog-nac," he said.

Diego laughed when he saw him pronounce the "g." "You don't say the 'g.' The 'g' is muda—silent—like me. You pronounce it co-ñac." He wrote a tilde over the "n." "It's a French word."

Mundo read the page and repeated slowly, "Cogñac. So what the hell are you, a fuckin' professor? You can't even talk and you're fuckin' correcting me."

"Don't get mad. And why do you say 'fuckin'' all the time?"

"Because it's a good word. If you don't like it, then look away." He took another drink. He looked down at his feet and looked at Diego. "How the hell do you know what the word sounds like? You've never even heard it."

"I read a lot. I go to the library. I had a good teacher—I learned

158

a lot of things. I read all sorts of things, and I read the dictionary. It tells you what words mean and it tells you how to pronounce them—even though I can't pronounce them all. I try to imagine it. I know a lot about the hearing world."

"So you read—OK—so what? Why do it when you can't talk?"

"Because when I know how a word is pronounced it helps me to read lips better. Like I told you, I had a good lip-reading teacher. She taught me a few tricks."

Mundo nodded. "You think you're pretty fuckin' smart, don't you?" He laughed. "So you read French words, right? What the fuck's wrong with Spanish? You think you have to know a fancy foreign language or something to show everyone you're smart?"

Diego shook his head. "I'm deaf. All languages are foreign."

Mundo laughed. "You're weird, man, you know?"

Diego nodded and smiled. "Yeah, I know. You know I read how they make cognac in a book about wines. I wanted to try the stuff, so I did. And I liked it. It cost me more than a shirt. I hardly ever drink it. Way too expensive."

"Don't you get bored at the library?"

"Sometimes, but I've never been stabbed in one."

Mundo laughed. "A que cabrón. You're a real smart mouth—even on paper. It's a good thing you can't talk—otherwise you would have been stabbed by now."

Diego laughed.

"You make noises, man, did you know that?"

"Yeah," Diego wrote, "deaf people can make a lot of noise."

Mundo nodded. "See, it's like the old lady says, we're all the same."

Nodding, Diego took a sip of cognac.

"I can't believe those goddamned pinche bastards threw me in the garbage. Man, to die in the streets is one thing, man, the streets, that's all right. But to die in a fuckin' trash can? Someone's gonna pay for this. I'm gonna get even."

Diego watched him as he emptied his glass.

"This stuff ain't so bad, man. I could get into this French shit. But I don't like their fuckin' language, got it? They sound like a bunch of pinche jotos—queers, you know? I got a sister who took

French in school. Thought she was hot shit. La cabrona wouldn't speak no Spanish. She thought she was too good. But she learned French, the bitch. Pendeja. She married a gringo and lives on the west side and votes on election day—the whole nine yards. Probably, she's gonna teach her half-breed coyote kids to speak French."

"I got a sister who's a pendeja, too," Diego wrote, "not too smart."

They both laughed. Diego sipped his cognac. He drank it slowly and let the warm liquid sit on his tongue. It made his mouth taste good. Diego poured Mundo another glass and offered him a cigarette. He smoked it in silence. Diego could tell he was in pain.

Diego watched him for a long time. Finally he wrote, "I got to go to work early in the morning. You can stay as long as you want. Doesn't bother me. I have some crackers and stuff if you get hungry. I'll bring some food home from Vicky's when I come home tomorrow. If you're hungry right now, I could go out and get something." He handed the note to Mundo who took his time reading it.

"No, man, I ain't hungry. Maybe tomorrow." He looked at Diego and nodded. "That's where I seen you. I knew that I'd seen you before, somewhere. That pinche that runs your place is the biggest asshole I ever met. Everyone calls him a sonofabitch. We're fuckin' boycotting his place."

Diego nodded. "Get some rest," he wrote. "I'll probably be gone by the time you wake up. Make yourself at home. I'll leave a note for Mr. Arteago—he's the landlord—and tell him I got a cousin visiting me. That way he won't say anything. You know, I think Mr. Arteago and my boss are related."

Mundo laughed and put out his cigarette, falling back into bed. He lifted his head and looked at Diego. "Now even my eyes hurt. I haven't read this much since I quit school." He laughed. Diego watched him as he mumbled himself to sleep.

In the dark, Mundo wondered about his life. He was getting too old to belong to the gang. Things were getting rougher and rougher. Maybe it was time to get out. He had held on to the idea of hand-to-hand combat with competing gangs, but he was losing the battle. Everybody wanted guns now and he didn't have the stomach for shooting people down—even those he hated. The knife was still his weapon of choice—the knife and his fists. Lately, he had been thinking he was getting too tired—too tired or old for all this shit. But it was all he had ever known. Maybe he would ask Rosie to marry him, but she would say no. He had asked her once already.

"Come on, you know you'll always be my baby."

She pushed him away. "I can't, Mundo, I just can't."

"Don't you love me?"

She kissed him on the cheek. "I love you. Eres mi vida. But I'm not going to marry anyone I can't grow old with."

"I'll grow old with you, baby."

She shook her head. "You'll be dead before you're thirty."

"But I'm alive, Rosie," he whispered in the dark. "Baby, I'm alive."

He slept most of the week; he didn't seem to be getting any better, though he didn't get any worse. Diego brought some food home from Vicky's every day, and although Mundo ate it all, he didn't seem to enjoy it very much. He didn't do anything all day as far as Diego could tell, except lie in bed. Diego brought magazines home for him to read, and it seemed that Mundo liked them pretty well, but he didn't say too much except that he liked the pictures. On Wednesday, Diego asked him if he was feeling all right.

"Just tired," Mundo said. "I just need to get some rest." Mundo wondered why this man cared, why this man wanted to bring him back into the world of the living. He thought it strange that the presence of this man made him want to be strong again. Maybe he had died, maybe this man was a spirit, a holy ghost. Maybe, he was being prepared for something. "And maybe I'm just going fuckin' nuts."

As he lay in bed, Mundo wondered why he had not died. He was getting tired of his life, and yet he felt powerless to change the way he lived. His gang and Rosario, that was all he loved. *What else is there*? He noticed that this deaf man had books in the room—they were nothing to him, they did not call him. He thought of his father, whom he had not seen since he was seven. He did not remember anything about him anymore except that he had once told him that the gringo would always hate him, and people like him. He remembered no words of love. He thought of his mother, who rarely smiled, the stoic resignation in her face. Only Rosario knew how to talk to him, and yet he felt she was leaving him. *"Rosie, tell me you love me." "It doesn't do any good, Mundo." "It does, it does do good." "What does it change? You stay the same."*

He pictured her dark eyes, her shaking head. He looked around the room. He hated when he thought too much. Thinking made him feel bad. "I'm going fuckin' nuts."

By Thursday Mundo looked stronger to Diego. Friday evening, when Diego came home from work, he found Mundo had taken a bath and changed into some of his clothes. "Hey, man," he smiled, "where'd you get this coat? It's wild, man. You dress like those old geezers that hang around Sacred Heart Church, you know that? You gotta do something about this, you got that? How do you expect to get yourself a good jaiñada?"

Diego looked at him. "What's that?" he wrote.

"What's what?"

"That last word—I don't understand that word."

Mundo looked at him and laughed. "A babe, man, a mamacita. An overnight special, know what I mean?"

Diego nodded. "How do you spell it?"

"Oh man, how the fuck do I know? It's not a school word, Diego. A jaiñada isn't something you spell—it's something you get. And I'm telling you, man, that you're not gonna get it wearing these clothes." He grabbed the pen and pad from Diego and wrote in large letters: JAIÑADA. He looked at the letters. "Something like that, man. Don't matter, anyway, how you spell it. Either way you got to get new clothes."

"I like my clothes."

"No, man, you gotta change your image. You gotta change your attitude, got it? That's what la teacha at La Jeff used to say to me all the fuckin' time. 'You gotta change your attitude, Edmundo.' "

"You got too much attitude," Diego wrote, "the wrong kind. "And what's La Jeff?"

Diego motioned him to stop. "What's La Jeff?"

"La Jeff's a high school. Only went there one year. Bunch of marranos teach there. Marrano City—pigs—that's what they are. Nobody has a name. And when la teacha remembered my name, she'd say it all wrong. Anyway, man, you gotta change your attitude." He walked over to Diego's desk and waved his suicide note in the air. "I read this, Diego. I'm not a good reader, you know? But I know what this fuckin' says, and I'm tellin' you, man, that you got the wrong idea. Shit, man. You thinking about killin' yourself is a pendejada—it's bullshit, got it?"

Diego stared at him, and pressed words on his pad angrily. "You shouldn't have read that. You shouldn't go around reading other people's letters." Diego ripped the sheet off his pad and threw it at Mundo.

Mundo picked it up off the floor and read it. "Relax, don't get all worked up. Easy, I'm on your side. You helped me out. I figure I can help you out, too, got it? It works that way, you know? And I say that it's a helluva lot better to start killing other people than killing yourself. Know what I'm sayin'? No te dejes. If you let yourself be pushed around, it's your own fuckin' fault—that's what my old man used to say. That's the smartest thing he ever said even though he is a goddamned liar. No te dejes, Diego. Your mom and your sister, they're gone, man. So what? Fuck it. You're not fuckin' dead, man. You think the fuckin' world cares if you kill yourself? You think they're gonna feel bad when they find your body smellin' up your apartment? That's bullshit. They're not gonna give a rat's ass. When I quit school, la teacha didn't cry. They don't give a pinche peso. Man, they don't know your name—and they don't wanna fuckin' know. They're gonna care when you fuckin' make 'em care. And that's the way it is."

Diego stood motionless. He shook his head. "So far, your philosophy has gotten you into a trash can. They left you for dead. Isn't the way you live suicide?"

Mundo crumpled up his note. "No. That ain't suicide. Suicide is when you wear these clothes, man. Suicide is when you take a knife and cut yourself until you fuckin' bleed yourself to death. I don't work like that, you know? When someone stabs my ass in the streets, it's because I've pissed them off so bad they want my pinche ass in the ground. But the motherfuckers know my goddamned name. I make sure they know, got it?"

"Pissing people off doesn't seem to be much of an ambition."

"Oh man!" Mundo shook his head. "You go to that goddamned library to learn things, but shit . . ." He stopped. He grabbed Diego's

163

letter and waved it around. "Just think about it." He threw himself on the bed. Diego looked at him. He was young. He didn't seem to be over twenty. Apart from the stitches on his brow, he looked like he'd never been stabbed.

Diego looked at him and shook his head. "Some day, somebody's gonna kill you."

Mundo laughed. "Yeah, man, just go to the fuckin' funeral."

Diego nodded and half-smiled.

"I'll be around, Diego. I know where to find you." He got up from the bed and headed for the door. He turned around and looked at Diego. He walked back toward the bed and picked up Diego's letter. "Tear it up." He handed it to Diego. Diego put it on his desk. "I'll see you around."

Diego nodded. "Yeah," he wrote, "see you. Come around to Vicky's sometimes, and I'll buy you a beer."

Mundo stared at the note and nodded. He untucked his shirt and strutted out of Diego's apartment.

As he walked back toward El Segundo barrio, Mundo fluctuated between exhilaration and revenge. "I want to find that sonofabitch—I'll find him and make him wish he never saw a trash can in his life." He understood being stabbed, but being thrown away? "One more fuckin' person throwing me away." Mundo wondered why the first thing he ever felt was anger. He pushed the face of the man who stabbed him away. He thought about Diego and nodded. He wondered at people like him—not that he knew many—not like him. He wondered why some people were kind and others were not. The strange, deaf man's kindness had helped bring him back to life, and he was suddenly happy to be alive. He wanted a beer, could almost taste it. He wanted to shoot a game of pool. He liked the feeling of the streets under his feet. As he walked, a cool breeze kicked up, and he promised himself he would pay the deaf man back. Somehow he would pay him back. He stared at the tatoo on his arm. How long could Rosie love a man like him? What could he do to make her stay? He wondered if life would ever be any different for him. Could he get rid of his fist and save his hand? He hated when he thought about things too much. It made him feel small and lost and hopeless.

7

His breathing was labored through the oxygen mask and it seemed to Jacob a sad and painful thing when sleep was something the body had to work for. He wanted to look away, and yet his dark lover was still beautiful to look at, too beautiful to be dying. He followed each breath, saw his chest rise up and down slowly like a calm wave on a quiet summer ocean. He rubbed his hand on Joaquin's arm, up and down to the beat of his breathing. It wouldn't be so bad if we could stay this way forever, he thought. Just like this. It would be good. He stared at his lover's body. Already it was going away, already he could see the bones through his perfect flesh more clearly than he had ever seen them. It was as if they were rising out of him like the morning sun rose out of a dark earth. Soon they would reach the surface.

He felt a touch on his shoulder. His body straightened, his back stiffened. His hand jerked up, and he abruptly turned around as if to strike the person who had just disturbed his world. The nurse took a step back—she was as startled as he had been. She stared into his impenetrable blue eyes. He relaxed and his arm dropped to his side. She smiled at him. "Sorry, she whispered. "I didn't mean to startle you. I shouldn't go around touching people. It's a vocational hazard."

He laughed nervously. "Guess I'm a little jumpy."

"Actually, you're a lot jumpy. You're entitled." Her voice was strong, friendly, disarming. She tried not to stare at him—something about him was disturbingly familiar. "You just missed the doctor."

"Damnit!"

"Not to worry. He said for you to call him this afternoon at his office." She spoke as she changed the bag to Joaquin's IV and made sure the oxygen tank was working properly. She touched his forehead, then softly combed his hair with her fingers. "He's nice-looking—beautiful, looks like a boy still," she said softly. She looked directly into Jacob's eyes. She wanted to ask him questions. She knew them, knew those eyes. She tried to remember where they'd met, maybe a long time ago—didn't it seem that she'd known him all her life? She felt a chill, ignored it. She even knew his voice—or was it that he simply reminded her of someone? She wanted to touch him. "You look like a boy, too," she said.

He wanted to ignore her, yet her voice made him smile, made him want to speak. "You always talk to your patients like this?"

"Only when they happen to be drop-dead gorgeous." She laughed. "Did I embarrass you?"

Jake laughed. "No. It's nice."

"Well, I'm a nice person. Damn fine nurse, too—my name's Lizzie. Did I meet you in a former life?"

"I never had a former life. Maybe we met in a bar."

She offered a handshake to Jake. "Lizzie," she said again.

Jake took her hand and shook it firmly. There was something about the way she touched him. "I'm Jake—and if I was straight I'd marry you." He was amazed that he'd said something like that to a woman. It wasn't his style to flirt—not even with men. He wondered what it was about this woman that made him want to be a boy.

"Sure you would. That's what they all say."

Jake laughed again. "Do you make it a habit of flirting with gay men?"

"Well, yes," she said. "It's safe."

He smiled. "Smart girl."

"Yeah, smart girl." She looked at her watch. "Listen, if you need anything just yell." She started toward the door, then turned around.

166

"You know, his eyesight's going. Doctor Michaelsen's going to put him on medication to kill the bacteria—"

"Does it work?"

Lizzie put her hands together as if she were going to pray, then placed them on her lips. She thought a while.

"Yes. Generally, it works."

"When doesn't it work?"

She was silent for a minute. "Sometime's the patient's very tired." She clicked her tongue against the roof of her mouth. "Anyway, Dr. Michaelsen said he'd fill you in when you called him at his office." Jacob shook his head, but said nothing. She patted the back of his head and walked out the door. A few seconds later she poked her head through the door again. "Yes, you can take him home. As soon as Tom gives his approval, you can take him home. He doesn't have to stay here if he doesn't want to." He doesn't have to die here, she wanted to add.

He turned around and stared at her. "How did you know what I was thinking?"

"Magic," she said. "If you work here long enough you can read minds." She disappeared down the hall.

What a strange woman, he thought, strange and beautiful and strong. He felt something urgent come over him. He shook his head. "This is crazy—she's just a nurse—she's just being nice. It's her job to be nice." He sat there for a long time and stared at Joaquin. He pushed his chair closer and placed his head on the bed and closed his eyes. He thought about one of the times he'd left him. He pictured the kitchen where they'd fought: *"You said you'd be home after work. Since when do you work until 11:30 at night?"*

"Oh great, J, now you're acting like a middle-class housewife."

"I'm not a housewife, and I'm not middle class you stupid sonofabitch. José, Mike, and Connie came to dinner—and you're the one who invited them. We ate without you. They send their regards." He grabbed a piece of cold chicken from the stove and threw it at him. *"We had chicken. It was good."*

"You do that again and I'll kill you."

"You have no imagination, you know that, Jake? You're a very old story: you drink too much, you go out with other men, you don't talk,

167

you don't know how to say I love you, you don't know how to say I'm
sorry—and you threaten people. A real credit to white boys everywhere."

"Shut up, J! Just shut your mouth—and don't open it until I tell you
to."

"What?"

"Shut up, I said."

"I'm going to bed, Jake. I can't talk to you right now."

"J, you walk out of this room, and I swear I'll walk out the door and
never come back."

"Don't make promises you won't keep, gringo."

"I'll keep this one, J."

"I'm going to bed." He picked up the piece of chicken from the floor,
and put it in Jake's pocket. "It's for lunch, darling."

Jake flung it from his pocket and tossed it in the sink. "Goddamn the
day I met you, Joaquin! Goddamn you!" "I didn't mean those things,
J. I was different when I came back, I was good, I was good to you
after that."

He felt J's hand on his head. "Are you beating up on yourself
again, Jacob Lesley?" His voice was weak, and a little distant.

Jake looked up at him and nodded. "I was only beating up on
myself a little. How do you feel?"

"You don't have to talk so loud—I'm going blind, not deaf."

He lowered his voice. "How do you feel?"

"I want to go home."

"I haven't talked to Tom, yet, but the nurse says it will be fine.
We just need Tom's OK, that's all. There won't be a problem."

"I don't give a damn what Tom says. Tell Tom I want to die at
home."

"You're not going to die."

"Don't be afraid, Jake. I'm not. I'm really not."

"J, don't—"

"Please, gringo. You never want to talk about this. You think if
we don't, then it will go away. You think if I take my medicine
then I'll get better? I'm not going to get better."

"You don't know that."

"Yes, I do."

"You're fine."

168

"No. I'm not fine."

Jake sat nodding for a few minutes.

"I'm begging you, Jake."

"Won't it get complicated at home?"

"Tom will help us."

"You just said you didn't give a damn what Tom said."

"I get confused. He'll help if I ask him." He swallowed hard, then looked into Jake's face. "He cares."

"I know."

"Do you mind?"

"No, I don't mind." He rubbed Joaquin's palm.

"Then I can die at home."

Jake nodded. "OK. Soon as Tom says we can go home, we'll never come back here again."

 **8**

"THE BODY IS open and porous. The body is open and porous." Lizzie found herself repeating this phrase as she took her morning shower. "The body can go anywhere. The body has no limits." She caught herself, became aware of the words she was uttering. Suddenly she wondered if words could be weighed. "There must be something physical about them. The body . . . What the hell am I saying?" She stared down at the drain in the bathtub. She wondered if she were going to leave her body again. Maybe she would fit in the drain; maybe she could become water and float below the city. She hugged herself. She felt her nipples grow hard, harder and harder until they hurt. She wanted to let herself go. She wanted to rip off her clothes and then jump out of her skin. She could press against the sky closer than she'd ever pressed against any man. The sky would never hurt her—not like men. "I can't, I can't. I'm late for work. Can I shed a body like an old coat?" She repeated her own name: "Lizzie" or was it "Maria de Lourdes?" The names sounded foreign to her as if they signified nothing. She laughed. How could she have ever thought her name or her body meant anything at all. Her names were strange, she had a strange body, and now she felt as if she could call herself anything since now she was a part of everything. She could call herself a man if she wanted to—or a frog—or the earth—or the grapes that grew

170

from it every year—or the new wine. Crazy. Crazy to have equated herself with her name and her body.

She had always seen herself as Lizzie the WASP who liked being a WASP and liked hating herself for it. But was she really Maria de Lourdes? What did that other identity mean? "Salvador," she said out loud, "I can call myself Salvador. I am my brother's body." She looked at her breasts. "Is this what makes me a woman?" For an instant, she wanted to cut them off. She shook her wet hair and tossed it around as if she wanted to shake it free from her head. She stared at herself as she put on her makeup. What a strange thing to be doing—putting on makeup. What a strange and stupid custom. What was she, now? Was she Mexican because her mother was Mexican? She looked at her skin. Nothing Indian about the way she was raised, the way she looked, the way she thought. She put on a pair of dangling silver earrings—they shook like wind chimes. She removed them. She pulled at her nose, her ears, her cheeks. She felt heavier than she'd been—but also lighter. She was relieved that the man she had called "father" for most of her life was not her father. But hadn't he been? Wasn't she his daughter? Was blood everything? Was it anything? "Stop it," she told herself. "Stop it! You'll make yourself crazy." She stared into the mirror. She was certain if she looked long enough at herself, she would begin to disappear "I have disappeared," she thought, "I'm gone." She laughed. "And since I'm gone, I'm going to quit my job. Ghosts don't need to work. I'll get a new name, a new house. Maybe I don't need a place to live at all. The former things have passed away." She drove to work singing. She was especially kind to her patients that day and felt so much love for them that her body hurt. She thought she was breaking. She wanted to tell them that nothing separated them now—except she knew it was a lie. Her body was healthy—theirs were not. It was a lie to think that nothing separated them, a lie, a lie, and she could not utter that lie and did not know why she felt it, so she just smiled and said nothing—smiled and felt sad because not everything the body felt was the truth, felt sad because she knew it was almost time to leave. At the end of her shift, she handed the head nurse a note she'd written during lunch. All the note said was: "I have to leave. I'm sorry, but I just have

171

to. This is an official two-week notice." She said nothing as she handed the note to Cassie.

Cassie read the note and nodded. "You can't. You're our best nurse."

"What does best mean?"

"It means the patients need you. You are so human with them."

"I don't know what human is anymore."

"That's a funny thing to say."

"Is it? Are these guys dying in here human? What's so great about being human? Give me a definition of human. Spell it out for me—it's not a word I know anymore." She was almost yelling. She was surprised at her own rage.

Cassie stared at her. "Lizzie? Are you sure you're OK? Maybe you just need some time off." She paused, stared into her face. "Look—just take a month—maybe you just need some time to think."

"About what?"

"I don't know. You're acting funny."

Lizzie smiled. "Yeah."

"Have you been to your doctor?"

"What the hell does a doctor know?"

Cassie laughed. "Nothing."

"Exactly."

Cassie reached over and touched her cheek. "Lizzie, please be OK. You're the best I've ever seen."

"The best what?"

"Just the best, Lizzie."

Lizzie looked down at the letter Cassie was holding. "I can't do this anymore."

"I don't want you back here tomorrow. I want you to take a month—then I want to see your ass back here, OK? No resignation, no two-week notice—just a little leave for a woman who needs some personal time. How's that sound?"

"It sounds fine," Lizzie heard herself say, but she felt hollow and numb. She reached over and kissed Cassie on the cheek. "I'll see you in a month." She walked slowly out of the hospital. She wanted to turn around and ask her patients for forgiveness; she wanted to say good-bye, but she had said good-bye too many times already.

Lizzie listened to the voice on the answering machine: *"Yes, Hello? Elizabeth? This is Mrs. Moncado, the secretary at Mission Dolores Catholic Church. You were in the rectory three days ago, and you asked me to let you know if I heard anything about a certain Mr. Salvador Aguila's funeral. Well, he was cremated a day after he died. Apparently, he left very explicit directions. But he also requested a funeral Mass here at Mission Dolores. A young man came in to make the arrangements. Anyway, I thought you'd want to know. There will be a memorial Mass for him this coming Monday at ten in the morning. If you need to call me back, you can just call me here at the rectory . . ."* Elizabeth liked the sound of Mrs. Moncado's voice. She played the message again—then again—before letting the machine go on to the next message. Conrad's deep baritone voice filled the room. His voice, like his presence, took up too much space. She pictured the five o'clock shadow on his almost-handsome weathered face, his thick graying hair, his deep-set olive eyes. He had a deceivingly kind face. *"Hi. Sorry I haven't been in touch. How are you? Uh, I was a little surprised by the message you left. Uh, well, actually, well, I've been doin' some thinking. Actually, we're not exactly meant for each other, are we? Listen, listen, we can be friends, right? Let's be friends, huh, Lizzie? Uh, give me a call, huh?"* She nodded, "Right, Connie, we can be friends—pure and chaste from afar." She laughed. She knew he would never call back, and she could see no compelling reason why she should try and contact him. *Actually, we're not exactly meant for each other . . .* He didn't know how to be friends with a woman—not that he knew how to be friends with a man, either. Maybe a dog—maybe he could be friends with a dog. "Poor Conrad," she said, "poor, poor Connie."

"Hi Sweetie, it's me, the very pregnant Helen Marsh. Do you think I made a mistake by taking Eddie's name? Sometimes I feel as if I should have kept my own damn name—but that would've been—well, it's too late—and anyway, I like his name. Can't you tell I don't have anything better to do with myself than to call and talk into your machine? It's the pregnancy. I'm getting a little anxious. I had false labor pains this morn-

ing. Oh, God, Lizzie, I'm terrified. And if you want to come and live with me until I deliver, I won't stop you—I really won't. How's that for a subtle hint? Please come—I'm making Eddie crazy. And I have something to tell you—it's about—well, it's about—damn!—I can't say this right. I want to tell you in person. I'm not who you think I am. It's a long story. Call me, and we'll have a long, long talk. See you soon, yes?''

There was a desperation in Helen's voice that unsettled her. She pictured what Helen looked like as she talked into the receiver, how she might tug at her long black hair, how her dark eyes would plead, how she might measure her words. She talked at the phone. "Helen, your voice is so pretty. Can I have it?" She took off her nurse's smock, her blouse, her long white skirt, then took off her bra and underwear. She walked to a chair in her bedroom and put on her white cotton robe, soft on her skin. She put a pot of coffee on the stove, a pot her mother had bought in Mexico when she had first been married. Elizabeth had retrieved it from the trash. She wished for a cigarette and somehow expected one to appear in her hands. She remembered a dream she'd had the first week after she'd quit smoking: She was walking down the street dressed in a long, black strapless dress as if she were going to a formal dinner. As she reached the place of the party, she had suddenly become nervous. She'd stuck out her finger in front of her and a cigarette appeared. She'd stuck it in her mouth and it had lit itself as she sucked on it. It was good. It was so incredibly good, the smoke tasting better than any lover she'd ever had. She smiled as she thought of the dream. The dream had come several times before it had left her in peace. What was she going to do with herself now that she'd left her job? She'd saved enough money to go on a trip, but now she thought she'd use the money to live on for a while. It would last six months— maybe a little longer if she lived sensibly. She laughed. "Shit, I haven't lived sensibly a day in my life." Her parents had been surprised she'd gotten herself through nursing school. She'd resented them for it—but even she had been surprised that she had stuck to it. She paced the apartment thinking—the thought of Salvador returning to her again and again. And then—from the hospital she had just left—the faces of two men entered her body or perhaps

174

just her mind. Whichever it was, she felt their presence as something physical. Then, they were gone. She was suddenly cold. She poured herself a cup of coffee and and added a little Kahlúa. She tried to place the identities of the two men whose presence she had just felt in her apartment. She knew them, remembered them, felt them move under her skin. Then she remembered she had flirted with one of them a few days earlier in the hospital—handsome and so scared, his lover mute in his sickness. They seemed to have become little boys, little boys lost in hospitals that threatened to steal the little bit of life they had left. She remembered how beautiful they were, how moved she was by what they felt for one another. She remembered the blond man, striking and chillingly familiar. She was angry with herself for not remembering their names. "It will come. Their names will come. And where in the hell do I know him from?" She wrapped her hands around the mug of coffee and took a drink. It was good. She walked over to the phone and brought it back to the table in the kitchen where she was sitting. She dialed Helen's number. She heard the voice on the other end. "You're not Helen," she said.

"No, but I'm her husband."

"Husbands don't count."

"I already know that."

"It's Lizzie."

"I already know that, too."

"How are you, Eddie?"

"I'm beautiful."

"Yes, you are. I was hoping you wouldn't find out. Wouldn't want you to get a big head. What would we do with you, then?"

"How come I'm allowed to have a big heart and not a big head?"

"Hearts and heads are different things, dear Eddie—and speaking of hearts, I would very much like to speak to the mother of your child."

"Ahh yes, the mother. The mother is cooking dinner."

"What?"

"Don't get mad—I'm not making her do it. She wanted to cook. We could be eating Frito sandwiches for all I care."

"Frito sandwiches?"

"I used to have them in college. If you put Tabasco on them, they're not half-bad."

"Yuck, Eddie. And your wife kisses you?"

"Oh, she does more than that."

"Not my Helen—I thought she was still a virgin."

They both laughed. "Let me get Maria Elena for you."

"Maria Elena?"

Eddie was silent for an instant, stumbled, then laughed nervously. "Yeah, I'm calling her that lately. She'll tell you all about it, I'm sure."

"Tell me what?"

"Let me just get her, OK?"

She sipped on her coffee as she waited for Helen to come to the phone. She wondered at Eddie's sudden nervousness, then laughed at the sound of Helen and Eddie laughing in the background. They always made her laugh. She heard Helen's voice on the other end.

"Lizzie! I've been needing to get in touch with you."

"Anything important or do you just want to see my face?"

"Well, of course I want to see your face, but I"—she stopped— "I have something I want to tell you."

"Well?"

"I don't want to tell you over the phone."

"You want me to drive all the way to Palo Alto just so you can talk to me?"

"I know you work, but—"

"Well, actually, I have a month off."

"You have a month off? Come be with me for a month. You can be here when the baby comes. He'll be here any day."

"He?"

"I have a feeling."

"Oh, a feeling? And what do you mean by 'any day'? I thought the baby wasn't due for another seven weeks. And first babies are always late."

"Always?"

"I'm a nurse—take my word for it."

Helen laughed. "Anyway, how come you have a month off?

176

Didn't you and Conrad take a trip not too long ago? How much vacation time do you get?"

"I'm on a month's leave."

"How come?"

"I wanted to resign, but Cassie wanted me to take a month off and think about it—so she gave me some time to think."

"That was generous."

"She's very generous."

"I thought you loved your job, Lizzie."

She took a deep breath. "Oh, Helen, I don't know what to say, what to think. I'm a mess."

"What's wrong, Lizzie? You sound exhausted."

Lizzie could bring herself to say nothing.

"Lizzie?"

"What?"

"Tell me."

"I told you I didn't know. I'm lost, Helen. Have you ever felt lost? I feel as if I'm alone, and I don't know what—" She began sobbing into the phone.

Helen let her cry. Finally she whispered, "Can you drive?"

Lizzie nodded into the phone.

"Lizzie?"

She took a few deep breaths, "Yeah, I can drive."

"Well, I want you to pack a few things—toothbrush, clothes, earrings—and I want you to get in your car and drive to Palo Alto and come and stay with me."

"But what about Eddie?"

"Eddie won't mind. Eddie adores you. I keep telling you he adores you."

Lizzie blew her nose from a roll of paper towels.

"Please come."

"I hate being a sympathy case."

"Don't insult me, Lizzie."

She nodded. "OK."

"OK, then. I'll keep the light on for you."

Lizzie hung up the phone, stared at it, then put on a pair of jeans. She put on a flannel men's shirt she'd inherited from a former lover, then started getting a few things together. "How the hell am I going to explain all this to Helen?" She shook her head so hard that she found herself out of her body. The two men whom she'd felt in her apartment came to her mind and occupied it as if it were an unpeopled country that they were claiming for their own. She found herself weightlessly floating toward an unfamiliar apartment house on Divisadero. It was nice, clean, well-kept, almost expensive. She found herself in their bedroom. A sandy-haired man was sitting on a big overstuffed chair and holding a thin black-haired man in his arms. They were whispering to each other. *"You have to let me go, Jacob."*

"Shhhh. Don't talk."

"You never wanna talk."

"What will happen will happen, J."

"Say my name. I want to hear you say my name."

"Joaquin."

"Say it again."

"Joaquin. Joaquin. Joaquin." He stood up, slowly, careful not to fall, careful to keep his balance, careful not to hurt the man he was carrying to bed. She had no idea why she was there. A part of her wanted to stay and watch them, but another part wanted to leave immediately. She was an intruder, a voyeur, a tourist in the land of someone else's pain. She willed herself to leave. As she left their apartment, she heard Jacob's racing heart. His rage racing through her like a river about to break through its own banks. Then the raging was gone. Lizzie found herself in her apartment again. She stared at her body lying on the floor next to the bed. She opened her eyes and stared up at the ceiling. She stood up, and repeated the men's names. "Jacob and Joaquin. Jacob and Joaquin. Jacob loves Joaquin. Joaquin loves Jacob."

She could have sworn she heard Jacob's voice in her head as she drove to Palo Alto. *"J, don't leave—never, never leave."* She wanted to hold him. She felt he had come to her before. She felt she belonged to him as much as she had ever belonged to anyone.

 **9**

May 7, 1992

Dear Jon,

Joaquin told me today that I have to let him go. "It's time, Jacob Lesley," that's what he told me. Spring is almost over, but it hasn't felt like spring. I met Joaquin in the spring. I left home in the spring, and I was a boy, but I didn't feel like one. Summer will be here soon, and the fog will be endless. I never liked summers in San Francisco. Joaquin won't die—not this spring. I won't let him. I'll make him live another year— and then another year after that. I will give him my rage.

Where do you live, Jon? I thought I saw you once in the street. I was drunk, I think. I haven't been drunk in ages. When Joaquin dies, I'm going to drink until I die. He's your age. Young. I've told you that before.

I wonder how much you remember. I wonder what they put you through. I'm not superstitious but I do believe there's such a thing as evil. Mom and Dad were evil. Then how come you're so good? Are you good only because I need you to be?

I wish I could see you. I say this all the time to you. Lately, it's not enough to write to you.

Joaquin is very peaceful about dying. He was always peaceful about everything. Why is it, Jon, that some men are born decent? Are they born? Are they made? I can't find a reasonable explanation for Joaquin's

179

goodness. There isn't one. I hit him once. I guess I told you that. Sometimes, I think I could live my life hitting face after face after face. I should have been a boxer. A gay boxer? How would the fans like that one? Maybe they'd like it just fine—people love a show—especially when freaks are involved.

We were together for a long time, and he loved me. I blame myself. I will always blame myself. I wasn't always so faithful. Then there was this thing, this disease—and Joaquin and I—we live it. Funny how love couldn't make me faithful—but a disease could. But it was too late.

I'm tired lately. I don't know if I'm at the beginning stages or if I'm just tired from the life we've been living. Bone tired.

Joaquin has dreams. We no longer make love. It's OK. I don't care about sex these days. I don't know that I care about anything. When he dies, I'll be alone. All the friends we have, we have because of him. He told me today he wanted a funeral Mass at Mission Dolores. He goes to Mass there every Sunday. I don't understand why a gay man would go to Mass every Sunday. He told me once, ''Look, gringo, Catholics aren't even good at heterosexuality. What do you expect? I go to Mass for my own reasons.'' He was pretty goddamned silent about those reasons. So he wants a Mass. He'll get a Mass. No Church is threatened by a dead fag—only a living one.

He wants his ashes spread over the desert. I promised him I'd spread his ashes near the ruins of Casas Grandes. He said he loved those ruins. He said he started dreaming wonderful things after he visited there. I don't even know where Casas Grandes is. I just know it's somewhere in the Mexican desert. I guess I'll have to make a trip there. I promised him. He asked me once if I prayed. I laughed. I told him I wrote disconnected letters to my brother in my journal. I told him that was all the praying I did.

When he sleeps he whispers that the earth is holy. Sometimes, when he says things like that, he scares me. The earth is just the earth, and that's all I feel. It's hard for me to have empathy for an inanimate object. Is the earth inanimate? Maybe not. Sometimes, I lose definitions of words I know. Joaquin says the earth is not inanimate. I don't think about it much, anyway. I only think about my job when I have to, and Joaquin— and you. I think about you all the time.

Joaquin's breathing is very labored. He's beginning to look dead. I want to die. I'm wondering if his memory—and yours—will be enough to keep me alive. Everything is too heavy. My thoughts, my body, my past. Everything is too heavy. Sometimes I'm so angry that I think I'll explode.

Joaquin sometimes fades in and out of reality, constantly crossing between fantasy and reality. He confuses the two. He no longer knows where he is. Sometimes, he's in Mexico and he's a boy and he asks for his mother. Sometimes he's in El Paso working as a busboy. He mentions a man by the name of Carlos. He says he can't die without seeing him one last time. And sometimes he comes back to me, here, in San Francisco.

I'm wondering why I never got in touch with you. If I would have tried to find you, maybe I would have succeeded. I think I say more when I talk to you than I say in real life. I don't talk to people much.

Are you me?

 **10**

WHEN EDDIE ANSWERED the door, Lizzie stared at him as if she expected him to look like a different man. Everything had changed. She smiled. She was relieved he looked like the kind and familiar man she knew—and yet she thought she recognized something about him, but she was unable to retrieve that something from her memory, from that place within her that recognized an identity that remained inarticulate, at the edge of her consciousness. She suddenly had an image of him sitting outside, the noonday sun shining on his face, and him writing carefully, in a black book— writing so carefully and sadly that he seemed to be writing an elegy. She couldn't see what he was writing, but he was thinking of a man, the man's name was—she could begin to make it out—

"Say hello," he laughed.

"Huh?"

"You OK?"

"Nothing a good drink can't fix."

"Not until you say 'hello.' "

"Hello."

"Hello, Eddie, you look better than the best pizza in Chicago," he said.

"Hello, Eddie, you look better than the best pizza in Chicago," she repeated.

"You're no fun. You didn't even sound like you meant it." He grinned, the light behind him making his face dim and unreachable as if he were only a silhouette. He reached for the backpack she was carrying. She watched him lift the bag and smile at her. She began to feel calmer in his presence. Eddie could be as calm as water in a glass. "Still," he smiled, "you said it, didn't you? It'll have to do. Bar's open—what'll you have?"

"Maker's Mark on the rocks."

"Ahhhhhhhh. The lady knows what she wants." Eddie took her by the arm and pulled her into the house. "It's the house specialty. How did you know?"

"I read minds."

"Hey, Maria Elena," he yelled up the stairs, "Our Lady of Palo Alto has just arrived."

"Why are you calling her that?" she asked.

"Calling her what?"

"Maria Elena."

"Well, we'll get to that." He didn't look at her face.

"You just turned red," she said.

He smiled nervously. Lizzie's presence suddenly embarrassed him. He felt silly and self-conscious. The game he and Maria Elena had played had been so silly, ludicrous. He felt ridiculous. She would look at them and laugh. "Be patient," he said, and kissed her on the cheek.

Helen was at the top of the stairs looking down at them. She smiled to herself as she saw her husband kiss her best friend. In another life, she would have been suspicious, jealous, protective. She would have wanted her husband to like her friend, but would have also demanded that he keep his distance from her. Lizzie enjoyed being a woman—that in itself was inexplicably threatening. She had often watched her husband as he laughed and listened to Lizzie's amusing stories—but she had always been more than just amusing. Eddie never hid his affection for her from the first time she'd introduced them to each other—and she had always managed to ignore her own ambivalence toward her husband's relationship with her best friend, a relationship that had life independent of her. Now as she watched them at the bottom of the stairs, the threat seemed as ridiculous as the silly name she'd chosen for herself. She repeated her own name, "Ramirez." She held on to the railing as she laughed. "It takes a while for me to climb up and down the stairs," she said. Lizzie watched Helen as she moved slowly toward her, she waited for Helen to reach the bottom of the stairs, and then kissed her friend on the cheek. "That backpack doesn't seem to have enough stuff for a long stay," she said.

"I'm only staying the weekend," she said. They walked into the kitchen holding each other. Eddie reappeared with a drink in his hand. "Here," he said handing the glass to Lizzie, "I'm going to bed."

"Stay," Helen pleaded.

Eddie shook his head, "Really, I have to go to bed." He looked straight into Lizzie's eyes. "You look a little beat up." He looked at his wife. "You guys need to—"

Helen looked at her husband and pleaded. He looked back at her with a look that said *"I don't want to get into this—you do it."* "Eddie," she said half-begging, half-demanding that he stay.

"I'm tired," he said firmly, "really tired."

Maria Elena nodded reluctantly. She wanted him to stay, wanted him to be a part of the conversation—and yet she understood that he did not want to repeat the story of his father to another human being. "You tell her," he'd said, "I don't mind—just let me be out of the room. Let me be absent." She placed her hand on his cheek.

Lizzie watched them and wondered why nobody had ever loved her like Eddie loved Helen. Sometimes she wanted to hate them for what they had. And yet she loved them and wanted to always love them. "Eddie," she said as Helen pulled her hand away, "pour yourself a drink. You might as well hear this."

"Hear what?" Maria Elena asked.

Lizzie hesitated, "Helen, something's happening."

"Her name's not Helen." Eddie covered his mouth as soon as the words came out. He shrugged his shoulders and looked at his wife. "It just came out—I'm sorr—see, honey, I should just let you two guys—"

"It's OK, Eddie."

"But you should have been—"

"Does it matter?"

"What the hell are you two talking about?" Lizzie asked. She looked at Maria Elena suspiciously. "If your name isn't Helen, then who the hell are you?" She volleyed her gaze back and forth from Eddie to Maria Elena. "Is that why you keep calling her Maria Elena?"

Eddie nodded. He tried to pretend he was invisible. He wanted to leave the room as graciously as possible. *"Do you love your father?" "Of course I love my father." "And your mother?" "Yes, I love my mother."* The business of revealing the truth was as impossible as keeping secrets. *"They hurt me, they hurt . . ."*

Maria Elena popped her knuckles.

"You only do that when you're nervous," Lizzie said.

"Do I?"

"Helen, will you tell me what the hell's going on!"

"Maria Elena," she said, "my name's Maria Elena Ramirez." Her voice cracked. As she articulated her name to her friend—her closest friend—she was completely embarrassed by the charade she and her husband had been playing. She felt stupid and awkward and self-conscious—the same way she'd felt the first time she'd been to a high school dance. But she wasn't a girl anymore. She was sitting in front of a woman she loved, a woman she respected, a woman she'd hidden from. *"Hide-and-seek at thirty-four. Shit."*

Lizzie's response was slow in coming. "What?"

"I'm not who I said I was." She stared at Lizzie's drink. She imagined how the bourbon would taste in her dry throat.

Lizzie sipped on her bourbon, then crossed her arms. Maria Elena and Eddie waited for her to say something. "It would be nice to have a cigarette," she said finally.

Maria Elena nodded.

"It makes sense," Lizzie said. "Your past was so vague. I was the one who had a million stories about growing up, and you, you never had any. It was as though your life began when you went to college."

"In some ways, it did." She squeezed her husband's arm. "In some ways I didn't lie, Lizzie. Life began with Eddie—it really did. Do you hate me for lying?" she whispered.

185

"It's too late to hate you," she said. She took another sip from her bourbon, then laughed. "And here I thought you were anything but a woman with a past." She laughed again. Maria Elena's back relaxed as she heard Lizzie's familiar laughter. It would be fine, it would all be fine. "I should have known," Lizzie yelled, "I knew you weren't Italian. Somehow I just knew—I just knew."

"You did not," Maria Elena objected.

"Never mind," Lizzie laughed, "Let's not argue. I want to hear—I want to hear everything." She became a little girl in the presence of her friend's revelation. It was as if she was waiting for her friend to sing her a favorite song. She played with the sweating glass of bourbon and rubbed the water into her palms. "And don't skip anything," she said, "I want it to taste as good as this drink."

Maria Elena smiled, and nudged her husband who was now sitting next to her and stirring his own drink with his finger. She slapped his wrist. "Eddie, you tell it."

"No way. I'm not telling my part again. You tell your part—she's *your* friend."

"Thanks a lot, Eddie."

"I didn't mean it that way, Lizzie—it's just it's—it's hard—you know? And you two are much closer, and you know how to talk to each other pretty well from what I can tell—so you don't need me for this. And anyway, I've always been a third wheel—"

"Isn't that a crock of shit," Lizzie laughed.

"I'll just slip into my room and read a good book, and you two can have a good talk."

"Coward." His wife stared at him.

"Ultimately, they're all the same," Lizzie said.

"I'm familiar with these tactics—and they're not working."

Maria Elena looked at him. His emotional reluctance was written everywhere on his face, in the way he was sitting. She wanted to tell him it was fine, that everything was fine, but she also sensed her words would sound hollow and condescending. She sometimes wanted to treat him like a little boy, but she was beginning to understand how much he had overcome to become the man he was. He had earned the right to say what he wanted, to speak about his life to whomever he chose. It occurred to her that some parts of his life would always be inaccessible to her. She tried to picture him telling Lizzie about his past, about his father. There was something wrong with the picture. *"Tell her anything you want. Just let me be absent."* She kissed him on the cheek. "Go to bed," she said. She could see his face relax as if he had just been given a reprieve from some command he could not carry out. "Lizzie and I have a lot to talk about."

He kissed them both on the cheek. As he climbed the stairs, he could hear their voices. He was happy to let the women talk, happy that they were friends, grateful that he could be alone. "I'll finish my book," he said to himself, but when he got into bed, he fell asleep after reading only a page.

"It's a goddamn fairy tale," Lizzie said looking at Maria Elena. "You married a nice-looking man who treats you nice and who turns out to be rich. It's a goddamn Victorian novel."

"It's not like a Victorian novel at all. Those things end with a marriage—our novel begins with one."

"A modern fairy tale, then? Even better."

"When you hear the rest you won't think so," she said, her voice almost dropping to a whisper. "How's this for a fairy tale? Eddie's very rich, Episcopalian Republican father sexually abuses his two sons. He turns around one day and kicks the oldest one out for being a homosexual. He keeps the younger one around for you can imagine what. How do you like that for a start?" Lizzie sat motionless. "I'm sorry," Maria Elena whispered, "I'm being glib."

"Be glib if you want," Lizzie said, "you're entitled—"

"You keep things in and all those things you have inside you—well, they kill you." The sound in her voice was no less angry because she could control it. She smiled. Lizzie was moved by her awkwardness, by the sound of the hurt in her voice. "My poor Eddie." She reached over and took a sip from Lizzie's drink. "One sip won't hurt at this point." She felt the cool bourbon on her tongue. "So," she continued, trying to smile, "my Eddie had this really shitty childhood with a mother who was emotionally abusive and a father who was sexually abusive." Her voice grew less clear, less defined. "Sounds like they were a helluva tag team, no, Lizzie? They kicked his oldest brother out when Eddie was seven. He hasn't seen him since. Eddie says his older brother beat them up before he left and they had him arrested." She stopped. "You know, I don't think they ever saw him—his parents, I mean. They had this wonderful child—and they couldn't see him. I think somehow he was always invisible."

"Until you," Lizzie said.

Maria Elena smiled. "Don't give me so much credit."

They sat in the quiet of the kitchen, Lizzie stirring her drink with her finger. "So, they died and left him all that money?"

"Oh, much better than that. These people never did things the easy way. Eddie got all the money when his loving mother decided to off his dad and then point the gun at herself. He was eighteen by then. I don't think he could ever deal with them, what they were, what they did, what they turned him into—so he just decided to lock them up in his memory forever. And then one day he met Maria Elena Ramirez, a.k.a. Helen Rosalie La Greca, and she was as eager not to have a past as he was. So we played a game: I won't show you mine, if you won't show me yours. And we still managed to have sex—"

Lizzie laughed.

"It's so stupid really. I feel so stupid, like an idiot. Anyway, it's a little more complicated than that, but that's the basic story line."

Lizzie leaned over the table and kissed her hand. Neither of them spoke for a long time.

"I wish I could have a drink," Maria Elena said, breaking the silence. "I haven't had a drink in seven months."

"Soon," Lizzie said, "very soon. I'm going to buy you a bottle of champagne."

"An unpretentious white wine will do," she said.

Lizzie polished off her drink. "Bartender, I'll have another."

Maria Elena poured her a generous shot. "Eddie said that when he was a kid, he used to watch his mother drink her bourbon. He said something strange: He said he wanted her to be as beautiful as the drink in her hand. I think he wanted her to hold him as carefully as she held her glass of bourbon."

Lizzie squeezed her hand. The room was silent again. Lizzie stared at the woman in front of her. She had always sensed something about them—about Maria Elena and Eddie—something about them didn't quite fit in this neat, polished neighborhood. They were like the golf courses she had seen in the desert—they simply didn't belong. She felt tears on her face. She felt Maria Elena's warm hands absorbing the salt that came from her body.

"Are you OK?" Maria Elena asked.

She smiled. "I'm not sad," she said, "just a little off center. She tugged at her earring, then took it off and placed it on the table. "Everybody has a story, huh? I have one, too—only slightly more outrageous than yours."

Maria Elena laughed. "I would expect nothing less."

"My name isn't really Elizabeth Edwards—that is, I didn't start off life with that name . . ." Maria Elena listened carefully to the story Lizzie narrated, not moving a muscle as Lizzie spoke about the incident at the hospital. She stared at Lizzie's throat as if she could listen closer by staring at the physical place where Lizzie's words were formed. ". . . so I had a brother," she said as she finished her story, "a real brother."

"But how do you know?" Maria Elena interrupted. "How could he be your brother? What about your other brother? How many brothers do you have?"

"Is there a limit?" They both laughed. "Haven't you ever wondered why my brother and I did not even remotely resemble each other?"

"It happens," Maria Elena said.

"Yes, it happens. But in this case we're both adopted—both of us from different families."

"It could be just a coincidence, Lizzie. This doesn't prove you're his sister. Even if you are adopted, it still doesn't prove you're related to Salvador."

"I asked my mother," Lizzie said.

"And what did she say?"

"She said my real name was Maria de Lourdes. She gave me

this." She took a letter from her purse and unwrapped it from the tissue paper she had placed around it to protect it. She handed the letter to Maria Elena who read it quietly.

"Incredible," Maria Elena said. "So if you're Salvador's sister, and he gave you his gift, then can you read what I'm thinking?"

"You don't believe me." She wanted to tell her about the silence and her baby—but she thought it was something she should keep to herself. It frightened her. She thought it would frighten Maria Elena, too. Always, there would be a secret that had to be kept out of necessity. She looked at Maria Elena. "I know something about Eddie," she said. "Do you want to know?"

"We're both named Maria."

"Yes."

"I like that."

Lizzie smiled. "Me too."

"Should I call you Maria or Lourdes?"

"I still feel like a Lizzie."

"Good." Maria Elena said, "Lizzie's fine." She shook her black hair forward, then backward again as if she needed to stretch herself. "So what do you know about Eddie?"

"Your husband keeps a journal. It's big—maybe notebook size— and thick. It's bound in black leather, and I think he usually writes in it during his lunch hour?"

Maria Elena nodded and smiled. "How did you know that?"

"When Eddie answered the door I saw him sitting on a bench outside in the sun—and he was writing in a black book, but he brought me back before I could see who he addressed his journal to. He addresses it to someone—a man. I couldn't quite see the name. But he looked very sad, your Eddie."

"His brother. He address his journal to his brother."

Lizzie nodded.

"And you?" Maria Elena asked.

"What?"

"Who do you address your journal to?"

"No one. I think it's weird that he talks to his brother in his journal. Damn weird." She couldn't keep a straight face. She broke out laughing.

"You're mean, Elizabeth Edwards. And you've had one too many drinks. Am I going to have to carry you to bed—a woman in my condition?"

"You sound like my mother, Helen."

"Helen who?"

"I forgot. If I call you Helen sometimes, then you'll have to deal with it, sugar." She laughed. "It's a small price to pay for deceiving your best friend."

Maria Elena laughed. "I'm going to bed—I'm tired."

"Not yet," she said, "I haven't even told you the best part. Did you know I could fly?"

"What?"

"I can fly."

Lizzie, Maria Elena, and Eddie spent most of the weekend talking. And talking and talking. There were awkward silences in between the words, and each still kept quiet about things they found necessary to keep only for themselves. Eddie cooked for the two women on Saturday, cooked because he loved to, cooked because it was his way of spending time alone—but also his way of communicating gratitude. He had always wanted a warm kitchen where people gathered. He had never known a warm kitchen in the house where he was raised, but he had visited the maid's house once, and he had found her kitchen to be a fine place to live. He had been six years old at the time, and he had asked her if he could live with her. He had always remembered that kitchen, remembered how that place had made him feel—like belonging. It felt like belonging. Standing over the stove, Eddie laughed at himself as he thought about how he and Maria Elena always fought over who would cook.

Saturday night, Eddie baked bread, and they rented old videos and argued over which were the best scenes. They laughed, and the laughter felt real and necessary and urgent. It was as if these three people were learning how to enjoy their new selves, getting used to new identities, new skins that were exposed to the air for the first time as if they had emerged from cocoons. They kept looking at each other to see if they had physically changed and were surprised that their bodies resembled their old shells. They often glanced at each other wondering at the strangeness of their lives, and each one, separately and together, was in awe of the lives each had led, in awe of this thing they were living, and each one was struggling desperately, if awkwardly, to respect the losses they had suffered.

Sunday morning, as Eddie was about to go out for a run, Maria Elena announced she was going to Mass.

"What?" Eddie asked.

"Mass," she repeated.

"Do you even know where there's a Catholic church?" Eddie asked.

"Of course I know."

"May I ask why?"

"To pray."

"To pray," Eddie repeated. "Sometimes, I don't know you."

"I go to Mass, sometimes, you know? Not usually on Sunday, but I go sometimes during the week. You don't have to keep a journal in secret anymore—and I don't have to be a closet Catholic."

Lizzie shook her head. "I didn't know you prayed."

"You didn't even know my name until recently." She placed her hand on her belly. "I want to go and pray."

"Want me to go with you?"

"Not really, Eddie." She smiled at him. "And anyway, you don't want to go. What would you do there?"

"Sit next to you."

"You can sit next to me when we watch television. This doesn't have to be a group thing." She noticed his look of relief.

"Just one more question, Nena."

"Anything."

"Are you going to raise our child Catholic?"

"I want to baptize him," she said, "the rest is negotiable. You don't want that, do you?"

"I'm not objecting, honey."

"I know that look," she said, "and you always call me honey when you disapprove of something I'm doing."

"She knows that look," Lizzie said—then started laughing, "and you always call her honey when—"

"Who hired you?" Eddie asked.

"I'm the sidekick."

"Oh—and what does the sidekick think of all this?"

"The sidekick thinks it might not be such a bad idea. I mean I was raised as a nothing. What's so special about that? Besides, the kid might learn something about prayer."

"Prayer? You've done much of it, have you, Lizzie?"

"Smart-ass. What does that have to do with anything?"

"Well, I just want to know on what basis you judge prayer as being something necessary. I mean, you obviously didn't arrive at that conclusion via the vehicle of experience."

"Via the vehicle of experience?" Lizzie asked.

"He talks that way sometimes," Maria Elena said.

"You know what I mean. Tell me why prayer is good."

"Because you empty yourself out," Lizzie said.

"Then is it the same thing as an out-of-body experience?"

"In a way."

"In a way?"

"Prayer is a centering."

"Why do we need to be centered?"

"Because if you don't feel centered, then you always feel like a wreck."

"How can you center yourself and empty yourself out at the same time?"

"I'm not good at theological debates," Lizzie said.

"I don't think this conversation qualifies as a theological debate."

"I hate to break up this discussion, but I'm going to be late for Mass," Maria Elena announced. "I better get dressed."

"I want to go," Lizzie said. "I want to go with you."

"Why?"

"Because tomorrow I'm going to a Mass—a Mass for Salvador. I forgot to tell you. And I won't feel so nervous if I've done it before." The thought of walking into Mission Dolores Church suddenly filled her with dread.

"Done what before?"

"Gone to a Mass."

"You're being ridiculous, Elizabeth," Eddie said. "It's not like a piano recital—you don't need to practice."

"But Catholic churches are so scary," Lizzie said.

"They're not going to bite off your valuables," Eddie smiled.

Maria Elena was amused by her husband's uneasiness. "Are you coming, Lizzie?"

"Lend me something to wear?" she said.

They headed for the stairs. "I'm going for a run," Eddie said. "Don't forget to pray for the mass of perdition—and for the homeless—and pray for a revolution—and pray that all polluters be punished for their sins—and—"

"If you have that many intentions, then I think you better say your own damn prayers," Maria Elena said as she walked up the stairs. She knew this was the beginning of a new battle. An old disagreement died, another was born. As Maria Elena dressed for Mass, she thought of her mother. She wished her mother had lived long enough to see her grandchild. Maria Elena wondered why she had omitted telling Eddie about how they had run away one night from their father as if that incident was a minor detail.

Eddie stood silently in the doorway and listened to them laugh as they changed in the bedroom upstairs. He remembered his parents had made him go to Mass every Sunday. He also remembered his mother had killed his father and herself on Sunday. *After Communion, they went to Communion, and then she came home and blew their bodies away. Good, religious, conservative people. "Get dressed, Jonathan Edward, God requires . . ."* He stood in the doorway cursing his father.

No one spoke about prayer or Mass when Nena and Lizzie walked back into the house that afternoon.

Lizzie cooked her favorite Sunday dinner, a roast with carrots, onions, garlic, and potatoes. Maria Elena baked an apple pie, and the kitchen was full of the odors and warmth and Maria Elena's body. Eddie was happy just sitting in the room all afternoon, writing and thinking and half-listening to Nena and Lizzie speak of small things—old songs, bracelets, movies they had loved in that time of life when they were becoming women.

194

Eddie read them a poem from a book he was reading and they listened to his voice. Maria Elena was not listening to what the poem said, she just listened to the fact of her husband's voice—it was soft and warm and she did not remember hearing anything as unthreatening as the sound that came from his body. She looked at Lizzie—she was very beautiful. Maria Elena set the table when it was time to eat, and she lit candles all around the dining room. Sometime between the salad and dessert, Lizzie had convinced Maria Elena to go with her to her brother's memorial Mass.

"But you didn't know him," Eddie said to Lizzie.

"Does that mean I shouldn't go?"

"That's not it," he said, "I think it's grand that you're going. It would be awful if no one went. It's just that it sounds so strange for you to refer to him as your brother."

"Was he less of a brother because I didn't know him?"

Eddie said nothing. "You're right," he said, and then he seemed to go away from them.

Maria Elena knew he was visiting with the memory of his brother. Too much of him would be missing until she found him. She thought of Diego, tried to keep his name from entering the room. Too much of her was missing, too.

Lizzie thought of Salvador, repeated his name to herself, felt his touch on her palm. *"You have a gift."* She thought of the two men, their names, Jacob and Joaquin. She knew she would go and find them and that their names would become as meaningful, as significant, as painful as Salvador's. She knew Joaquin would die, the image of him on his deathbed became as real to her as the smell of Maria Elena's apple pie. She felt she was at the beginning of something and she knew that the two people in this room would be a part of whatever was coming—and so were the two men. She could still picture the blond Jacob holding the dark Joaquin. She wondered how it could be that these men's names were already holy on her lips. She did not know them. How could she love them? But she did love them, already, loved them almost as much as she loved Maria Elena and Eddie.

They ate dessert in silence. They were all a little tired. And a little sad.

Eddie got up and served more coffee. "It was a nice weekend," he said.

"It was lovely," Lizzie said.

"Lovely," Maria Elena repeated.

Maria Elena dipped her hand in the holy water font and crossed herself as she walked into Mission Dolores Church. She breathed in the years of incense that poured out of the walls. She lit a candle and whispered a prayer from her childhood. Lizzie followed behind her in silence. She was glad Maria Elena had come with her, and now that she was in the church, she wondered why she had been so afraid of it, but wondered, too, why it still looked so familiar. She was beginning to believe she'd had a former life. When Maria Elena finished her prayer in front of the image of Our Lady of Guadalupe, she took a seat in the third row. Lizzie nudged her as they sat down. She pointed at a man who was sitting alone. "There's nobody else here." She looked at her watch. "It's ten o'clock sharp." As she spoke, an altar boy and a priest robed in white moved toward the altar. Maria Elena stood up, and Lizzie mimed her friend's actions. The priest kissed the front of the altar and lit the Easter candle. It went out almost immediately. He tried to light it again. It stayed lit for a moment, flickered, then went out again. He shrugged his shoulders. He then faced the empty pews and the three people in the congregation.

"He's handsome," Lizzie said.

"Shhh, it's a church not a bar."

"You sound like an old lady."

"Priests are celibate."

"I'll bet."

"Good morning" the priest said. He had a nice voice, Lizzie thought. Maria Elena nodded. "Let us begin this memorial Mass in thanksgiving for the life that has been bestowed upon us in the name of the father and of the son . . ." He crossed himself as he spoke.

I hate words like "bestowed," Lizzie thought.

She noticed a brass urn sitting at the foot of the altar.

The ritual was simple, stark, serene. The light through the windows made Maria Elena think of the cathedral in El Paso where her mother had taken her to church as a child. Lizzie imagined what it would be like to be a believer. Somehow, she couldn't picture herself as a believer. Still, she was moved by what was happening before her—the light, the incense rising as the priest blessed the book, the candles burning all around them. It would be a great place to make love, she thought. The priest was graceful and sincere. He was around forty and he seemed a very calm man. When he read from the book, his voice was neither dramatic nor perfunctory. He enunciated each word clearly. When it came time for him to preach a sermon, he said very little: "I did not know Salvador Aguila . . ." He continued talking but Lizzie's mind wandered. She remembered feeling Salvador's strong hands on her palm, the sound of his voice in her body. She thought of her mother and suddenly she was sorry she had not told her about this Mass—her mother would have come. She would have wanted to be here. But maybe, she thought, it would have been too painful. She remembered what she said—that she had been in love with him, wanted him more than she had wanted her. As she thought of her mother, she stared at the statue of a Virgin with a bleeding heart. She placed her hands over her mouth and trembled. *"I know this place."* And then she remembered what she had been unable to remember—the dream— the dream she'd had—a terrible dream that had frightened her. *"I didn't have a body, I couldn't touch my mother . . . and there was a man, a man."* She stared up at the priest who was pressing his mouth together, and placing his finger on his temple. "God only breathes through us. I believe this. I believe that God's breath in the world changes with each death, with each birth . . ." His voice seemed good and warm, but she wondered if anything he was saying had anything at all to do with her. Did his life—this priest—did his life have anything at all to do with hers? She saw the priest sit down and bow his head. *"Jacob, the man in my dream was Jacob."* Everything in her dream became more vivid than the present. *". . . And the sun was setting—or maybe it was rising. God, I hope it was rising. Yes, it must've been ris—"* She felt herself coming out of her body. She willed herself back. Willed herself. Lizzie focused on

Maria Elena's hands folded in prayer until she was certain she would not float away from herself. She took a deep breath. She wondered about this thing called "prayer"—what was it? Why did people do it? She smiled. There was a tingling in her body. She tried to ignore it. She wondered about the life her brother had lived, what kind of man he had been. He seemed to think of himself as selfish—but people were often very hard on themselves. Maybe he had been a very kind man—maybe he had been decent and generous. Maybe he had loved deeply. Maybe he had been lonely—maybe he had been many things. But he had given her his gift. He could have died without giving it away; he could have taken it with him to the grave. He could not have been such a bad man, and she was certain he did not deserve to die as young or as painfully as he had. No one deserved that. Not her brother. She felt tears in her eyes and then a certain numbness. She didn't want to feel anything. Why should she feel anything for this stranger, this brother who was now even more unreachable than he had been when he was alive. Then, as if from nowhere—or perhaps from a less conscious place in her memory—something that resembled rage began to run through her, and her heart began to beat faster and faster, racing, raging like a tuna caught on a hook. It was as if her father was in her—and she wanted to kill him—even if she had to kill herself to do it. *"I hate you. I'm glad you're not my father."* She had the urge to leave her body again. If she left—just for a moment—then she could escape the rage. *"Free, look I'm—"* She was floating in the church just as she had been floating in her dream—it was exact. She was as light as the incense, as light as the words of the priest, as light as the colors streaming through the stained glass windows. *"It would be so pure to live like this—to be nothing but being, no longer obsessed with becoming."* At last she was perfect. She stared down at Maria Elena. She felt bad that her friend was burdened with a body. She saw Maria Elena reach for her arm—her body's arm—not her arm— she had no need of an arm. In the dream, she had been afraid, but now that fear was gone—absent, banished. She heard Maria Elena's voice. "Are you OK, Lizzie?" She sensed her friend's panic. She entered her body again—for Maria Elena.

"Are you OK?"

Lizzie smiled at Maria Elena and nodded.

"Did you go away, Lizzie?"

She nodded and tried to focus on the priest. The hatred she had felt for her father passed like a tornado that had touched down, then went on its way. Now, she only felt the exhilaration of having left her body behind. *"I can control it. I can."* She felt happy and rested. She smiled to herself and touched Maria Elena's hand. Lizzie watched the young priest closely as he motioned through the rest of the Mass, the ritual cleansing of his hands, the words he whispered, half to himself, half to God. *"Lord, wash away my iniquities, cleanse me of my sins."* She wondered about his sins. She wondered why he poured a drop of water into the wine. She looked up at the Host as he lifted it, and jumped at the sound of the bells the altar boy rang. When the Mass was over the priest and the altar boy disappeared down the aisle. Maria Elena and Lizzie sat in stillness for a moment. Suddenly, Lizzie felt as if she were about to leave her body again. She held on to Maria Elena's arm. "Pull me back," she gasped.

"Lizzie—what's wrong?" The sound of her voice was enough to keep her from leaving her body.

"I almost left again," she said.

"Again? Jesus—"

"Let's get some air."

As soon as they stepped outside, Maria Elena looked Lizzie over. "Well, you look fine—never better."

"I've never felt better."

"Well, if you feel so good, then why the hell are you trying to leave yourself?"

"If you could do it, you'd do it, too—it's why I've never felt better. It does wonders for your complexion."

"Don't be a smart-ass, Elizabeth."

"We're at church."

Maria Elena was about to scream at her when she noticed that the only other person who had attended the Mass seemed to be waiting for them at the bottom of the steps. Maria Elena nudged Lizzie and they both looked at him. He was tall and thin and had fine, light brown hair. He hadn't shaved, and he seemed very ordinary until he smiled. His teeth were even and white, and Lizzie thought he was very beautiful. She smiled back at him. She walked up to him. "Did you know him?" she asked.

He nodded. "I'm his executor," he said—then laughed. "He didn't leave much. He was lucky: He had insurance. He held the urn in his arms. "It paid for his cremation. He said he had a sister. Are you his sister?"

He nodded. "Can you prove it?"

"That's nice and friendly of you."

"Sorry. I don't mean to be a hard-ass. I knew Sal for a long time. We were good friends. He was good to me. He wasn't good to most people—but he was good to me. He helped put me through law school. I owe him. And I won't have him ripped off after his death."

"If it's about money I don't want it."

"No, don't say that. If you can prove you're his sister, it's yours. It's not very much—ten thousand dollars. He said if you didn't turn up in a year, then I could keep the money. But he said you would. And he said you'd be wearing long earrings. And so you are. He had a gift—"

"I know," she said.

"I didn't get a chance to see him when he went into the hospital. He died before I got there. I'm glad. He was very sad at the end."

She nodded. "I know. I met him in the hospital. I'm a nurse at St. Mary's. A strange and lucky coincidence."

He didn't seem surprised. "Not a coincidence. He knew."

Maria Elena stood next to them listening. She felt a chill run through her.

"I'm Lizzie," she said. "Well, my birth name was Maria de Lourdes Aguila. But I've known myself as Elizabeth Edwards for most of my life—until I met Salvador." She reached out to shake the man's hand.

He smiled as he gripped her hand. "I'm Daniel—Daniel Murphy."

"And this is my friend, Maria Elena."

They shook hands and nodded at one another. "Nice to meet you," Maria Elena said, "you look familiar."

He stared at her for a moment. "Yes," he said, "you do, too. Did I meet you at a party or something?"

200

"Maybe? I can't remember. I'm certain I've seen you. I can't place where."

"Are you married?" He looked at her stomach. "Sorry—it's none of my business."

"Yes," she said, "I'm not offended—it's not good to make assumptions."

He nodded. "Maybe I know your husband—maybe we met somewhere through your husband. What's his name?"

"Eddie Marsh."

He laughed. "Eddie Marsh is your husband?"

"Yes," she said. "What's so funny about that?"

"Nothing—I've known Eddie for years. We've probably met before at some function or other. I handle all of your husband's legal matters."

She smiled. "It's a small world."

"Yes, it's very small, and very mean," he said.

"Well, if you're a lawyer, it's mean," she said.

"Ahhh, yet another admirer of our profession."

Lizzie laughed. "My father wanted me to be one of you people."

"Stick with nursing," he said. "It's better for your soul."

"Yes, well, I'll trade you the condition of my soul for the car you drive and the house you live in."

He smiled—then laughed. "I get your point." He looked at Maria Elena. "I think I vaguely remember meeting you. You weren't pregnant, though." He smiled. "I see your husband often. Actually, we're pretty good friends."

"Well, Eddie doesn't mix business and pleasure." She smiled at her own response.

"Smart man." He turned his attention to the urn he was clutching. He handed it to Lizzie. "He's yours," he said.

She stared at the urn she was now holding. "Aren't you going to find out if I'm really his sister?"

"I'm satisfied. He told me his sister would have light brown hair with red highlights and that her name was Maria de Lourdes—and that she would go by Lizzie. I'm satisfied." He handed her his card. "Call me about your brother's will." He laughed self-consciously at himself. "I sound like a lawyer." He laughed again.

"You always laugh at yourself?"

"Always."

Lizzie tugged on her earring, smiled, then looked directly at him and tried to read his face. "You're not surprised by any of this, are you?"

"I knew your brother for a long time—nothing that ever happened while he was around surprises me—*nothing*."

Lizzie nodded. "I don't want his money," she said. "Can't we just give it away?"

"Anything you want," he said.

"Just give it to someone who needs it."

He nodded. "And his ashes—"

"His ashes? Did he want them scattered somewhere?"

"He went to high school in El Paso, Texas. His parents moved there—they had family there or something like that. Anyway, he said there was some kind of holy place—Christ the King—on some mountain. He said he wanted his ashes spread there. Something happened to him at that place—he was pretty vague about it."

"El Paso," Maria Elena repeated, "small world."

"Huh?" he asked.

"El Paso—it's my hometown," she said.

"You know the place Sal talked about?"

"Yes," she said, "I know the place. People go on pilgrimages there."

He looked at Lizzie. "Your friend here will help you take care of it, then."

They nodded. He shook their hands and started to walk away, then turned around and watched them. "Did he give you his gift?" he yelled.

"How did you know?"

"Just a hunch." He smiled. Lizzie heard his voice inside of her. *Use it well, Lizzie.* She smiled back at him.

11

October 9, 1984

Dear Jacob—

Today I was walking down the street, and I saw this guy who looked like you. I opened my mouth to call your name but nothing came out. That's him, I thought, that's my brother, Jake. But when I looked closer, it wasn't you—it wasn't you at all. He was big, blond, and he had this heavy walk and he had a very serious way about him. He caught me staring at him. He gave me a dirty look. I got kind of nervous. He followed me down the street, grabbed me, and told me he didn't like faggots. I just looked at him. I wanted to say something to him. His hate was so pure it was almost holy. I thought he was going to kill me, beat me until I was nothing but a torn-up rag. He dropped my shirt collar, and then grabbed me by the neck. Everything became instinct, and we were both animals. I kneed him right in the balls—just a reflex. He doubled over. I wanted to hurt him. He was bent over trying to hold himself up. "I don't like blonds," I said. I think he was surprised. Surprise—that's always the way to win. That's how Dad won with us, wasn't it? He just came to my room one night to tuck me in, and then—well, surprise! Hell, I didn't even know what the hell was going on. Except that I understood pain— and I have understood pain for a long time. I sometimes see men that

203

look like Dad, and my mouth gets dry, my hands tremble, my back aches. I used to want to run. Now, I want to hit them. Maybe that's better—I don't know.

I seem incapable of getting close to anyone. I've only had sex twice in my life—and I can't say I enjoyed it very much. I just wanted it to be over with. Yesterday, this guy in one of my classes tried to put the move on me. I wasn't offended. I was in his apartment—we were studying. We had a beer. He put his hand on my thigh. He tried to kiss me. I started laughing. I didn't feel anything. Nothing. I wanted to feel something. I wanted to feel what he felt. I didn't feel anything. I just laughed like an idiot. Anyway, we're still friends. He's a nice guy. There's this girl I know. She's pretty, beautiful. Really beautiful. I catch myself watching her, studying her body, wondering what she feels like, wondering if I could love her. I want to get close to her. I want to hold her and memorize the pores on her skin. I don't know how. I don't know anything about being close to people. It wasn't something we learned in our family, was it?

I keep thinking of that woman I saw. I wonder what she's like? She looks Mexican—or maybe Italian. She looks a little sad, but when she smiles—I want to hear her laugh.

Have you ever made love to someone you loved? What was it like? I'm going to be twenty-one in a couple of weeks. I always think I was born on such a sad day. This guy asked me what I was doing on the day John Kennedy was assassinated. I told him I was busy being born.

I never told you, did I? I found them. I'm the one that found them. I came back from a camping trip on a Sunday night. And they were lying there. It was disgusting, their bloody bodies lying next to each other. My mother, my father. When I called the police I wanted to say, "I killed them." I wanted it to be true. I wanted to make it seem like I killed them. I couldn't make myself touch the gun. I couldn't go near them. I just stared at their bodies, and I didn't even utter a prayer. Am I a bad man because I did not forgive them—even in death, I did not forgive them. I do not forgive them now. They sent you away from me, sent you away because they sensed how close we were—they must have hated that. People who can't love resent people who do. You know what? After I called the cops, I didn't feel sad, and I didn't feel disgusted. I felt relieved. I felt weightless. I thought, "My God, they're gone. They're gone and I'm still here." When the cops arrived, I cried. They thought I was crying because I was afraid. I still feel guilty for feeling happy.

Maria Elena was mesmerized by Eddie's handwriting. She touched the letters. She could hear his voice reading it to her. She imagined the look on his face as he handed over his journals. It wasn't a look of defeat or surrender. It was as if he was completely unafraid, completely open, as if his body had become indistinguishable from hers. She looked at her hands and half-expected to see her husband's fingers. All these words, she thought, and he's given them to *me*. She looked at her stomach and rubbed it gently. "Your papa's very beautiful." She looked at her watch, then stretched herself out on the couch, and kept reading.

July 12, 1985

Dear Jake,

I'm getting married tomorrow. I know I'm still kind of young, but I'm twenty-three. That's old enough, I guess. I just want to be loved—that's not so strange, is it? I haven't written to you in a long time. I haven't been thinking about the past too much lately. She doesn't know about you. I told her I had a falling out with my family. That's kind of true, I suppose. I never thought I would be happy—not like this. I sometimes panic and think it's just an emotion that will pass. I thought I would always feel alone, and now I don't remember what it was like before I met her. I think our bodies change when we love someone. The first time I made love to Helen, I went home and went for a run. I wanted to run and run and think of her body, the way it felt, the way I felt when I came in her. I felt as if I had emptied out my entire body, and now she was carrying me around. And I, I was carrying her around too. And she was so light, her laugh inside me. I see her eyes everywhere I go.

I promise I will always be good to her. I promise I will remember what has happened to me—and I will never repeat it. I will bury everything about the past today—except you. I will never bury you. I will carry you everywhere I go.

I want someday to be a father. I never thought I'd say and feel that. I used to think that to have a body was nothing but a burden. But that was before I knew that people could be kind to the body—like her. It sounds like a strange thing to say, but I know you know. I want to be a father, Jake. I want to teach my child to be kind, and I will love that child like no child has ever been loved—and that child will love the staying earth . . .

Time had no meaning that day, not for her, just the words her husband had written, his voice, his hurt, his haunting vision. Reading his words made her hunger even more to find her brother, a hunger that was growing and growing like a twin to the child she was carrying. She was certain Eddie would love him, both of them addicted to books. She tried to picture them in the same room, two men with dark eyes and smiles on their faces, and her child between them. Eddie, Diego, Jacob. Eddie, Diego, Jacob.

She whispered these men's names carefully, as if, by uttering them in a certain way, she could make them all appear, photograph them, embrace them, show them her repentant heart. "Someday they will live in my house, someday—"

When Eddie walked in the door, she looked surprised. "What are you doing home?"

"I live here," he said, "and I only work until five."

She looked at her watch. "Oh damn—and I didn't even make dinner."

"Have you been lying there all day?"

She waved one of his journals in the air. "I've been reading a good book."

"Ahh—I've read it. The author could have used a good editor."

She just stared at him.

"Come here," she said.

He sat next to her on the couch. She placed her palm on his cheek. "You're going to be a wonderful father."

"I used to think I would be."

"What happened?"

"We got pregnant."

She laughed.

"It's real now, Nena."

"You won't be like your father, Eddie."

"Well, there's more than one way to be a bad father. What if—"

"Shhh. You worry too much."

"You worry, too."

"Thank God we worry about different things."

"Aren't you scared, Nena?"

"No."

"You sound so certain."

"I want this. I'll love him."

"Still think it's a going to be a he?"

"Yes."

"We're certain about a lot of things today, aren't we?"

"And mostly I'm certain that I'm crazy about my husband."

"Your storybook husband?"

"Yes, that one."

"Introduce him to me sometime."

She handed him one of his journals. "Here," she said, "He's here."

 **12**

EVERY DAY, Joaquin grew weaker and weaker, lighter and lighter. He felt as though he was being transformed from a solid into a gas. Some days he was sad. Other days he was euphoric. A part of him was in mourning for what he was losing. Another part of him looked forward to dying. Some days, he said nothing. Other days he would talk to Jake all evening, and his voice was as strong and as deep as the Pacific beyond the Golden Gate.

They no longer shared the same bed, no longer woke up feeling each other's skin, smelling each other's breaths. Every morning, Jacob would walk into Joaquin's room and wake him. He would bring him water or juice and sometimes hold him or just look at him. He would go to work slowly and reluctantly. Joaquin would push him out the door with a voice that could still be strong: "We need the money—and besides, Tom comes by every day—he has a key. And I get visitors. And José cooks me lunch, and if José can't come, then he calls Mrs. Cantor who sits and reads to me after she makes me eat her soup—the best chicken soup you ever ate. There's nothing better than soup from a Jewish mother. That's the truth, Jacob. I'm fine." But he was getting thinner and farther away, and sometimes he was lost as if he didn't know where he was, and his eyesight was growing worse and worse, and some days he couldn't see at all, and the world was dark for him. Jacob felt he was slowly disappearing from the world, but he kept himself from mourning because he was afraid of what might happen to him if he let himself think about the word "death." There would be plenty of time for mourning, for thinking, for being sad after J was gone. He wasn't responding to any of his medications, almost as if nothing on this earth had the power to affect his body. Whatever medication Tom tried, Joaquin's body rejected—or ignored. Tom looked at Jake soberly one evening and said a little numbly: "He wants to die, Jake—all we can do is make him comfortable." Jacob nodded. *"Comfortable? Comfortable? A helluva doctor we have—a helluva doctor."* He went to work, came back home, read the newspaper to Joaquin, and at night he would sip a beer and wonder how long they would live like this. Four weeks passed, and strangely, their lives took on an air of normalcy, of familiarity—even of a strange and peaceful calm. Friends still visited them—Mike and Connie Sha and José—and there was still some laughter in their house. Joaquin made jokes about his blindness, and kept his grief at bay, but once, in the middle of a joke, he wept. "I want my eyes. I want them back." Jake held him, and that night they made love, both of them knowing it would be the last time. As Joaquin fell asleep, he thought that the only thing he would miss about the physical world was Jacob's touch. He wanted to tell him that, but thought it would only make him sad. He fell asleep in his arms. After that, Joaquin's body would no longer desire anything but death.

Joaquin sat on his bed and thought of Jake, tried to remember the color of his eyes. He asked himself if his life had meant something. He laughed. He wondered why the time he had spent on the earth had to mean anything at all. It occurred to him if his life had a meaning, he couldn't possibly know what it was. Before she died, his mother had said that love was all that mattered. As he sat there, he didn't know what she had meant. "Jake, is love all that matters?" He thought of his father, and about the time he and his brother caught him with another woman. He thought of how his father had never been capable of being monogamous, had never been capable of communicating affection, had never been capable of love. Love was always one woman away. His mother must have known, and yet she never said a word. In some ways she had never existed in his world. But the reverse was also true: In some ways, he had never existed in her heart. They protected each other from the elements. If his father had not died, she would have remained his wife. She had not loved him. He had not loved her—and yet she is the one who had said: "Love is all that matters." What did she mean by love?

He thought of his father's mustache, his eyes that never looked directly at him, his smile that hid everything he thought or felt. *"I didn't turn out to be at all like you, did I Dad?"* It seemed to him that his father was standing in front of him, and he was wearing that impenetrable look he wore as other men might wear hats to protect them from the sun. He nodded at him. *"Not like you at all, Papá."* "Speak Spanish," his father said. Joaquin shook his head. *"Aren't the dead bilingual, Papá?"* His father shook his head. *"Entonces, vete. Ya no te quiero ver. Ya se acabó todo, tu vida, mi vida, la vida de tu esposa. Ya se acabó el tiempo de las palabras."* His father opened his mouth as if to speak, but Joaquin stopped him. *"You're a ghost with no power in my house. Te me vas! No te quiero en mi casa."* His father disappeared from the room. He was glad he had stopped him from speaking. He would have only voiced his disapproval, but he suddenly wondered what part his father would have disapproved of most: the part of him that loved men, the part of him that had abandoned Mexico, or the part of him that had played the same patient role as his mother in the face of the repeated indiscretions of his lover. *"You wouldn't understand, would you, Papá—everything that is me, me, Papá—Joaquin—so foreign to what you were. Do you disapprove of me as much as I disapproved of you?"* His father had disappeared from the room and he was still trying to explain. Twenty years and another country later, and he was still trying to talk to a man who had not been born to listen. *"Will I be your son till the day I die? It shouldn't matter so much, but it does. Goddamnit, it does."* Is this what his mother had talked about when she talked about love?

He heard the doorbell ring. He wondered who it could be—didn't they know he was dying? "I'm dying," he wanted to yell. "Go away." Why were they still coming? To see—to see the show, to see the magic man do his disappearing act? "Look, I am walking on a wire, and I am going to fall gracefully, so gracefully that you won't even notice when I hit the ground." He felt his mind leaving his body. He tried to focus on the color of walls in the room. If he could only name the color, his mind would come back. He focused his eyes on the things in the room—his saints, his candle burning in the room. He could see them despite the fact that everything else was blurry and dark. He imagined himself to be lying in a coffin. "Someone is at the door. I can reach it, I can reach it. I can make myself open the door, I can make myself speak." He found the knob and pulled. He stared out into the hallway of the apartment. He saw nothing. He felt the air in front of him with his hand. "Is someone there?"

"Yes. You must be Joaquin."

The voice was soft and familiar. A woman, he thought, the voice belongs to a woman. He looked out into the void and said nothing.

"Joaquin?" the voice asked.

"Help me. I can't seem to see. Can you help me?"

The woman took him around the waist. "Let's get you back to bed," she said.

Her arms were almost as strong as Jacob's. "Who are you?" he asked.

"Let's just get you back to bed first, shall we?"

"Did someone send you—did Jake send you?"

She sensed the panic in his voice. "Dr. Michaelsen said I might drop in and see you. I was your day nurse at St. Mary's hospital."

"Tom, Tom sent you?" He seemed relieved, more focused at the sound of his doctor's name.

She helped him into his bed.

"I remember your voice. I remember your voice," he said. "You said Jake and I were beautiful—is that what you said?"

"Yes."

"I remember your voice—a good voice."

She looked around the room, everything so neat and orderly. "Is Jake at work?"

"Yes. He gets home around five-thirty."

Joaquin looked so thin and hungry. "Would you like some tea? Something to eat?" She wanted to make him strong.

"Crackers," he said, "Crackers and orange juice. Tom sent you?"

"Yes."

"I remember. Your name's Lizzie."

She smiled at him though she knew he could not see her. His mind seemed better. Yes, he was better. She grabbed his arm. "Don't be afraid," she said. "I'm your friend."

He nodded. "I need to use the bathroom. Will you help me?"

She took his hand and led him slowly into the bathroom. She helped sit him down on the toilet. "I'm so much worse," he said.

She combed his hair with her fingers. "I'll wait outside. Let me know when you're ready." She walked back into Joaquin's room. She picked up a photograph of Joaquin and Jake that was sitting on the dresser. She traced the frame with her finger and stared at their images, Joaquin with his dark eyes and perfect skin and perfect teeth and Jake with his fine blond hair and eyes that burned a hole in your skin as he stared at you—even in a photograph. She was not surprised they had met, not surprised they were lovers, and she was not surprised to be standing in this room. She looked up and saw Joaquin standing in the doorway between the bathroom and the bedroom. He hung on to the wall as if it were his life. "Are you there?"

"I'm here," she said. "I'm just looking at a picture of you and your lover."

"Yes. It was taken at the beach. Tom took it."

"It's a wonderful photograph. I didn't know Tom was such a good photographer."

He placed his head against the doorway. "Tom wanted to be an artist. Sometimes, I think he's sorry he became a doctor. He wanted to please his father." His voice was so light, almost as fine as powdered sugar. "Are you holding it in your hands?"

"How much can you see?"

"Not very much. Everything's a little fuzzy, kind of dark. A little bit. I can see a little bit—but I can't see what you look like, but you're wearing a white blouse." He paused, then seemed to go away from her. "And a skirt with flowers. My father could have never understood all this."

She walked over to him and placed her hand on his cheek. "Well, fathers are sometimes a little limited—they can't help it. Maybe it's our fault. Maybe we shouldn't try to please them."

He leaned against her as they walked toward the bed. When he felt the blankets, his hands trembled. She helped him slip under the blankets.

"Do you love yours?"

"My father?"

He nodded.

"No."

"Me neither. Well, he's dead. But if he were alive, I wouldn't love him."

"It's OK," she said.

"I shouldn't hate him—he's dead."

She sat on the edge of the bed and placed her hand on his forehead. "Forgive yourself," she whispered. "It's you that matters now."

"I don't know you," he whispered.

"You know me well enough."

"It's easy to forgive everyone but yourself."

"It's possible."

"You really think so?"

She squeezed his arm. "Yes. Still want the crackers?"

"No. I want to sleep."

His breathing was labored. She reached over and took his wrist. "I'm going to take your pulse."

He laughed. "I'm dead."

"Funny man."

She looked at her watch and counted. She took his hand when she finished. "I think I'll have Tom come have a look at you. You know, most doctors don't make many house visits—you're lucky."

"He was in love with me once."

"Well, it must've ended well."

"It never started." He breathed in deeply, then coughed. His coughing continued for several minutes. She handed him a glass of water with a straw. When he stopped, he sipped on the water. "He never told me. I just knew. Nothing ever happened. Sometimes, he looked at me—and I knew what he was thinking. I don't think he ever thought Jake was good enough for me. Don't tell him I said that. He's a good man, such a good man. I always wanted to make them like each other."

She listened to his voice. He was sick but could not keep himself from caring for the living. They always did that, she thought. All the men she'd seen on the ward—they were always taking care of the living—even when the living didn't give a damn. It made her angry. When would it be their turn to be cared for, to be loved? He groaned quietly as if he were trying to embrace his physical pain as he would a lover.

"Are you taking anything?"

"No. Tylenol."

"That's all?"

"I'm dying naturally." He smiled.

"A poster child for a drug-free America, huh?"

He laughed. "Bad joke, really bad." He coughed again. She waited for him to continue coughing, but he stopped. "I'm beginning to look like a figure from el Día de los Muertos." He seemed to be falling asleep as he spoke—too tired to finish his sentence.

Lizzie sat and watched him. "Gringo, corazón. Corazón." He kept whispering those words over and over. She knew what the words meant. When he was finally asleep, she walked into the living room and looked around for the phone. She reached into her purse, pulled out a phone book and looked for Tom Michaelsen's phone number. The phone was sitting on top of a baby grand piano. She wondered who played it. As she reached for the phone, she noticed a picture of a little boy in a gold frame. There was something very familiar about the face of that child. She picked it up and stared at it. "I know this man." She shook her head. "That's impossible." She finally put the picture back where it had been. The boy was six or seven and his smile was sad. She was certain it was not a childhood picture of Joaquin, and she was equally certain it was not his lover's image—Jake was too blond. She had seem him often in the hospital, and he could not have had dark hair as a child, though there was an unmistakable resemblance. "I know this man. I know I know this man." She shook her head. She picked up the phone and dialed Tom Michaelsen's office. "Yes, this is Elizabeth Edwards from St. Mary's Hospital, and I'd like to speak to Dr. Michaelsen—it's about one of his patients." She waited for several minutes, then heard Tom's voice.

"What can I do for you, Lizzie?"

"I'm over at Joaquin Villanueva's house—"

"What the hell are you doing there?"

"Nurses can make house calls, too, Tom."

"I didn't know you knew him. He's never mentioned you."

"I don't know him—not really."

"You just decided to drop in on him, huh? Just looked up his address and stopped in to see a strange man you didn't even know?"

"I had a dream, Tom."

"What the hell are you talking about, Lizzie?"

"I'll tell you some other time. Look, I think you should drop by this evening and take a look at Joaquin."

"Does he look worse?"

"Well, I don't know what you mean by worse—but he shouldn't be left alone anymore. Can he afford a nurse, Tom?"

"No way in hell."

"And I suppose his lover needs to keep working?"

"Same as the rest of the world, Lizzie. He needs his insurance."

"The world sucks, Tom."

Tom said nothing on the other end. "Yeah," he said. "So what else is new?"

"Look, I take it they have a few friends?"

"Yeah, some."

"How about if we make a shift schedule?"

"A what?"

"You know—people who can take shifts watching him."

"What are you—a one-woman hospice?"

"People shouldn't be alone."

Tom laughed.

"Don't laugh, Tom, I'm very serious."

"I'm not laughing, Lizzie."

"Yes you are. I can hear you."

"Well, I'm only laughing because I'm happy."

"You're happy?"

"Yes, you're the angel these guys needed."

"An angel, huh? Just wait until they get my bill."

Tom laughed again.

She remembered working with him at St. Mary's when she had first started on the ward. She had loved him for the way he touched his patients—and for his laugh. He was the only doctor she truly respected.

"Can you wait there until Jake gets home?" he asked.

"Sure. I don't have any plans."

"You're a saint."

She laughed. "An angel and a saint? A saint who likes to wear long earrings and have affairs with men who are bad for her."

"But never at work—which reminds me—why aren't you at work?"

"I'm on vacation."

"So you visit dying men on your vacation?"

"Well, I'm not going back—so I'm not in a hurry about anything."

"You're not going back to St. Mary's?"

"Don't say anything, Tom. I haven't told them yet."

"We have to have a long talk, Elizabeth Edwards."

"Yes, we do, Tom Michaelsen. In the meantime, I'll wait for Mr. Villanueva's lover to come home. I'm sure he'll be surprised to find me here."

"Tell him I'll drop by this evening."

"Bring something for his pain."

"Whose?" he asked.

She had no answer. She hung up the phone and stared at the picture of the little boy, trying to remember who he was. Lizzie looked at her watch: It was nearly five o'clock. She walked into the kitchen—it was clean and sunny and looked as though it belonged to someone who liked to cook. Jake didn't look like the type who'd spend his time in kitchens. She was certain the kitchen was Joaquin's territory. She opened drawers and cabinets and found everything in its place. She put on a pot of coffee. She found herself with the urge to cook. "I shouldn't do this in a stranger's home," she said out loud. She couldn't resist the kitchen. She had always wanted a room just like this one. She wanted to give herself to the room. She opened each cabinet door. She saw pasta shells and a bag of sun-dried tomatoes in the cupboard. She eyed some canned tomatoes, cans of soup, olive oil. On the kitchen counter she spotted a wooden bowl full of onions and garlic. She decided to make dinner. "I'm nesting again. I must be getting ready to have my period." She shook her head and laughed. "The body does such funny things to you." She found a large skillet just perfect for making a red garlic sauce. She poured in olive oil and diced some garlic. When the oil was hot, she added the garlic and sun-dried tomatoes. She let it fry for a minute, then turned off the stove. She opened a can of whole tomatoes and threw it in the pan. She smiled as she worked. Within minutes, she had added fresh basil, oregano, and a touch of cinnamon. Soon, the entire apartment smelled of oregano, tomato, and garlic. She heard the front door open, then heard Jake's deep voice. "Who's here?"

"In the kitchen," she yelled.

He walked into the room and looked at her. "Do I know you? Who the hell are you? And why are you cooking in my kitchen?"

Lizzie looked at him and almost winced. She was completely embarrassed, and somehow the words in her mind stumbled into each other but would not fall out of her. She had no real explanation. She was surprised he didn't recognize her—but why should he? She was only a nurse in a hospital. Her heart hurt. She felt stupid for feeling so hurt. She looked at him and realized she should say something—anything. "I'm sorry," she said awkwardly. "I got carried away. You have such a lovely kitchen—and I—I'd been wondering how Joaquin, how he was—how he was doing—and I just found myself at your door—it's strange, I know, but it's as simple as that." She could feel her face turning red.

"Are you a friend of his?"

She looked at him. "Well, no, not really. Don't you remember me?"

He looked at her strangely. "No." He looked at her more closely, a look of recognition moving over him. "You're the nurse."

"Yes—I'm the nurse."

"Lizzie," he said. "Your name's Lizzie." He smiled, then nodded. "And you like to flirt with gay men because it's safe."

"So you remember me?" She began to feel more at ease, less like an intruder.

"I'm sorry I didn't recognize you." His initial sense of violation disappeared from his voice. His words became calm, even friendly. "But that still doesn't explain what the hell you're doing in my kitchen."

"I liked it—it made me want to cook."

"That's it? That's your answer?"

"Yeah, that's my answer. You want some coffee?"

"Are you nuts?"

"Completely."

"You just walk into strange people's houses and cook dinner?"

She looked at him, shook her head, then shrugged. "I'm sorry. I should leave. I really don't know what I'm doing here. I just wanted to see how you two were doing. It was perfectly innocent—and perfectly pushy. I'm sorry." She tugged at her earring, then popped her knuckles. "I talked to Tom. He said he'd be by this evening. I don't think—" She stopped herself. She started toward the living room. "Look, I'm sorry. I really don't know what I'm doing here." She looked at his face. It was a hard face, though she sensed he could be very soft. "I'll just get my coat and purse." She walked out of the kitchen toward the living room where she'd left her things.

Jake said nothing. He found himself following her into the next room. Lizzie looked up at him and smiled as she walked out the door. He watched the door shut behind her. It bothered him that her smile seemed so sad. He threw himself on the couch, then undid his tie. "What am I doing?" He kept staring at the door. He thought a moment, thought how it would be nice to eat dinner with her, to talk to her, to have company instead of just waiting for something to happen. She didn't actually feel like a stranger, though he wondered why. He found himself running out the front door of his apartment. He looked down the dark hallway, but there was no sign that she'd even been there. He ran downstairs and looked down the street frantically, afraid she had disappeared from his life forever. *Why am I so afraid of losing someone I don't know?* He was relieved when he spotted her walking down the street. "Hey!" he yelled, "Lizzie!" She was too far down the street to hear him. He ran toward her yelling, "Hey! Hey, Lizzie!" By the time she heard her name being called and turned in the direction of his voice, he was standing next to her. "You might as well stay for dinner," he said. He was a little out of breath.

She thought a moment, then played with her dangling earring again. "We don't know each other. Sometimes I do stupid things—"

"Please," he said, "I'd like you stay. I mean, you're not really a stranger."

She thought a moment, then smiled. "What are we having?"

"Pasta," he said.

"I love pasta—how did you know?"

"I've always had great instincts." They both smiled.

As they walked back up to the apartment, she had the feeling she had talked to him many times before. She thought of the dream. He had been in her dream before Salvador had given her his gift. *How strange. How strange and lovely.* As she made the final preparations for dinner in the kitchen, she listened to him talk about the past few weeks—what his life had become. He talked to her as if he had been living alone, as if he had been separated from every human being in the world. She knew immediately he was letting things out because he was more hungry for human contact than for food. He was like an overinflated tire—if he didn't let some of the air out, he was going to explode. She listened, sometimes asked questions, but was happy just to let him talk. She could detect the rage in his voice, the frustration of being unable to find his way out of his own apartment—but there was something else, too—a kindness, a kindness in his voice that was strong and familiar and intimate. His voice sounded very much like someone else's—she'd heard this voice before—she was certain. She kept thinking of the picture of the little boy. She was about to ask him about that boy when he excused himself to check on Joaquin. He was gone for a long time.

As she set the table, the doorbell rang. She waited to hear if Jake would answer it. It rang again. She heard Jake's voice from another room. "Will you get that, Lizzie?"

"Sure," she yelled. She opened the door and smiled at the man standing in the dark hallway. "As I live and breathe, it's Doc Holiday."

"Still here, huh?"

"I made dinner."

"How did you know I hadn't eaten?"

"Well, while you go check on your patient, Doctor, I'll go and put more water in the soup."

"Where'd a city girl come up with a country saying like that?"

"Lots of country boys up in my ward."

"That a fact?"

"Yup," she said as she walked back toward the kitchen.

He followed her. "I didn't know you knew these guys so well."

"I don't. I told you—I had a dream."

"You had a dream? And in the dream you came over to this apartment and made dinner?"

"Actually, in the dream, I was sitting with Jake—and he was dying."

"It's not Jake whose sick—better inform your dream maker."

"Some day he will be—and I'm going to be there."

"Well, you certainly are sure about your future."

"Tom, please don't make fun. I'm taking some time off—and I'd like to make myself useful."

"You want to come work for me? I could use you. Jesus Christ, could I ever use you."

"I don't particularly care for doctors—why would I work for one?"

"All doctors are evil?"

"OK, you're fishing for a compliment. Yes, you're a good doctor, and yes, I've always liked working with you. And you don't treat nurses like shit, which is saying something when it comes to members of your profession. I even like you, Tom. There, I've said it. Are you happy now?"

"Yes. So why won't you come and work with me?"

"The word 'with' is better than 'for'—I like that."

"Well?"

"We'd kill each other."

"Maybe—but what a way to go, huh?"

"Thanks for the offer, Tom, but—"

"Don't say no—just think about it. I don't need an answer right this minute. Consider yourself to have a standing offer."

She nodded as she filled a pot with water and placed it on the burner. "Make yourself useful and put another plate on the table."

"Well, well, the medical profession shows up in force—and just in time for dinner."

Tom looked up at the sound of Jake's voice. "Hi," he said. "Lizzie here invited me to dinner."

He grinned at her. "She takes a lot of liberties." He'd changed into a pair of jeans and a deep blue T-shirt; he looked relaxed and somehow more vulnerable than when he was wearing a starched shirt and a tie.

"You look nicer," she said.

"Hey, you don't like white guys in ties?"

"I like ties," Tom said.

"Yes," Lizzie laughed, "I know, but won't you take yours off while we eat?"

There was a sudden quiet between them, almost as if they all remembered at the same time that there was a man in the other room, a man who could not eat, a man who would never again enjoy the kind of affectionate small talk they were all enjoying in that warm room that smelled of olive oil, garlic, and tomato. No one made an attempt to say anything. They looked at each other knowingly. It was as if Jake could allow himself to be vulnerable so long as words were not involved. He could allow Tom and Lizzie to comfort him so long as they did not speak. At that moment they shared something that resembled intimacy. A recognition passed between them, a sense of belonging. Elizabeth kept herself from weeping as she sensed the depth of compassion in Tom's body, the great sense of sorrow in Jacob's face. Their emotions were overwhelming to her. Her lips trembled, and she placed her hand on her chin to calm herself. Jake poured his two guests a glass of wine

221

without asking if they wanted any. He poured himself a glass of mineral water. He sat down at the table as Lizzie rinsed the pasta shells. "I'll step in and take a look at him," Tom finally said.

"He's sleeping," Jake said. "He's peaceful right now. He didn't sleep well last night."

"Did you?" Tom looked at him sternly. "You have to rest, too."

"I can't sleep. I have no right to sleep when he can't."

Tom nodded. He rubbed his neck and looked up at the ceiling. There were tears in his eyes, then suddenly they poured down his cheeks. He tried to calm himself, but found he could not make himself stop. He placed his open hands over his face and sobbed into them. He took a few deep breaths, then moved his hands away. "I'm sorry. It won't happen again."

"Don't be sorry," Jake said.

"I'm a doctor."

"You're just a man."

Tom was surprised at the softness in Jake's voice. They caught each other's glances, then looked away. Elizabeth watched them and wanted to weep until her tears washed away the smell of sickness in Joaquin's room. Tom looked up at her. "You're awfully quiet."

She smiled at him. "I'm going to sit down now, and you're going to serve us."

"But you're up already."

She sat down on the chair. "Now I'm down." Tom rose from his chair obediently and began to serve them all dinner.

Jake laughed. "Where did you come from, Lizzie?" She could tell by the tone in his voice that he liked her, that he was grateful she was there. This was not a man who laughed often. She was glad she could bring something of value into this house. It occurred to her that she had been much too self-absorbed for most of her life. She thought of her dream, how she had held the healthy man sitting next to her as he broke in her arms. Maybe her dream would not come to pass. Maybe this man would be spared.

 **13**

ONE DAY, feeling restless and a little bored with his routine, Mundo showed up at Diego's apartment and waited for him to come home from work. He sat on the concrete steps, smoked cigarettes, and wondered what the hell he was doing here. He wanted to do something for Diego, but he was at a loss. *What the fuck can I do for anyone?* He rose from the steps, put out his fourth cigarette, and decided to leave. *I should stick to playing pool.* But just as he started to leave, he noticed Diego walking up the hill to his house. He sat back down and lit another cigarette. *Too late to leave.* He erased the doubts from his face, and leaned on the steps as if he owned them.

Diego noticed someone sitting at the top of the steps to his apartment house. Even from far away he knew it was Mundo. His posture and jet black hair attracted the light around him. He waved. Mundo cocked his head and smiled.

Diego walked faster up the hill to his house. Mundo tossed him a pack of cigarettes as he reached the steps. "Merry Christmas from one of the barrio elves."

Diego caught the cigarettes and put them in his shirt pocket. He took out his pad as Mundo moved down the steps. "So what brings you to Sunset Heights? Did you miss the mountains?"

Mundo read Diego's note and laughed. "Yeah, man, I liked the pinche view."

"Really?"

"Look, Diego, I'm not into looking at the scenery. If it doesn't have a woman in the picture, you can just forget it."

Diego shook his head. He noticed Mundo was dressed up. He was wearing a dark red shirt and some well-pressed khakis. A gold chain on his wrist showed off his thick veiny arms. "Do you have a date or something?"

"Nah, man, no date tonight. Got in a fight with my woman. I'm laying low for a while."

"What's her name?"

"Rosario."

"Is she like her name?"

"Like how?"

"Like a prayer?"

"She makes love like a prayer, I'll tell you that." He puckered his lips and whistled.

Diego laughed. "You love her?"

Mundo shrugged his shoulders. "La Rosie?" He nodded. "She wants me to go to college. After that, she says maybe we'll get married."

"What's wrong with that?" Diego wrote firmly.

"You been reading too many stories in the library about houses with picket fences, you know that? In El Segundo we ain't got no picket fences. We got kids, concrete, policemen, and the migra—that's what we got."

"So move somewhere else."

"There ain't no place else. What the fuck am I gonna do where I don't belong? What am I gonna do in gringoland?" He lit a cigarette. "I thought you and me would go out. You know, drink a few brews and shoot the breeze. We got time and we got money."

Diego looked down at himself, and looked at Mundo's nice clothes. "I don't go out much."

"I figured that out already, see? That's why I'm here." He stretched out his arms and lifted them up. "I'm here to save you from your fuckin' boredom."

"I didn't know I was bored," Diego wrote, "and I didn't know I needed saving."

"That's the problem, man. You're pretty smart—you got yourself a good head—but you're a pendejo, got that? There's more to life than thinkin' about things—you gotta do things—all kinds of things. Just call me your guardian angel who's gonna show you some things about living."

Diego smiled and wrote: "You're not my idea of an angel."

Mundo looked down at the bold letters and shrugged his shoulders. "My old lady says the same thing."

"How come you're not out with your friends instead? Am I a project or something?"

"No, man, you got it all wrong. It's not like that. Look, Diego, all I want to do is buy you a few beers. You did me a favor, Mundo doesn't forget." He snapped his fingers and pointed toward Diego. "C'mon, let's do some serious drinking. Get drunk and be somebody. You can talk to me about your pendejo boss at Vicky's, and I can tell you about how I caught up with one of those bastards that threw me in the garbage. You should have seen the look on that motherfucker's face when he saw me. That sonofabitch is gonna walk crooked for a year. Maybe he's never gonna have sex ever again." He smiled.

"How come you fight so much?"

"Gotta make up for people like you, see? I bet you never got into a fight a day in your life."

"Nobody bothers me."

"That's bullshit, Diego. That asshole you work for, he bothers you. I bet that sonofabitch treats you like a fuckin' dog. Pigs like that think they own people."

Diego could see Mundo's anger. "Why does it bother you? It's me who works for him."

"It bothers me because the world is full of motherfuckers like that pinche—and it's not just you who works for people like that—it's everybody in the fuckin' barrio."

"Well," Diego wrote, "what am I supposed to do about it? Are you going to give me a job?"

225

Mundo laughed. "Nobody works for Mundo. And Mundo don't work for nobody, neither. This vato," he said pointing to himself, "ain't never gonna make nobody else rich. They hire you to clean their shit-stained bathrooms and make them smell like no one ever crapped in there and they don't pay you nothin' because they tell you they can't afford it, and then they go home and drink wine that costs them twenty bucks a bottle. Fuck that, man, this baby don't work to make the gringo rich."

"My boss isn't a gringo," Diego wrote.

"That's worse than being a gringo. That pinche sold out his own people. He makes money in the barrio and then spends it on the west side of town. Your boss is the worst kind of pinche there is, know what I'm sayin'? He can bite my hairy ass."

"What do you want to do about people like him—line them up and shoot them?" Diego shook his head.

Mundo snapped his fingers and spun himself around. He aimed his fingers at Diego like a gun and laughed. "They should die real slow, see? Burn them or something and make barbecue out of them—that's what pigs are good for."

"But it's pigs like that that give people like me jobs."

"Man, that guy has you right where he wants—right under his foot."

"Maybe," Diego wrote, "but being under my boss's foot keeps me from getting wet. It's kind of like an umbrella."

"But it don't rain in El Paso, Diego, know what I'm sayin'? And someday that bastard you work for is gonna step down on you real hard."

"I got a strong back—stronger than his foot."

Mundo laughed. "I don't know if you're a pendejo, or what, but me, I got feet for the street." He did a dance step on the sidewalk. "And I got hands that like to touch women real nice or to bust people's faces in." He smashed a fist on his own open palm. "Magic hands and magic feet, see? I don't think too much about my back."

Diego laughed. "In that case, my back is magic, too."

"If you say so, my man—if you say so." He snapped his fingers. "Let's make it—let's go have some brews. You like beer?"

Diego nodded. He looked down at his clothes again. "You want to wait while I change my clothes?"

"Yeah, I'll wait down here for you."

Diego went into his apartment and looked through his closet. Mundo was right, he thought, his clothes were boring. He put on a clean white shirt and some black pants, washed his face and combed his hair. Diego studied his face. It wasn't bad, he thought. Sort of a friendly face—it wouldn't scare anybody off at least. He was too thin, though. "I don't have a body like Mundo's," he told himself. "It's not a body that was made for dancing." He rolled up the sleeves on his long-sleeved shirt. Diego gave himself a hard look in the mirror. His heart pounded. It was the first time in his life that he was going to a real bar. Vicky's didn't count. He skipped down the stairs and lit a cigarette.

Mundo looked him over. "You know what, if you got yourself some new clothes you could get a babe like that—easy." He snapped his fingers. "You dress like an old rukito."

"New clothes won't make me hear."

"No, man, you got it all wrong. Women don't care about ears—they care about other parts. Know what I'm sayin'?"

Diego laughed. "So where are we going?"

"I thought we might check out this new place—downtown. It's got a pool table, the whole bit. It just opened up this week. It don't even have a name yet. I'll teach you how to play pool."

They walked down the street in the early evening, Mundo talking and talking. Diego read his moving lips and watched his hands move in the air like doves as they walked toward the nameless bar.

14

THE MORNING WAS COOL. Eddie sat at the edge of the bed watching Maria Elena sleep. He'd been sitting there for almost an hour. Lately, he had taken to thinking he might forget what she looked like if he didn't sit and memorize her face. He wanted to hold her and make sure she was real. On certain days he could not believe she loved him, that anyone could love him. But she was there, pregnant and lovely in the morning light of the early summer. He quietly walked out of the room and made his way into the kitchen. He drank his coffee and stared at the poem he had been writing. It had been a long time since he had tried writing a poem. Something about the way Maria Elena called him corazón made him want to pick up a pen and write a poem for her. She had begun teaching him Spanish and he felt himself changing as he learned her language. Eddie had never realized that languages were so physical, the way he carried them around with him—the way they carried *him* around. He had lost all interest in work. He had lost all the interest in the life he was living in Palo Alto. He no longer lived there. He felt as cool and clean as the light on his wife's face. He was happy it was Saturday. Saturdays made him feel younger and lighter—like a schoolboy free of the burdens of learning things he had no interest in learning, things somebody mistook for knowledge.

Today, he wanted to know, to acquire new knowledge. He wanted to drink his coffee and stare at his wife.

Things were almost perfect. There was still the space reserved for his brother. Eddie was tired of feeling the emptiness of that space. He wondered if his brother's presence would make his life perfect. "Well," he thought, "the hell with perfect. Happy is better. Happy would be good." Maybe Nena would find Diego. He could sense her hunger for her brother. He could see it when she spoke his name. Maybe he would take her to El Paso and they could look for him. Maybe they would both find the missing pieces of themselves and they would be whole.

Eddie stared at the blank pages of his journal. He had nothing to say to his brother today, nothing at all. It made him sad to think he felt so empty and wordless. His words to his brother had kept him alive for the many years he had lived alone, had kept him alive long enough to meet the woman who married him, the woman who had loved enough to hold him even when he was far away from her—far away from himself. He wondered to himself how he could love this woman so much and still feel this emptiness. It was not her fault, he thought, his life was too heavy for her to carry. His writing would help her carry the load.

Eddie had been writing to his brother for as long as he could remember. He had lost what he had written as a child. But he had saved every piece of writing he had ever written since he had been in college. He had learned to write and think clearly by writing in his journal, he had learned to understand himself, to see himself through his writing. If he had not written, he was certain he would have disappeared.

He read over the poem he was writing for his wife. He wanted to give her the finished poem when the baby was born. He stared at the words. Today, they seemed meaningless, but he needed to finish it. It was important to make sense of the chaos—it was essential. Eddie would write his way back into meaning—then he would give it to his wife.

I will be a good mother. Maria Elena stared at her naked body in the mirror. She studied it. She rubbed her hands on the tight skin around her baby. *I will love you and I will cherish all your days and I will tell you everything about the history of the world, how it came to be, how we must save it, and I will tell you the sad stories of our lives and how we found happiness, and how strong you made me feel when you were kicking me—kicking me to let me know you were alive. Little boy, I will love you more than any child has ever been loved.* She noticed she was weeping. She thought of her mother, how she yearned to have her here, here in this room to show her that she had carried her child as carefully as any child in any womb had ever been carried. *And I will tell you how your grandmother suffered, how she loved—and how she saved her children. You will carry her name in your heart, and carry the voices of your people . . .*

"Eddie? Eddie. Wake up." Maria Elena whispered his name loudly, but her voice did not wake him. She laughed at herself for whispering. There was no one in the house but them. "Eddie?" she said out loud, "Eddie?" She shook him.

"Uh."

"Eddie—wake up."

He rolled over slowly.

"What?" he was still more asleep than awake.

"Eddie—my water broke."

"What?"

"My water bag broke."

"Oh my God!" He jumped up from the bed, slipped on a pair of jeans that he'd left lying on the floor, and threw on a T-shirt. "Don't be nervous."

Maria Elena took a deep breath. She was sitting awkwardly on the bed. She had neatly dressed herself in a thin cotton dress. She seemed excited, but there was a decidedly calm look on her face. She imagined herself holding her baby, touching the soft skin of her child. She was ready.

"I should pack," Eddie said.

"I've packed already."

"You got everything?"

"I got everything."

"Why didn't you wake me?"

"Eddie, just take me to the hospital."

"Oh my God," he yelled, "we're going to be parents."

He laughed and screamed and jumped all the way to the car. "Be quiet, Eddie, you'll wake the neighbors."

He honked the horn as they left the house. "We're gonna have a baby!" he yelled out the window as they drove away. "And he's gonna be hell!"

Despite the pains that made her body feel as though her back might break, Maria Elena laughed at her husband. She was glad there was so much of the boy in him—it would make him a good father. He kept staring at her on the way to the hospital.

"Keep your eyes on the road," she said.

"It's three-thirty in the morning," he said. "No one's out but us."

A baby, she thought. She squeezed her husband's arm as she felt another contraction. "Jonathan Edward Marsh, drive like hell. He wants out—and he wants out now!" She took a deep breath and trembled. The pain was harder on her body than she'd imagined. A baby, she thought. My God, I'm going to have a baby. "A baby!" Eddie yelled as they pulled up to the hospital.

15

For two weeks, Mrs. Cantor came every morning and left when Lizzie arrived at noon. On Tom's suggestion, Lizzie had arranged a schedule with her, and a few friends often came for a few hours, giving them a chance to take care of their own chores. Lizzie was given a list of phone numbers of people who had offered to do small things for either Jake or Joaquin. Old friends of Joaquin's, Mike and Connie Sha came by often just to sit with him and talk. They were shy at first, and their calmness disturbed her. One afternoon, Mrs. Sha arrived unexpectedly and shoved Lizzie out the door insisting she had to get some fresh air: "It's so lovely today," she said. "Take a walk, buy yourself something at the store." She went out for a long walk and was happy not to think about anything. She bought herself a deep blue sweater, and picked up some groceries on the way back. When she returned, Mrs. Sha was holding Joaquin in her arms, and Mr. Sha was telling him a story. It was obvious to Lizzie that they had claimed him as a son.

Before they left that afternoon, Mrs. Sha offered Lizzie some manzanilla, Joaquin's favorite tea. "When our Xin Wei was sick," she said softly, "Joaquin was the only one who didn't stop coming. He was with us till the end. My sister said my Xin Wei had shamed our family. Joaquin wanted to know why any illness should mean shame. He was angry with her—but my sister only said what I had been thinking." She squeezed her husband's hand.

"We will not leave him." Mr. Sha spoke slowly and softly as if to make her understand that they must be kept informed of Joaquin's health.

"I promise to call whenever he needs anything—anything at all. Jake will do the same."

They seemed reassured.

Mrs. Sha and Mrs. Cantor made it their job to make sure there was something on the stove or in the oven. "He won't eat," Mrs. Cantor complained as Lizzie walked into the apartment every afternoon. "Two weeks and he hasn't eaten enough food to feed a pigeon. My husband was like that near the end." Elizabeth always kissed her before she left and told her, "Not to worry, Mrs. Cantor, I'll eat it. I eat enough for both of us." Mrs. Cantor always managed a smile. "My son should have married such a girl." Lizzie would hug her, and she would look into her eyes and say, "I adore you, Mrs. Cantor." Mrs. Cantor never left the apartment until she heard Lizzie's words.

These were days of quiet waiting, everyone at their stations as if they were soldiers waiting for the enemy to attack. Jacob kept Joaquin's veladora burning. "The candle has to stay lit, Jake," Joaquin ordered from his bed, "day and night it has to burn—and it has to be the candle of the Sacred Heart." The candle burned on the dresser where Joaquin kept his two statues—San Isidro and Our Lady of Guadalupe. "They were his mother's" Jake explained. "He's always lighting candles for some lost cause."

"Who the hell is San Isidro?" Lizzie asked.

"He's the patron saint of farmers. His mother's father was a farmer—it belonged to him. The statues are all he has."

"Oh," Lizzie said quietly.

"They won't help," Jake mumbled.

"Maybe not—but at this point they're as good as any doctor."

Jake shook his head in disgust. "Lizzie, I thought you were more levelheaded."

Lizzie said nothing, but she made a mental note of the fact that

Jake always made sure a new candle was lit before the old one went out. Everyone had their separate relationship to the candle—including Mrs. Sha and Mrs. Cantor. They always reminded Jake when the candle was getting low even though he needed no reminders. "What is this thing with the candle—everyone's worried about the damn candle, and nobody's Catholic but Joaquin."

Some days Joaquin was talkative, and he spoke easily to Lizzie about his dreams, about how his mother was coming more and more often, about how he would send his father away when he came into his room: "I never loved him. He never loved me either." Sometimes she felt as if she was his priest, Joaquin confessing all his sins including the fact that he was living outside of the sacrament of marriage. Lizzie never knew whether to smile or cry when he said those things—so she smiled and told him that everything was fine—everything forgiven. Sometimes, he would stretch his hand toward her face and feel it. "It's a good face, a very good one, the best I've felt in a long time." Sometimes he would drift off into a world that was his alone and say nothing, just mumble to himself in Spanish. Sometimes his questions made no sense: "Do you still have that penthouse in New York?" he once asked her. "No, my darling," she said, "I sold it." He addressed her as if she were his mother. "¿Por qué no lo dejaste?" "¿De quién hablas?" she asked. "Mi papá—¿por qué no lo dejaste?" "I loved him," was all she said. "Why are you speaking English, Mamá—you don't know English." "I learned," she said. He nodded. "It's an ugly language, isn't it? You should try spelling in it sometime—la cosa más fea del mundo." Another time he insisted she take him to the airport. "If you don't hurry and dress me I'll miss my flight." "The hell with it," she told him, "let's stay home. We'll play Scrabble instead." "Scrabble instead of Mexico City—are you crazy?" "It's just that I'm tired," she said, "I want to stay home." "I'm tired, too," he said—and fell asleep. And another time he insisted to be taken home. She was unable to convince him that he *was* home. When Jacob walked in, he verbally accosted him with all of his strength: "Why did you move me into this house, you sonofabitch? I loved our house—and you sold it right under my nose." Jacob soothed him by promising to buy their old house back.

234

By the end of the week, he had completely stopped eating. All he had was an IV to keep him from becoming completely dehydrated. Mrs. Cantor announced to Lizzie she couldn't come and stay with him in the mornings anymore. "I just can't take it anymore," she said, trying not to cry. "My heart can't take—please don't think that I'm abandoning him. He and Jacob Lesley have been such wonderful boys—so nice, so nice—it's just that I can't see him like this anymore." Her eyes were as gray as her hair, and Elizabeth held her as she sobbed.

"It's OK, Mrs. Cantor, you've done what you could. Jacob would have been lost without you."

"So many boys have been coming by," she said straightening herself out. "I'll bring food by every day. It's too much work for Mrs. Sha—and she can't make a chicken soup to save her life."

Elizabeth smiled. "Perfect," she said.

"I've given him his last kiss," she said. "And you tell Jacob Lesley I'll be bringing by some food." She left the apartment slowly and looked toward Joaquin's room as she stood at the door. "And make sure his candle doesn't go out—and when the time comes make sure the priest comes. He wants a priest."

Before Lizzie had the chance to acknowledge her adamant reminder, Mrs. Cantor left the apartment. *I won't cry. I will not cry.* She poured herself a cup of coffee and sat down. She tried to empty herself of all thought. She took off one of her earrings and rubbed her earlobe. She looked at her watch. She walked into Joaquin's bedroom. His breathing was loud and labored. She touched his forehead. He was sweaty and had a temperature. He opened his eyes. "Is that you, Lizzie?"

"Yes," she said.

"I'm cold."

"I'll get you another blanket."

When she touched him, she knew he was not afraid. He only wanted to rest. There was something very peaceful about him and Lizzie could almost touch it. Lizzie was happy he was calm. It was she who was afraid—and so was Jake, and she could not make what she felt go away.

"Tell him not to be afraid. Tell him I dreamed about his heron."

"Yes," she said. She wrapped him up in blankets.

"Will you tell him?"

"I'll tell him."

"Did I ever tell you I hate Mexico?"

"Shh," she said.

"I hate the U.S., too."

"It doesn't matter."

"It *does* matter," he said as if it were urgent that Lizzie understood.

"Shhh." He could hardly breathe at all. Dementia, she thought. "Don't talk."

"Do you understand me, Lizzie?"

She could see he wouldn't stop until she agreed on the importance of his point. "You're right, amor," she said.

"The United States is barbaric," he said.

"Yes, amor," she said.

"And Mexico, too. Barbaric."

"Shhh."

"I'm right about this. I insist on it."

"Of course you're right, corazón."

She held his hand until he fell asleep. She kissed him on the forehead and left the room. When she walked back in the living room, she reached for the phone. She stared at the picture of the young man. She had not thought of the picture since the first day she had been in the apartment—but as she sat there waiting for Tom to answer his phone, she felt a sense of urgency about the boy in the picture.

"Hello."

"Yes, I'd like to speak to Dr. Michaelsen. It's about one of his patients. It's very important."

"Who should I say is calling?"

"Elizabeth Edwards. It's about—hell, he'll know."

"Can you hold?"

"Why the hell not?" She was annoyed. She stared at the photograph, those familiar eyes, the well-defined chin, the soft lips.

She heard Tom's voice on the other end. "Yes, Lizzie, what's the news?"

She put down the photograph at the sound of Tom's voice. "I

don't get a good feeling here, Tom. I'd drop by after work and park myself for a while if I were you. You got big plans tonight?"

"Just dinner with Rick."

"Tell him to come say his good-byes—if he wants."

Tom said nothing for a while. Lizzie didn't mind the silence.

"Sure thing, Lizzie."

"See you this evening, then."

"Lizzie?"

"What?"

"Are you as tough as you seem?"

"No." She quietly hung up the phone.

Sometimes the smell of death or dread of an impending unknown is in the air like the smell of corn tortillas at a market in Juárez or the smell of sulfur near an oil refinery or the smell of eucalyptus after a rain. The smell is strong, overwhelming, irretrievable, and it loiters in the air like a prostitute waiting to be picked up. Some people know—without knowing—that something sad or good or significant is going to happen. They smell, they sense what is coming in the air and they prepare themselves as best they can, prepare and brace for the impact. Sometimes they hide the preparations even from themselves. When Jacob woke that morning, he sat up in bed and knew. He remembered his dream. The heron had come to him again. He was young and he was walking along a beach, the red sun rising, the lyric lake so perfect and blue and shining that it seemed as if it had been created out of nothing only the day before. A heron as white as any angel he had dreamed of as a boy flew out of the water flying toward the red sun. As he watched it beating its wings against the bluing sky, the heron suddenly stopped beating its wings. Something interrupted its perfect flight toward the sun. Its wings stretched out, they froze, unable to move, and it began falling back toward the lake. "Fly!" he yelled, "Fly!" But the bird was deaf to his voice. The grace and strength having left the white heron, his heart was no longer able to withstand the labor that life asked of it. The heron, falling toward its death—its wings outstretched—offered no resistance against its fate. It fell quietly, graceful even in its final descent. "Fly!" Jake yelled, his face growing older and more desperate with each passing second until he was old and weak and wrinkled. "No! No! Fly!" He watched as the heron splashed into the shining lake and sunk into its drowning waters.

THE END AND THE
BEGINNING
OF THE WORLD

 1

July 15, 1992

I got a check in the mail today from Eddie. All the note said was: "Lizzie, I don't want you to worry about money. All kinds of love, Eddie." I called him on the phone and told him I couldn't accept his gift, but I knew I was going to take it. I needed it. I hate needing it. Maria Elena must have blabbed about my pathetic finances. I wish I didn't need money, not me, not any of us—it's so violent to need it. Last week, I dreamed I was homeless, nowhere to go. I was sitting on a street corner and I would call out the names of people I knew as they passed me. They just looked at me with the strangest eyes, and I knew there was no longer anything human or recognizable about me—not my voice, not my face, not anything. I was separated from everything that had come before. I wanted, in that dream, to leave my body—but the power to leave myself was gone. And I knew I would be homeless forever.

I keep wishing I could live in a kind and decent world. Everything I see makes me cry lately. I went out to the grocery store to buy some things for Joaquin and Jake. I ran into someone I knew from the hospital. He'd almost died, and there he was laughing and breathing and we sat down on the curb together to talk. It was such a miracle that he was there. And this guy passes us, stares at us. "Faggot," he said. I could hear the hate in his voice, as clear and sharp as a dry twig breaking beneath a heavy

241

foot. And I wanted to grab him and shake him and tell him that I hated him, too. I wanted to slap him and never stop slapping him and ask him again and again: "How does it feel to be hated? How does it feel?" And, not an hour later, as I walked with a sack full of groceries down the street, some guy eyes me, and I wanted to be nice, so I smiled. Goddamnit, I smiled at him. And he says, not a hint of shame in his voice, he says: "Baby, you look good enough to fuck. I could fuck you till I died." I looked at him. He was waiting for me to say something back. The sonofabitch was hoping I'd smile. "I'm not your toilet," I yelled, "so stop pissing on me." He chuckled. What gives people the right? I'm tired of the world— goddamnit I'm so tired. If I didn't have a body I wouldn't be tired.

So I keep wanting to leave my body. When I'm a part of the air, I don't need money, I don't need food, I don't need to hear human voices, I don't need to touch bodies, and I don't need to be touched. I don't need anything. Joaquin says the best part of dying is that you begin to stop needing.

This evening I left my body because I hated it, wanted to be rid of it. It was an escape, a vacation, and I didn't want to feel. It was so lovely to be a part of the night, to be all colors, to be a star that had nothing to do but shine. I was gone a long time. I didn't really want to come back. I could have wandered for weeks in the desert of nothingness and never once been thristy. I'm so pure when I'm out of my body. I think I came back because Eddie sent me the money—and because of Jake and Joaquin, and the heron in their dreams.

August 12, 1992

Joaquin told me to bring him flowers today. He said it was the Day of the Dead. I told him it wasn't November yet, but he wouldn't hear of it. "No, no, it's the Day of the Dead—and I'm mostly dead, so bring me flowers." I didn't argue with him. I told him I'd bring the flowers. Joaquin and I have been speaking a lot of Spanish to each other. Me and my perfect pronunciation of that language. And it's mine, that language, mine, and yet it's no more mine than English. I don't feel Mexican. I don't feel American, either. I'm disoriented and disjointed and fragmented *lately. I hate all these confusions. I want to go to a place where I'm pure, where I'm certain*

The night Maria Elena had her baby, I dreamed about his birth. In the dream, we were all celebrating in a huge room. It was like New Year's, and amid all the laughter—and Eddie's smile—his son started to grow up right in front of us. Right then and there, he turned into a young man. When I spoke to him, he shook his head. And then I spoke to him in sign language, and he spoke back to me. We spoke to each other for hours, our hands dancing like leaves falling from all the elm trees in the world. When I woke up the next day, I called Eddie and left a message on the machine. He called back and told me the baby was perfect. But I know he isn't. I know what the silence meant. But there was another man in the room, and I remembered him when I spoke to Eddie on the phone and I knew that man's name—Diego—and he looked just like Maria Elena. And I know I'm going to meet him.

I went to speak to the priest at Mission Dolores. I told him everything about what's been happening to me. I told him about leaving my body, about reading minds, about seeing things in the future. I seemed to need to tell him that I didn't believe in God. I didn't have to ask him if he believed me—I could read him easily. He believed every word. He wanted to know if I was going to be all right. I told him I didn't know. I told him I was scared. I told him the world had changed, and I didn't know how to change with it. He smiled. And when I cried, he held me, and he told me I would learn to live a new life. He seemed so certain.

Joaquin keeps lingering. It's as if he's doing a slow fade. Every day he grows a little paler. I sometimes think he'll turn into a ghost before he disappears. He seems to always take care of all of us, instead of us taking care of him. And I'm sitting here in this cold summer night wondering why it's the dead and the dying who are always remembering the living. When will the living learn about the dead? When will the living learn about the dying?

Lizzie opened the door before the doorbell rang and smiled at her mother as she stood in the dark hallway of the apartment building.

"You knew I was standing here?"

Lizzie smiled, "I didn't want to make you wait out here—too cold." She took her mother by the arm and pulled her into her living room. She kissed her, then kissed her again. "Coffee?" she asked.

The old woman looked into her daughter's face as if she were afraid that face would soon be disappearing. "It's cold—even for a San Francisco summer. It's warm in here, though."

"Too warm?"

"No, it's nice—wonderful. My circulation isn't what it used to be." Elizabeth listened to her as she walked into the kitchen. Her mother stopped talking.

"Keep talking," she said, "I'm listening."

"I don't like to yell through walls," she said.

"Oh Mom, it's not angry yelling, it's just talking yelling." She walked back into the room holding two mugs of coffee. She handed one to her mother. "Just like you like it—black and bitter."

Her mother smiled appreciatively as she sipped on the coffee. "You make good coffee."

"So are you going to tell me why you've come to visit your daughter?"

"Do I need a reason?"

"Mom, I can count on one hand the number of times you've visited me. If you just felt like talking, you'd have called me on the phone." She squeezed her mother's hand. "So what's the occasion?"

"You tell me—you knew I was at the door. You're gifted, no?"

"I can't read minds at will, Mama, it just happens sometimes."

"Have you left your body lately?"

Lizzie shrugged her shoulders. "I'm learning to control that one."

"Where did you go last night?"

"How did you know I had one last night?"

"Maybe I'm gifted, too."

"Seriously, Mama."

"Seriously? You look too thin."

"I look too thin and you've been talking to Maria Elena."

"I still call her Helen."

244

"You're so stubborn, Mother—it's not a real name."

She looked straight into Lizzie's eyes and smiled. "You don't seem to mind *your name*, and it's not real either—and me? I'm not your *real* mother—you don't seem to mind that either."

Lizzie sipped on her coffee. "I like Lizzie just fine. And, Mama, you're as real as I need." She let out a laugh, calm. "You sure it's not too strong for you?" Her mother shook her head. "You're real to me, Mama—and you shouldn't have driven all this way in this cold. I would have been happy to drive to Palo Alto."

"You hate Palo Alto—and the drive did me good. I'm not on my deathbed, you know—and I needed to get away from Sam. You don't look like you're getting enough sleep."

"What did Maria Elena tell you?"

"She said you looked too thin and that you were working too hard for no money. Who are those boys, anyway?"

"They're not boys, Mother, they're men. And one of them is dying."

"And Elizabeth Nightingale has to stick her nose in everybody else's business."

"Mama, this isn't negotiable."

"What if you—what if—"

"And AIDS is hard to get—if that's what you're worried about. You didn't come here to lecture me about that, did you?"

"You quit your job, you go and practically live with two gay men, you start talking about revolutions, you start losing your interest in sex, you start reading people's minds, and you leave your body every Tuesday and Thursday. What the hell are the people who love you supposed to think?"

Lizzie laughed. "I'd forgotten how theatrical you could be, Mama. Revolution, Mama? In this country? Ludicrous. When I say stuff like that, do you really think I'm taking myself seriously? Do you think anybody else does? Certainly not you, Mama. And anyway, my views aren't new—and I don't leave my body only on Tuesdays and Thursdays. Sometimes I take myself out on a Saturday night. It's like a date. *And who told you I'd lost my interest in sex?*"

"Helen's noticed. She said you looked tired, preoccupied, and that you haven't mentioned sex with a man in over a month. She said she'd never had a conversation with you when that didn't come up at least once."

"That's ridiculous. Men have never been that important to me."

"Ha! Men are all you've ever lived for. Boy crazy. You've been boy crazy since you started ovulating—and you started rather early as I recall." She sipped on her coffee. "You were such a lovely child. Stand up. Let me have a look at you."

Lizzie put down her cup of coffee and sighed in disgust. "Mom?"

"Just do as I tell you."

Lizzie stood up, pretended she was modeling a dress for a prospective buyer, then lifted up her skirt and stuck her ass at her mother. "Done with the goods?"

"You *have* lost weight. You look different. Come here." Lizzie obediently sat next to her mother. "Lizzie, what is it? I just know something's wrong. Is it your brother? Is it that we lied to you?"

Lizzie sat back on the couch and stared at the framed poster on the opposite wall. "I don't know," she said quietly. "It's everything. It's as if I have to learn what it means to be alive. Every damn thing's so strange to me—my body, my voice, the way I look— and I fluctuate between exhilaration and despair. I've always been emotional—but not like this, Mama. It's never been this bad. My feelings are killing me." She leaned her head on her mother's shoulder. "Tell me what's wrong, Mama."

"I wish I could."

"Stay the night? Can you, Mama? Can you hold me?"

"Yes," her mother whispered. "But you have to hold me, too."

"I promise," she said, "I promise."

2

February 1, 1988

Jon,

When you were five, you used to worship me, "Jacob, Jacob!" you used to yell, "I love you, love you."

You used to follow me around the house if I wouldn't play with you and you'd yell my name until I couldn't stand it anymore and played with you.

I used to carry you. When you were a baby, I used to like to hold you. Mom would take you away from me because she said I'd drop you. But I was always careful with you—more careful than her. Sometimes I would just put you on my shoulders and give you rides all through the house, and then we'd go outside and I'd toss you in the air. You were so little. You used to sit on the lawn sometimes and play with bugs. You could play with insects forever and you would never kill them. You were as careful with bugs as I was with you. You were good with bugs and animals and people.

I taught you to swim, do you remember?

I wonder what kind of man you are.

Are you still careful? Are you still good with people? Did he damage you so deeply that you live somewhere alone and far away from everybody around you? I hope you're not like me. I push people away all the time, always have. Even Joaquin—even him I pushed away. Except now that he's dying.

Do you ever wonder where desire comes from? I never desired clothes or houses or property. I desired men. I wanted all of them. Where did I get that?

I keep going back to the house where we lived. I keep going back. I keep going back to that house to find you. Funny thing about that house we lived in, I keep finding things.

Today I remembered the first time I ever had sex. I don't remember the event being very thrilling. Maybe a little. I was nervous. Uptight. I was scared. Hell, I was terrified. I was sixteen and it was with another guy. My best friend. We couldn't look at each other afterward. We never talked to each other again after that. We were ashamed. I was. He was. Maybe he's gay. Maybe he isn't. Don't know. Don't think it matters. Now, I'd like to go back and tell him everything is OK, tell him it doesn't matter. Why is everything always such a big deal? I was just a kid. And I felt bad for months. I was so ashamed. Isn't it stupid, the things we suffer over? And where the hell does shame come from? Joaquin says that a conscience is not possible without shame . . .

I found out today I was HIV positive.

J is beginning to come down with symptoms. I want him close, now. And now he'll be getting farther and farther away.

I'm scared, just like when I was a kid. And I'm so fucking angry. I can't even tell you. I'd like to break the earth in half. Maybe not the earth. Maybe just the people.

Today, I hate anybody who's healthy. Joaquin doesn't hate. But I hate, and it's so real, so fucking real. When I found out Dad had bothered you—I hated. That's how I hate now. When I punched Mom out, I hated, and really it felt so goddamned good to hate—I mean really hate her and hit her. I could have hit her until my arms fell off their sockets. I hate so much sometimes that I think I'll just explode. But it's like food, sometimes. It's what you're used to eating—and you have to eat something. Joaquin always wanted to make me into a calmer man. I think he feels that if he had loved me more, then all that rage could have been converted into something more positive. He is more than I ever deserved.

 **3**

Mary sat at the usual table waiting for Diego to walk through the door of Sol's Barbecue. He had never been late before, and she was uncomfortable sitting alone in a public place. She was afraid Diego would not show up—leave her sitting alone. They would ask her to leave—she knew it. Maybe no one would notice her. But people had always noticed her. "I was pretty and men liked pretty—and women liked pretty, too. Crazy—crazy isn't pretty. I'm better, really I'm better." She looked down at herself. "Maybe I'm better, but I'll never be pretty again," she whispered. She looked around the room nervously and distracted herself by playing with her newly painted nails. The lavender of the hard nail polish looked purple against her pale skin. She smiled at her hands as she stretched them out in front of her. She snapped her fingers and giggled. She looked up and watched Diego as he skipped through the door, and noticed the lightness of his footsteps. As he waved, her fear disappeared. "Johnny—hey honey," she said, "see my nails! Ain't they somethin'?"

Diego nodded at her. He wanted to reassure her because she seemed to always need to be reassured. He kept smiling at her almost stiffly. He had a large box in his hands tied with a huge pink ribbon. He placed it on the table in front of her and smirked.

Mary looked at the box and pretended a casual interest. Diego said nothing, but played with the pink ribbon. Finally, she was unable to keep her silence. "That's an awful big box, Johnny."

"Want to know what's in it?" His hands skipped happily as he wrote.

"I figured if you wanted me to know, you'd tell me. Ain't that right? My mama said men don't care for women who want to know too much."

He moved the box toward her side of the table. "For you," he wrote in capital letters.

"Oh!" She took a deep breath like an actress in a play, the whole restaurant hearing her breathy exclamation. "Ain't that somethin'." She looked at the box and then looked at Diego. "You're so good to Mary! How come you're so good, huh, honey?"

Diego shrugged his shoulders. "Tomorrow's Easter," he wrote. "I thought you should have something special. Go ahead and open it."

She looked at the box again. "What a pretty pink ribbon. I just love pink, Johnny, pink reminds me of the songs birds sing—I've always thought that." She stopped talking and looked around the room nervously. "Ain't that silly?" She undid the ribbon slowly. Her eyes opened wide and her hands trembled.

Diego kept his eyes on her face.

Mary finished unwrapping the box clumsily. She tried to remember the last time anyone had given her a gift. *"Do you like it, Mommy? Do you really, really like it?"* *"I love it, my angel, the most beautiful dress ever made—and you bought this for me—all by yourself?"* *"Daddy helped, Daddy helped . . ."* She could feel she was going to cry. *Just don't cry, just don't.* She took the lid off the box. *Just keep acting, just say words.* She sat motionless for an instant, staring at the contents of the box. "Oh! My word, Johnny! If that ain't the most gorgeous thing I ever saw. Oh! My sweetest Lord, ain't that nice? Oh, sugar, you shouldn't have."

"Do you really like it?" Diego wrote.

"Oh, Johnny, I love it. I adore it! You are absolutely the kindest man I ever met." She kept staring inside the box. "I just can't believe it." She put her hand on her chest as the tears ran down her face.

"Don't cry, Mary," he wrote.

She wiped her tears with a paper napkin and looked at Diego's note. "I'm sorry, honey, it's just that I'm a damn fool sometimes. Ain't it just like a woman to spoil everything with tears? Ain't it though?"

"Tears are nice," he wrote, "like rain."

She shook her head gently as she read the note. "Johnny, you're sweet—you're so, so sweet." She folded up his note with her lavender fingernails.

"Don't you want to model it for me?"

She reached over and gave Diego a kiss on the cheek. She smiled and took the white, wide-brimmed hat out of the box. Little yellow flowers were sewn into the borders and a wide yellow ribbon adorned it. She combed her hair back and put the hat on, tilting it to one side. She stretched her arms out as wide as she could. "How do I look?" Mary placed a finger under her chin. Diego stared at her painted nails. "I knew I should have painted my nails yellow— I just knew it."

Diego smiled. "Purple's fine."

"You really think so?"

Diego nodded.

"You know somethin', honey? I ain't had a hat like this since I was a little girl. My mama used to buy one for me every Easter, and she used to take me to church, and I'd sit and stare at my white shoes and roll my white socks up and down—up and down—and I was so happy, Johnny. Life is good to children, ain't it, sugar?"

Diego nodded. He wanted to tell her it wasn't true, wasn't true at all. "You want to go to church with me tomorrow?"

Mary stared at his written question. "Which church you go to, Johnny?"

"Usually Sacred Heart, but sometimes the cathedral."

"Oh, I like that one," she said, "all them windows. It reminds me of a garden—like I died and went to heaven."

"You want to go with me? We can go to church there if you want?"

She thought a minute. "Well, honey, I ain't never been to one of those church services before."

"You've never been to a Mass?"

She nodded, "I ain't Catholic."

"It doesn't matter, does it?"

She tilted her hat to the right, then to the left. "I guess you're right, a church is a church, ain't it? And I sure would like to wear my hat to church—it being Easter Sunday and all."

"I'll meet you at the plaza. We can walk from there, OK?"

"Oh! Yes, Johnny! That would be so lovely." She placed her hands on her cheeks; her worn face blushed; she looked down at the skirt she was wearing. A new hat and no nice clothes, she thought, they'll look at me, they'll all look at me. *Everyone's always staring at us. Can't take it, anymore, goddamnit! Get yourself to a place where no one will have to see you. You're always causing a scene—just get the fuck out of my life* . . . She looked down at her bag, and was immediately lost in a thought.

"Something wrong?"

She stared at Diego's note and then his eyes. "Johnny, honey, Mary's got to get busy." She leaned over and kissed him again. "Mary's got to run." She took her hat off and placed it carefully in the box. "It's a treasure, Johnny." She smiled at him.

"Where are you going? We haven't had lunch yet."

"Mary's got to go find something to wear." She took some crackers off the table, placed the hat back in the box, and rushed out the door. Diego shook his head and laughed. She came rushing back in, breathless, and asked, "I nearly forgot, sugar, what time do I meet you at the park tomorrow?"

"Ten o'clock?" he wrote. She took the note and put it down her blouse.

"Tomorrow at ten. Mary's gonna look fine, sugar. Sun's gonna shine for Mary."

Diego winked at her. She winked back as she hurried out into the city.

Diego got up from the table and headed toward the shops on Stanton Street. He thought maybe he'd buy himself a new shirt. Maybe even a tie. He thought about what Mundo had told him about his clothes. He walked into some shops and finally decided to buy a yellow shirt and a gray tie. He tried on the shirt and looked in a mirror. The color looked good on him, he thought. He nodded—and kept nodding. Mary would like it—even Luz would like it. Maybe he should get a hat, too. He looked at all the hats they had, trying them on, one after another—a black one, a white one, a gray one. The hats made him look like a little boy playing dress-up. He remembered the hats the men used to wear when his mother took him to church. The men would take off their hats, make the sign of the cross, and hold them over their hearts. He had thought at the time that they looked very holy. He decided to buy an imitation gray fedora. He looked in the mirror and smiled to himself. "If that doesn't get me some good stares," he said to himself, "then nothing will. It would be nice to be looked at."

When Mary arrived back at her apartment, she frantically looked through her closets for the right dress. Finally, she found one—yellow with printed white flowers. She tried to shake the wrinkles out of it. She looked in the mirror as she placed the dress in front of her. She wondered if Diego would like it. He was a kind man, and he would say he liked it even if he didn't. She imagined herself standing in front of him, and him reaching over and kissing her. His kisses would be soft. He would not know what to do, but she would show him. She felt as if she had come back from a long journey. *I don't want to be me anymore. I don't need*— She noticed a man standing in her doorway.

"Put it on," he said.

She stared up at the voice. She knew who he was. She had noticed him watching her on the street, staring, staring.

He moved closer to her. "Put the goddamned dress on," he said.

She froze. She had never heard him use that tone.

"I'll scream," she said.

"I'll kill you if you do,"

She felt herself slipping away as she took her off her clothes. She felt the feel of the dress she had found just for Diego on her skin. She felt hands push up the dress. "Diego," she whispered as the man entered her, "Diego tell me it's you, tell me . . ."

4

August 12, 1993

Dear Jake,

Jacob Diego Marsh was born yesterday morning. "He's so beautiful, Eddie," that's the first thing she said. It was still dark outside, but it was almost dawn. He was three weeks late. Nena was very brave. The minute she was having hard labor pains, she lost her English completely. My Spanish is still really bad, so I didn't know what she was saying—except my name, and I now know the word "dolor," and now I really know how to perfectly say "Dios mío." I'll never forget those words, or how she looked. Her sweat smelled new and fresh like a tree after the rain.

She was strong, Jake, incredible! I thought she'd take my arm off its socket. And yet when it was over, she kept staring at this little child. She kept repeating my name, "Eddie, Eddie," she kept saying. "Look. Look what we've made. Look, amor." I know I was just one more man staring at his wife holding their new child—just one more man among a million others. One more child. Before I had him, in the back of my head I asked myself: "Does the world need another child?" And I know the world doesn't need him, doesn't need him at all. But, Jake, I need him—and Nena needs him. And if we do right by him, maybe he will do something good for the world, something really good, so good that the world will be

254

changed forever. I'm probably thinking the same thoughts as the million other fathers who had a child today. Maybe we are all hoping the same things.

It's so strange, Jake, to hold a child—and to feel that kind of love. Did you know that when you love a child your heart hurts. I didn't know that. It hurts. It's the best pain (sounds ridiculous, doesn't it?)—but it's the best pain—to feel the heart literally hurt, strange and awesome and, well, mortal. Jake, I'm a dad. I was too happy and tired and excited to sleep. I just wanted to be with her and with him, and I wish you could have been there so you could have driven me home and listened to me babble about the whole thing. I'm a father. In my cynical moments, I think to myself that I'm just perpetuating a system that's gone bankrupt. Isn't that what our parents tried to make us do? They thought we'd grow up to be big white boys who believed in big white gods. And we didn't, did we? Tell me we didn't, Jake.

He has Maria Elena's eyes, and his skin is going to be dark. I can tell. But he has light fine hair—maybe he'll be blond like you. Actually, right now it's fuzz, but I think he might have your hair. It's not my hair, that's for sure. He's very handsome. He has some very Indian features— Maria Elena's genes. I want him to know all about you. I want him to know all about his past. I'm not going to hide anything from this kid— I swear I'm not—not about the country he lives in, not about the rich and the poor, not about sex, not about the families he comes from. I want him to know. I want him to carry that knowledge in the deepest parts of him. I don't want him to wake up some day and say: "Why didn't they tell me? Why didn't they trust me with the truth?"

It's very beautiful outside. The baby and Nena are coming home today. I'm bringing them home. I'm taking a month off from work. Actually, I don't know if I'll ever go back. Every day I sit there and think I'd rather be someplace else—doesn't matter where. But it does matter where—I just don't know what I'd like to do. I have choices. The rich always do— that's what Lizzie always says. She's right. I'm wasting my life for a buck I don't even need. If I hate my job, then why keep punishing myself. Punishing myself is so easy—for what? For surviving? Right after Mom killed Dad, and then herself, I had a dream. I dreamed I was in the room, and it was me killing them. I woke as I put the gun to my own head. I sometimes think I should have died with them. Then it would be *over for all of us. But then I think of Maria Elena. And now I think of my son. Maybe that's why I wanted to have children—I'm hoping they'll set me free. I hope they'll give me another chance at something, another chance at my own life. I hope I'm not too heavy for my son. I hope he'll be strong enough to carry his father in his body. One way or another, the poor little guy is stuck. If I believed in God, I would ask him to make me a good father. Please.*

MARIA ELENA WAS WADING through the waters of one of Eddie's journals as he stood over the stove and stirred the soup he was making for dinner. She held the baby in her arms as she read. "He doesn't weigh very much," she said half to herself, half to Eddie.

"Well, give him a break. He's still little. He doesn't talk yet, either."

"He's awfully quiet."

He nodded, only half-listening to his wife. The olive oil where he'd planned to sauté the garlic was beginning to smoke. "Oh shit!" he said. As soon as the words were out of his mouth, the smoke alarm began blaring. Nena jerked at the noise. "Turn that thing off!" He placed the pan in the oven, and climbed on a chair and reached for the alarm. He screwed it off the wall and took the battery out. The kitchen was quiet again.

He looked around the room. "Did you hear that?"

"What?"

"The baby?"

"What are you talking about, Eddie? He's an angel—just look at him."

"Why isn't he crying?"

"What?"

"Nena, that thing should have scared the hell out of him. Startle reflex—we all have startle reflexes. He didn't hear it."

She looked at her son still lying peacefully in her arms. She had noticed it, too, though she'd said nothing. She was working hard at ignoring the fact that he didn't respond to noises. She didn't want to know. "He's fine, Eddie."

He shook his head. "If you don't take him to the pediatrician, then I will, Nena."

She nodded. "Take him, then. He's going to tell you he's fine." She wondered why she was fighting what she already knew. *He's awfully quiet.* She stared at her husband. She expected to see anger, but there was no anger in his face. Instead she saw the face of a worried father. She knew her husband was staring at the face of a frightened mother.

"Are you OK?" he asked.

"I'm fine."

"You look upset."

"The fire alarm startled me."

"Me, too," he said.

"We'll be fine," she whispered to herself.

 **6**

January 1988. San Francisco

"Jacob Lesley, I'm not feeling very well lately."

"You're working too hard, J."

"I'm not working too hard—I've never worked less in my life."

"Maybe you're coming down with a cold."

"It doesn't feel like a cold."

"You're not a doctor. How the hell do you know?"

"I know what a cold feels like, gringo. My lymph glands feel hard as a rock. Feel." Joaquin took Jake's hand and placed it on one of his glands. "See?"

Jake nodded. "It's nothing, J." He started toward the door. "Take an aspirin. I'll take you out to dinner."

"An aspirin, Jake? You want me to take an aspirin?"

He heard the anger in Joaquin's voice. "Don't worry. Where does worry get you? You're always worrying about everything. Lymph glands get enlarged for everything. They're like little penises—they get excited all the time. Doesn't mean a thing."

"What if—"

"You're fine."

"Right." Joaquin shook his head.

Jake pulled him against his chest. "It's OK—don't overreact. It's Tony—his death has you a little rattled."

"It isn't that. And how come you get to overreact about everything—and I don't? You get to yell and kick and scream. You kicked the door down once, the goddamn bedroom door! I can't even breathe too deeply because—if I do, I'm labeled theatrical."

Jake smiled. "See, you're getting that thing you get in your voice—like you're in a play. That's why I married you, for your sense of humor—your sense of drama."

"Are we married?"

"Yes," he said, "absolutely."

Joaquin pretended to be comforted. "Go to work," he said. When his lover walked out the door, he shook his head. "I'm sick," he whispered. It was no use to talk about it with him. Jake always avoided everything—and when he finally faced things, he faced them with a fist. "I'm sick, gringo." He trusted his body. There was a reason he was bone tired, a reason why his glands felt like he was carrying a second set of testicles under his chin. He was carrying a weight, a heaviness he'd never known, and Jake was adding to it by his disgusting arrogance. He was going through an immortal phase—something he had skipped while growing up. He had survived his childhood, had survived his mother and his father, had survived a hundred lovers and at least that many fistfights. Jake had survived his drunken self-destructive twenties—after that, he thought he could keep everything at bay just by not being afraid. Joaquin sensed this visitor—this thing he had—would pound at the door—was pounding even now—would pound until he let him in and embraced him, until he let him take his body, his mind, and his life away like a strong wind stole the tiny seeds of a dandelion. He took a shower, slowly examining his body. It looked the same—a little weight loss but he was busy, yes, that was it, he would slow down and eat more. As he shaved, he couldn't ignore the pain of his enlarged glands. Don't panic, Joaquin, it's not that painful. You can't even tell by looking. You can never tell by looking. He shook his head as he looked himself over in the mirror. "You look great," he set aloud, "just great." His heart raced. An anxiety attack, it's just an anxiety attack. Panic held him now. He reached for a cigarette, then lit it. He trembled as he smoked it. He smoked another.

He felt calmer. He walked into the bedroom and lit a candle. He always lit candles for special intentions. Jake hated them—especially because he never told him what the special intentions were.

He had stayed awake at night worrying—worrying and listening to Jake snore. He snored so quietly, a man at peace, a man resting from his labors, a man who had earned these quiet, necessary hours. Jake was so sure they were safe, so untouchable, had convinced himself they had escaped. They alone had escaped. For a second, Joaquin hated him. He felt the pain near his throat. He dressed himself after he lit his candle and walked slowly toward the free clinic. He didn't want to go to Tom. He would go to Tom later. The counselor spoke to him in a soft, clear, tenor voice—was he sure he knew the facts, yes, yes, he nodded, knew them all. A man with warm hands drew the blood, and he thought his body was a strange and foreign thing. Did anybody know their body— did anybody? He looked away—didn't even feel the needle take the blood. He signed something. Results in two weeks, maybe less. He walked away. He decided he wouldn't come back, forget he had ever come here, live a long and happy life.

The next two weeks were a daze. When people spoke to him, he wanted to tell them to shut up; he watched their lips, wanted to grab their words from the air and shove them back down their throats. When Jacob talked, he pretended to listen. He did a lot of smiling. He felt like crying all the time. He made love to his Jake—almost like normal, only it was just a body thing—not a heart thing. His heart could do nothing but worry and mourn. During the day, he took walks, talked to himself, thought about his life. Hadn't it been good—hadn't it been a good life? If he was negative, he would praise God the rest of his days, be kind to all of the people in the world, be grateful for everything—good and bad—in his life. If he was negative—then he would never let himself feel this heavy again, and he would lighten burdens everywhere he walked. Were November's night sweats really the flu? If he was negative—he would . . . For two weeks, he hoped. He knew, but he hoped. Was it so bad to hope? After all he had done, the life he had lived—the men he had loved—he still hoped? When the kind man in the free clinic told him as kindly as was humanly possible that he was positive, Joaquin almost smiled. It was almost a relief—to know. To finally know. He would never know anything like he knew this. *Knowledge was power—it was true. Maybe he would live a long time. There was still a life to be lived. I'm only twenty-five, I'm only twenty-five. People live a long time. Yes, people live a long time. More than ten years, and maybe they'll find a cure—in my lifetime? In my lifetime? Ten years, yes, that's a long time. I'll be thirty-five by then. There is still a life to be lived.*

When Jacob opened the door, Joaquin smiled and hugged him. He looked into his eyes. "I'm positive," he said.

"What?"

"A couple of weeks ago I went to the clinic." He paused and looked at the expression on his lover's face. "Would you like a drink?"

"Yes," he said.

He poured a lot of bourbon into their glasses—just a little ice. He handed one to Jake, the cold of the cubes still on his skin. Jake sat on the couch and said nothing.

"Why didn't you tell me, J?" He sounded numb and far like a light breeze against the growing grass.

"You didn't want to hear it."

"That's not true," he said.

"You told me to take aspirin," Joaquin almost yelled back.

Jake nodded his head up and down as if his head were a buoy in the ocean. He finished his drink in one gulp, got up from the couch and fixed another. He sat down right next to Joaquin. "We should have gone together."

"It's OK," Joaquin said.

"Call Tom."

Joaquin nodded. "I'll call him. You should go, too."

He nodded. "Yes."

They finished their drinks. Joaquin started for the door. "I think I'll take a walk." His back was toward his lover. As he opened the door, he felt Jake's hand pulling him back inside. They stood in the doorway and looked at each other saying nothing. "I'm sorry," Jake said. "Forgive me."

In all of the years they had been together, Jake had never said "I'm sorry." He was not the kind of man who ever overtly asked for any kind of forgiveness for any reason. After a fight or a disagreement, he would simply make some kind of gesture—dinner, a movie, a quiet weekend.

262

He was better at gestures than at words. "After all this time, you don't know that I've forgiven you?"

Lizzie stared at Joaquin's burning candle as she sat in the room.

"Will you miss me when I die?"

"I thought you were asleep," she said softly.

"Will you miss me?"

"Funny man," Lizzie said, "Always being funny. I'll miss you, miss you, miss you." She pushed his hair off his face.

"Three times."

"Three times for luck."

He laughed. "Jake says you have out-of-body experiences."

"Yes," she nodded, "I do."

"I'm about to have one, too," he said.

She smiled crookedly.

"Jake doesn't believe you—about your experiences."

"I know. Did you expect he would?"

"No—I guess not. Tom believes you. Tom says you're real, the real thing."

"As opposed to what? As opposed to whom?"

Joaquin ignored her question. "Lizzie, did you dream me?"

"Yes," she said.

"Am I your dream?"

"You are much more than *my* dream. So much more than that, my love."

"But don't we invent each other?"

"What a strange thing to say."

"Isn't it true, though? Don't we just make each other up?"

"Well, in a way. I guess so. Still, we're real aren't we?"

"I don't know anymore. Except my body, it hurts. That's the only thing that's real." He sipped on a glass of water. "My throat's so dry. Did you know that I was born in the desert? They say you return to where you were born when you die. Already my mouth is full of sand." He stared up at her. "My mother used to say there was a grain of sand for every human being that was ever born and died. When I die, I will become a grain of sand."

She nodded.

"You're a very kind woman. Why did you come here? Was it my mother, did my mother send you?"

"No, not your mother. You asked me to come—don't you remember? I heard you. You asked me. And so I came."

"I remember," he said, "yes." He took another sip of the cold water, the sweat running down his face like the sweat that used to run down his chest after a run. "I used to be very healthy, you know? You never knew me when I was—will you take care of Jake?"

"Your job isn't to worry about Jake. Jake will be fine."

"No, he won't."

"I'll see to it," she said.

"And you'll help him find Jonathan?"

"Jonathan?"

"His brother."

"Yes, I'll help him find Jonathan."

"Read to me," he said.

"What should I read?"

"Anything. Anything to help me sleep, to help me dream."

"Well, I should have brought my journal—that would make you sleep." She laughed. "Though I doubt it would help you dream."

"Will you?" he asked. He smiled. "Will you?"

"Yes."

She brought her journals the next day. For two weeks, she read him sections, different entries, she smiled as she read parts of them. It didn't seem that it was her life at all. She laughed at some of her entries. They seemed to have so little to do with anything that was real. Well, what was the harm? She liked reading them to Joaquin— it made her feel as if she were keeping him alive. He would stop her sometimes and ask her questions. "You have bad taste in men," he said once.

"Well, not always," she said. "You're a man, aren't you?"

"Queers don't count."

"*You are a man,*" she said deliberately, "a man. And queers count."

"OK," he said.

Joaquin looked up at his lover as he bathed him. He almost enjoyed the feel of his soapy hands on his skin. He was calm and steady and careful. "I won't break," he said.

"You might."

Joaquin smiled. "How did it come to this?"

Jake stopped washing him, and sat down on the bathroom floor staring at his lover. He tried to imagine Joaquin as he used to be. He was the same man. He was not the same man.

"Don't look at me," Joaquin said.

"What will happen if I look, J?"

"If you look at me too hard, you'll make me want to live."

Jake looked down at the floor. He stared at his hands.

"It's hard for you, isn't it, Jake?"

"I'm not dying, you are."

"I'm the future."

"J, if you're the future, I could do a lot worse." Jake placed his hands in the water, cupped them, and held as much water as he could in them. He lifted his cupped hands in the air. If I hold my hands very tight, he thought, then the water will stay. But already it was pouring through his fingers. He slowly let the water go back into the bathtub. Joaquin stared up at the ceiling as if he were trying to imagine himself somewhere else. "Joaquin, are you afraid?"

"Someone in the village where I was from was always dying. They used to ring the church bells and we'd go. I grew up kissing other people's caskets before they lowered them into the ground— that was my life. And how many friends have we lost, Jake? Death after death after death. I'm sick of it. I'm sick of grieving. You want to know if I'm afraid? Sometimes. Sometimes, I'm terrified. But most of the time I'm not. Why the hell should I be afraid, Jacob Lesley? Hell, I'm more afraid that this will go on forever."

Jake looked down at the floor as Joaquin spoke.

"Look at me. Don't look at the floor. You've spent enough time looking at it—you stare at that floor as if you might find a cure down there. It isn't there, gringo. I know you don't want me to die, but I don't want to live, anymore. I don't. I don't. Look at this body. I'm suffering, Jake. I know how to spell that word now—I know what that word means. I know every letter of that sad and ugly word. Do you understand? Do you know what that is?"

Jake nodded. "Let me help you out of the tub." He helped Joaquin up, his bony body trembling. He imagined that the drops of water dripping from his body were tears. His body was crying. He dried them off. He carried him to bed, and stared at his eyes. They were still the same.

December 24, 1972

It was a cold night to be crossing the river. Joaquin could see his breath in front of him, and he tried to catch the warmth with his hands, but his hands were too small and too slow. His coat was too thin for this weather. His mother whispered that the desert was being unkind to them tonight. She had always said the desert was a fickle god not to be trusted. She stopped and rubbed his arms and legs. She whispered words in his ears that sounded like prayers. He hugged her when she finished and told her he was not afraid. He lied, but he did not want her to know. He had never felt so strange, nor had he ever felt this scared. He was glad it was cold: His mother would think he was shaking from the cold. He wanted to go back to the village. He wanted to go back to the house where he had been born. But he did not tell her what he felt. She should not be worrying about him, not now. She was doing this for him. Yes, that's why they were doing this. He watched his mother as she walked through the desert. He thought there would be nothing when she died. She had always been there from the beginning, and the world seemed hard to imagine without her smile or her touch or her voice. He smiled at her. When she died the world would end. He told her he was fine. He was fine. The man leading them said they had to hurry. They walked quickly like pilgrims reaching their shrine—at last—happy at last because they had been afraid they might not find what they were seeking. When they reached the river, his mother made the sign of the cross. The river was not very wide. He thought it would be much bigger, much wider. It was not far to the other side.

A man, bigger than his father had ever been, carried his mother on his shoulders. Another man carried him into the river. The water was cold on his legs and he thought he might freeze. He wondered how the men could be so strong. They laughed softly as they crossed. He wanted to be strong like them, laugh like them. They were afraid of nothing. No one spoke and it was so quiet. The world had ended. There were not many of them, twelve. Before they had crossed the river it began to snow. Joaquin looked up at the snowing sky and caught a snowflake on his tongue. "It is a sign," one of the men said. He did not say what the sign meant, but his mother nodded. The whole earth was red from the glowing sky and he thought it was the end of the world. He could see everything from here. When they reached the other side of the river his mother said everything would be different. "We will be richer here," she said, "but we will not be happier. And even if I have to live here—I will never die here." And then he knew. It was the end of the world.

The cold summer left them. Autumn was warm. The Day of the Dead came and went, and still Joaquin breathed. Miraculously, a day before Thanksgiving, Joaquin rose from his bed and wandered into the kitchen where Lizzie and Jake were drinking coffee, his IV at his side. "Who's going to make the turkey?" he asked. They stared at him.

Jake hugged him and smiled, then looked at Lizzie. "She is," he said.

She had planned to be with Maria Elena, Eddie, and the baby. She nodded. "And Jake will make the stuffing."

"He's a terrible cook," he whispered.

"It'll be good," Jake laughed, "I promise."

He nodded. "Fine."

That evening, Lizzie baked a pumpkin pie, following her mother's exact instructions. Joaquin, who had somehow received a few ounces of strength from some unknown source, sat at the table and watched her roll out the dough.

"Have you ever made tortillas?"

She laughed. "No."

"You have the hands for it," he said.

"Oh?"

He stuck his hands out for her to see. "I do, too."

Jake watched them as he stood at the door. He held two bags of groceries in his arms.

Lizzie looked up at him. "Did you get everything?"

He nodded. He placed a turkey in front of Joaquin. "Is it OK?"

"It's wonderful, it's a wonderful turkey."

The next day, Joaquin actually ate. He ate slowly, but he ate.

"He's going to live," Jake thought. But Lizzie knew Joaquin had gathered all his remaining will to pay a last visit to the living. He wanted to eat with them one last time.

"He wants a priest, Lizzie. How the hell do I get one—and when the hell is he supposed to come? Shit. Shit, shit, shit." He ripped the newspaper he was holding in half.

Lizzie took the pieces of paper from his hands. "I know one," she said softly.

"You do?"

"Well sort of. I met one when I went to Salvador's funeral."

"Salvador?"

"My brother. I told you the story."

"Yeah. Right."

"Why do you have such a hard time believing my story?"

"Maybe because it's more than a little strange."

"You mean, as opposed to *your* life story."

"I haven't told you my life story."

"But if you told me, what would you do if I just dismissed it because it was so outrageous?"

"It is outrageous. I don't believe it myself."

"You don't believe your own life? Well hell, no wonder you don't believe mine."

They both laughed—hard—as if they could have just as easily been screaming or crying.

Jake looked up at Lizzie from where he sat. "How is it that he's lived this long?"

"He's waiting for you to let go."

He nodded. "Will you call that priest, Lizzie?"
"I'll go see him. I'm sure he'll come."

"Peace be with this house and with all who . . ."

The priest's sober voice filled the room. There was something calm about the whole scene. Everyone was still, motionless, out of respect for the ritual, but also out of a kind of discomfort. Ritual was a place where Joaquin had lived, the rest of them were only onlookers, distant participants. Mrs. Sha held a candle in her hand. Mr. Sha had his hand placed on his wife's back. Lizzie stood at the foot of the bed next to Jake. She held his hand. They almost looked like husband and wife. The priest blessed a bowl of water and sprinkled it with a branch of cedar.

"Like a stream in parched land, may the grace . . ."

Jake felt the cool drops of water fall on his face. He wished Joaquin had not asked for this. He watched his lover lying on the bed, eyes open, head nodding. He watched him cross himself as the holy water fell on him. He stopped listening to the words. It would be better if he stopped listening. He watched the priest as he anointed Joaquin's forehead, the oil glistening in the dim light of the room and it seemed as if there was a star on his skin and Jake wanted to make a wish. "I wish he were well. I wish he could live to be old." He kept himself from hearing the words the priest was uttering— it was enough just to watch. It was enough to have eyes. What were these words, anyway? What power did they have? What would it change? His body is rotting, and we are whispering prayers. But Joaquin looked peaceful. He seemed to grow calmer and calmer as the rite progressed. The priest anointed Joaquin's hands, said a prayer, then anointed his feet, then anointed the place in his chest near his heart. When he had finished, he fed Joaquin a Communion wafer that looked to be as white and weightless as a summer moon. "Food for the journey," the priest said.

Joaquin whispered, "Amen," and ate. Outside, an early January rain pelted the parched city.

 **7**

"WHAT DO YOU MEAN he's deaf?" She pointed her chin
at him as if it were a knife, as if she might stab him with it.

He reached for her hand. She pulled her hand away, turned her
back on him. "No."

"Honey, he's healthy in every way. It's no big—"

"*No. I said no. He's perfect.*"

He touched her back. Again she moved away. "What's perfect,
Maria Elena?"

"I don't want to talk to you right now."

"Shoot the messenger, is that it?"

"He's my son, damnit. I didn't want him to suffer. You don't
know—"

"Oh, I get it, yeah, I want him to suffer. I want him to go through
life without hearing my voice, without hearing yours. I want that?
What are you saying?"

"You don't get it do you, Eddie?"

"What? Talk to me."

She shook her head. "Not now."

Eddie pulled at his hair. "Not now," he said through his teeth.
"Going at this alone, are you?"

"What the hell's that supposed to mean?"

"It means what's a marriage for, Nena?"

270

She stared out the window.

"Good girl." he said shaking his head.

"Don't 'good girl' me, Eddie."

He stared at the back of her head. "I think I'll just leave and come back when you're not so angry. Maybe you just need to be with your anger for a while."

"Grief," she corrected.

"No," he said, "I know grief, and I know anger—and this is definitely anger."

She grabbed his alarm clock and threw it against the wall. It broke into several pieces.

"It's definitely anger," he repeated.

She threw a book he'd been reading at the same wall.

He watched it bounce on the wall and land on the floor, pages dog-eared and folded. "You have a hell of an arm. At least the baby didn't hear it."

"Get out!" she said.

He left the room, paced his office, then went downstairs and paced through every room. He walked slowly out of the house.

At four o'clock, Maria Elena began watching the clock. She fed the baby, held him. He was good; he liked to sleep. She watched his tiny mouth sucking on her breast. She felt sad and numb, and did not sing to him. What did it matter? He could not hear her voice. Eddie would have sung anyway. Her mother used to sing to Diego: "He can feel it," she said, "he can feel my voice running through his body. It's different than hearing, maybe better." "*Jacob Diego, is it true? Can you feel my voice?*" She put him down in his basket. "Such a tiny boy," she said.

She carried the baby into the kitchen in his basket. She set him down on the table and began cooking dinner. She chopped the carrots and onions as if they had somehow offended her. She stared at the stove, stared at the table, stared at the cabinets.

The stew was done by seven—she'd never made it before—it was a stew her mother had made. She wondered why she'd made it. This was peasant food—more potatoes than meat—a bad cut besides. She wasn't poor any longer, no longer just the daughter of a wetback. Look at this kitchen, she thought, it's mine. But as she

271

tasted the stew, she smiled. It was good. She could almost smell her mother and the small apartment they had lived in on Ochoa Street after they'd left her father. She looked at the clock: seven-twenty. She put a lid on the stew, turned off the burner, and left the pot on the stove.

The baby was still sleeping. By eight, no Eddie. By nine, she'd fed and changed the baby again. She sat in a rocking chair in the living room and began singing to him, singing a song she remembered, a song that meant nothing to her. She didn't even know she remembered it—and she was not really aware she was singing it:

> Hush my babies, go to sleep,
> I know your eyes are sad
> But Mama's here, she'll keep you warm:
> Sleep safe, sleep calm, sleep deep.
>
> Go to sleep, now all of you,
> Your Dad is drunk and gone.
> But he'll be back soon—sober
> Don't count the days, they're long . . .

A month ago she had been happy. A perfect baby, a perfect husband, and even she was becoming something that resembled that word. Finally, perfection. She laughed. Maria Elena wondered why she was so attached to this thing called normalcy. What if Eddie didn't come back. Hadn't she acted perfectly disgraceful? Hadn't she wanted him to leave her alone? ''Good girl.'' She thought of her mother and her father, she fought remembering how they lived. She stared into her son's eyes, who stared back so intelligently. She wanted to know what he saw, and wondered if children loved. No, they only had instincts, they only had needs. They needed to be fed and cared for, needed to be protected, and perhaps he was beginning to recognize her as his protector. She wanted him to hear her voice, though somehow she had sensed something in her pregnancy, and sensing it, she had insisted all the more he would be perfect. She laughed at herself. "Perfect"—that word had no meaning. It had no meaning whatsoever. Only the dead were perfect—because they were dead. Her mother used to say that. Her mother's face and the memory of her voice had been returning slowly, and she found herself speaking to her more and more since the birth of her son. Now she felt even closer to her because she would come to know everything her mother had known. Two mothers. Two deaf sons. She looked around the room and shook her head. But her life would not be like her mother's. She was not poor, and her husband was not like her father, and there was no going back—even if she lived the rest of her days in El Paso, there was no going back to the way she had lived. She had crossed a line, and now there was a wall that prevented the return. The gates had shut behind her. If she went back, what would her life be like? But she still remembered. And she could not make herself cease from that labor. *Her mother was sitting on an old rocking chair. As she sat on the floor and colored in her book, she looked up at her, and her mother smiled. "Mama, does it hurt if you're deaf?"*

"No. It doesn't hurt him. Nothing hurts."

"Will he ever talk?'

"No, m'ijita, nunca."

"Who's going to talk for him?"

"We are."

"What about when he needs to go to the bathroom—how will he ask?" Her mother smiled. "M'ija, there are other ways to talk."

"What other ways?"

"Some people talk with their hands."

"Oh," she said, then continued coloring.

She heard her father walk through the door. He was always noisy. She picked up her coloring book and crayons from the floor and sat perfectly still. Maybe he would not yell. Maybe he would go to bed. She could smell the liquor on his breath even from where she sat, and it became the only smell in the room, the only smell in the entire house. His black eyes seemed to be more red than black, and his whole body was on fire with a rage that she knew nothing about, but it scared her. He started shouting that there was no food. "Pero sí hay comida," her mother insisted. He grabbed the baby from her arms and shook him. He tossed him on the couch as if he were a lifeless doll, but the baby, not being a doll, began to cry. Her father seemed not to hear his son crying. Her mother shouted, yelling, "No, no, no." Her mother tried to reach for her baby, but her father stopped her and shoved her back in her chair. Then I will pick him up, she thought, so she ran and gathered her brother in her arms. Her mother nodded at her, and almost smiled. Her brother did not seem to be hurt, and she held him, and rocked him in her arms. She went to the corner of the room, the corner where she went when she was afraid, and there they sat, she and her baby brother. She heard her father yelling at her mother. He began to hit her, hit her and hit her and hit her. She couldn't watch, never could watch this scene that had repeated itself for as long as she could remember. She closed her eyes and prayed that her father would go away and never come back. She did not look up until the room was silent. When she opened her eyes, her mother's nose was bleeding and she was lying on the floor. "Dame comida, cabrona," her father said. Her mother picked herself off the floor slowly and went to the kitchen. She began warming up his food, which had grown cold because he had spent hours in a place where men drank.

She rocked her brother in her arms and he was sleeping again. He was a peaceful child, and he was fine, and she was happy he had not been hurt. Her mother held some ice in a cloth and pressed it against her face as she stood over the stove. She walked into the living room and watched her as she held her baby brother. "He's OK, Mama," she said. Her mother nodded, her tears glimmering in the light of the room. But tonight she was wearing a rage she had never seen, and though she did not speak, she knew something else was going to happen. "¡Tengo hambre! ¡Vieja inservible!" her father yelled as he sat at the table staring at the empty plate, a plate that had been sitting there placidly for hours. Her mother said nothing. She warmed some tortillas on her comal, served him beans and papas con chorizo. "Good," he said and ate. When he had finished, he said nothing. He stared at his wife as if he might hit her again, as if he might kill her. But he was too tired to hit her again, so he stumbled into the bedroom and shut the door behind him.

Her mother told her to put on her coat. And her mother, too, put on her coat. "No digas nada," she said, and so she sat perfectly quiet watching her mother. She watched as she tiptoed into the bedroom. When she opened the door, she could hear her father snoring. Her mother came out with some clothes. She went back into the bedroom and came out with a suitcase. She put her clothes in the suitcase, then went into the other bedroom and came out with some of her daughter's clothes. "Where are we going?" she whispered. "Shhh," her mother said. She stuffed

*everything into the suitcase. "Carry your brother," she said as she
wrapped him in another layer of clothing, "it's cold outside." She carried
him carefully, as carefully as she had carried anything in her life.*

*They walked in the cold for a long time. They came to a place. Her
mother knocked on the door and waited. A woman answered the door
and let them in. Her mother cried for what seemed an eternity, and the
other woman held her and kept telling her everything was going to be
OK. The woman looked over at her and her brother and told her she
would make a good mother some day.*

Maria Elena fell asleep clinging to her son. She was dreaming he
could speak. She woke up wondering where she was. Eddie was
sitting across the room. "Have you been there a long time?" she
asked him softly.

"Maybe an hour," he said—his voice as soft as hers. "Can I hold
him?"

She nodded.

He walked across the room and took him in his arms. "He's so
small." The baby started to cry. "Shhhh, baby, it's OK. It's just your
daddy."

He sat in the chair next to his wife.

"Did the doctor say why?"

"Well, the long and the short of it is that they don't know. It's
just a defect, Nena. Did you know that dimples were weaknesses—
tears really—tears in the tissues surrounding the mouth. Weaknesses. Defects. Is there any reason why we should value hearing
any more than we should value silence?"

She watched her husband holding their son. He was so in love.
With him. With her. "Eddie, I didn't mean to send you away."

"It's OK."

"There's deafness in my family."

"Don't, Nena. Does it matter, Nena? If you would have known
he was deaf before you had him, would you have aborted him?"

She shook her head.

"Then we chose him." He kissed his son's forehead. "We chose
you."

"Yes, we chose him."

"And we can teach him to give the hearing community hell."

"I hope so." She was crying.

"Cry only if you're happy."

"Happy? It's a lot to ask."

He laughed. "Nobody knows what the hell it is, anyway. And nobody's ever answered why we're supposed to think it's good. Do you know any happy people?"

"Well, everybody lies, Eddie."

He laughed again. "We're all so greedy." He looked down at the baby. "He's handsome, isn't he?"

"Que hombre tan lindo," she said.

"I know what that means, Nena."

"What? What does it mean?"

"It means I'm a good cook."

She laughed and shook her head. She pretended she was still angry. "I made dinner and you never showed up."

"I'm sorry," he said, "I was trying to make you regret you'd sent me away."

"It worked."

"I'm sorry." He stared at Jacob Diego. "I bought some books," he said.

"What kind of books?"

"You know about deafness, about learning sign language—stuff like that."

"He's not even two months old. And besides, I know a little sign language. I can teach you some. I'm rusty, but—"

"But what?"

"We need to find him," she said.

"Who?"

"Diego."

"We could hire someone to find him—we could hire—"

"I want to find him myself. I lost him—now I can damn well find him."

"OK," he said, "but can we eat first?"

"You're the one was out cattin' around. You warm up dinner."

"Cattin' around? Me? Monogamous Eddie?"

She took the baby from his arms and put him in his basket. She

276

took her husband by the hand and led him into the kitchen. "I'm starving," she said, "and I want some wine with my dinner. Do you know how long it's been since I've had a glass of wine?"

Eddie watched Maria Elena as she put the baby down, toothbrush clumsily moving back and forth in his mouth. He, in the doorway between the bathroom and the place where he slept, and she, sitting on the bed almost oblivious to his presence and yet she felt him, and she wanted to tell him never to leave her, but she knew he would not, so it was better to think it and not say it. She pulled her hair back, and Eddie trembled, not a big tremble, not the kind of tremble a boy feels the first time he is confronted with an object of desire but a different kind of tremble, one much saner and knowing and familiar, a tremble that wanted, wanted to be touched but no longer wanted to swallow because he had learned not to want everything, not to be greedy, not to demand that she be there for his use—but something beyond all that. When he had first loved her, that is what he had wanted to do—swallow her—swallow and be swallowed as if he wished for a kind of immolation, but now that kind of violent passion was irretrievable, and his body did not miss it. His body had changed and had learned to be more generous, though he did not name it that. His wants and needs were simpler, he wanted to look at her and hold her and sleep inside of her and be grateful for her skin and be at peace. He walked back into the bathroom, finished brushing his teeth, and looked at himself in the mirror. He wondered if he looked all right. Not so young anymore, well, not old, just thirty, this was better, did she think so? He walked into the bedroom and stood at the foot of the bed. She was undoing her braid.

"I like your braid," he said. "How come you never wore one until now?"

"I don't know," she said, "my mother wore one."

"Is that why?"

She shrugged her shoulders.

He stared at her.

"What?"

"How long has it been?" he asked.

"Since my mother died?" she asked.

"No," he said, "not that. I wasn't thinking about your mother at all."

"What were you thinking of?" She laughed.

He kept staring at her, trying to keep himself from smiling.

"Me," she said. "You were thinking of me."

"Don't be so self-centered—I was thinking of someone else."

"I don't think so," she said. "It's me you were thinking of. Yup. Me."

He jumped on the bed, and kissed her back.

"Do you remember the first time we made love, Eddie?"

"It was in my apartment. You came over with Hunan chicken. And I was dessert."

She laughed. "I thought I was dessert."

"Don't be so sexist. And besides you practically raped me."

"Rape is a strong word, Eddie."

"OK—it wasn't rape—it was—it was—"

"It was what?"

"It was great."

"Well, except that your bed broke."

"Yeah, and I never even made you pay for it."

She took off her clothes. "I'm a little flabby," she whispered, "and I think I've forgotten how to do it."

"I'll teach you," he said, "we'll take it slow."

She undressed him, and he let her touch him wherever she wanted. They pressed against each other. Their talk disappeared. They did not need to say each other's names. They stared into each other's eyes, not even noticing the soft smiles, just the eyes—and she, she did not care about her own identity for the moment, what she was, what she meant, she only cared and wanted to be a part of him, and not only him, but a part of the world, their child, her brother, the world she had left. She felt poor again, without possessions or the need for them, and she wanted to stop running away from the people and the desert that had formed her and given her an identity, however changeable and fragile. She, she thinking and knowing their love had changed and was no longer the stuff of idiotic and self-centered lovers who forgot about everybody who lived and breathed outside their bedroom. And he, he felt his heart pounding because he had forgotten about the physical pounding of the heart when it loved, but remembered as he pressed himself into her—and that pounding was not a hurt, but a joy, and he knew it was a joy. And he, too, no longer wanted to exile the violent world because he felt himself to be a part of everything—and was glad— and he wanted to heal the earth and everything that was wrong with it and be grateful for it because it had given him breath, because it had given him this woman, because it had given him a son. And he thought suddenly that there was still hope, and that this hope was not merely for himself because it was no longer acceptable to want it just for himself. And he thought their love had changed and was no longer made of only feelings and silences and privacy, but that it was something that belonged to the communion of the living and the dead. And she feeling the genesis of compassion as if good- ness was beginning to arise out of her not because it was pleasurable but because gratitude demanded something in return. And he crying, tears coming out of him like a spring in the desert, and she not recognizing the tears as tears, but as water, a water that was putting an end to the drought that had been her life. And both of them knowing their love had changed. And he thinking that love was work, and happy to be employed in the labor. And she thinking that most things she'd learned were nothing but lies to keep her from looking directly at the world, but just then all those lies seemed insignificant—but so did the necessity for speech, and he thinking that irony and distance were nothing more than masks of inadequate men, masks he had worn because he had not believed intimacy was possible, but it was, it was—and suddenly they, he and she, gasped, together gasped. And there was a moment of nothingness and they wrote the book of hope on that blank page in that instant. And she laughed. And he laughed. And neither of them cared nor wondered about where laughter came from. But still they did not speak. And somehow they knew they weren't in love with their silence anymore, with the isolation and despair they'd somehow inherited from the generations that had come before, no longer in love with their senseless and unnecessary unhappiness. And they were both sure they had died a kind of death, and knew that when they woke, they would not be able to return to the old dispensation.

And they slept.

 **8**

SUNDAY MORNING, Diego woke up late. The sun was shining, and he saw the bells moving back and forth in the tower across the freeway. He remembered the drawings he'd done for his mother when he was small. Mostly they were drawings about Jesus and his miracles. His mother used to write him little letters about Jesus and how he suffered and died and about how he came back to life. He saw the bells—and for an instant he held the image of a boy holding a picture of Jesus and giving it to his smiling mother. Now, he thought, if only Luz would come back everything would be fine. Maybe she'd learn to get along with Mary now that she talked less about being the Virgin.

Diego took a hot bath and changed into his new clothes. He straightened his tie and imitated Mundo's strut in front of the mirror. He smiled to himself and walked out the door wondering what Mundo would say if he saw him dressed so fine. He walked past the steps that went nowhere. Today, he didn't climb them. The sun was bright and there wasn't any wind, just a quiet breeze, and the pigeons were flying everywhere, their wings moving like the bells. Diego thought they looked like colored paper in a parade. At San Jacinto Plaza he sat on a bench and waited—he was early—but it was good to sit in the spring sun and wait. "It is Easter," he thought, "everything is alive, maybe even me." Some tulips were swaying in the breeze and the yellow dots on the green stems reminded him of the hat he'd bought for Mary. He expected her to arrive in a new white dress with white shoes and a smile wider than the brim of her hat. He waited. By ten-thirty, she still had not arrived. By eleven o'clock there was still no sign of Mary. He undid his tie. He took off his hat, played with it. He waited in the park all afternoon.

He walked back home, put his hat back in the closet and took off his yellow shirt. He took out his suicide note and read it over carefully making notes in the margins. "Crazy gringa," he said to himself, "she probably just forgot." He went to the evening Mass at the cathedral. There wasn't a choir, no Easter songs—just a few people who had missed the morning services.

He thought about Mary all evening. He had the strangest feeling about her. "She didn't forget," he kept writing over and over on his pad. *She didn't forget.* He had a bad feeling, felt uneasy. Something shot through him like a bullet—something was wrong. He knew something had happened. He'd had this feeling before, he remembered. His mother's face flashed before him. He couldn't fall asleep. Finally, after lying in bed for hours, he dozed off uneasily and dreamed of Mary. He saw the dead look on her face, and the yellow flowers splattered with blood. He woke up sweating, and looked into the darkness. Taking a deep breath, he lit a cigarette. He tried not to think about his dream, but it seemed so real—as real as the sweat that ran down his back.

On Monday, he asked Mr. Arteago to call his boss at home and tell him he was sick. Mr. Arteago was very nice about it and asked if he needed anything. Diego shook his head. He knew his boss would be furious when he showed up on Tuesday, but he didn't care. He was going to find Mary. He couldn't think of what to do as he walked around downtown looking for her. He kept thinking about his dream and kept searching.

By noon he was tired and drenched—confused. He needed help, tried to think. Mundo—Mundo would know what to do. If anybody could find Mary, he could. But he had no idea where he could find Mundo, either. He headed for La Fe Clinic, and went inside to look for Carolyn, the nurse. "I'm looking for Mundo," he wrote when he found her. "It's important that I find him. Can you help?"

She looked at him blankly. "I don't know, Diego. I don't know anything about that guy except that he and his friends are always trying to put the moves on me."

Diego looked at her, lowered his eyes.

She picked up his chin. "Look, Diego, I'll ask one of the other nurses. I'm sure one of them knows something about him. Everybody around here knows the gang members—they're everywhere."

Diego waited for her in the waiting room. The room was crowded with mothers, children, and old people. Usually, he tried to imagine what their lives were like, but today he had to find Mary, could think of nothing else. In his mind, he tried to erase the splattered blood he'd seen on Mary's hat. Maybe she was all right—maybe he was getting all worked up over nothing. Maybe he was finally cracking from all the years of working in the dark at Vicky's.

Carolyn returned to the waiting room and motioned Diego over. "Carmen says Mundo moves around a lot. A friend of hers knows him, and she says he's a member of the T-Birds. I don't know if that helps much," She looked at him softly. "Are you in trouble? Are you all right?"

Diego stared into her green eyes. He wanted to fall into them. He shook his head and wrote, "Thanks, I think that bit of information is enough to go on. I hope so, anyway."

"Let me know if I can do anything, OK?"

Diego nodded. "If you weren't on duty, I'd kiss you." She read his note and laughed.

He shook her hand and hurried out the door. He wandered around the Alamito projects until he spotted a group of young men tossing a football down the middle of the street. As they walked toward him, Diego was disappointed. He could see they were too young. Still, he thought, they might be able to help. He motioned them over.

They ignored him.

He motioned them over again.

One of the young men pointed to him and looked at his friends.

They stepped over and one of them asked, "¿Qué quieres, ese? You need somethin'?"

Diego wrote on his pad. "Look, I'm deaf, and I'm trying to find a friend of mine. His name's Mundo—you know him?" They gathered around the note and stared at it.

"We know lots of Mundos," one of them said.

"The one I'm looking for has a scar over his eyebrow and belongs to the T-Birds. You know that gang?"

They looked at Diego's note and said nothing.

"Look, damn it," he wrote, "I'm not a cop—and I'm not the migra or anything like that. I just need to find him."

They looked at him without saying a word.

"Look," he wrote, "I got five bucks for the guy that can bring him to me. Whoever brings me the Mundo I'm looking for from the T-birds will get the five bucks."

"Make it ten," one of them said.

"I'm not the Juárez Market," Diego wrote, "five bucks."

"Forget it then."

Diego nodded. "All right—ten bucks. Bring him to San Jacinto Plaza. Tell him the deaf guy's looking for him. Tell him *today*."

They read the note and all of them nodded. Diego headed for San Jacinto Plaza and again he waited.

Half an hour later, Diego looked up and saw Mundo standing in front of him. He recognized one of the young kids who was standing next to him. "You lookin' for me, Mr. Diego?" Mundo cocked his head and rubbed his chin.

Diego reached out and shook Mundo's hand. He looked at the kid as he reached into his pocket.

"Don't pay him," Mundo said. "This kid knew exactly where to find me. He just wanted your money—don't give 'em nothin'." He put his hand around the kid's neck and playfully choked him. "He don't need your money, got it? He's only gonna throw it away on some girl who don't give a damn about him."

Diego handed the kid a ten-dollar bill. "A deal's a deal," he wrote.

Mundo motioned the kid to take the money. "Now beat it, and

the next time Diego here needs a favor you don't charge him. You got that?"

The kid nodded and smiled. He strutted away.

Diego watched him go. "Did you teach that kid how to walk like you?"

"You should learn to do it. You drag your feet when you move, see—people don't respect that. But you didn't go lookin' for me to talk about my walk—what's shakin'?"

"I need your help."

"So shoot."

"Help me find a friend."

Mundo looked at him. "So you think I'm some kind of fuckin' private eye?"

"I'm serious. I need to find this friend. Something's happened to her."

"Is she your new woman?"

"No. I don't have a girlfriend. Is that all you think about?"

"You bet. A good street fight and a woman . . . man, that's what it's all about."

Diego shook his head.

"Man, you're so fuckin' straight, Diego. What you gonna do with your life. Too uptight, see?"

"Skip the lecture, Mundo," Diego wrote. "Teach me about life some other time. Right now I have to find my friend. She's been missing since Sunday, maybe even since Saturday."

"How do you know she's missing? People disappear all the damn time, but they always show up again. I got some friends who don't show up for weeks. Don't mean nothin'."

"She didn't show up on Sunday. We were going to meet here at ten, and she never showed."

"Just 'cause a woman don't show don't mean nothin'—they do it all the time. She forgot or she didn't feel like seeing anyone—they're like that. They don't mean nothin' by it."

"No, she didn't forget, and she didn't change her mind. Something happened. I've looked everywhere all morning—I can't find her. Something bad has happened."

"Goddamnit, Diego, look what's happening to you! Your hands are shaking—you can't even write straight. Maybe she's visiting one of her friends or something—or her mother. You worry too damn much."

"Goddamnit! I don't worry too much. Something's happened to her."

"How the hell do you know?"

"I had a dream."

Mundo shook his head as he read the simple statement on Diego's pad. "Man, what's wrong with you? Dreams? You're as bad as the old ladies—"

"You think only women believe in dreams?"

"Look, Diego, everyone has dreams, know what I'm sayin'? I ain't sayin' nothin' bad about dreams, but you don't go lookin' for someone just because you had a dream. That's bullshit. This woman's drivin' you crazy—just relax, we'll have a beer—talk about it."

"Are you going to help me or not?"

"Look, I'll do what I can. But I think she just stood you up."

"Mary wouldn't do that. She's a little crazy, well, she's a lot crazy, but she wouldn't stand me up."

"Her name's Mary? You got yourself a gringa?"

Diego glared at him. "Where do you look for missing people?"

"What does your gringa look like?"

"She's about five-foot-six, has blue eyes, dirty blond hair, wears piles of weird clothes, carries a bag with her all the time. I don't think she has a place where she regularly stays. She lives out on the streets I think—and she thinks she's the Virgin Mary."

Mundo laughed. "I know that pendeja—everybody knows her. She's a fuckin' pain in the ass. What the hell are you doin' hangin' around that pinche broad?"

"She's not a pendeja."

Mundo shook his head. "Look, man, sharp guy like you—she's not worth your time."

Diego got up from the bench and wrote angrily on his pad: "Just forget it. I thought you'd help me. I should have left you in the trash." He ripped the note off his pad and shoved it in Mundo's hand. He walked toward his house, turning his back to

Mundo. Mundo read the note and chased him. He took him by the shoulder and tried to talk into his face. Diego pulled away and kept walking.

Mundo grabbed him again. "Look, Diego, calm down—don't get excited. I didn't know you had such a bad temper."

"I don't have a bad temper," Diego scribbled. "You could piss anybody off."

Mundo threw his hands up. "I didn't say I wouldn't help you. Pinche Diego." He lit a cigarette and offered it to him. Diego shook his head. "Come on, take it—take it."

Diego took it, put it in his mouth, and took a deep drag.

"I'll find her, man—I'll find her." Diego wasn't watching his lips. Mundo touched his arm and made sure Diego watched his lips. "I'll find her, goddamnit."

Diego said nothing. He tried to keep himself from crying.

"Look, just go home, Diego. I'll get back to you. If she's in this pinche city I'll find her. You got the right man for the job. Just wait for me at your place, got it?"

At about four-thirty in the afternoon, Mundo found Diego sitting outside the steps of his apartment. His pallid skin had turned red in the sun. There was a pile of cigarette butts at his feet. The day had grown hot and windless, and the thick smog hung in the air like the cigarette smoke in Vicky's Bar. Through the dense air, the Juárez mountains seemed to have moved farther and farther away. Diego could do nothing to pull them back toward him.

Mundo looked down at Diego but said nothing.

"Did you find her?" he wrote after a while. It wasn't really a question.

Mundo nodded, unable to speak.

"Well?"

"You're not gonna like it—it's not a good scene." Mundo kept shaking his head.

Diego lit another cigarette. He offered one to Mundo. Mundo took it, but did not light it. "Where is she?"

"You really want to know?"

Diego nodded. He stared out at the Juárez mountains.

"It ain't nice—I don't think you really want to see."

Diego wasn't watching his lips. He just stared out at the mountains. "They seem to be getting farther away," he wrote.

Mundo stared at the pad. He sat next to Diego and took him by the shoulder trying to make him look up. "I said it ain't nice. You shouldn't see her—won't change nothin'."

Diego looked at him blankly. He wrote on his pad: "Did you know that Carlota's jewels are buried out in those mountains?"

"Who's Carlota?"

"She was Maximilian's wife—the Empress of Mexico."

Mundo looked at him strangely. "You're goin' crazy, ese—snap out of it."

Diego nodded. "Take me to her."

"You sure? You don't look so good. I don't think you should see her."

"I'm already deaf—but I'm not blind. I can see—I want to see."

Mundo nodded, and lit his cigarette.

They walked toward downtown, both of them dragging their feet. On Santa Fe Street, Mundo noticed a cloud of thick black smoke coming from the south side of downtown. He pointed up, and Diego's eyes followed his fingers. "Let's go check it out."

Diego shrugged his shoulders and followed Mundo. The smoke led them to Sacred Heart Church. When they arrived, the fire engines, policemen, and a silent crowd of watchers all stood in the middle of the street. Firemen raced to put the fire out. Mundo watched Diego as he made the sign of the cross. Out of respect, he bowed his head. Diego searched the faces in the crowd, most of them as silent as he was. He sat next to Crazy Eddie who was sitting on a curb and crying. "What happened?" he wrote.

Crazy Eddie raised his arms, but he let them fall as if they were too heavy for him. "My church—my church has burned down." Diego handed him a handkerchief. Crazy Eddie wiped his tears on the handkerchief, wrapped his arms around himself, and rocked himself on the sidewalk.

"It's OK, Eddie," Diego wrote. "The outside is still standing. Look, it's only the inside that's gone. They'll fix it."

"It's the inside that counts!" he yelled. Diego watched his contorted face. He put his arm on Eddie's shoulder and nodded that it would be all right. Eddie did not believe it.

He stared at the firemen who had put out the last of the flames and were trying to get people away. Some women gathered, some of them crying, others speaking to each other; and the children began playing in the puddles of water left on the street. Everywhere, people's lips began moving. Diego saw one of the cops saying: "All right, it's all over. Everybody go home," but no one moved. Some of the firemen dragged out some of the statues from the church—all of them covered in a black film. The women clapped.

"Hey, the santos survived the fire," Mundo said.

"I didn't know you were religious," Diego wrote.

"Hey, man, I'm religious—made my First Communion and everything. I even got a rosary." He pulled it out of his pocket and showed it to Diego. "See—it goes everywhere I go. Yeah, God saved those santos."

"But he didn't save Mary," Diego wrote.

They walked to the morgue in silence.

 **9**

"I HATE THIS BLIGHT." Jake sat in the kitchen staring out into the darkening San Francisco sky. "It's like a fire that spreads and refuses to go out."

"I hate it, too," Tom said.

"But you're not losing your lover."

"No, I'm not losing my lover." He wanted to comfort this hard man, but there was nothing he could say. And anyway, Jake would refuse to be comforted. Tom felt almost as lost as the man sitting next to him—and angry, but he knew Jake would not be the one to listen to him or even see that other people were losing Joaquin, too. For a minute, he hated Jake for isolating himself and all the resentments came flooding back into his body. But Jake had built walls around himself all his life—he had always been like that, lived like that, made a virtue out of living like some goddamned cowboy in a movie. But hadn't he been taught to do that—hadn't they all? To be alone in grief was to be strong. Tom did not want to be alone, did not want to be strong. Jake stared out the window. Tom stared at Jake. Sometimes, I hate being a man, Tom thought. Whoever invented it should be shot.

"Is life simple for anyone?" Jake asked. His question hung in the air like the evening rain. He looked at Tom.

"Is life supposed to be simple, Jake?"

"Maybe for some—don't you think?"

"Everybody gets to stop breathing some day. Is that simple enough?"

"We're talking past each other."

"Yes," Tom smiled, "we always have."

"What will happen now?"

Tom shrugged his shoulders.

"Joaquin's the only thing you and I have in common, Tom."

"That isn't true."

"Isn't it, Tom? He's the only thing that comes between me and chaos. He always mediated our—our—whatever it is we have."

"Why can't you call it a friendship?"

"Is that what it is?"

Tom wanted to tell him he was an ass. He wouldn't. Not tonight. "You're very hard sometimes," he said. He looked at Jake with a look that almost resembled disgust. "Tell me something, why do you find it so difficult to belong?"

"Belong to what?"

"Never mind—it doesn't matter."

"Want some coffee?"

Tom nodded.

He got up, ground some coffee, and put on the kettle.

"I love him, too," Tom whispered.

"Did you say something?" Jake asked.

"I said I love him, too."

"I could have lived without hearing that," Jake said.

"I could not have lived without saying it."

Lizzie walked into the room. She stared at the two men. No one said anything. They pretended they had not been talking—and Lizzie pretended she had not heard the last part of their conversation. They all waited for the coffee in silence, each one separate, isolated, alone as if they had told each other there could be no touching. Jake thought of nothing but the great sadness of his life. There was nothing now, that is all he thought, and suddenly he decided that after Joaquin took his last breath, he would drive to the Golden Gate Bridge and take a plunge. He pictured himself dead before he hit the water like the heron in his dream. Tom tried to keep from howling, tried to keep from hating Jake, hating him not only because he was so hard and self-centered, but because he would learn nothing from this, he would be as isolated and ignorant about the world he lived in as he ever was. Jake was incapable of learning anything. Jake was capable of feeling—what was that? What was feeling without thought?—I feel bad, I feel good, I feel sad. Was that what living was? What was great about that? All Jake could do was feel, and he hated him for that. Without wanting or needing to, Lizzie could hear what they were saying to themselves. And since she overheard, she could not stop herself from intervening. "You won't," she said.

They both looked at her.

"What?" Jake asked.

"You won't jump off that bridge," she said. "I'll chain you to your bed if I have to, but you're not taking a dive—not tonight—not ever."

Jake stared at her. "How did you—"

"Shut up," she said, "I'm talking. And you," she said turning to Tom. "You will stop being angry with Jake. You will stop hating him. Tonight, we will respect the dying. All you can think of is your own grief—is that all? There's a man in the other room—and he is dying. Why aren't you thinking of him—of him, damnit—him! And I want a cup of coffee."

Jake served her a cup immediately. She took a sip of the hot, bitter liquid. It was strong, she thought. She stared at the two men in the room. "I'm sorry," she said, then smiled. No one spoke. Jake served Tom a cup of coffee. He squeezed the doctor's shoulder.

Lizzie felt Joaquin's heartbeat as she sat quietly drinking her coffee. The two men said nothing. There was so little to say. Lizzie felt Joaquin's heartbeat grow weaker, felt him struggle for each breath. He thought of nothing now—only of taking one more breath. The world and the people in this room were no longer his business. Then she felt a terror, as if his body had become her body, and his body had decided to wage one final battle before retreating, run one final race before resting. She felt her own heart racing as if she were running the final race with him. He was young and he was walking toward the edge of the river, and he was with others, and there was a woman there. *Mama.* She smiled at him, at who? At her? She was there, she could see. The river was cold and it was night and he was crossing the river—is this the end of the word?—and suddenly the waters came over him, he was sinking, his heart was racing, could no longer breathe, it was going to burst, his heart, her heart—it—they—were going to burst. Lizzie felt the coldness of the water and the taste of a snowflake in her mouth. She felt afraid, could not breathe. She had never been this close to anyone, not like this, never like this. She grabbed Tom's arm. "What is it, Liz?" he asked. She looked sick and frightened and far away and it seemed as if she were dying.

Lizzie took a deep breath. She looked at Jake. "He's going," she said. "Jake, he's going."

Jake and Tom ran out of the kitchen, not out of any real belief in Lizzie's words, but out of instinct. They were irrational animals running without knowing why, running because they were afraid, running because it was all they knew how to do now, and they had become all instinct. Mr. and Mrs. Sha, and Tom's lover, Rick, who had been sitting in the living room talking and keeping vigil ran into the room after them—they too ran out of instinct like a crowd running together toward an unknown goal, something leading them in the same direction like lost pilgrims in search of an altar or anything that would pass for a shrine. Jake grabbed Joaquin from the bed and picked him up. He sat on the chair and held his fragile body in his arms. "It's OK, J. You can let go. You can let go now. I'm here. You can let go." Jake heard himself speak the words he had sworn he would never speak. Tom watched them, his grief too great, too heavy to allow him to move. Joaquin' breathing filled the room. There was nothing in the house except Joaquin's breathing, just his breathing and this handful of people who sat—motionless— motionless because movement seemed so futile, so insignificant— and their communion was delicate because the man who had brought them together was leaving them, and perhaps after his passing they would no longer belong to each other. There was nothing, nothing but his breathing, nothing else. And then there was quiet. And no one noticed the room was dark and that the candle had gone out. There was only this silence and this darkness and then suddenly, one by one, the room was full of their sobs.

In the kitchen, Lizzie heard Jake's words: *"You can let go now, J."* She felt herself floating away. She saw her body sitting limp and lifeless on the chair. She felt Joaquin's passing in her body, a nothingness with no point of reference. There could be no point of reference. There was a space within her, and yet she was nothing but space. And there was a freedom. It was not nothing—she knew it was not nothing. Tom walked into the room and touched her lifeless body. She looked up at him from her chair. "Are you OK?" he asked.

She nodded.

"I could have sworn you were dead when I touched your arm." He shook his head and stared at her. He looked frightened.

"Tom?"

"Your hair," he said.

"What?"

"It's white."

She nodded. "I felt him. When he died. I felt him when he died." she said, her voice beyond any sadness. "His candle went out." She took his arm. "Don't be afraid." Lizzie's voice helped calm him, but he trembled as if he were cold. She rose from the chair and held him. She sat him down on a chair and handed him a whiskey. "Drink it," she said. He poured down the drink. Lizzie walked into Joaquin's bedroom, and stared at Jake sobbing into his dead lover's body. "It's time to give him up," she said softly. She gently took the dead man out of Jake's arms. Mrs. Sha was beside her helping to carry him. They placed him softly on the bed. Lizzie felt strong. She'd never imagined her body could feel this way. Mr. Sha covered him with a clean white sheet. She relit the candle that had gone out and placed it on the nightstand next to his body. She led Jake out of the room. Tom thought it odd and stupid and unnecessary to pronounce him dead, but it was his job, and somehow, despite the heaviness he felt, he called the coroner and gave him the appropriate information, the time of the death, the cause. It was official, and yes, he would contact the funeral home. But he waited for that. He would call them later. He sat a while in his friend's room. Of all the men he had seen die, of all the men he had buried, this one cut him, cut him deeply and he felt himself bleeding. "I'm not even forty," he said to himself "and I have known too many deaths." He was fighting despair, a despair that wanted to claim him—but he fought it. He fought it, and wondered why.

Tom sat and sipped a cup of coffee in the living room. His lover sat next to him saying nothing. It was as if there was so little air in the room that no one spoke in order to preserve the little oxygen there was. Jake sat on a rocking chair—close to Tom. Mr. and Mrs. Sha sat quietly on the couch drinking tea. Mrs. Sha wept silently. Lizzie thought it was odd she made no noise. Lizzie ached for someone to break the silence. Jake said nothing, just looked down at the floor. In the dim light, his hair looked darker, and he looked much younger—like a boy. Lizzie stared at him. He looked exactly like someone she knew. She stared at him for a long time, then suddenly looked at the picture on the piano. "Oh my God!" she yelled. "Oh my God! Every day in front of my nose, every damn day and I— Oh my God, Lizzie, you idiot—you're a such an idiot!" She banged her open hand on the piano.

Tom looked up at her as if to say, *What now? Your hair has turned white, we have lost our Joaquin, we have fought with each other and ourselves and outside it is the coldest day of the new year and we are too tired to say or do or think anything. What more—is there more?* Jake didn't seem to hear her at all.

"Jake?" she said. "Jake!"

He looked up as if to ask why she was yelling. He wore the same look as Tom. What more?

"Jake—what's your last name?"

He stared at her blankly. "Marsh," he heard himself say. "What a stupid question to be asking." He looked at her strangely, almost disapprovingly. "You've practically lived here for months and months—and you don't know my last name?"

"I never thought about it. We didn't discuss your name or your life, did we? How often did we talk about ourselves? I'm such an idiot."

He looked at her blankly. "What difference does it make? It's just a name."

"No, it's not just a name."

"What are you getting so excited about, Lizzie? I'm tired. What does it matter? If it makes you feel any better, I don't know your last name either. You're Lizzie, that's who you are. What's a god-damned last name?" He leaned over and placed his head between his hands. "Lizzie," he said almost without emotion, "you're hyster-ical. Is it our turn to calm you down? Is this your way of helping us deal with grief?"

"Edwards," she said, "My last name is Edwards." She smiled, then broke out laughing.

"Why do you look happy?" Tom asked. "It's a strange time to look so happy."

"Jake," she said almost yelling, her heart beating as fast as the wings of a hummingbird, "I know your brother."

"What?"

"Your brother. All this time, I've been sitting here—and me a seer—and I couldn't see—I know your brother."

"Yes, you said that," Tom said.

They both stared at her.

"I can't take this, Lizzie," Jake said. "Don't do this—"

She stuck out her hand and pointed her open palm at Jake. "Wait," she said. She grabbed his picture. "I kept staring at this picture—he looked so familiar. Of course he's not this young any-more—he's thirty. And nobody calls him Jon-Jon, and nobody calls him Jonathan. I didn't know his name was Jonathan. I know him only as Eddie. Eddie Marsh—the sweetest man I've ever met."

"When's his birthday?"

She knew why he asked. She smiled knowingly. "November 22, 1963. John Kennedy."

"John Kennedy," he repeated softly. Jake clenched his teeth. The thought occurred to him that he had lost his mind, that he had died along with Joaquin, and had gone to hell and Lizzie had become the devil and would tempt him with news of his brother forever. But he knew he was sitting in the same room he had sat in for the last ten years. He wanted to ask Joaquin what to do, he wanted to tell him: I have found my brother, I have found him. He is alive— but Joaquin was not there, Joaquin was not alive, could not hear, could not see the great reunion. Was this true? Was this strange woman telling him the truth? Who was she? Where did she come from? He knew nothing about her, really. Could it be? After all this time, was this woman sent to bring him his brother? He was lost now, he knew he had gone completely mad. He remembered reading about his parents' death in the newspaper. He had felt like this, devastated and elated all at once, and all he wanted to do was wander outside and live as homeless and confused as he felt, and be away from anybody who even pretended to treat him like a human being. A human being? What was that, anyway? He stared at his skin. Joaquin had told him that his skin was everything. *"It's white, Jake, and it will always be white, and mine is not, and that is what we are,"* but he had spoken those words in anger because someone had called him a spic, and he had been hurt. Joaquin? Joaquin, why are you dead? He was suddenly cold and he wanted to be warm and yet he felt he would never be warm again; who was hot enough to thaw his frozen skin? He knew sounds were coming out of his mouth because he felt something, his own sounds, but he was not speaking a language. He looked at Lizzie. He had known her less than a year and yet he believed in her compassion, had grown to rely on it. He kept his eyes on her, and they calmed him and so he felt himself stop his screaming. But he wanted to yell more, yell and yell and yell in grief for his dead Joaquin, the only person who had ever made him shake like a leaf in the wind out of pure love, and yet he believed what this woman had said, believed she had found his brother, and so he wanted to shout "I have found him, I have found him." Lizzie grew dim, he couldn't see her. It was as if he was looking through a windshield in a rainstorm. He heard himself howling, he felt the noises he was making. He could not stop the howling that came from within him.

Jake felt Tom's arms around him. He did not have the strength to push him away. He was unable to speak for a long time. Finally, he found the words, and speaking them he felt he had regained his intelligence. "Call him," Jake said softly. "Tell him his brother needs him."

 **10**

THE DETECTIVE at the morgue uncovered the body and looked at Diego. "You know her?" His voice was as aggressive as his movements.

"Yeah, he knows her," Mundo answered. "I already told you that, man, can't you speak English?"

The detective ignored Mundo and continued staring at Diego. Diego looked up at the tall, graying man and nodded.

He stared at Diego with straightforward gray eyes. "What's her name?"

"I already told you that," Mundo said. "Goddamnit, her name's Mary."

Diego grabbed Mundo's shoulder and put his finger on his lip. "Her name's Mary," he wrote. "I'm deaf."

"Yeah, I told him already," Mundo answered.

"Mary what? Does she have a last name?"

Diego thought a minute. "Ramirez," he wrote.

Mundo stared at him.

"Ramirez?" the detective asked. "She doesn't look Hispanic to me."

Mundo clicked his fingers. "She ain't Hispanic, man, she's a Chicana, you know? A Chicana—what the fuck's a Hispanic?" He clicked his fingers again and did a dance.

The detective stared at him. "I'm talking to your friend. And this is a morgue not a dance floor." He looked at Diego again. "She doesn't look Mexican to me. Does she look Mexican to you?"

"Hey, you're harassing him," Mundo said, "chill out."

"Her husband's name was Ramirez," Diego wrote.

"Where is he now?"

"No one knows. He took off years ago."

"How many years?"

"Ten, fifteen—hard to say. She didn't talk about him much."

The detective looked hard at his handwriting. "Where did she live?"

"She didn't have a home. She lived on the streets. I don't really know, I thought she might have lived somewhere. She never talked about it."

"I thought you were friends?"

"She kept secrets."

The detective shook his head, a hint of disgust in his expression. "Secrets, huh? Can you tell me anything about her?"

"Not much really," he wrote. He stared at the dry blood on Mary's skin, her ripped clothes, the yellow dress with white flowers. He took a deep breath.

"Are you gonna be all right?" Mundo looked at the detective. "Go easy."

Diego placed his hand over his eyes. Mundo moved next to him and shook him softly. "You gonna be all right?"

"I'll be all right," He wrote, "I'm fine."

"Was she a prostitute?"

Diego clenched his teeth and glared at the detective. He pointed his jaw at him as if it were a dart, an arrow about to be let loose. He dropped his pad on the floor. The detective reached down, picked it up for him, and handed it back to him. "Can you tell me anything else?"

"I don't think she had any relatives," Diego wrote. "No children that I know of. She carried a bag with all her clothes. She had a box with a new hat in it, a white hat with yellow flowers. She was supposed to meet me on Sunday morning. We were going to Mass together—she was my girlfriend—and she wasn't a prostitute."

The detective read Diego's note and nodded. "But you can't be sure she didn't have a family."

Diego shrugged his shoulders.

The detective looked at him with his harsh gray eyes. "What's your name?"

"Juan Diego Ramirez."

He rubbed his thumb against his lip. "What a coincidence," he said, "you have the same last name as she does." He smiled.

"I hate your pinche smile," Mundo growled. "It's making me sick. I get violent when I get sick."

The detective smiled more deliberately.

"A lot of Ramirezes in this town, wouldn't you say?" Diego handed him the note.

The detective nodded. "I guess there are. Still, it's an odd coincidence, don't you think?"

"You callin' my friend a liar?" Mundo gave him a threatening stare. "Like you say, it's a coincidence. These things happen all the time. I never ask a woman her last name before I go out with her, you know? Don't care if she has my last name or not—don't give a damn—y ya no chingues."

"Speak English," the detective said as he moved his thumb away from his lip.

"Be careful, Mr. Dick-tective, I could make you look like Mary here. You want to lie next to her, frozen with that smile of yours?"

Diego took Mundo by the shoulder and shook his head. He wrote firmly on his pad. "Look, sir, if you don't believe me, then that's your business. If you think I killed her or that I have some kind of reason to lie about this, then you have a right to your suspicions— I suppose that it comes with the badge. But I've told you everything I know and now it's my turn to ask a few questions. How did she die? Who did this? Where did you find her? Who did this to my Mary?" He placed the note firmly in the detective's hands.

"You talk an awful lot for a deaf guy, don't you?"

"I'm gonna bust your fuckin' face, dickhead." Mundo tightened his fingers into a claw, then clenched them into a fist.

"And I'm gonna throw your ass in jail. I know all about you—

I'm sick of dealing with your types. All you do is litter up the streets. I'm going on a cleanup campaign."

"Go ahead, baboso," Mundo yelled, "throw my ass in jail. I've been there before, but I've never been there for knifing a cop. If I'm gonna go, I'm gonna go happy."

The detective smiled and put his thumb on his lip.

Diego shoved a note in the detective's face. "What happened to Mary? It's your job to find out."

The detective's face turned red, then white again as he flipped the note to the ground. "They raped her. They raped her and then they stabbed her. Looks like more than one man. They found her body in an alley—downtown. She was wearing that hat you just described."

Diego nodded. He couldn't control the tears welling up in his eyes. He must've made some kind of noise because both the detective and Mundo stared at him. He took Mary's hand and rubbed his tears into her cold skin.

"Hey, Diego, chill out—calmate." Mundo turned Diego toward him, making sure he could see his lips. "She's not gonna wake up, man. Those bastards that killed her, they're gonna rot in pinche hell."

Diego stood still, unmoving, stood as though he would never move again.

The detective looked at Diego carefully. "Look Mr. Ramirez, I know this stinks—it stinks to high heaven. Look, I believe you. I know this is hard—I don't know if we'll find out who did this. It could have been anybody—the streets just aren't safe anymore." He looked at Mundo. "Look, you can go by and pick up her personal effects at the station. I have her bag and her hat, just like you said. You can come by and pick up the stuff. Just come and sign for her things. We won't be needing them." He paused and looked back at Diego. "Can you arrange a funeral for her? If you can't, I know who you can talk to at the county office."

"I can handle it," Diego wrote. "I got someone who can help."

The detective slapped him softly on the back. "Take a piece of advice: Stop hanging around with your sidekick—you don't need him. You keep hanging out with him and there's gonna be a lot more trouble coming your way." He walked out of the room. Mundo flipped him the finger as he walked past him.

"Mary used to do things like that," Diego thought, "crazy gringa."

"You're crazy, Mundo," he wrote. "Why do you always have to threaten people?"

"Control makes me crazy," he laughed. "So, where to now? You look like you could use a drink."

"I have a plan," Diego wrote.

"What plan?"

"First of all, we have to find the nurse, Carolyn, at the clinic. I bet she can arrange a funeral. After that I have to talk to Gonzalo and ask if he'll give me some time off."

Mundo looked at him and nodded. "You go to a lot of trouble for your friends, don't you?"

"I don't have too many of them."

"Is that why you gave La Mary your name?"

"What was I supposed to say to that cop? Was I supposed to tell him she was the Virgin Mary? Anyway, why should she die without a last name? Why shouldn't she have a decent funeral? She never hurt anybody."

The nurse agreed to arrange the funeral. "We have a social worker that knows all the ropes," she said, "I'm sure it won't be too difficult. I can arrange something."

Mundo smiled at her. "I bet you can arrange a lot of things."

She looked at Diego. "How come you hang around with this dirtbag?"

Diego shrugged his shoulders and wrote, "He's all right. If you knew him, you'd like him, too."

The nurse smiled. "If you come back tomorrow by noon, I can let you know what we've been able to arrange, OK, Diego? Go home and get some rest—you look like you could use some sleep."

"And you make sure to get a Mass? We need to have a funeral Mass. Maybe at St. Patrick's—Sacred Heart burned down today."

"I know," she said, "the whole barrio's buzzing about it."

He smiled at her and slowly walked out the door. He headed for Vicky's Bar. Mundo followed him out the door.

"And when we get to Vicky's," Diego wrote, "let me do all the talking. You handle my boss like you handled the detective, and I'll be out of a job. Just promise me you won't say anything unless I tell you."

"Yeah, yeah, I promise—whatever you say. You're the boss."

Diego wanted to throw up at the smell and the darkness as they entered Vicky's Bar. His boss was busy cleaning up for the evening shift. He looked up and stared at Mundo and Diego. He walked up to the bar with a frown on his face and found a pad. "I thought you were sick."

Diego shook his head.

"His friend died. Somebody killed her. Diego here's not doing too good. You know how that goes, right?"

Diego's boss gave Mundo a cold stare. "I thought I told you to keep out of my place." He pointed toward the door. "Get out!"

Diego wrote on his pad. "Why do you want him to leave? He's my friend."

His boss read the writing and began to write something. Diego grabbed his arm gently and pointed to his lips. His boss looked at him oddly.

Diego looked at Mundo and nodded. "He can read lips," Mundo said.

"You been making a pendejo out of me all these years? You get your rocks off making me look like an asshole? I ought to fire your deaf ass."

Diego shrugged his shoulders and bowed his head.

"Finish cleaning this place up," he said as he handed him a wet cloth. "People will be coming in for their evening drinks and I haven't even had time to set up the bar yet."

Diego shook his head. He put the dirty rag on the table next to him. "I'm not working today," he wrote.

His boss picked up the rag and threw it across the room. "God-damnit! You want to eat, then get to work."

Diego shook his head. "I need the rest of the week off. A friend of mine died. I'm sick."

His boss read the note, paused and broke out laughing. "A week off?" He laughed again. "I'm gonna tell you what, Diego, you don't show up tomorrow morning, and you're fired. You got that?"

Diego nodded. "Well then, will you at least let me off for my friend's funeral?"

The boss shook his head as he read the note. "You already took one day, and you even lied about it. I give you weekends off, don't I?"

Diego nodded.

"Well, schedule your funeral on the weekend. Come in the rest of the week like usual and just forget about the whole thing. Drop it, and I'll drop the little detail of you not letting me know about you being able to read lips."

"I need to go the funeral," he wrote. "It's very important to me."

"If it ain't your own, then you don't need to be there."

"I'm going anyway."

"You go, and you're fired."

"It's just for half a day."

Mundo kept looking over Diego's shoulder to see what he was writing. "Tell that asshole to shove his job up his ass." Diego wasn't watching his lips but he saw his boss yelling at Mundo. "Get the hell out of my place you sonofabitch, good for nothing, cabrón marijuano."

Diego looked at Mundo. "Quit!" Mundo yelled.

He looked at his boss. "I need the job," he wrote.

"You fucking right you need the job," he said. "And don't ever bring your friend with you again. What the hell are you doing hanging out with people like that? And be here tomorrow."

Mundo spoke into Diego's face. "Tell him to shove his fuckin' job."

Diego stood motionless, not knowing what to do. He wanted to throw a chair at his boss; he wanted to sit himself down and be a customer and drink himself into unconsciousness—but he needed the job—what would he do? Who would hire a deaf-mute with a high school education? What could he put on a job application? "I'm deaf. I went to high school. I can read lips, but I know a lot because I'm an eavesdropper and because I go to the library and read things. I can make Mexican food and mop a floor." He kept staring at his feet. He looked up at his boss, who was waiting for an answer.

"I loved my friend," he wrote. "I think you're cruel."

His boss put his arms around the back of his head and stretched out. Diego hadn't expected to change his mind, but he hadn't expected him to be this hard—not even him. "So I'm not St. Francis," he told Diego. "But then, you already knew that, didn't you? I don't pay you enough to like me—I just pay you enough to eat. And that's why you're still here, isn't it?"

Mundo reached for him and took a swing, just missing him. He glared at Mundo and made a fist.

"Come on, you silly bastard, let's have at it!" Mundo began dancing in circles around Diego's boss. "Come on, take a swing—I'd love to kick your ass from here to Albuquerque."

"Go ahead and take a swing at me. Just one swing and you're in jail and your friend, Diego, is out of a job."

Diego pulled at Mundo's arm. He motioned him to stop. He looked at his boss, a big man, tall, a hard face. Diego hated him. "I'll be here tomorrow," he wrote, but before he handed him the note, Mundo grabbed it and crumpled it up. He jumped in front of Diego's boss and grabbed him by the collar and yelled something in his face. Both of them clenched their jaws and they remained frozen for a few seconds. Mundo pushed him to the floor, but before Mundo could kick him, Diego stepped in between them.

Mundo smiled, then laughed. "It's all right, Mr. Diego, I'm not gonna hurt the sonofabitch." He stared down at Diego's boss who was lying on the floor. Mundo kept his eyes on him, smiling, and spoke calmly. Diego saw the quiet expression on Mundo's face, totally in control, almost peaceful. "Señor Asshole, I'm gonna tell you something—are you listening? My friend, Diego, is taking the rest of the week off, see? He's gotta take care of some personal

306

business, got it? Who knows, he might even visit our friends at the IRS or something and find out what he can do about a pinche boss who don't pay no minimum wage or nothin'—but he might not, got that?—you never know. He'll be back next Monday and his job better be waiting for him, and if it's not, well then I'm gonna burn your fuckin' place to the ground. If you don't believe me, just wait and see. And after I burn this hellhole I'm gonna find out where you live, and I'm gonna burn your house, too—with you in it. You got that? You like pushing people around, you like to play hardball. Well, me too—I'm a pinche all-American." He ripped his shirt open and showed off the scar on his side. "See this? The bastards tried to kill me, and I didn't die. I'm hard to kill. It's like this: You ain't no St. Francis, and I ain't no St. Francis neither."

He looked at Diego and smiled. "Let's go, Diego." He looked down at the bitter face staring up at him. "Diego here will see you next week. Come Monday, if he's still got a job, you'll never see me again. If he don't, well, Vicky's Blue Bar is history." He jerked his head toward the door, and strutted out. Diego followed him.

Mundo walked toward the 7-Eleven across the street, his shirt open, his chest bared to the sun. Diego could hardly keep up with him and had to chase him into the store. Mundo bought a six-pack of beer and a pack of cigarettes. Diego wrote him a note while he paid for his goods. "You promised me you'd control yourself."

"No harm done—you got the week, didn't you?"

Diego nodded. "Yeah, but it was a hell of a way to get it."

"People don't listen when you beg. People who beg are invisible—just ask the beggars on the street."

The man at the counter put the beer in a bag and handed Mundo his change. "I know a place where we could drink our beer," Diego wrote.

"Lead the way. You're the man in charge."

"Like hell," Diego wrote.

 **11**

WHEN LIZZIE'S VOICE had disappeared and Eddie heard only the dull, motonous tone of the dead phone, he sat in the quiet of his office. He felt dizzy, the room spinning around him. He put his head on the desk. The room slowed down. He felt sick. He reached for his trash can and tasted the watery salt in his mouth. He felt his stomach go into spasms. He stared at his own vomit in the trash can. He stood up and walked around the room. "An office," he said, "why do I have an office?" His father had had an office. Now, he had one, too. He laughed. He remembered the day he and his brother had accidentally broken his father's lamp because they'd been running and running around his desk. His father had hit them both with a belt. "*A man's office is not a place of play.*" Eddie remembered the day his older brother had sat on his bed and promised him everything would be all right. It was the last time he'd seen him. Seven years old. Now he was thirty. For twenty-three years he had thought of his older brother. He had become addicted to thinking of him. Now, he was afraid. What if they had nothing to say to each other? What if there was nothing left between them? He felt numb and paralyzed and tired. He sat back down on his chair and turned off the light.

He sat in the darkness for a long time. In his mind his brother had been good; he had been a strong, protecting angel; he had loved him and been faithful to his memory. And now, on this cold January night, it was time to meet his brother, not the brother to whom he had addressed his journal, but the brother he did not know, *that* brother, the brother who was a body and mind and a heart, a heart that had been beating without him for twenty-three years. But there had been a death, so then why was there this life? His brother would be grieving, and what good could he—a stranger—do him? What words were there for him from a man who would show up at his door saying, "I am your brother and this is my wife. She is beautiful, and this is my son, who is also beautiful—do you see all that I have? I am a lucky and fortunate man, and fate has smiled on me, do you see?" Would that comfort his brother? Would his presence remind him how poor and cursed his life had been—he with a dead lover and a grieving heart? How could he go to him like this? He's going to hate me. My brother doesn't know me. I don't know my brother. Maybe they would just look at each other and turn away in disappointment and say to themselves in tired voices: "This is not the one I have been waiting for—he is not the one." What then? What would happen then? He remembered Jake sitting on his bed that last evening when he'd been so sick, and he had promised he would make everything OK—had he promised that?—or had Eddie only made that up? What had happened, what had really happened? He had written a script with the information he had, but most of it was fiction, and like all fiction, it was as powerful as any truth and he had mistaken it for truth. Yes, this was the way history was written, his and his brother's and the world's. He felt sick and heavy, and yet his brother was alive. It was true, the brother who was lost, who perhaps had been wandering the country homeless and poor and had fought many demons only to find more demons, who was tired—but who had survived all the tempests. His brother was alive. He was alive. Or was Eddie having a dream? He would wake up any minute and find himself in his bed and ask his wife, "Have you seen my brother?" and she would look at him oddly but with compassion and say, "Amor, it was only a dream." Eddie felt the weight of the disappointment. But he was here in his office and it did not feel like a dream, and he felt the weight, the weight of a loss he had known for years and years and years—and now the weight was about to be lifted. He walked into the bedroom. His wife was dressing herself. "What are you doing?" he asked.

"I'm getting dressed. I'm going with you."

"What?"

She looked at him. "You're in shock, amor. I'll drive."

"What about the baby?"

"The baby's going with us."

"We'll wake him?"

"Well, he'll learn early that life has its interruptions. Someday you can tell him about this night, and you will tell him that he was there. You can begin the story by saying to him, "One cold winter night, your Aunt Lizzie called us up to say . . ." She smiled at him. "Get dressed."

Eddie looked completely lost, confused, disoriented. He was glad to be told what to do. "What should I wear?" he asked blankly.

She smiled at him, went to his closet and picked out a deep blue pullover sweater. "Here," she said handing it to him, "you look beautiful in this." She sat next to him on the bed. As she held him, she could hear his heart beating. "You're trembling, amor."

"Yes."

"Be happy, corazón."

"Am I dreaming?"

She placed her hand on his cheek. "Do you feel this hand?"

He nodded.

"It will be good," she said.

"How do you know?"

"I know."

"I don't want to go."

"You're crying."

"What if he doesn't want me there."

"He told Lizzie, 'Tell him his brother needs him.' Those were his words."

"Did he really?"

"Yes, really."

He took a deep breath. He felt cold. "It will be good?"

"It will be good."

He watched her bundle the baby and pack a few diapers in a bag

310

she used for him. He was getting bigger and bigger every day. She picked him up. He cried. "Shhhhh." She placed the baby in his father's hands. "Make him calm," she said to her son.

Jake and Joaquin's apartment had emptied of people. The Shas prayed over Joaquin's body once more before they left. Mrs. Sha expressed the feeling that Joaquin's spirit had brought the two brothers together because his love had been so great. He had conjured the Chinese wind, and that wind had blown them together. Mrs. Cantor, who claimed to have felt Joaquin's passing had shown up at the door a few moments after Lizzie had called Eddie and Maria Elena. Tom explained what had occurred as simply and succinctly as he could. "But of course," Mrs. Cantor said, "it was like this in the old country. Things like this happened all the time, and no one thought anything about it. Perhaps the old times are returning," she said. "It's a sign. Elijah," she whispered, "Elijah may yet come—but probably he won't show up in San Francisco." Tom smiled at her, and she insisted on praying a very short kaddish in praise of God and for her friend though she said it wasn't orthodox. Even Jake was moved by her prayers in Hebrew. She promptly served everybody a glass of wine. "It's good to toast the dead," she said. And so they drank to Joaquin. Tom listened intently to the mourners and their theories. He only knew that Lizzie's hair had turned white and that she had a gift. His culture gave him no entry, no access into the evening's happenings. His father had been a rationalist in the extreme, but it did not prevent him from being moved by the evening's events and the voices of the people in the room. Coincidence, Tom thought to himself, the coincidence of Lizzie knowing two men who happened to be brothers—that was all. On the other hand, there was the matter of Lizzie's white hair, and her out-of-body experiences and her being able to read minds, however unsystematically. Tom neither dismissed her experiences nor theorized about them. He merely sat there and breathed in the evening just as he would take in the salt air when he walked on the beach. Breathing it made him feel clean. He was sad and exhilarated, sad and exhausted—and yet somehow he felt he could go without sleep for days. And he knew he would never forget anything about this night, and the people who were present, and what he had felt. He would keep this night and honor it just as he kept his parents' photograph in his house.

One by one, the visitors left despite the urge they felt to see and touch the lost brother. They were embarrassed enough by their voyeurism to excuse themselves. Tom stayed because he was waiting for the funeral home to come and pick up Joaquin's body—it was something practical he could do. And, for some inexplicable reason, Jake had asked him and Lizzie to stay behind and be with him because he didn't want to be alone with Joaquin's body, and because he wanted to be with someone when he met his brother: "Stay. Just in case."

Lizzie answered the door to Jake and Joaquin's apartment before the doorbell rang. "I thought you'd take longer."

"Oh my God, Lizzie! Your hair—what in the hell happened to your hair? It's white! You dyed your hair white!"

Eddie only half-listened to his wife. He looked frightened and fragile, and didn't seem to be affected by the color of Lizzie's hair.

"I didn't dye it. You think I'm crazy? It's a long story."

"I'll bet. You know everything's beginning to be a long story with you, Lizzie. And to think I liked you so much because you were so uncomplicated. Are you going to let us in?"

Eddie was beginning to turn as white as Lizzie's hair. He wiped his sweaty palms on the thighs of his pants.

"Are you all right?" Lizzie asked.

He shrugged.

She took him by the arm and led him inside.

He looked at the comfortable living room.

"Jake's in the shower," she said. "He was nervous, and suddenly he had to take a shower. Poor man, he's been through hell, and I picked a helluva time to put two and two together, didn't I?"

Eddie nodded despondently.

She shook her head as she watched this man in front of her who had become deaf and dumb. She looked at Maria Elena and took the baby from her arms. "I'll take him," she said. "Oh, look at you, such a pretty boy, and so good."

Eddie stepped into the room and stared at the man sitting on a chair. The man smiled at him. "I'm Tom," he said, "I'm a friend of your brother."

"And his doctor," Lizzie added.

"I don't know why that matters," he said, "unless, of course, you feel ill."

Eddie managed an awkward smile. "My name's Eddie," he said.

"The young man in the picture," Tom said.

"The picture?"

"Yes, the picture." He pointed at the piano.

Maria Elena picked it up and stared at it. He had changed a great deal—and yet he hadn't. It was clearly her husband. She had memorized his eyes that were at once happy and sad, and she immediately recognized that familiar half-smile that sometimes made it so difficult to tell whether he was happy or angry or melancholy or aloof. She handed the photo to Eddie. Eddie stared at the boy. "I look sad," he said. "I was sad." He handed the photo back to his wife. He clenched his jaw shut as if by doing so he could prevent himself from feeling or remembering.

Eddie looked up, and across the room, he saw a man wearing jeans and a black sweater. He was standing in the entryway between the hall and the living room, standing and staring as if he were lost in a strange place. He might have been eighteen with his fine blond hair and muscular body, eighteen and on a football team and ready to carry a little boy of seven on his shoulders through a large house. The man's gaze was steady and straight. Eddie wanted to pronounce the man's name. It was him, it was true, but he couldn't speak as if he were in one of his own dreams where he became paralyzed and couldn't move or yell for help. Maria Elena watched her husband. She wanted to hold him, yet knew this was not a time for her to be with him. This was not her place, her moment—she would have to refrain from touching him. She moved closer to Lizzie and grabbed her arm as if it were the only thing that kept her from falling off the earth. Eddie clenched and unclenched his fists, then tried to smile, his lips quivering, and he thinking of nothing except his brother's name. And Tom watching Jake watch his brother. And Tom thinking: "I have never seen a face that was breaking with joy, and now I have seen it and seen it on the face of the angriest man I have ever known, and so this must be a miracle." And Jake thinking of this boy whom he had wondered about for years, this boy who was no longer a boy, this boy who had become a man he could no longer carry on his shoulders, a man—twenty-three years, a lifetime, and he was standing in his house, and he did not know if his tears were for his grief or because suddenly there was no grief. And for a moment he hated his parents more than he had ever hated them because it was they who had prevented them from being brothers as if they could not stand any kind of love whatsoever because they were sick and envious and greedy and so they had to put a stop to the affection their sons shared. He hated them, and yet that hate, furious as it was, passed quickly and silently because the man in front of him demanded his attention and there was no room for that hate—not now, and so he let that hate fall away and he felt light and weighed no more than his hair. He felt his teeth chattering, and so he placed his hands over his mouth and he yelled into them, and then he breathed into them as if he could catch everything that was coming out of him. And Lizzie, thanking her brother for giving her a gift, a brother she, too, had been separated from because a man who masqueraded as a father had decided that only one of them was worthy of recognition and so banished the other. So she crushed her father and spoke her brother's name with respect though he had died hated and alone and exiled, and she thanked him for giving these two men to each other, and feeling the iron grasp of Maria Elena's fist, she put the baby down because he was sleeping and she held the woman whom she loved as much as she loved life itself. And Maria Elena knowing that life would never be the same. And all of them thinking that this was the end of the world, and all of them wondering if this silence could ever be surpassed or ever be broken. And Eddie thinking: "If only I can say his name, if only I can make myself speak it, if only—then I will know" And then finally taking a deep breath and saying that name: "Jacob." And having spoken, he repeated it: "Jacob." And he walked over to him and pulled his brother's hands away from

314

his mouth and held them and said, "It's me." And Jacob falling into his younger and smaller brother's arms and weeping and holding him closer than he had ever held all the anger and rage and sadness of his days, and Eddie holding him closer than he had ever held any man, and he kissed his brother's head over and over and over, never tiring of his task.

 **12**

I hereby bequeath everything I have to Jacob Lesley Marsh. It's not much, but I just wanted to make sure everything was official. I know he hates religious icons of any sort, so I want him to find a good home for them. I won't define a good home, but what I mean by that is that I don't want him to throw away what belonged to my family. I have a life insurance policy worth $65,000, and Jake is the sole beneficiary. He is to use the money to pay a private detective to find his brother. I'll rest better if I know he's found Jonathan. I also ask that my ashes be spread over the desert of Casas Grandes. I have already spoken to Jake about these things, but I thought I'd speak from the dead just to remind him. And Jake, remember, I want a Mass, damnit—and wear something nice out of respect for the dead.

Joaquin's handwriting was simple, clear, without any affectation. Tom and Rick had witnessed and dated it two months before he had died. He stared at the paper, then handed it back to Tom. "He shouldn't have left me that kind of money."

"Why the hell not? It's not exactly a fortune."

"For us, it was a fortune. It makes me feel bad."

"Because he wanted to leave you with something?"

"I don't want anything."

"He loved you."

"I can't take it."

"You're a real pain in the ass, you know that?"

"Why don't you just leave me alone, Tom?"

"I can't. I'm trying, but I can't."

"What if you're not wanted?"

Tom walked away from him.

"Come back here," Jake said. Tom kept walking toward the kitchen. Jake followed him. "I was joking," he said. He smiled at him. "It's hard for me," he said. "I won't forget what you've done—what you did—for him—for me. I won't."

Tom nodded. "And will you promise not to be so cold with your brother—will you promise to be good to him?"

"Yes."

"Are you really going to move in with him and his wife?"

"He insisted. They both insisted."

"When?"

"Any time I want. I'm going to take care of stuff around here. Maybe a couple weeks."

"You're actually going to take something from someone?"

"He's my brother."

"There are lots of us," Tom said.

Jake said nothing.

"Will I see you?"

"Of course you'll see me—you're my doctor."

Tom poured himself a cup of coffee. "Lots of people at the funeral," he said awkwardly. "People loved him."

"Yeah," Jake said. "I just remembered—"

"What?"

Jake walked out of the room and returned with a jacket in his hand. "He wanted you to have this. He said he lent it to you once, and you looked good in it."

Tom took it carefully. "Thanks."

"Thank Joaquin."

"I wish I could, Jake." Tom finished his coffee without trying to say anything else.

 **13**

AT THE TOP of the steps that went nowhere, Diego and Mundo sat among the powdered pile of bricks and drank their beer.

"What a strange day," Diego wrote.

Mundo laughed. "Makes me feel good."

"Not me," Diego wrote, "if I had more days like this, they'd have to put me in a mental institution. My nerves are shattered."

"Look, ese, you gotta learn to fight back. See that shit of a detective—he hates me. He hates me, but he respects me—just like your boss. They'd love to see me get blown away, but they hate you, too, Diego, got that? They hate you maybe even more than they hate me. They'll never like us—so where the hell does that leave us? Screw 'em, that's what I say. All we can do is fight 'em till they're as worn down as we are. They want somethin' from me, then they're gonna have to fight me for it—the same way they make me fight for what I want from them."

Diego stared at the expression of anger on Mundo's face—but there was more than anger—something better than anger. "That was great," he finally wrote, "what you did to my boss—it was one of the greatest things I've ever seen." He broke out laughing.

Mundo laughed with him, laughed and stomped the ground. Chugging his beer, he opened up another one, and took a swig.

318

"We gotta let 'em know," he said. "You sure got a loud laugh for a deaf guy."

Diego nodded. "Too bad I can't hear it." He finished his beer and Mundo handed him another. "You think he'll fire me?"

Mundo shook his head. "That chickenshit won't fire you. He won't screw around with the gangs—he doesn't have the balls to screw with us, you'll see. I've met a lot of guys like him, talk big but their balls shrink real fast. Next Monday you'll still have a job, you'll see."

"I hope so," Diego wrote. "Who the hell's gonna hire me?"

"Hell, lots of people would hire you."

Diego nodded, but he didn't believe him.

Mundo chugged his second beer and crushed it in his hands. He threw it down the steps and followed it with his eyes. He scratched at one of the bricks he was sitting near. "Look at this, Mr. Diego, they just fuckin' fall apart when you touch 'em."

Diego reached over and touched one of the bricks. It crumbled in his hands. He played with the red dust and let it run through his fingers.

Mundo opened another beer. He crushed another brick.

Diego thought of Mary, her purple fingernails digging into his memory. The sun was setting, and the blue sky around the edge of the mountains was turning pink. He watched Mundo's hands, his blue veins popping out. His hands were alive, Diego thought, so alive.

"Thanks," Diego wrote. "Thanks for helping me out. Now, *I* owe *you* one."

"Friends don't owe," he said. It seemed strange to Diego that Mundo's eyes could turn so angry then be so soft. The eyes he looked at now seemed incapable of violence. "But don't think about it too much, Diego. You think too much about things. I had a good time today—but I didn't like seeing La Mary that way. It's bad luck to see dead people like that, Dios la tenga en paz. My old lady always says things like that—I guess it sort of rubs off on us, huh?" He took another swig from his beer. "I should have bought more than just one six-pack." He looked at Diego with his black eyes. "How come you gave Mary your last name? She's a gringa—she ain't no Ramirez."

319

"I told you I didn't think anybody should be buried without a last name."

"Why yours?"

"I didn't have anything else to give her. Besides, I told you: I liked her. She wasn't really my girlfriend—she wasn't a jaina or anything like that—I just liked her."

"You shouldn't go around liking too many people. Things happen—and then you're fucked."

Diego shook his head. "It's good to have friends."

"Yeah, well, I ain't saying it ain't good to have friends, but goddamnit you don't have to pick all the fucking locos in the pinche world, do you?

"Well," Diego wrote, "you going to tell me your friends aren't crazy?"

"Just some of them," he laughed.

"You're crazy," Diego wrote, "and I picked you, didn't I?—picked you right out of a garbage can. Of course, I should talk, huh? Look at me, my only hobbies are walking the streets, reading in a library, and writing a suicide note."

They both broke out laughing. "Yeah, I don't care what you say, I don't believe it—I ain't no pinche loco. I'm just tryin' to get by, that's all. Different people play different games, and I like to play my games out on the streets. I ain't crazy. You ain't crazy, neither. You just think about things too much."

"You would too if you were deaf," he wrote.

"Maybe," he said, "but Mary—she was crazy. I mean she was really crazy as they come."

"I don't think Mary was that crazy. I think she was pretty smart."

"She thought she was the Virgin Mary! You call that smart?"

"Sort of, I think."

"Maybe you're crazier than I thought."

"Yeah," Diego wrote, "I can't explain it. I just think she was very smart—she knew lots of things."

"Like what?"

"She wasn't afraid to touch me. She wasn't afraid that my deafness would rub off on her."

Mundo didn't say anything after that. The sky was a bright pink;

320

the edges of the mountains grew red like the color of the bricks. "In a minute," Diego wrote, "I won't be able to see your lips."

"Yeah, and I won't be able to read your handwriting." Mundo finished his beer. "Look, I'll come by your place tomorrow."

Diego nodded. "Will you come to Mary's funeral?"

"Sure."

"Can you bring some friends?"

"Yeah, I'll bring some of the T-Birds."

"Can you get some of them to be pallbearers?"

Mundo laughed and shook his head. "Yeah, I can handle that, no problem." He turned around and walked down the steps. Mundo wished Diego could hear the sound of his walk. He stayed among the bricks and watched the red of twilight turn to deep blue then black. He walked back to his apartment.

He took out his suicide note and read it. He thought about his sister. She really wasn't that stupid, Diego thought, but he hated her because she could talk—no, he hated her because she'd left him, left him alone, and never wrote back. The last letter he'd written had been returned with a note on the envelope: NO LONGER AT THIS ADDRESS. He wondered what she looked like now. He wondered what Luz looked like now, too. Maybe she looked different in Chicago, maybe she'd changed. And then Mary jumped into his head—Mary—she would have looked pretty in her white dress. Pretty Mary.

The pictures in Diego's mind kept spinning around. He saw Luz laughing, throwing her head up toward the sky, and Mundo grinning. He asked himself if they had ever thought of suicide. He'd read somewhere that everyone had some kind of death wish—something in everyone wanted to die. He picked up his pad without thinking. He saw his fingers moving across the paper as if he were watching somebody else's hands: *Do I want to be dead*? Other people were alive, at least it seemed that way to him—other people. Mundo and Luz and Crazy Eddie and Mary. Mary had been alive. His head pounded. He saw Mundo drinking a beer and crushing a brick; he saw Luz clapping her hands and Crazy Eddie pointing his finger toward God. He saw Mary's bloody body and a white hat that never got to see the inside of a church. He tried to read his suicide note again. Luz said everybody needed someone to fight with. "You have your letter." But you can't buy a hat for a letter—letters don't wear hats. He shut his eyes and dreamed that he and Mary were sitting in a church. The light from the stained-glass windows made them look like figures in a coloring book. His mother watched them sitting there.

In the morning, Mundo came by, and they walked to La Fe Clinic. By then, it was almost noon, and Carolyn told Diego that everything had been arranged. "I've seen to a Mass at the cathedral—the whole nine yards." She smiled at him.

"Are you Catholic?" Diego wrote.

She nodded. "Not a very good Catholic, but good enough to give street people decent funerals. Don't ask me why—it makes me feel better."

Diego smiled at her.

"I know one of the priests at St. Patrick's," she said.

"Is he your confessor?" Diego asked.

Carolyn laughed as she read Diego's question. "No, I don't have a confessor."

"Don't you have any sins?" Diego held up the note and laughed.

"If I had a confessor," she said smiling, "then the poor guy would be overworked." She looked at Mundo. "I'll bet you could use a confessor."

Mundo grinned and nodded.

She was surprised he didn't have a retort. He seemed almost nice today, something soft in his eyes.

Mundo kept smiling good-naturedly, nothing lecherous in his look. She was surprised by the warmth she sensed in him. *Don't get sloppy, Carolyn.* She looked at Mundo and laughed. "Why are you smiling so much?"

He shrugged his shoulders. He seemed almost shy.

"I don't always got something to say," he said finally, "sometimes I just listen."

"And you smile when you listen?"

He nodded.

Really, he was very beautiful, she thought. He couldn't be any older than twenty-two—just a little more than a kid. She shrugged her shoulders and laughed to herself. Carolyn took her eyes off Mundo and looked straight at Diego. "The funeral's scheduled for Thursday morning at ten. She's going to be buried at Concordia. That's where they bury them, the people who don't have anybody get buried at a section of Concordia. At least they're still saving spaces in the ground for the Marys of the world."

"You knew her?"

She nodded. "I used to give her clothes. I also . . ." She stopped. "Never mind. The funeral home wants to know if you have any clothes to dress her in. There's blood all over the dress—they're keeping it as evidence."

Diego handed her a note: "No clothes."

"I'll find something," she said.

"It's not too much trouble?"

"Diego, if things were too much trouble, I'd quit my job." She looked at Mundo. "So are you guys a team now?"

"You wanna join?" Mundo asked.

"You handing out T-shirts?"

Mundo smiled at her. "Yeah, sure—you want T-shirts, you'll get T-shirts."

She avoided his smile and looked straight into Diego's eyes for a second, and nodded. "I'll be at the funeral."

Diego touched her hand, then squeezed it.

"You have nice eyes," she said.

"What about me?" Mundo asked.

"Those eyes of yours are too damned mean to be nice." *They're nice, too.* She looked at him. "Thanks for helping Diego out."

"I owe him."

"At least you pay your debts," her voice was soft. She cleared her throat. "See you at the funeral."

"You're very nice," Diego wrote, "very kind."

"Not to everyone." She looked at Mundo, then back at Diego. "Keep him out of fights and trash cans." She laughed, walked away, and took a patient into one of the doctor's offices.

Mundo nudged Diego. "She was nicer to me today, don't you think?"

"You were nicer, too," he wrote.

As the two men walked out of the clinic, Diego spotted Tencha sitting at her usual post. He asked her if she would go to the funeral. "Pobrecita," he wrote. "No tiene a nadie. No podemos dejarla sola ¿verdad?"

Tencha stared at his note and agreed. "Claro. Mire, Señor, tengo una comadre que me puede cuidar el puesto mientras voy a la misa. Nadie debe irse al otro mundo sin ser acompañada. Tenemos que encomendarla a Dios."

Diego smiled at her, and thanked her for agreeing to attend Mary's funeral. He was happy she would be there.

Diego made his way to Fifth and Oregon, Crazy Eddie's usual post. He wasn't there so Diego waited for him. About twenty minutes later, Eddie showed up, he and his worn Bible. "Will you go to my friend's funeral?" Diego asked. "She was very holy." Crazy Eddie stared at the note.

He pushed his glasses up, and they slid back down. "Yes," he said with his thick lips. "Funerals are important. To pray for the dead is a good thing."

Diego shook Crazy Eddie's hand and gave him a note with the time and place of the funeral. He turned around and saw Mundo standing across the street. He walked over and handed him a note: "You been following me?"

"Yeah, just checking out your scene, got it? I was wondering when you were gonna spot me. You know, someone could kill you easy. You got to pay attention, you never know when someone's out to get your ass." He paused, "and you know something else? All the people you talk to are nuts, just like I said—nuts."

"Bring your friends to the funeral." he wrote. "You got the pall-bearers?"

"Yeah, I got 'em."

"Good—and don't make fun of my friends. And tell your T-Birds to dress nice—they're going to a lady's funeral."

"Look, after the kind of clothes you wear, you're telling me to dress nice? We're all gonna look sharp, baby, like brand-new knives waiting to be used."

"I'm going to dress sharp, too," Diego wrote, "you'll see."

 **14**

EDDIE SAT IN HIS living room holding open a book of poems and reading it half to himself and half out loud. His son was in a basket next to him, and occasionally he would look down and smile at the sleeping infant, rock him, then continue reading. Jake sat across from him. He was reading an old newspaper. They had been sitting there for hours only stopping to change or feed the baby. Jake watched his brother change, touch, and talk to his son, a son who could not hear voices. Already, he was learning to crawl, trying to escape the grasp of his father. "Where you going?" Jake asked. "Nowhere to run, kiddo." He picked him up, swung him in his arms, then placed him back in his basket.

Neither of them was in the mood for speaking. Sometimes, they asked each other a question or two from across the room, then continued reading.

"Is that what passes for conversation in this house?"

Eddie and Jake looked up at Maria Elena.

"This is public space," she said. "Can't we just talk to each other?" She grabbed the book away from Eddie's hand and shut it. "Your brother is sitting over there," she said. "Talk to him."

Jake smiled nervously at Maria Elena. She smiled back. "You can talk, too," she said. "This house has been too damned quiet. If you're both going to be so mopey, then I'm going to dress you both in black." She walked across the room, took the newspaper away from Jake, kissed him on the forehead, and held it up in the air.

"You're a madwoman," Eddie said, "I married a madwoman."

"I think we should all talk about something."

"Is this like a planned activity at camp?"

"I wouldn't know—I never went to camp."

"You're a reverse snob, Nena."

"Honey, you would be, too, if you were me." She took the baby out of his basket and placed him on the floor. He began crawling back and forth between his parents.

"Are we talking now?"

"No."

"Pick a topic, then, Nena."

"Houses."

"Houses? There's a topic. Past houses? Future houses?"

"This is the only house I've ever lived in."

"Really, what about when you were growing up?"

"Eddie, I lived in the projects."

He was quiet. "You never told me you lived in the projects."

"Now you know. It's not past houses I'm interested in—let's talk about future houses." She had a curious smile.

"We're not finished with past houses."

"I told you—no houses in my past."

"I still own an old one."

"What?"

"My parents' house—I still own it." He looked at Jake, who was looking at him as if he were crazy.

"The house we grew up in?" Jake asked.

"Yeah," Eddie said. "What other house would I be talking about? I had a dream once that I burned it to the ground."

"Great dream," Jake said.

"Awful dream," Nena said.

"Great dream," Eddie said. "The flames were beautiful."

Jake pictured his parents' huge mansion going up in an apocalyptic flame. "You still have that place? You still own it? Really, Eddie?" His voice was suddenly loud and animated.

"I pay someone to stay in the chauffeur's house just to watch the place."

"Why didn't you get rid of it?"

"I don't know. I couldn't decide anything about that house—so I just kept it. And I didn't need the money so I kind of just forgot about it. I didn't want to think about it. I never touch it, just like I never touch their money—which reminds me, Jake, do you want it? The money, I mean?"

"How much is it?"

"Funny you should ask. I just talked to my lawyer today—"

"The nice man I ran into with Lizzie at Salvador's funeral?"

"The very one. He said, by the way, that you were lovely. And he also said I was worth about thirty-eight million dollars."

"Thirty-eight million dollars!"

"And change."

"And change?"

"You want it, Jake?"

He stared at his younger brother in disbelief. "I'd be homeless a million lifetimes before I touched that money."

Eddie stared at his brother's face, contorted in anger at the mention of his parent's money. "Maybe we should burn it along with the house."

"With all the hungry people in the world, you would burn that money? What are you, nuts, Eddie?" Maria Elena asked.

"I thought you didn't care about the money."

"I don't, I mean, *I don't want it*—but that doesn't mean you couldn't do something responsible with it."

"It's dirty money—really dirty."

"Oh, and the money we live on now is so clean? Life happens to be a little dirty, Eddie. Wouldn't it be lovely to live so purely?" There was something bitter in her tone and Eddie could taste it. "Since the subject is houses, how many houses could you build for people who have nothing?"

"We can't save the world—not even with thirty-eight million dollars."

"Saving the world?—is that it, Eddie? Oh that's damned arrogant." She picked the baby off the floor, and put him back in the basket. "He's getting too big for this. He'll be walking in no time." He fell asleep as soon as she put him down. "This kid will sleep through anything—except the night." She laughed, then looked at Eddie again. "I don't understand you sometimes, I really don't, Jonathan Edward Marsh. You and your left-leaning ideas—oh, they're all very well and good, and admirable—but since you can't save the whole goddamned world, then you won't save any of it. That's such California horseshit."

He nodded, and looked down at the floor.

Jake watched his brother.

"How come you guys are always looking at the floor? What the hell is down there?" She heard the tone in her voice and caught herself. "I'm sorry," she said softly. "It's none of my business—"

"No," Eddie said, "you're right."

She smiled at him. "And in the meantime, that money could get us into a big house."

"What?"

"I've been thinking," she said, "and Lizzie and I have discussed it."

"Oh, you and Lizzie have discussed it?"

"Yes, we have. We want to buy a house."

"Oh? Is that why the subject is houses."

She nodded.

"You have something in mind?"

"Not the house—just the city."

"I bet I can guess."

"El Paso, Eddie."

"El Paso? You're moving to El Paso?"

She nodded.

"You gonna take the husband and the baby with you?"

"Of course, I am. And the brother-in-law, too." She looked at Jake trying to read his reaction. "You like the desert, Jake?"

"Never been there."

"Well, it's not exactly a gay mecca—but *it is* near Casas Grandes. And the town is full of Latino men." She winked at him.

He smiled at his sister-in-law. She was kind and funny and passionate and he wondered for an instant what it would be like to love her.

"But what about our lives here?" Eddie said.

"Eddie, you hate it here."

"Oh yeah," he said, "I forgot." He laughed. "Can we leave tomorrow?"

"You're a very goofy man, sometimes, you know that, Eddie? And how come you didn't tell me you quit your job."

"You didn't ask."

"I knew you were going to say that—and it's a completely unacceptable answer."

"Who told you I quit?"

"Your boss called. I took the call. He wanted to know if you'd changed your mind. I told him fat chance in hell."

He laughed. "Good girl."

"Don't good girl me, Eddie. When were you planning to tell me?"

"Today. Right now. I was going to tell you right now." He moved up to her and kissed her. "You want to find Diego, don't you?"

She looked into her husband's eyes. Today they looked green and not so dark. "He's going to need someone who'll understand." She looked at her son. "You have a very persuasive way of changing the subject. Next time just tell me, OK?—yes, I want to find him. I had a dream about him. I woke up with his name in my mouth, and I had to say it over and over: Diego, Diego, Diego—and all of a sudden I felt I was in the middle of the desert."

"We could hire someone to find him, Nena."

"Why are we always hiring someone to do our dirty work?"

"OK," he said. "It was just a suggestion."

She made a face at him, then laughed.

"El Paso," he said.

"But, Eddie, I have to tell you that El Paso's not Palo Alto, and it's not Berkeley and it's not San Francisco. No coffee shops filled with yuppies in formal attire, no bookstores—no bookstores, Eddie! You won't like that, and it's hot, and there aren't any art flick movie houses, and no tulip trees, and no bicycle lanes. It's not like anything you've ever known. And you'll trip over the poor. You'll look across

329

the river and see Juárez, and you'll see wealth in El Paso, and you'll see businesses, and you'll live next door to a poverty on a scale you've never seen. Rough edges, Eddie, a lot of rough edges. And you won't like the pollution."

"I could go," he said. "At least we won't be living like this." His arms flew over his head in circles. "I hate how we live. We make everything so neat, overconstruct everything: nice lawn, porch, dogs—"

"We don't have a dog, Eddie."

"Sorry. You get the picture. We're so smug here. When was the last time you were in East Palo Alto? Shit, that's poverty, too—and it's awful, but we don't want to see it. Remember the riots, Lizzie? When the students from Stanford were marching on the streets, a woman said to me, 'Oh my God, they're coming.' It just fell out of her mouth—just like that. She didn't know it was the students— she thought it was the people from East Palo Alto, and she finally voiced what everyone here fears—that all those people were coming into our nice neighborhoods to take away what we worked so hard to get." He laughed and looked at his wife. "I could leave all this behind in a second—Italian bakeries, bookstores, everything." He looked at his brother. "Will you go, Jake?"

"I could go," he said. "I'm done here in this part of the world. It's a place, a beautiful place with beautiful men and beautiful places to eat—and I'm done with it. It was only home because Joaquin was here. I haven't been feeling so hot, you know? El Paso doesn't sound like it's a bad place to die. From the sound of things it's already a bit of a cemetery."

Nena laughed. "Well, it isn't that bad."

"We'll go then," Eddie said.

"We'll all go." There was a smile in Maria Elena's eyes as she spoke.

"But first," Eddie said as if the thought had just occurred to him, "Jake and I are going back to say good-bye to a bad memory."

"The house, you mean?"

Eddie nodded.

"You're not really going to burn that place down, are you?"

Eddie bit his lip.

"I know you, Eddie," she said. "I can read you like—
"A journal."
"Yes," she said.
Jake smiled.

"There isn't any breeze tonight," Eddie said, rubbing Maria Elena's back. "I love the feel of your back when it's damp with your sweat."
She laughed softly. "I know."
"Are you sorry you married a gringo?"
"What in the hell makes you ask that, Jonathan?"
"Jonathan? You never call me Jonathan."
"Well, you're acting like a Jonathan."
"What in the hell is that supposed to mean?"
"It means your question is ridiculous."
"Maybe you should have married one of your own."
"One of my own? Oh, Eddie, you are my own."
"But I'm not, Nena. I'm this rich—"
She placed her hand over his mouth. "Be quiet. Go to sleep. This conversation is too silly to have." She didn't let him say another word, just kept her hand over his mouth until she could tell he would be quiet. "Listen to me," she said, "I married the right man." She rose from the bed, and lit a candle in front of Joaquin's santos.
"What are you doing?" he asked.
"I lit a candle."
"What for?"
"So you and Jake would come back safely from your trip to La Jolla." She got back into bed and turned her back to her husband.
"I guess Joaquin's statues found a good home."
"They're not statues—they're santos."
"Santos," he repeated. "Do they hear?"
"About as well as anybody else."
"Will they put gas in my car?"
"Eddie?"
"What."
"Put a sock in it."

He kissed her back softly. "I'm just teasing," he said. A sudden breeze blew softly through the room. The light of the candle swayed softly back and forth and the light in the room flickered gently. The shadows on the walls and the ceiling reminded Maria Elena of her childhood. She used to pray for her father to stop drinking. But the candle in the room kept the darkness away, kept it from swallowing her and her house and her mother.

"Eddie, you're not really going to burn that place down, are you?"

Neither Jake nor Eddie spoke as they drove up the hill. The Southern California sky was calm and clear, and though it was still winter, it might have been spring. As they drove through the neighborhood where he had spent the first eighteen years of life, all Jake could think of was the day he was arrested. *Are you Jacob Marsh? . . . You're under arrest for assault . . . I should have killed them . . . Jake, has Dad ever touched? . . . I swear if you ever touch him again I'll cut your balls off and stuff them down your . . .* Jake looked at his brother, who was driving the car. He seemed so unscarred, almost innocent—like the sky. He wondered how some people managed the virtue of serenity as if cruelty and violence had no power over them. Jake felt nervous, scared, edgy—he'd felt this way every time he had approached his home when his parents had lived there, when he had lived there with them. His palms were sweating. *They're dead. Can I say good-bye to him? No. We can take care of . . . They can't hurt me anymore.*

"Are you all right, Jake?"

He nodded. "It's spring again. It's hard to believe that after this winter, there could ever be another spring." He laughed. "Anyway, in La Jolla, there was never a winter—not really."

"Mom," Eddie said, "Mom was winter."

"She was, wasn't she?"

"Why do you suppose she was so cold, Jake?"

"She must have come from a long line of sick people."

Eddie nodded. "Maybe. But how do you account for us?"

Jake laughed. "Geez, sport, we're on our way to burn our childhood home—we're as sick as they come."

"Guess so," Eddie said, laughing as hard as his brother. "You know, Jake, Mom was really a freak about her family history. She had all kinds of picture albums and things—they're still in the house. Dad had some, too. Should we save them—from the fire I mean?"

"No. Let the whole goddamned family tree die."

Eddie turned into the driveway. The house looked empty and sad, but the lawns were still well kept. "The guy who lives in the chauffeur's house keeps up the lawns—it's part of his job. The neighbors don't like weeds." He stopped at the gates, took out a set of keys from his pocket. He looked at his older brother. "Here," he said, handing him the keys, "You do the honors."

Jake took the keys, jumped out of the car, unlocked the gates, and waved Eddie to drive in. He jumped back in the car without shutting the gates behind him. He looked at his brother and smiled awkwardly. "Are you nervous?"

Eddie nodded. "Why are we doing this?"

"We have to."

He stopped the car in the circular driveway in front of the house. They both walked around the grounds in silence, afraid to enter the house. "It looks like Frankenstein's castle," Jake said.

"Are we going in?"

"Guess so."

Jake looked through one of the windows. "Jesus, the furniture's still there."

"I didn't get rid of anything. It's all just been sitting here."

"There's gotta be an inch of dust everywhere."

"We can write our names on everything."

Jake laughed. "When you were little you would have said something just like that."

"Nobody changes completely—not even you."

"Wouldn't it be great if we could?"

"No. No, it wouldn't, Jake." They walked around to the front of the house. "Open it," Eddie said.

Jake stared at the door. *I swear if you ever touch him again . . . One more step, Dad—just one more step. I'll kill you—I swear I will . . . Pederast! I looked it up in the dictionary when I was nine. You're a goddamned monster, Dad . . . We found all those magazines underneath your mattress . . . And I'm taking Jon-Jon with me . . . We can take care of everything . . . There's one thing I always wanted to do, Mom.* He placed the key in the keyhole and turned it. The knob turned in his hand. The door opened. Eddie watched his brother walk through the door. He saw himself running up the stairs, the house so quiet. He saw himself staring at the blood and the two corpses, and thinking they were no more and no less ugly than they had been when they had been breathing. He saw himself picking up the phone and calling the police. "Come and get them," he had wanted to say, "come and take them to a place where no one will see them." He felt his knees shaking, he couldn't move, he wanted to get in the car and drive away. He felt confused, his heart thumping in his chest like a fist hitting a wall. He had felt this way when his father was on top of him. He couldn't breathe. He felt his whole body tremble—then felt his brother's hand on his arm. "It's OK," he said. "They're not here, Eddie." He felt his brother's hand wipe his tears from his face. He heard his voice: "They're not here, Jon, they can't hurt us anymore." It was a good voice. He felt he could walk. He reached for his older brother's hand—he held it tight. They walked inside together and stood in the entryway, two little boys holding hands, overwhelmed by the enormity of a long journey. Having arrived at this place, their eyes did not ask, "Have I come home again?" but asked instead, "Now can I rest? Now have I earned my rest?" And Jake thinking that good things could not be born in houses like this because they were not meant to house people but things, and Eddie thinking that he would never forget this moment because he had just seen the past, and his future would not look like this—not like this—never like this—his future would look like a house where people lived and breathed and fed each other food.

They walked around the house saying nothing, going from room to room. It was like a museum where the retired arms of war were kept. They examined everything asking themselves if it had been real—were we here? Did we fight this war? Remember this battle—remember that one? They looked at each thing in the house distantly, curiously. Yes, it was nothing more than a museum—and like most museums the artifacts seemed out of place, valuable in a strange and removed and unnecessary way—and so, not valuable at all precisely because they were no longer necessary, no longer a part of the daily lives they led. What was valuable now was the hand that each brother held, the life that each brother had led, but this house was not valuable, this house was good kindling since the civilization it housed was long dead and not worth preserving in the memories of the living.

"I used to give you rides on my back," Jake said quietly.

"I remember."

"You wanted me to carry you everywhere. 'Carry me,' you used to yell, 'Carry me, Jake,' and I would have carried you until my back broke." He picked up an oil painting from one of the walls and tossed it as if it were a ball. The frame shattered as it hit the floor. "I wanted to take you with me."

"I know."

"I'm too old to carry you, now."

"It was bound to happen, old man," Eddie laughed—they both laughed.

"Can we torch it now?"

"Let's wait until it's dark—we can watch the flames in the night."

"What if they catch us, Eddie? What will we say?"

"We'll say we came back to see our old house. There's no insurance, anyway, I cancelled it a long time ago. We'll say it got dark and we lit a candle, and that it caught something on fire, and that we couldn't put it out—and that we barely escaped with our lives."

"Did you bring a candle?"

"Yup."

"Smart kid."

"Yup."

They sat perfectly still in their parents' bedroom, a sanctuary neither one of them had ever been allowed to enter. Jake lit one of the carpets— it was old and it lit as easily as paper. The room caught fire quickly, the flames burning higher and higher, as yellow and red as anything he'd ever seen. Eddie pulled him toward the door, coughing. "Let's get out of here, Jake." Jake was reluctant to move, his feet planted on the floor as if he were rooted and the floor was the soil that gave him life. He thought

of Joaquin, his hundred indiscretions, he thought of the heron dying in flight and wondered how it might feel to die, to burn with this house. He would be dying soon, anyway. This would be over quickly, no hospital rooms, no IV, no complications of the body caving in on itself. It would be better to burn with the house, and he could die with it. It would be like becoming one of Joaquin's candles. The room filled with smoke, and he could hear his younger brother calling him: "Jake! Jake! What's wrong? We have to get out—" His voice was distant in his ears, but he remembered a little boy who loved him and had treated him as if he were as valuable as the air. He felt his brother trying to pull him toward the door. "Jake!" And suddenly that voice became more real and urgent than the smoke and the flames and the burning room. He felt his feet run toward the door.

Suddenly, as if he had reentered his body, he was alive and vibrant and happy, and he laughed as he and his younger brother ran down the stairs. He looked up and saw the flames shooting out of his parents' bedroom. They found themselves in the living room. Jake stood in the middle of the room and started dancing and jumping and yelling, soaking wet in his own sweat. Eddie watched him and was terrified at the look of joy on his face. "Let's get out of here, Jake!" He grabbed his older brother by the shoulder and spun him around. Jake looked at his brother and laughed—then walked toward the door, the house filling with smoke. Eddie followed him out of the house, leaving the door wide open. Jake calmly slammed the door shut: "Burn, baby, burn!" he yelled. "Burn!"

"Jake, Jake, wake up. Wake up!" He felt Eddie shaking him awake.

"Huh—what?"

"You were having a nightmare."

"What time is it?" He stared at his brother who sat on the floor next to the couch he was lying on. He watched the candle flicker on the coffee table.

"It's late," Eddie said.

"I was dreaming. We burned it, me and you. We burned it. I wanted to burn with the house. You called me back."

Eddie said nothing as he listened to Jake's voice. "You want to stay here tonight?" he asked after a long time.

"You don't want to burn it, do you, Eddie?"

"This house—it can't hurt us anymore."

Jake sat up on the couch. "How long was I asleep?"

"A couple of hours."

Jake lit a cigarette from the flame of the candle. "And you?"

"Oh, I took another tour of the house."

"So we won't burn it?"

"We already have," Eddie said.

Jake smiled.

"You're not disappointed then?"

Jake shook his head. "You know what Joaquin would have said? He would have said that we came to pick up our ghosts."

 **15**

"I'VE SOLD EVERYTHING."

"And you gave the money to the poor."

"Actually I pocketed all the cash."

"So what are you going to do with all the dough?"

"Buy another set of earrings, and then I'm going to move to El Paso."

"El Paso? Do you know how to spell it?" The two women stood in the middle of the living room amid half-packed boxes and stacks of books. "Did you really sell everything, Lizzie?"

"Well, almost everything. I kept all my earrings, I kept a few sentimental kitchen utensils, I kept my first IUD, which I had bronzed—"

"Are you serious?"

"Of course I'm serious. Do you realize that if I hadn't worn that thing, I would have probably wound up pregnant and marrying Michael Topp?"

"Michael Topp? Where do you find these guys?"

"Can you imagine me as Mrs. Michael Topp? So I've kept it as a good luck piece. And I kept my clothes, of course. Well, I'm actually giving my brother a couple of my dresses." She gave her friend a knowing look. "Remember when you said that dress of his was probably his girlfriend's? Well, it wasn't."

"Did you stick your psychic nose in his bedroom one night?"

"Actually, I wanted to, but I refrained. I found out the honest way—I asked him. He said the only way he could get excited was by wearing women's clothes." She laughed triumphantly. "I love being right."

"Did he model one for you?"

"I asked him to—but he wouldn't." She laughed. "I was right— I was right."

"You love being right too much, if you ask me," Maria Elena said. She tried to keep herself from smiling.

"Oh, and the bed, well, I burned the bed."

"You didn't."

"I was afraid it would talk."

"You really burned it?"

"Actually, I sold it to a couple of guys who were moving in next door. I warned them the bed was cursed but they liked the price— they couldn't resist."

Maria Elena placed some books in a box. "That man has books everywhere. I wonder if he would mind burning a few of them before we moved."

"Does he read them?"

"Yes. All of them. That's the good part. The bad part is that he wants to talk about them." She looked around the room for some tape to seal the box. "He actually follows me from room to room sometimes, reading passages of books to me." She caught a glimpse of Lizzie's hair as it caught the morning sun. "I can't get over your hair."

"Lovely, isn't it?"

Maria Elena laughed as she headed toward the kitchen. "You want some coffee?"

"No thanks." Lizzie looked around the disorganized room. "Why don't we just go to it?" She followed Maria Elena into the kitchen. "Where are those boys, anyway? When the packing begins, they disappear—but call them into the bedroom and they're ready."

"The boys are at their lawyer's."

"Oh yeah, what are they doing there?"

"They're talking to him about what they should do with the house—he's going to help them dump it."

"I still think they should have burned it."

"It's not a game, Lizzie."

"I know. It's very serious. Serious business burning down houses. How come they didn't do it?"

"They thought better of it. They can't just go around burning old houses down."

"Why not, Helen? It's their house. I'd have torched it."

"Big talker. And the name's Maria Elena."

"I slip sometimes. It's a big ugly house—someone *should* burn it."

"You've never even seen it, Lizzie."

"I've heard enough about what went on in that house—that's reason enough to watch it crumble to the ground—in flames, baby, in flames. Besides, who's going to buy it? Who wants to buy a house where people committed murder?"

"Oh, someone will buy it."

"What if someone doesn't?"

"Who cares, Lizzie? Let it sit there and rot."

"Oh, you don't care if it sits there and rots, but you don't think it should be torched."

"I'm much more patient than you, Lizzie." She laughed. "And a lot less theatrical."

"You're funny, you know that? About certain things, you'll talk till the cows come home—about other things, you just want to shut up, and hope it will go away."

"Like what?"

"Like parts of your past, like," she hesitated, "like—your son."

"What are you talking about, Elizabeth Edwards?"

"Promise me you won't get mad."

"I won't promise anything."

"Then I won't talk, either." She looked toward the half-packed boxes in the living room. "We should get packing. What room should we do?"

Maria Elena shook her head in exasperation. "OK, I promise I won't get mad."

"OK, I'll tell you—but I've changed my mind about the coffee."

Lizzie watched her friend as she put the coffee on. "Are you sure we're going to be able to live in the same house?"

"Are you worried?"

"I've always lived alone."

"I've *never* lived alone. Couldn't afford it. It's not so hard to live with other people, you know?"

"Well, not if you don't talk."

"There you go again."

"Have you told Eddie your father beat your mother?"

"I told him he was a violent alcoholic—and that my mother couldn't take it anymore."

"And you call that revealing secrets?"

"There are always more secrets. You tell one—and another one pops up."

"Yeah, right."

"You're telling me you don't have any secrets?"

"Yes. It's just not a way of life."

"Bullshit."

"I tell you everything, Nena."

Maria Elena laughed victoriously. "We'll live fine together. I'm not worried about us at all." She bit the inside of her mouth. "Jake looks a little tired, don't you think? How's his blood count?"

"Medium."

"Medium?"

"In the seven hundreds."

"When the time comes, it's going to be hard on Eddie. It'll be hard on you, too, Lizzie."

"Maybe he'll live for a long time. Medium is good."

"Something tells me he won't."

"Oh, so now you're a seer, too."

"Sometimes. And then of course, there's your dream, isn't there?"

Lizzie nodded. "I know, but let's not talk about it, not today. Today, let's talk about gardens and new places and the ba—Hey, where's the baby?"

"Eddie and Jake took him."

"To the lawyer's?"

"You knew he'd be deaf, didn't you?"

"Yes," she said softly.

"And you didn't tell me?"

"You didn't want to hear it, Hel—Maria Elena. I don't have to be psychic to know what you could and couldn't hear."

"When did you know?"

"When I felt him kick. When you took my hand and placed it on your belly. I was here having dinner with you and Eddie one night—and all of a sudden the room was sad and silent, and I didn't know what it meant. But later, I knew." Maria Elena handed her a cup of coffee. "Remember when I was here right after little Jake was born? He was lying there perfectly still. And I let out one of my barroom laughs, and the baby didn't respond—and you knew. You knew. That knowledge was a kind of dying for you, and I felt it, but you pushed that knowledge away with everything you had. It was as if you were concealing something that could never be concealed. And you knew—and I knew—so what was I supposed to do? So I did what all good friends do—I played stupid."

Maria Elena looked down at her hands. "It's hard, Lizzie. You'd think at this point I could say anything I felt, speak about all the ghosts—everything. I keep so many things—old habits are so damned hard to break."

Lizzie took her friend's hand and kissed it. "I know," she said, "especially when those nasty habits helped you to survive." She kissed Maria Elena's hand again. "It's like smoking cigarettes: The more you smoke them, the more they become a part of you. And pretty soon you need them."

Maria Elena inhaled loudly, held her breath, then exhaled. She shook her head in disgust. "I'm glad you're so pushy. Never stop being pushy. Did you dream anything else?"

"I dreamed about his birth. He grew into a young man right in front of us. There we all were in the delivery room—you still recovering and your son already grown up, but when I spoke to him, he just looked at me and shrugged. And your brother was in the dream."

"Diego? Diego was in the dream?"

"Yes."

"You're sure."

"I'm sure. Dark eyes, slender body, lips—"

"He's alive, then?"

"I'm sure of it."

"What else? What else?" She squeezed Lizzie's hands.

"That's it."

"That's it? I wish we were there already."

"Let's pack then, Nena." But as she spoke the words, she began traveling to another place, a place Maria Elena could not follow. She stared into her cup of coffee as if she were searching for something crucial, urgent, a key to a door she had to open. In that instant Maria Elena recognized something very sad in the way her friend was holding herself. Lizzie was tired. She was paying a heavy price for her gift—and something else.

"What is it, Lizzie?" Maybe she didn't want to move with them to the desert. The thought of leaving her behind seemed unimaginable, and yet her distance seemed more real than the cup of the coffee she was holding. *"Tell me you're not changing your mind."* She was afraid to ask, afraid she would say she wasn't going. "You don't have to go, you know? I thought that's what you wanted—a new life, a new place—that's what you said. A new life because you'd shed the old one. 'New wineskins for new wine,' you said. But maybe—not everyone belongs in the desert."

"I've been having dreams, Nena."

"Tell me." She felt her lower lip quiver.

"About the desert—they're mostly about the desert." Maria Elena felt calm as soon as Lizzie said the word "desert," felt as though she were stepping on sand and smelling a chamizo and squeezing that desert bush's olive leaves between her fingers, the smell of the rain exploding onto her hands. Lizzie's voice was becoming a dry breeze blowing across the droughted sand. Maria Elena could almost feel the grains blowing across her body. This woman who was speaking to her had become the drought, but she had also become the rain. "And we are all there in my dreams—all of us—you and the baby and Diego and a dark woman dressed in simple clothes who has the worn look of a woman who has worked all her life and is tired because she was expected to carry too big a piece of the earth, but that dark woman is smiling and kneeling on the ground.

She's praying. I can almost hear her Spanish—even now. Eddie is holding Jake in his arms and Joaquin is bathing naked in the river, perfect again and at peace—like a boy—and from the river he is calling Jake to come: 'Come,' he whispers. And Eddie finally lets him go, his tears as clear as the waters of the river. I'm standing next to Diego—but someone else is there, and I can't see who she is—but I know it's a she." She looked at Maria Elena and trembled. "I have to go with you and Eddie to that border. I know I have to go—and I want to go. Already, it's a part of me. I can sometimes taste it when I wake. I mean, Maria Elena, look at me. Who the hell am I? I'm sometimes a body, and sometimes I'm not a body. I'm a Mexican and I'm not a Mexican. I'm a middle-class WASP, and I'm not. I'm a twin, but my twin is missing." Maria Elena stared at Lizzie completely mesmerized by her voice. "Ever since Salvador gave me this gift, I catch myself repeating: 'My name is Salvador.' " She looked at Nena and tried to smile. "I never used to ask myself why I was born. Now, I ask it all the time."

"Why does that make you so sad?"

"Something's very wrong," she said. "I feel as if something is wrong."

"Are you seeing something or is it just nerves? Maybe it's Jake. Maybe you sense his illness. In the dream, he's going away from us—is that it?"

"No, it's not just nerves—and it isn't about Jake. It's something else." Lizzie shrugged. "I'm a very bad psychic." She laughed and gulped down her coffee. "Let's get to work. We have a lot of packing to do." She stood up and stretched toward the ceiling and yawned. "I've got to get more sleep. Which way to the first closet?" Her face turned as white as her hair as soon as she'd finished speaking. "No," she whispered. Her eyes became distant and cloudy.

Maria Elena reached for her arm. She was cold and trembling. "Are you leaving?" she asked. "Lizzie?"

"No," she said again.

"What?"

"How did you get in here?"

"Lizzie?"

"No, don't."

"Don't what?"

"Who are you? What are you—"

"What's happening, Lizzie?"

"Don't hurt me. Please don't—"

"Lizzie!" Maria Elena tried to keep her from shaking. "Lizzie?"

She froze in Maria Elena's arms. She trembled as if she were coatless in a freezing rain. "No! Please, no! Take anything you want. I can't—don't hurt—How did—please—"

Maria Elena tried to hold Lizzie up as she fell to the floor on her knees. "Lizzie, what's happening? Lizzie!"

Then she was calm again. Lizzie knelt on the floor and was perfectly still. Maria Elena knelt next to her and placed her head on her lap. "Lizzie?"

She opened her eyes. "Mama," she said. "Mama! No. We have to go and help her."

"What?"

"Just take me, Nena!"

"You just had a seizure, Lizzie! You need a doctor."

"That was no seizure. That was my mother!"

"What?"

"My mother, Nena! My mother!"

Lizzie ran toward the door the second Maria Elena's car stopped in front of her parents' house. She banged on the door. "Open the door—open the goddamned door! Open this door goddamn—" Somehow, in her panic, she remembered she had a key. She reached for her purse. It wasn't there. "Damn! No!" She banged on the door again, oblivious to the fact her fist was throbbing from hitting the door again and again and again. As she leaned into the door, she felt it open slowly. She saw her mother, bent and crooked, lean against the doorway and sway. She looked as if she had been broken by a wind, her bones no longer able to hold her up. Her clothes were washed in sweat. The old woman strained to make out who was standing in her doorway, her hands groping in front of her, groping, reaching—trembling and reaching. "My glasses—"

Lizzie and Maria Elena stood in front of the old woman, breathless and paralyzed by the terror they saw in the woman who stood in front of them. Instinctively, Lizzie reached to help her mother remain standing. The old woman flinched. "It's OK, Mama. It's me, it's Lizzie."

"Thank God," she sobbed. She fell into Lizzie's arms, no longer able to hold her own weight. She winced and sobbed and was utterly confused. Maria Elena helped lay her on the floor carefully.

"Who did this to you? Where is he? I'll find him, Mama. God help him when I do. I swear I'll kill that—"

The old woman did not speak. She was too hurt and far away and confused to hear her daughter's voice. Maria Elena took Lizzie's shoulder and shook her gently. She looked at Lizzie's mother. "Where does it hurt, Rose? Are you hurt?"

The old woman slowly pointed to her chest.

"I'm going to call an ambulance. You're going to be just fine. It's me, Rose, Helen Marsh. Do you remember me?"

The old woman nodded and groaned quietly.

"It's all right, Rose, we're here now." She placed her hand firmly on Lizzie's trembling back, then went to find the telephone. When she returned from calling an ambulance, she placed a blanket over the old woman's shaking body. She watched Lizzie weeping as she knelt beside her. She clenched her fist and slammed it against the wall. "I'll kill whoever did this," she said, "I swear I'll kill him."

Maria Elena shook Lizzie gently. "She's just frightened, I think. She'll be fine. She'll be just fine."

Lizzie could not hear Maria Elena's voice. "I'll kill them all," she said.

"I'm old and tired," she said. Rose spoke to the yellow roses in the vase. She couldn't smell them. Why couldn't she smell? Was she half-dead already? She reached for a rose, ripped off a petal, squeezed it between her fingers, and breathed in the fragrance. She didn't know if the smell was really present or if she was merely bringing her memory into the room. But the smell was there, and that was all that mattered. She laughed to herself. She remembered the smell of her father's sweat, the way he used to tease her, hold her, make her feel as if she were the only person in the world. He used to care for roses in his garden and place them in a vase for her mother. He could make things grow. His life had seemed so easy and simple, his love so uncomplicated. She closed her eyes and willed him into the room. She opened them and half-expected him to be standing there, thin and strong, his kind brown eyes taking her back to that Iowa cornfield she'd left for that ambitious man she'd married. "Papa, I married badly," she said, "just like you." She tried not to think of her mother, how badly she had treated him, how she seemed to enjoy humiliating him in public. She tried to remember something happy, something that would remind her she was once alive, something that would redeem the life she had led. She tried to picture Lizzie's face, her dangling earrings reflecting all light. At least she'd had Elizabeth. For all of her rebellion, for all of her stubbornness, for all of her verbal rages, Rose's daughter had been the only presence in her house that had made her feel as if she were more than an inanimate object. She was tired. She closed her eyes and slept:

"You what?"

"I told her."

"You told her!" She felt the coldness of his stare.

She stared right back. "She knew anyway, Sam. She knew."

"I should have never let that girl into this house. I should have let her go with her brother. How did she know? How?"

She shook her head. "I won't tell you."

"I want to know!"

"You're drunk, Sam."

"You promised me. You said you'd never tell."

"You had no right to ask, damn you! Damn you!"

He banged his fist on the table. "Who told her?"

"Her brother, Sam, her brother." She tried to calm him. She wondered why she still needed to make things right with him when they had been so wrong for so many years.

"I hate you," he said.

"I want to leave."

"You'll leave with nothing."

"I don't care."

He stormed out of the house slamming the door. Rose sat alone in the late morning light. She woke to the sound of a broken window. A big man with a blond mustache stood over her. She came down the stairs. "Who are you? What do you—" She felt his hand against her cheek. Run, I have to run. She managed to free herself from him for an instant. She took a step. He pulled out a knife and it sparkled like a diamond in his big hands. She dropped down on her knees. "Take anything you want."

"Please," he said. "Say please."

"Please."

He smiled. She felt she would die there, no one would come to save her, Sam would not come to help. Sam was gone. They would find her there, they would find her dead. She closed her eyes, her heart pounding against her chest as if it were a hammer knocking out her ribs. She could not move. The door! Someone was at the door. Go away. Go away and let me die. I want to die. The door, I have to—

Rose made herself wake. She expected to find the man—he was gone. She looked up and saw her daughter standing over her. The younger woman smiled at her mother and wiped the sweat from her face. "It's OK, Mama, it was only a dream. He can't hurt you, now. You're safe, Mama." Her voice was as soft as the rose petals in her father's garden.

"You won't let him come here, will you?"

"He won't come here, Mama." She bit her lip to keep from crying as she stared at her mother's face. "He won't hurt you again, Mama. Everything will be fine—everything will be beautiful."

"And Sam?—why didn't he come, Lizzie? Why didn't he come when I called his name?"

"He wasn't home, Mama."

"I'm his wife—"

"Shhhh, Mama. He was gone."

"I would've heard," she said, "I would have done something." Her throat was as dry as the yellow hills of the California summer. "He doesn't care. He doesn't care. And that man. I heard a window break, and he had a knife—" Her voice cracked. Lizzie didn't know who to hate more, the man who broke into the house, or her father who was gone, always gone. Lizzie handed her mother a cup of water and held her head as she sipped from a straw. Her lips trembled as she drank. "I told him you knew about your mother—Sam, I told him. And I told him I wanted to leave. He was angry. And he left the house. He doesn't care, Lizzie. He doesn't care. It's my fault, It's all my—"

"Don't you ever take the blame, do you hear? Never! It was them, damnit, it was them." She placed her head on the bed and cried. *"It was my fault, Mama, it was all my fault."* Her mother combed Lizzie's hair with her fingers. When she had had enough of her own tears, she lifted her head and laughed. "We're all so arrogant," she said, "we always think everything is our fault." She smiled at her mother. "You're so beautiful."

The old woman smiled. "I'm not. I'm not beautiful."

"Don't argue, Mama." She kissed her on the cheek—softly—so as not to hurt her. "I'm taking you with me," she said.

"I don't know anything about the desert," the old woman said, "and I'd only be in the way. I'm getting old."

"Should I throw you away, then—because you're old? I can't leave you, Mama. Don't make me leave you."

"Don't cry, child. It always hurt me so much to see you cry." Rose nodded at the young woman. "I'll go then. El Paso is as good a place as any for an old woman to rest." She laughed, "Do they have roses there?"

"We'll grow them, Mama."

16

"YOU HAVE A LOT of nerve walking into my house." he said. "You swore you'd never come back. What do you want?"

"Nice to see you, too, Pop." She maintained perfect control. *I promised her.*

"You could have knocked."

"I have a key."

"What do you want?"

"I came to ask you to leave while she comes and gets her things."

"You can both go to hell together."

She gave him a hard stare. "What happened to you? When I was a child you were kind."

"I don't owe you any explanations," he said quietly, his voice almost soft.

"No, I guess you don't. And I don't owe you my life—and neither does my mother."

"She's not your mother."

"More than you'll ever know."

"If you knew—"

"I don't need to see my mother through your eyes. She's invisible to you—she always has been. Why can't you see her?"

"I can see just fine. What would you have done—either of you—what would you have done without me?"

"What would you have done without us?" Lizzie felt strangely alive, almost drunk. She was stronger than him, now. She wondered why she had feared this man for all of her adult life, but wondered, too, where he had placed his kindness. She could see how much he hated her. Those hard eyes were a wall, and she did not know how to make that wall crumble. "My mother's coming for her things," she said casually, "and I'd like it very much if you let her pack her things in peace."

"She can leave with the clothes on her back."

"If you don't do me the courtesy of making yourself scarce for one miserable afternoon of your more than miserable life, I swear I'll beat you like a drum—and if you don't think I'm willing or able, try me, old man." *I'm breaking my promise. Be careful, Lizzie.* She took a deep breath, then smiled.

"This is my house, damn you—my house."

"Who cares? No one wants it but you. I just want you to make yourself disappear for a few hours. If my mother wanted to, she could take you for the financial ride of your life. You're getting off cheap, so don't push me. All you have to do is step out of this place for one crummy afternoon. It's not so much to ask, is it?"

He sat down on the chair that had conformed perfectly to his shape over the years—it was as deformed as his old body. He stared into the room seeing nothing in it—nothing but emptiness. He nodded and kept nodding.

"I'm sorry," she said, her voice raw and careful, "I'm really sorry it had to—"

He held up his hand to quiet her. "Not another word. Please." His voice sounded hollow and numb. He walked slowly toward the front door, his body bent with the years. He opened the door, took one last look at Lizzie, then walked out the front door. "I'll be back by five," he said softly.

She nodded, unable to speak.

He shut the door behind him.

She had come here expecting some kind of victory. This was not a war anyone had won. She understood perfectly why Jake and Eddie had thought of burning down their childhood home—and

351

knew why they had been powerless to do it. Nothing could bring down the houses of the past.

There wasn't much in the house Rose wanted. She wandered from room to room occasionally picking up an object, then setting it back down. Such a large house, she thought, all this space, all this nothingness, all this time in this nothingness. She opened her hand, and grabbed at the air, nothing in her tight fist. Nothing. But she had chosen this house, and chosen to live with the man who bought it. Over twenty-five years in this damn house, and she couldn't think of anything she wanted to take with her. Rose walked into her bedroom—she and Sam had slept apart for years. She had hated sleeping with him—and yet she had waited for him to suggest they have their own rooms. She did not remember ever having enjoyed sleeping with him. She had long forgotten his touch. The last time they had made love, she had risen from the bed and vomited, not caring whether or not he heard her spilling her guts out over the toilet. The very thought of him inside of her made her feel like vomiting again. How had she allowed herself to live in this house for so long? She began taking her clothes out of the closet. She examined each dress, wondered where she had bought it, why she had bought it, where she had worn it. So many clothes. She must have thought they were important. Why else did she have so many? In the back of the closet she found a box. She knew what was in it. She placed the box on her bed and stared at the dress. She tried to picture herself on her wedding day. Had she been pretty? How had she looked in this dress? She felt it, stared at it, felt it again, then shredded it with her bare hands. It tore like paper. "My arms are still strong," she thought.

Jake took a final stroll through the city. He had taken the train in from Palo Alto, walked up Fourth Street, then slowly made his way up Market Street into the Castro. *Last summer, my J was dying. Why am I still living?* He'd lived in this town since he was twenty, and every inch of it was familiar to him. He could daydream and walk to an appointed destination without even being conscious of where he was going. This town is what he knew, and it was his as much as any town could ever be. It was all he had known for twenty years, and he'd never imagined he'd ever leave. He felt numb and empty, a hollow man. If he cut himself open at that very moment, he was convinced nothing would come out but stale air. No blood. He had never thought of this place as home, not really. There was no home. There was only Joaquin. There was only his brother. He had lost Joaquin, and found his brother on the same night. Jake entered a store and bought a pack of cigarettes. He lit one, sucked the smoke into his lungs, then blew the smoke out of his nose. As he stood on the sidewalk, he noticed a young man staring at him. Jake thought of another life he had lived, a life where he would have smiled at the youth, taken him home, then forgotten he'd ever met or touched or wanted him. He remembered when he had first arrived in this city, how it had made him forget that he'd had a previous life. He had loved that amnesia. And now there was just this dull feeling of a sidewalk under his feet. Why, then, had he come? Why did he need to walk its streets a final time? Why the need to be alone in this town one more time as if he were meeting a lover one last time, looking into the familiar eyes as if seeing them a final time would make the memory easier when the time came to remember? And he would remember. San Francisco had given him Joaquin—and so he was paying it his final respects. *I'm leaving, J.*

He found himself standing outside of Tom's office without even realizing he'd walked there. And becoming conscious of where he was, he entered the reception area. He nodded at the receptionist. "I'd like to see Dr. Michaelsen."

"Do you have an appointment, Mr. Marsh?" She remembered his name. He thought it was nice to be remembered.

"No, but can you please tell him I'm here?" He sat down and waited. *Maybe I should leave.* He looked at the door, at the patients waiting to see the good doctor. *What the hell am I doing here?*

Tom opened the door. "Jake, come on in." He seemed genuinely happy to see him. He followed Tom into his office.

"How are you feeling?"

353

"Fine, Tom," he said. "Well, sad sometimes." He cleared his throat. "Well, I'm not here about my health."

"Social visit? I only have two more patients—you want to have coffee?"

He cleared his throat again. "Well, actually, I have to get back to Palo Alto. We're leaving in the morning."

"Leaving?"

"Yeah, I'm moving to El Paso with Eddie and—" He couldn't finish the sentence. His eyes welled up with water, though he made no noise, would not allow himself to sob.

Tom nodded. "I'm sorry to see you go," he said. "It won't be the same without you."

"This town won't miss me."

"Not this town, Jake. I meant my life—it won't be the same without you—or Joaquin."

Jake smiled crookedly. "You're a real charmer, Doc."

"So I've been told."

They sat in an awkward silence for what seemed an eternity to both of them.

Jake rose from his seat. "I just wanted to say good-bye." He smiled crookedly again, "If you're ever in El Paso—" He laughed. "You won't—" He stopped, swallowed hard, then nodded. "Listen, take good care."

Tom placed his hand on Jake's shoulder but could not bring himself to speak. In that instant, he hated being a man, hated that he could not bring himself to sob because he felt like sobbing, embrace because he needed to embrace, to speak and to tell this hard and unforgettable man that he had come to respect him—forgive him—and even to love him. "Good-bye, then," he said slowly and sadly and carefully, the meaning of those words as sad as anything he'd ever spoken.

Jake waved awkwardly, then left the office silently as if he wanted to make no noise as he left, perhaps because then no one, not even himself would notice that he was leaving a whole life behind and the man who most symbolized that life, the man who had taken care of his lover, the man who had told him he was HIV positive. He turned around as he opened the door. He saw that Tom was crying, and he knew he would remember him this way. "You're a good doctor," he said, then shut the door behind him. He smiled to himself. There was someone to say good-bye to after all, he thought as he walked toward the train station. Jake yelled into the street. He listened to what his shout sounded like—then shouted again. It was not always a bad thing to feel pain.

"Are you awake, Eddie?"

He broke out laughing. "I wish to hell I wasn't." He placed his head on Maria Elena's stomach and kissed it. "Are we going to have sex?"

"At this hour of the morning?"

"We used to."

"We were younger then."

"Oh, and now we're so ancient." He laughed again. "I like to feel your skin. You have a small mole right there." He touched the inside of her thigh. "You excited?"

"About the move or about where you're touching me?"

"The move."

She moaned.

"Is that a yes?"

She moaned again. She heard the baby cry. "Feeding time," she said. They both laughed.

He turned on the lamp and watched his son nurse.

"Are you watching him or me?"

"Both."

"Be honest."

"Mostly him. He's newer."

She laughed.

"He's getting too big to still be nursing. He's practically walking."

"I only nurse him at night, now."

"He eats solid food, Nena."

"He's still a baby."

"He's almost a toddler."

"Almost—but not quite."

"He's going to be walking—and you're still going to be breast-feeding him."

355

"He's one year old."

He smiled as he watched them—then started laughing.

"Why are you laughing?"

"Because I'm scared."

"Are you, Eddie?"

"Yes."

"What are you going to do on your last day in Palo Alto, amor?"

"I'm going to take you and Jacob Diego for a walk in the evening and sit in the park and read you a poem."

"Read me one now," she said.

He thought a moment, then smiled. He walked out of the room, then reentered waving a book at his wife.

"Where did you find that?" she asked.

"In your secret hiding place."

"You rat!"

"Shhhh, the baby's sleeping."

"He can't hear."

"He can feel."

"I can't believe you spy on me."

"I don't spy on you—I was packing. When one packs, one finds interesting things—and I found this book. It's a great book, you know?"

She nodded. "I was selfish—I didn't want to share. I wanted it to be mine."

"I'm sorry," he said. "I won't read the poem if you don't want."

"No, read it."

"Are you sure?"

She nodded.

He opened the book, kissed his wife, kissed his feeding son, and cleared his throat.

"I love you," she said.

"Shhh." He cleared his throat again and began reading:

> My vision of hell is the large moving van
> I am condemned eternally to pack and unpack
> as payment for my middle-aged foolishness.
> Twice I moved my heavy household coast to coast

and right back, unwilling to give anything up.
Possessions battered from being crated,
friends lost, things bent beyond straightening.
All for learning: If you're here, you can't be there . . .

Maria Elena listened to her husband's voice and smiled at him. He was the desert after a storm, calm and clean and smelling of sated earth. There was an innocence about him, an innocence no one could take from him—beautiful—especially when he was lost in what he was doing or reading. She could stare at him for hours, and seeing his face, she could find pieces of her life she had lost. He had written his voice into her skin and listening to him was almost as physical an experience as feeling his hands on her body. She wondered to herself how her life had happened to her, how he had happened to her. "Eres un milagro," she whispered. She rubbed the back of her baby's head, and thought it all must be a dream, this child, this man, this light in the room, this bed. It seemed she had forgotten her life before him, and now she was beginning to remember again. She wanted a part of her life back, wanted to retrieve it and give it to her husband, and give it to her child—and give it to the brother she had tried to pretend no longer existed. Home, she thought, I'm going home. Her heart jumped as if it were reaching for the city of her birth. Place mattered. Brothers mattered. She had dreamed of the river, and she tried to remember what the river was saying. No, it was not the river who had been speaking, but her. *It was a prayer, a prayer to the river. River . . . Diego . . . Home . . . River . . . Diego . . . Home.* She stared at her husband. What if he hated it there? What if he hated her for dragging him into a place that was foreign and strange and barren?

Once on a bus in Dime Box, Texas,
a woman who had flagged us down
said to the driver as she sat close behind him
and unpinned her hat: "One place
is as good as another when the heart
grows cold." "What's that?" the driver
said, glancing back in the mirror.
"One place is as good as another," she said.

Eddie shut the book. The baby was sleeping. Maria Elena let the quiet in the room surround them. "I liked the poem," she said finally. "It's the last one in the book."

"Is it true?" he asked. "Is one place as good as another?"

She shook her head.

"Will you make love to me?" he asked, his dark eyes wide and pleading.

She put the baby down in his crib. He kissed her. When she tasted him, she thought of the river and tried to remember the prayer in her dream.

Lizzie watched her mother sleeping in the bed next to her. *She's looking old. How many years for her? Is it the years that mattered? But at least she wouldn't die in his house.* She kissed her on the cheek softly, then silently slipped out of the room. No one was awake, not Eddie nor Jake nor Nena. Not the baby. The house was quiet, hollow, stripped of the things of the living. Lizzie stared at the bare walls of the living room—she imagined her name on them. She sat on the back steps in the cool morning. The bridge, she thought, I want to see the bridge. She shut her eyes, felt the weight of her body disappear. She looked down and saw herself sitting on the steps, her white bathrobe rippling softly in the breeze. She felt herself moving toward the city, and found herself astonished as she saw the buildings on the horizon. San Francisco, the only city she had ever loved. Lizzie wondered how she could leave this place so easily. It had meant so much to her, the city where she had learned to care for someone other than herself, the city where she had learned about death, about the dying, about the fragile, ephemeral beauty of the body and how the body suffered and yearned and loved. She remembered the first time she'd ever seen the skyline at night. She'd thought the lights of the buildings were more brilliant than the stars. There was no place on the earth like this city, and yet she was leaving it freely. There was another city in her future. She had dreamed it. Lizzie drifted toward the bay and the Golden Gate Bridge. She thought of her father who was not her father and who had brought her here once when he still had some kindness in him.

She took herself to the very top of the bridge, then let herself drop into the water. She floated down, down, faster, faster until she felt she had ceased to be—nearer and nearer to water, and as she was about to go into the depths, she pulled herself back up toward the sky. If she would have had a voice, she would have laughed out of pure joy.

Lizzie was back in her body again. Jake was sitting next to her, his hand trying to read her pulse. She turned to him.

He seemed more curious than frightened. "Were you away?" he asked.

"Joaquin told me you didn't really believe."

"I felt you. You were gone. How will we know when you're dead? What if you don't come back some day?"

"I'm not afraid."

"I am," he said. "I don't want to die."

She took his hand, opened his palm and rubbed it. "What are you doing?" he said.

"I'm trying to give you my gift."

He laughed. It was a beautiful thing to say. He slowly moved his hand away from hers. "Where did you go?" he asked.

"I went to say good-bye to an old lover."

"Will you miss him?"

"Yes," she said.

17

TUESDAY NIGHT, Diego spent the evening alone. He was tired, but he tried to keep himself from falling asleep. He was afraid of the dreams, but he wasn't strong enough to fight sleep. He saw his mother: She was young and was wearing a turquoise cotton dress and her long, dark hair was shining in the sun. In the dream, she had Indian features but white skin. She was holding his sister in her lap. They were yelling and looking for someone. He felt himself in the dark, almost as though he were in a coffin. "I'm right here!" he yelled. "Do you see me? I'm right here!" His voice never reached beyond the darkness. His mother and sister kept looking for him, asking for him, yelling for him. He could see their moving lips. "We're over here! We're over here, Diego!"

He woke up with a headache. The sun was coming up and the shadows in his room were cold and unfriendly. He filled the tub with hot water and soaked himself, feeling the wet heat against his skin. He remembered how pretty his sister had looked when she wore her dark red dresses. It made her skin look as gold as the color of cognac. He remembered she once smelled like the rain. He saw a face, a little girl, saw how she looked at him, felt sorry for him because he was different. And then he remembered how she used to tell him to go to his room and hide when her friends came over. He saw himself looking in the mirror when his sister led him to his room. He knew she was playing with her friends. Diego looked in the mirror to see if he was ugly, and the little boy he saw *was* ugly. He saw his mother's face—crying. She sent him to a school where everyone was nice, and he had friends. They learned to talk with their hands and look at people's lips. His teacher was so beautiful, and he wanted her to be his mother. He felt bad because he knew his mother knew what he felt, and he never looked at her in the same way ever again. Their faces wouldn't go away. They covered him like the hot water in the tub, and he wondered if he had ever loved them.

All day Diego thought of his mother, and his sister. He wondered what city his sister lived in—maybe Chicago, maybe El Paso. He pictured her face at their mother's funeral—accusing him. He pictured the casket, the flowers, remembered everything as it was except that he could not remember how she died. Maybe she had just died. Diego didn't remember. He was nineteen when it happened. *He should remember*—why couldn't he remember? He felt the steam clean his body; he washed himself and stuck his head in the water and wanted to stay there. Fragments of Mary's clothes kept appearing before him like pieces of glass. He was afraid of cutting himself.

Diego got out of the tub and made some hot coffee. He dressed himself and shaved in front of the mirror; he looked at himself like the little boy he remembered. But I'm not ugly, he thought, maybe I was never ugly.

He took a cup of coffee to his desk and stared out at the purple Juárez mountains. He tried to erase the memories. He concentrated on the colors and shadows in the mountains. "They're really brown," he thought to himself, "they're not purple—it's just the sun that makes them look that way." He tried to think of nothing. He finished his coffee and filled his cup again. He emptied the dreams out of his thoughts, out of his room. Diego left his building and walked to the bridge; he sat where Luz used to meet him and tried not to cry. He wanted to cry for Mary because they killed her; he wanted to cry for his sister because he had learned to hate her; he wanted to cry for his mother and for himself because he couldn't remember how she died and because he was thirty and was still afraid. He saw the river, and it seemed to him to be the same color as the inside of Vicky's Bar. He saw himself jumping off the bridge, and wanted to jump, but stopped himself. I still have a funeral to attend. He walked by Sacred Heart Church and stared at it. The outside was still the same, but inside it was nothing but black dust. The church was gone.

Diego wandered around the city. He sat on a bench at the plaza and waited for the sun to set. When it got dark, he went to bed. He saw a car coming down the street. He saw the space where his mother's face was supposed to be. The space looked at him. He saw the car. He heard a scream. The car tried to stop, couldn't stop— his mother was gone. He woke up. He didn't want to go back to bed. It was four o'clock. He made coffee and lit a cigarette to help him stop trembling.

He put the hot cup of coffee to his lips, and looked up. His mother's broken body was standing in front of him. He dropped the cup on the floor. His mother was gone again. He remembered, saw her throwing herself in front of that car. It happened in the spring. She did it right in front of him, threw herself down on the street. He put his face between his hands: It wasn't my fault, he thought, not my fault. But he knew his sister would always blame him, and he would never find either of them again. He thumbed through the pages of his suicide note, and wished his mother had left him a letter.

Diego went back to bed and stayed there all day. He was cold and the dreams, Mary, his mother, his sister, covered him like blankets making him colder. He felt he would never be warm again. Thursday morning he woke up, was lost, and the coffee was more bitter than usual.

As Diego sat on the steps of his house dressed in his tie, yellow shirt, and imitation gray fedora, Mundo came by in a parade of three cars. Mundo's car led the way, a canary yellow '57 Chevy with gleaming chrome rims. A deep blue '65 Mustang followed and the third car, a '71 cherry red El Camino revved its engine as it came to a stop. The cars sparkled, newly painted, as clean as any- thing Diego had ever seen. The cars were full of dark-faced young

362

men dressed in white shirts and dark hats, young men who looked as if they were going to a wedding. As the cars reached a full stop, Mundo jumped out of the first car. "What do you think? The streets got style when we travel." He took out a handkerchief from his back pocket and polished the car he was driving. "Gotta treat these babies right." He took a good look at Diego, puckered his lips; and whistled. "Now we're cookin' with gas, man—now we're lookin' good. Any woman you want is yours, man—I know what I'm talkin' about."

Diego smiled. "You like the hat?"

"It does something for you. All you need now is to grow a mustache, and then you're gonna be one mean man. They're gonna call you El Vato de Sunset Heights—I'm serious, ese." He clenched his fist and thrust it in the air. He motioned his friends, nine of them in all, to get out of the cars. All of them moved toward Diego and Mundo—slowly. Graceful. Diego thought they all looked like dancers. Mundo looked them over and began introducing them.

"This guy," he said pointing to a dark, hazel-eyed youth with a gold chain around his neck, "his name's Kiki, but they call him El Guante. He's got big hands and he used to play baseball—great hands." El Guante stuck out his hand and gave Diego the handshake of his life.

"You ever hurt anybody with those hands of yours?" Diego wrote.

El Guante looked at Diego's note strangely. "I don't like to hurt no one, but sometimes it can't be helped, you know?" He nodded seriously.

"El Guante's gonna make a great pallbearer," Mundo said. "He's got the most experience of any of us. He's been a pallbearer seven times."

El Guante smiled.

"Maybe you should stop hanging around him, Mundo," Diego wrote, "all his friends are dying."

Mundo laughed and turned to the guy standing right next to him. "And this guy, this here's El Kermit. His little sister says he talks like the frog on *Sesame Street*." El Kermit smiled and tipped his hat.

A small guy with rough hands and tattoos all over his arms moved

363

forward and shook Diego's hand. "Indio," he said, "sometimes they call me Apache." His muscular arm rippled as he shook Diego's hand.

"And this guy, here, is El Güero. He looks like a gringo, but he's all right. He doesn't like to talk English because of the way he looks." El Güero cocked his head toward Diego and took a drag off his cigarette.

"And this guy," Mundo said nodding to the driver of the blue Mustang, "is El Romeo. His last name's Romero. The women love his ass." He looked very plain to Diego, but his skin was dark and smooth. El Romeo shook Diego's hand and took his shoulder with the other. "Sorry about your girlfriend," he said. His eyes were black and intense and looking at them Diego knew why they called him Romeo.

"The rest of these guys just came along for the ride." Mundo pointed to three guys leaning on the El Camino. "I thought you'd want to meet the pallbearers—I picked the most experienced guys. We've all done this before—last year I did it twice, but like I say, El Guante's the best, but all of us are good. I got the best for La Mary."

Diego smiled and shook Mundo's hand. "You guys got some weird hobbies," Diego wrote. El Güero stretched his neck out to read the note Mundo was reading. He tried to keep from laughing, but couldn't control himself.

As they were getting into the cars, Mundo took him over to the side. "They like you, I mean it. El Güero doesn't laugh at too many things." Diego stuck out one of his thumbs in the air and cocked his head. As soon as Diego got in the front seat of the car that Mundo was driving, the engines roared and the cars drove slowly toward the funeral home.

The man in the dark suit stared at them in a controlled manner. He eyed Mundo carefully. Diego handed him a note. "We're here to accompany Mary Ramirez's body to the church. We'd like to view the body." Mundo looked over his shoulder as he wrote.

"Hey," Mundo whispered to Diego, "you got a real smooth way of saying things. You could be a writer."

The man in the dark suit stared at them.

"He's deaf," Mundo said.

The man's expression remained the same. "Are you next of kin?" Diego nodded.

Mundo pointed to his friends. "And these guys here are all the pallbearers." He looked at them in a professional manner and smiled courteously. He handed a box of carnation boutonnieres to Mundo. "You may put these on, please."

Mundo took the box and lined up the T-Birds like soldiers and pinned a flower on each guy as if he were giving out medals.

The man showed them to a small room with faded carpeting. Mary lay in a cheap, cardboard casket.

He looked at Mundo. "You have fifteen minutes before we're scheduled to leave for the church."

Diego knelt before the casket, took off his hat and made the sign of the cross. Behind him, Mundo nudged the T-Birds, and they all took off their hats, knelt on the floor and bowed their heads. Diego stared at Mary's powdered face and wished he could see her eyes. Watching her face, he tried to pray, but he could do nothing, could not even remember his childhood prayers. He did not feel the tears falling down his face. Mundo stared at him, and watched him watch Mary.

The man came in and motioned to Mundo that it was time to go. He placed his hand on Diego's shoulder, but Diego did not seem to notice his touch. He shook him gently until Diego looked up at him. "It's time to go."

El Guante, El Kermit, El Romeo, Indio, Mundo, and El Güero took the casket to the limousine. They followed the black shiny car in their bright yellow, blue, and red cars; the chrome wheels filling the streets with reflections of light.

The priest met them at the entrance to the church and sprayed the casket with holy water. "Baptized into Christ's death," he said. The T-Birds moved the casket up to the front of the church, moving slowly as if they were hearing music. Tencha and one of her friends were standing at the front of the church. Carolyn and Crazy Eddie were there, too. That was all. It was the best I could do for you, Mary, Diego thought, the best.

He stared at the flame of the Easter candle. The colors in the stained glass reminded him of the T-Birds' cars. He watched the priest like he had watched other priests a thousand times before. He had their actions memorized.

Concordia Cemetery was full of weeds and trash delivered there by the El Paso wind. It looked more like a dump than a cemetery. It was only cleaned once a year when the prisoners from the county jail were let out to clean it, but that wasn't until the summer, and it had been almost a year since its last cleaning—a year's worth of old newspapers lying up against the gravestones. Diego watched the priest read the final prayers: "May the angels carry you to paradise; the saints rise up to greet you . . ." He handed Diego the crucifix. Diego clasped it in his hands, squeezed it so tight that it dug into his skin. Mundo and the T-Birds placed their carnations on top of Mary's cardboard casket. Carolyn brought a rose.

Mundo helped Diego to the car and held him up. He would have fallen without him. On the way back to Diego's house, they stopped and picked up two cases of beer. They went inside Diego's room, and there they all drank. Carolyn brought in a basket of fruit, but she didn't stay long. "Call me if you need anything," she said.

Mundo pulled out a bottle of cognac and handed it to Diego. "Just don't ask me where I got it. Drink."

Diego poured himself a glass and drank as he watched the T-Birds drink their beer. He made no real attempt to watch their lips. They're like their cars, he thought. Mundo watched him out of the corner of his eyes as he laughed with his friends. When the beer was gone, they each shook his hand and left. "I'll come by tomorrow," Mundo said.

Diego was glad they had left. He was tired and fell asleep on the floor. He woke up in the afternoon and went to the store. He bought a can of spray paint and when he got home he opened the window and spray-painted his suicide letter so it couldn't be read by anybody.

He sat in his room and waited for the sun to set. When night came, he sat in the darkness and didn't turn on the lights. Around midnight he walked over to the barrio and found a space on a wall. He sat in front of the space for a long time and howled into the empty streets. When he was too tired to cry anymore, he spray-painted a new sign: THE VIRGIN IS DEAD.

Mundo watched him as he wrote the words on the wall. He could read what Diego had written clearly—the streetlight burning right above them like a worn out, dying sun. He watched this strange, innocent, unreachable man howl in the street like an animal, like a wounded coyote separated from his pack. Diego's voice was strong in its sorrow, as strong as any wind Mundo had ever felt. He was not so speechless after all, Mundo thought. *Every man has to have his say.* He followed his friend back home to make sure no one would harm him, followed him like a protecting angel. When Diego was back in his apartment, Mundo saw a light appear through the window. He walked back to the place where Diego had written his words. He traced the letters with his finger. "The Virgin is dead," he said out loud. And then he screamed it.

 **18**

TWO CARS AND A van are driving along the southern New Mexico desert. Two women, two brothers, an old woman and a baby—they are traveling away from the westering sun as if they are being beckoned by something they cannot resist. The gravity pulls them and they are tired of fighting. They drive free into that something they've never known. That unknown something does not frighten them.

The dark-haired brother is thinking about how his wife will look in the desert, how her dark eyes will look like coal against the endless sky, how she will grow more beautiful than the yucca in bloom, how her hair will turn the color of the earth, how her face will mirror the blinding sun and burn itself into his eyes. He wonders if she will love him less in this desert. He is looking across the great expanse—and knows he is even smaller than he ever thought. He is beginning to feel a kind of thirst he was never known. And the dark-haired man's brother is thinking: "I have found my brother, but I have lost my Joaquin. And now I am moving toward a strange doorway, but I do not know that place." But as he looks at the clouds, dark as anything he has ever known, he thinks: "I have lived in a doorway all my life. Perhaps I am going home." He drives one of the cars alone, and yet he does not feel as if he is alone anymore. He takes out a cigarette from his pocket and smokes it.

He thinks of his dead lover, and how he once walked up to him in a bar, took a cigarette out of his mouth, kissed him, then placed it back in his mouth and said, "Promise me you'll quit, gringo." He smiles at the memory. "I'll quit when I get to the promised land." He laughs to himself, and wonders at the large sky in front of him. He has never seen anything as large, as forbidding. It is startling and vast and as deep as the death he feels inside himself. He can see the storm across the desert and knows he is driving toward it. He wants it to swallow him. He lets out a puff of smoke through his nose. He sees lightning in the distance, then hears the thunder. It is like the sound of an earthquake, he thinks. *I have lived through earthquakes*. And the dark-haired woman holding her child in her arms is thinking: "I can smell it already—home—I can smell it, my mother, my brother, my skin." "Do you see?" she whispers to her deaf son. "This is what you are made of." And the other woman whose hair is much older than her skin is thinking: "This is the place I saw in my dream. Now it is more than a dream." And the old woman is dreaming as she sleeps: "Yes, this will be a good place to die."

The old woman continues to sleep as her daughter drives them into the storm. The daughter breathes in the smell of the desert, pungent and sweet. It makes her want to lick the earth, kiss it, take it into herself, take her clothes off and make love to it, the sand warmer and softer than any man's hands. She thinks: "The clouds are as dark as Joaquin's eyes in his final days." She is startled by the sound of the thunder. She remembers a storm in Chicago when she was five. She had been playing outside, not noticing the gathering clouds. When the thunder and lightning began, her mother rushed outside and carried her indoors as the rain poured down around them, carried her as if she were the rain itself. She remembers the smell of her mother's neck. She places her right hand on her mother's lap for a few seconds then places it back on the wheel. Soon, they will be driving into the torrent. She thinks she has heard this thunder in the last breaths of her patients who died too young, too alone, too angry. She knows she has heard this thunder. Soon, she thinks, we will be surrounded by the rain.

The caravan slowly reaches the center of the storm, the darkness enfolding them like a hungry lover who has been celibate for too many years. Slowly, they stop by the side of the road and wait for the downpour to cease before they continue traveling. The lightning strikes and strikes, the thunder surrounds them. And the man with the cigarette thinks: "Joaquin said the earth was animate and holy and now I know it is true." And then he thinks: "I have struck and struck—I have been the thunder," and the old woman—now more awake than she had ever been—thinks: "I have felt the thunder all my life and I am not broken," and her daughter, whose hair is as old as her mother's, looks out into the great storm and thinks: "I have dreamed of being the thunder, and will become it," and the dark-haired man looks in awe of the rain and thinks: "I have hidden from the thunder all my life, and now I must stop hiding," and then he thinks of the time he trembled in his wife's arms and told her about a cruel father whose thunder almost broke him as a boy; and the woman holding the child wants to yell for joy at the sound of the crackling sky: "I have come back to the thunder." She feels the rain pulling her to itself. Unable to contain herself any longer, she places the child in her husband's arms and runs out of the van into the arms of the rain. She begins dancing in the mud by the side of the road. The other young woman runs out of her car and begins to dance with her. They take each other's hands and swing each other in a circle. The dark-haired man watches his wife and her friend dancing in the mud, unafraid of the thunder, unafraid of the rain, unafraid of the anger of the skies. Through the sheets of pouring rain, he sees and hears them laugh. He sees them imperfectly, but knows he is seeing the perfect image of freedom.

CARRY ME LIKE WATER

 1

IT WAS DARK and cool in the desert, the night air scented with the sharp smell of the rain bush. Maria Elena looked over at her husband as they were nearing the city of her birth. "It smells like God," she said. It was hard to see his tired smile in the darkness of the van. The lights of the instrument panel allowed her to vaguely make out some of his features. She tried to picture him in the daylight, all the shadows of his past that had covered him like a shroud, banished, exiled from his face.

He took his time acknowledging her statement as if he had to think very hard about what she had said. "What is it that makes the air smell like that?"

"Chamizos," she said. "Gringos call it the rain bush. There's another name, too, creosote, I think."

"Say it again," he said.

"Chamizos," she repeated.

"Chamizos," he said slowly. "It feels good in the mouth." He laughed. "And it smells like God, huh?"

"Yes."

"You know what it really smells like?"

"What?"

"It smells like—like when you gave birth to little Jake. It smells just like that."

"Really?"

"It came from somewhere inside you, that smell. Fresh and sharp like an undiscovered spice."

Maria Elena squeezed his arm. "You're a funny man, Eddie."

"A tired man," he said almost inaudibly.

"We're almost there."

"I wonder how Lizzie and Jake are holding up?"

Maria Elena ignored her husband's question. He had asked it in a distant voice—he neither needed nor wanted an answer. His question was just taking up space in that tired kind of tone that most questions have at the end of a long journey, the voice as numb as the traveler's feet.

"EL PASO CITY LIMITS," he said, reading the sign. "Nena, you're home."

"You, too," she said.

Home, he thought. The desert felt strange and uncomfortable—a shirt that fit too tight around the neck. "It's dry," he said. "Even after a rain—it's dry."

They said nothing else as they reached the lights of the city. He saw a hotel off the freeway. "That one OK?" he asked her.

"Your call," she said.

"It's your town."

"Yeah, but they're not *my* hotels." she said.

He nodded and smiled as he pulled the van off the exit ramp. "Sunland Park Drive. What the hell kind of name is that? It sounds like a retirement village for veterans of foreign wars."

"It's a racetrack," she said. "My father used to gamble there."

"I thought you didn't know your father?"

"Well, my mother used to say he threw all his money away at the track—there and at the cockfights."

"Cockfights?"

"You never heard of cockfights?"

"Yeah—I just thought they were a thing of the past—also illegal."

"They're not a thing of the past, Eddie. And since when has illegal stopped anyone from gambling?"

Already it was a strange world, and he felt like an alien. Whatever he had been in California, at least he had not felt foreign. This didn't feel like anyplace he knew or had ever been. He chastised himself for his thoughts. All he had seen was a sign that read: EL PASO CITY LIMITS. But the lights, he thought, the lights of this city in the desert seemed unearthly to him, and he felt he had left the world completely behind. He felt almost dead. Maybe I'm just tired, he thought. Eddie wondered if this place would ever feel like home. It will be enough to see her happy, he thought. She will make it habitable.

Maria Elena stared at him as he drove. She decided she liked his outline in the darkness of the van. "When I moved to California, Eddie, it didn't feel as if it would ever be real again."

"You read my mind."

"But what if this place never makes you feel real, amor?"

"One place is as good as another," he said—then laughed. "I'm with you and that counts for something. And I have a son—and I have my brother back. That's real enough, yes? To want more than that is just greed." It will be fine, he thought. Eddie listened to the words he had just spoken. Yes, they were good words. They were the right words. All he had to do was believe them. He wondered why he felt so uneasy when he had been ecstatic to leave California. *Just believe the words.* He pulled the van into the parking lot of the Holiday Inn. *See, they have Holiday Inns.* Jake and Lizzie pulled up behind them. "All here?" he yelled as he got out of the van and placed his feet on the firm pavement of the parking lot.

"All here," Jake yelled as he stepped out of the car.

"All here," Lizzie yelled slamming her door.

"Not quite," Rose said quietly in the dark, "I'm too old to be all here. But the air here after a rain"—she paused—"you know it's been years since I've lived in a place where it rained in August." Lizzie could see her smile in the dimly lit parking lot. Her mother would like it here, she thought. It was enough of a reason to have come.

All of them seemed content to stay in the parking lot, stretching and talking, none of them caring to move toward the lobby of the hotel.

"Has anybody thought of where we're going to live?" Jake lit a cigarette as he asked the question.

"Oh Jake, I wish you wouldn't smoke—you're going to make me start again," Lizzie said sniffing at his smoke. "It smells like a banquet. I've never been this hungry."

"You always used to say that when you were a little girl. I've never been this hungry."

"I mean it this time, Mama."

Rose laughed in the darkness.

"I repeat—has anybody thought of where we're going to live?"

"Jake, you think I dragged you to El Paso without thinking of where we were going to live?" Maria Elena asked.

"Actually, yes," Lizzie said.

"Wrong. I called a realtor—and we're looking at a house in the morning."

"Actually, *I* called a realtor," Eddie corrected.

"You—me—what's the difference," Maria Elena said.

"There's a difference," Eddie said.

"I hope the house is big," Lizzie said.

"Eddie told her 'big'—didn't you Eddie?" Maria Elena leaned against Jake's car.

"That's what I told her. I told her, 'We want old, we want wood floors, and we want big.' 'I have just the house,' she said. Well, we'll see. It's in a place called Sunset Heights."

"Nice name," Lizzie said.

Jake laughed. "Sunset Heights? It sounds like a soap opera."

"Don't be mean, Jake—it's nice."

"Ahh, a hometown partisan."

"Oh, Jake, go to hell," Maria Elena said. "Are we going to check into this hotel or we just gonna pull out some beer and have a Texas tailgate?"

"I vote for a bed and cup of hot tea," Rose said.

"Mama's tired," Lizzie said. "Let's go in."

"Welcome to El Paso," Maria Elena said.

"Are you happy?" Eddie asked.

"I don't know. I feel like we've been wandering around in the desert for a lifetime."

376

"It's only been three days, Maria Elena."

"*It was a lifetime*," Maria Elena repeated.

"Uh—huh," Eddie yawned. "OK, a lifetime."

Lizzie carried the baby in her arms as they walked toward the hotel lobby. He was getting heavy, already learning to walk and Lizzie felt his growing weight. *Was it already over a year that this child had come into the world? My God, what a year.* The world had ended and begun again, and here she was in El Paso. El Paso—what a strange name for paradise. She laughed. She was tired. They were all tired, all of them exhausted and hungry, looking for rest.

Maria Elena smiled as she stepped out of the van, the baby in her arms. She thought of her childhood. She remembered the run-down apartment house in this same neighborhood—the last place she'd lived before leaving for California. "Oh, Eddie, it's a wonderful house."

"It's a little big, don't you think?" Jake asked. "And a little run-down."

"The realtor said it needed a little work—'mostly cosmetic.' " He tried to sound optimistic. "A little paint, a little this, a little that—it'll be fine."

"Yeah, sure," Jake said. "Don't be such a sucker, Eddie."

Lizzie shook her head and glared at him. "Oh don't be such a spoilsport, Jacob Leslie." She kissed him on the cheek, took the baby from Maria Elena's arms and placed him in his uncle's arms. "Just hold him and be quiet. Be a nice uncle—and try not to talk." He kissed his sleeping nephew softly. Lizzie looked at the huge house in front of them. "I like it. It's big, but it doesn't wear a sign: RICH PEOPLE LIVE HERE. It's really kind of simple looking. And look—a big front porch. It looks like the South."

"How many bedrooms?" Rose asked.

"Eight." Nena said, "One for me and Eddie, one for the baby, one for Jake, one for Elizabeth, one for you Rose, one for Diego when we find him—and two left over for guests."

"Guests? We want guests?" Jake asked.

"Shhh. You'll wake the baby," Lizzie said.

Jake smiled. "The baby can't hear—and he's practically a toddler."

"He'll be as big as his uncle," Lizzie smiled, "And what's wrong with guests?"

"Why not open a hotel?"

"This is communal living, Jacob."

"Are you sure we should all be living together?" Rose asked.

"Why, Mother? Are you afraid it's illegal?"

"Don't make fun of your mother, Elizabeth."

"Oh, Rose, it'll work out just fine," Maria Elena said, quietly nudging her husband.

"Yeah," Eddie grinned. "We couldn't possibly be more difficult to live with than your former husband."

"Very funny," Maria Elena said.

Rose broke out laughing. "Well, actually, it was funny, wasn't it? You'd have to go a ways to be harder to live with than Sam," she said, "but somehow living with so many people seems a little unnatural."

"Unnatural?" Jake asked. "You mean like homosexuality?"

"Stop it," Maria Elena said, trying not to laugh.

"It's a serious question," Eddie said. "What the hell's natural? What's so natural about living alone? Is it unnatural to live in packs?"

"Well," Lizzie said, "look at us. Tell me we're not all a little perverse."

"Speak for yourself," Maria Elena said, "I happen to be a mother."

"What does that qualify you for?" Lizzie asked.

"When the hell is the realtor coming?"

"Be patient, Jake."

Jake kissed his nephew again. "I haven't got an ounce of patience—I never have. You should know this about me." Just then the baby started to cry. Jake bounced his nephew awkwardly in his arms trying to make him stop. "He wants you," he said handing the baby to his brother.

"Thanks." Eddie felt the baby's diaper. "He's wet. Jake, it's time you learned how to change your nephew."

378

"Isn't that the mother's job?" As soon as the words came out of his mouth, he saw the look on his sister-in-law's face. He noticed a car drive up and park directly in front of the van. "Real estate agent's here," he said as he walked toward her. "Hello," he said, "I'm Jacob Marsh."

"Valerie," she said, "Valerie Miller." Her handshake was firm. She didn't look like a Valerie, he thought, more like a Marian. "I'm sorry I'm so late."

"It doesn't matter," he said, "we were enjoying looking at the house from the outside."

"Are you the man I spoke to on the phone?"

"No, that would be my brother." He pointed at Eddie who was changing the baby on the seat of the van. "The new father over there."

The woman smiled.

"He likes to change babies," Jake informed her.

Maria Elena smiled as they approached her. "I'm Maria Elena Marsh," she said, "I'm dying to see the house."

"It was built in 1915," she said sounding exactly like a woman who sold houses for a living. "It was built by a David Victor Macias who fled Mexico during the Revolution. There were rumors he was a gunrunner." The enthusiasm in her voice, however sincere, made Lizzie feel like a tourist. She was glad to fall behind and listen from a distance. "And on the third story, there's actually a ballroom. You can use it for anything you like—even for throwing balls." She laughed. Eddie managed a chuckle—he always accommodated strangers. Maria Elena dropped even farther back, content to let her husband and brother-in-law deal with the realtor's anecdotes.

"Do they go to school to talk like that?" Maria Elena whispered as they entered the house.

"Behave yourself," Lizzie whispered back. "She's nice. I can tell."

"Maybe so, but someone should tell her we're not buying the house for snob appeal."

"It doesn't matter, honey," Rose said. "Just let her talk—she's harmless. She looks like she's honest, anyway." Rose had managed to end up with the baby. "I'll catch up with you later," she said as she sat on the steps of the front porch. As Maria Elena walked through the front door of the house, she looked back and saw Lizzie's mother holding her son. She thought of her own mother, how she had watched her hold her brother every night, how she had worn a look that said he was everything in the world. She had hated her brother on those nights, had wanted to be held, had wanted to be as loved as he was. She sometimes still felt her mother's warmth in Eddie's arms as he held her at night. Sometimes, she wanted him to be her mother—her mother and her father and her husband and her lover. She wondered if he knew these things. "Stop it," she told herself—but she knew that living in this neighborhood would bring back all the memories she carried. The commands Maria Elena spoke to herself would not send the visitors away. They would come to see her in this house—they would come and they would stay. It was a better thing to welcome them than to try and exile them. She walked into the house. She heard voices echoing from upstairs. She took off her shoes and felt the cool wood floors beneath her feet. It was big and old and dusty. The walls needed painting, but the house was solid, strong, well built—and in its day it must have been as elegant as the woman who first owned it. It would never be elegant again, but it would be a clean and happy shelter. Maria Elena remembered seeing this house from the outside when she was a little girl—like the other big houses in this neighborhood, it was something that was meant to be seen only from the outside. Her mother used to clean houses like this, she thought. *I've come back, Mama. I've come back to find him. Will you help, Mama? ¿Me oyes? Yo sé que me estás oyendo. It was wrong of me to leave, but I'm back now, Mama.* She sat down in the middle of the dining room and looked out into the backyard through the French doors. She imagined herself making love to Eddie on this floor. She imagined her brother sitting across from her. She imagined having a thousand conversations with Lizzie and watching her son learning to walk on the floors of this house. *"I want this house."* She felt the spirit of the house, and knew it was good. Perhaps it was her mother. She knew it would bring her blessings.

"Nena!" She heard her name echoing down the stairs. "Nena,

come and see!" She rose slowly from the floor and made her way up the stairs. Eddie was leaning over the railing. "Nena, it's incredible. It needs a little work—but it's really incredible!" He looked like a college boy.

She smiled at him calmly. "Tell the realtor we'll take the house," she said softly.

"But you haven't seen it all," he said.

"No, amor, but you have."

He laughed. "I didn't know you were so spontaneous."

"After making love to me for more than seven years, you think I can't be spontaneous?"

"The bedroom's different."

"Nope."

As she reached the top of the stairs, Jake walked up to his brother and put his arm around him. "Great house," he said— "not as big as the one we grew up in—but much simpler. Lots of light. Did our house have light, Eddie? I don't remember."

"I don't remember light."

"Lots of light in this house," Maria Elena said. "They call it the city of the sun."

"This house?" Jake asked.

"No—the city."

"Well, I haven't seen much of it—but I can tell you this much, Nena, it's not San Francisco."

"Are you two fighting?" Eddie asked.

"No, honey, we're not fighting—we're just relating." She winked at Jake as she spoke. "Where'd you put the realtor?"

"She's on the third floor talking to Lizzie—turns out she's an ex-nurse—and they're talking shop."

"Does Lizzie like the house?"

"Are you kidding—she loves it. She says she wants to live in the ballroom—windows on every side. She's decided she wants to paint."

"And maybe," she laughed, "she'll give us lessons on how to leave our bodies."

I'm leaving mine soon enough, Jake thought.

Maria Elena stood between them and took each of them by the arm. "Give me a tour of my new house."

"I didn't know looking for a house would be so easy."

"Jake, everything is easy when you have money."

Eddie noticed the bitterness in her voice. It was like a grain of sand in his eyes.

 **2**

On Monday morning Diego walked slowly and carefully through the darkness of the downtown morning as if he were walking on bodies he thought he might crush as easily as leaves—no one on the streets but him and the weight of the things he felt. The dark sky was turning pale blue and he wondered if his boss would be at Vicky's waiting for him to return, waiting with extra work, waiting with a face that made him feel as though he should be invisible. He imagined his boss's face, hard like the street he walked on, like the concrete of the gray jail. Normally, his boss didn't show up at Vicky's until noon, but he sensed he would be there on this morning, there, waiting. It felt strange to be walking back to work after a week's absence—he had never been free of work for a whole week, and now he felt as though he had been gone for a lifetime, and had forgotten about that previous life. He didn't want to be walking toward Vicky's—not anymore—that path too much like the steps that went nowhere. He dragged his feet on the sidewalk as he approached the faded blue building. He read the hand-painted sign on the wall: VICKY'S BAR. He hated the hand that had painted it. Diego stared at the letters as if by staring at them, he could erase not only the name of the place but the whole damn building. He put his key in the door and walked in. The lights were on, and his boss was waiting for him, his face sagging with wrinkles, and yet the wrinkles were anything but soft—ungiving as if his wrinkles had hardened permanently. His skin looked like cracked stone. Diego shut the door behind him and stood motionless.

His boss glared at him. "Give the kitchen a good cleaning before the day's over. Wax the floor before the noontime lunch crowd. You're working late every day this week until you catch up on your work—and no overtime pay. You got that? And I'm cutting your salary to two seventy-five an hour." He held up a sign that read: $2.75. "Did you get that, deaf man?"

Diego paused and then nodded.

"I'm surprised you had the nerve to come back to work."

Diego did nothing, just stared at his lips.

"You're pretty brave when you have that hoodlum with you." He took off his apron, then came out from behind the bar and handed it to Diego. He grinned: "So long as we understand each other we'll get along fine"—he paused—"like we always have." He walked back to the bar and picked up his briefcase. "I've been working my ass off all week. I'm going home, but I'll be back around noon—and the place better look good."

Diego walked into the kitchen and began preparing the food.

His boss walked in a few minutes later and stared at him. Diego tried to ignore him, tried not to look up from his work, but he could feel his boss's eyes crawling on his body like roaches. Diego felt him as he left the room, and he took a deep breath. He lit a cigarette. When the food was prepared, he stepped out into the small dining room and bar. His boss was gone. Diego shook his head as he looked at the filthy floor. He took out the ammonia and the mop and stacked the chairs on top of the tables. He scrubbed the floor and then waxed it. It shone like the T-Birds' cars. He lit a cigarette and stared at the drying floor from the kitchen. All the dirt was gone. He smiled at his good work. "Magic hands," he thought, "like Mundo's." The first customers walked in and sat down at a corner table. Diego smiled at them and brought them a menu.

The week went by slowly. "This will never end," he wrote when he got back home each night, "it will never, never end." He worked late every evening until Vicky's was spotless. He didn't write any notes to his boss all week, not once. His boss gave him orders when he came in around ten o'clock. He seemed happier now that he knew Diego could read lips. He always ended his orders with: "Did you get that?" When he spoke too fast, Diego would shake his head. "Idiot, pay attention," he'd say, and repeat the command. Diego hated him more than he had ever hated anyone. His hate for his sister wasn't like this, he thought, not like this at all. Sometimes even his hands itched as if they were on fire when he saw his boss's face. He scratched at them. This is hate, he thought, this is really hate, and he wondered if he would ever feel anything that made him feel as sad or alive as this hate that blew through him daily. "Magic hands," he thought to himself, and laughed. He even had a dream that he could hear, but the only thing he heard was his boss saying, "Did you get that? Did you get that? Did you get that?"

Sunday morning Diego woke early. It was late May, and soon it would be summer. The winds had come and gone. He didn't bother with coffee; he didn't brush his teeth; he didn't shave; he didn't wash himself. He put on his dirty clothes, and before the sun rose he walked through Sunset Heights and stole flowers from people's gardens until he had a large bouquet. He went downtown and bought a newspaper from a machine and wrapped the flowers carefully on a bench at San Jacinto Plaza. He took a long walk toward Concordia Cemetery. It took him over an hour to walk there, but he had not minded the walk. Diego placed the wilting flowers on Mary's unmarked grave. He pulled the weeds and raked the litter away with his hands. He placed a note with the flowers on the ground: "I'm going to get you a marble marker."

The sweat rolled down his face and burned his eyes—the loose dirt from the graveyard stuck to his sweaty skin. He stared at the colors of the flowers and remembered the tulips he had seen at the plaza on Easter Sunday. He clenched his fist and his teeth, turned from the grave, and headed toward downtown. By then, it was almost noon. He thought of going back home, but decided to keep walking. He wandered toward Sacred Heart Church and watched the workers rebuilding it. An old lady came up to him and asked him something. He didn't understand what she was saying. He shrugged his shoulders, and she repeated her words but her lips were too difficult for him to read.

"¿Que no entiendes español?" she asked.

Diego took out his pad and wrote: "Señora, no oigo. Nací sordo. Si habla despacio y con cuidado la puedo entender." He showed her his note.

"Ay," she said, "pobrecito. Dios lo ha de cuidar. Mire, estamos juntando dinero para renovar nuestra iglesia que se quemó."

Diego stared at the raffle tickets in her hand. GRAND PRIZE: BRAND-NEW LINCOLN CONTINENTAL. DONATION $1.00. SPONSORED BY THE DAUGHTERS OF THE BLESSED VIRGIN MARY OF SACRED HEART CHURCH. Diego smiled to himself, knowing that he would buy a ticket. What was he going to do with a new car? He didn't even know how to drive. He smiled at the old woman and took a dollar out of his pocket.

"¡Que lindo muchacho!" she said. "Tan amable."

He smiled at her as he put his raffle ticket in his wallet, and watched the workers that kept coming in and out of the church. He wondered how long it would take before they finished rebuilding it.

As he stared at the doors of the church, Luz appeared in front of him—out of nowhere like a vision, like the Virgin of Guadalupe had appeared to the Indian Juan Diego.

He shook his head and wondered when the dreams were going to go away. He closed his eyes and opened them again. Luz was still there—in front of him—standing like a statue. He smiled at the image.

"So," Luz said, "why the hell are you buying raffle tickets from old ladies, my Diego? You really think you're going to win the pinche jackpot?"

He stared at her, wondering when she was going to disappear. Maybe she wasn't there. Maybe she didn't really move her lips, maybe he was dreaming. Maybe he had gone crazy. He wanted to write on his pad and show her his handwriting, but he was afraid. Maybe she'd disappear. He wanted her to be real.

"Well, Dieguito," she said, "no kisses? Not even a pinche abrazo?"

He reached over and touched her arm, real skin—it was her. He smiled at her, touched her face, and did not want to move his hand away. He looked into her bright brown eyes and hugged her, held her in his arms for a long time, the tears from his face rolling off onto her shoulder. She let him cry and softly rubbed his back. Finally, he let go and looked at her again. She wiped his tears with her wrinkled hands, and Diego stared at her eyes that sparkled like the water in the river.

They sat at the corner, and Diego took out his pad. "Don't ever leave El Paso again, Luz. You understand?"

"No, my Diego, I'm never leaving El Paso again, that's for damn sure. If I'm going to be screwed over, I'd rather be screwed over in El Paso."

"I never thought anybody could look so good," he wrote. "You look beautiful."

Luz grabbed his hand and squeezed it. "Ay Dieguito, you think I'm Miss America or something. Not only are you deaf, querido, but you've gone damned blind." She threw her head up and combed her hair with her fingers. "Look at me, Diego, I look like a dried-up prune. I smoke too damn much—it's wasting me away. The cigarettes and the pinche floors I clean, they're going to kill me. I feel like shit, Dieguito."

"But you're home now, Luz."

"Yes, I'm home, but I lost my house in Juárez, and now I don't have a pinche place to live. I think I'm going to look for something here in El Paso." She paused and took a deep breath and coughed. "I have enough money. I worked my ass off in Chicago, and now I'm going to rest a while, Dieguito. I'm going to have to go back to work, but I can rest a while."

"You'll find a place," Diego wrote, "something nice. There are lots of places here."

"Never mind nice, Dieguito, just some place with a bed and a kitchen."

"I've never had a place with a kitchen," Diego wrote, "the only kitchen I know is at Vicky's Bar."

"You still working for that pinche?"

Diego nodded. "Where else?"

"You shouldn't work for him, Dieguito. I see you're still letting yourself get run over by everybody. God is going to lose patience with you. Carlos told me your boss has a brother who works with the migra. A bunch of bastards in that family—the poor mother. You should refuse to work for people that are in with the migra. Aren't you afraid God will punish you?"

"Being deaf is punishment enough. If God punishes me for working at Vicky's then he's a bad God. Why are the wrong people always being punished?"

Luz looked at his answer and laughed. "Ay Dieguito! You always have something to say, don't you? What would have happened if God had given you a voice? You'd be running this city and those pinches on city council would be working at Vicky's."

Diego laughed, his dark eyes lighting up in Luz's presence. She had brought something back to him, something which only she could give. "I can't believe you're home—I just can't believe it. Everything's going to be all right—I can just feel it."

"Yes," she said, "here we sit in front of this damned church that burned down." She stopped. "Did a gringo burn it down?"

Diego looked at her and grinned. He shook his head.

"Just thought I'd ask," she said. "Anyway, like I was saying, Dieguito, here we sit in front of this burned down church, and you're still living in that apartment with that pinche, cheap, poor excuse for a landlord and you're still working for that bastard at Vicky's and I don't have a place to live, and you're telling me everything's going to be all right. Some things never change, Dieguito. You're beautiful, my Diego. A piece of work, you are, amor."

"But you told me we'd win someday, remember?"

"I've changed my mind, Dieguito. Thank God that I'm still pissed off, otherwise I'd just lie down and let a car run over me."

Diego looked at her. He shook her gently. "Don't ever say that," he wrote. "*Never say that.*"

She thought a moment, and looked at him. "I was just joking, Diego. The car that runs over me is going to wind up in a dump. I swear I'll come back from the dead and haunt that damned driver until he prays to God to take his worthless life. I was just joking."

"Don't joke about that."

"Why are you so uptight, Dieguito? What's wrong?"

"I'll tell you later," he wrote. "Anyway, when did you get here? Tell me about your trip."

"This morning. I flew in from Chicago. I had to spend the pinche night at the Dallas airport with all those flashy people. I swear, I'll never understand the gringo—never. You should see the way they dress. Unbelievable, my Diego. Women paint their hair the same color as their nail polish, and their clothes are bright and baggy. Everybody is wearing baggy. Nothing fits anybody. They pay good money for clothes that fit too big. And they laugh at the way we paint our houses. I'll never understand them, it's just not possible— I could watch them and watch them and never have a clue. The pinches laugh at us, and think we want to be just like them."

"Was it a nice airport?"

"You ask the damndest questions, mi Diego. Are you sure you're not part gringo?"

"Maybe I am," he wrote, and laughed. "I read in the newspaper that Dallas had one of the most modern airports in the world."

"Yes," she nodded, "it's all very modern. It could use some graffiti if you ask me, Dieguito. Some parts of Chicago, mi amor, are just wonderful. Lots of graffiti. I read a sign there, and it said: THE RICH ARE SWINE. It was beautiful, just beautiful, mi Diego. The rich hate to read shit like that—it really pisses them off. I hate the rich. But that airport was too damned clean. And the chairs were uncomfortable. Who could sit on them? You'd think that the people who know so much about sitting could make some comfortable chairs, and they got little stores everywhere—twenty dollars for a T-shirt that says DALLAS. You know what I could do with twenty dollars? And me, I don't even want people to know I've been to that damned city. Screw their T-shirts, Dieguito."

"They have a famous football team."

"What is that to me or you, Diego? What does a football team have to do with our lives?"

"I don't know—I've never watched a game."

"You're not missing a damned thing, Diego—not one damn thing. People will throw money away on a goddamned ticket to a game— but they won't put a dime in a beggar's cup."

389

Diego was sorry he'd raised the issue. He smiled to himself. She hadn't changed a bit. "Did you like the flight?" he wrote.

"What's happening to your handwriting, Dieguito? You're beginning to write like an old man."

"I'm tired, that's all. Tell me about your flight."

"Well, the flight, it was a beautiful thing. I felt like a bird. We flew right through the clouds." She clapped her hands and laughed. "And Diego, my body felt—I don't know—it felt good. And the stewardess brought me a beer, and I never wanted to set foot on the earth again. You should try it sometime. But then you know what happened? As soon as we landed at the airport, the migra stopped me. I swear those bastards follow me around everywhere I go. They're a curse, Diego! As soon as I got off the plane, a migra dressed in blue jeans asked me for my papers. The sonofabitch asked me twice! His Spanish was the worst thing I've ever heard. Just listening to it made me want to hit him. I gave him one of my looks, one of those looks that told him he'd better protect his balls if he asked me anything else. And then he asked me a third time. I wanted to kill, Diego, just kill. God knows I don't like to speak English to gringos, but I told him, 'If you ask me for my papers one more time I'm going to go get my son, the lawyer, to drive one of those damn green vans up your ass.' He said he was going to haul me in. He knew I was a citizen, the pinche, just by the way I answered his question. But the sonofabitch wanted some respect. Respect is one thing he'll never get, not from me. He asks people for their papers for a living and the cabrón wants respect. He wanted me to be nice to him. I just walked away, Diego, just turned my back. He didn't even go after me. If he would've followed me, I would have screamed, Diego, I would have screamed and let the whole damned airport think he was a molester. That's what they are: they're molesters. And poor Carlos, those bastards got him—but the last time I heard, he'd left El Salvador again. His gringa girlfriend sent him money to bribe his way out and get back to Chicago. He's going to make it. Believe me, Diego, Carlos is going to make it. That gringa loves him. And Carlos, he loves her, too. And that gringa's pinche mother's going to lose her mind when they get married. I didn't use to believe in purgatory, but now I've come around. I hope the Church is right about that—and I wish I got to choose who'd have to spend a lot of time there." She reached for a cigarette and laughed. "Yes, mi amor, there's going to be a wedding. Carlos and his gringa, they're going to be happy!"

Diego watched her clap her hands and joined her. Luz lit her cigarette. She inhaled deeply and stared out into the streets. "The streets are nicer here than in Chicago." She reached for Diego's hand. Diego felt the softness of her age, the softness of her skin that was no longer tight around her bones. They sat on the corner in silence until Luz finished her cigarette.

"I'm going to have to go and stay with a friend in Juárez until I find a place. She has my books, my furniture, and my altar. On Monday, I'll start looking for a place to live."

Diego watched her lips, her graying hair. He put his pen on his pad, and pressed down. He stopped before writing anything down.

"You were going to write something," she said.

He nodded.

"What were you going to write?"

"You know how I don't like Mr. Arteago very much," he wrote, "he's so cheap. No air conditioner, no heat. I was thinking that if you found a place to live with two bedrooms, then maybe we could be roommates. I'm easy to live with. Wouldn't you like to be my roommate?" He watched her read the note. Diego tried to keep himself from looking too eager. He kept his gaze focused on the pad he was writing on. "And neither of us would have to live alone. It's not good to live alone, Luz. I don't like it."

She put out her cigarette and lit another. "Yes," she smiled. "But only on one condition."

"What's that?" Diego wrote.

"You have to quit your job."

"That's crazy, Luz. I can't do that."

She clapped her hands and pinched his cheek. "Ay Dieguito! It's a wonderful idea! You could finally live in a house with a kitchen, and we could live very well, the both of us. Hell, it would be great. But I won't live with you unless you quit working for that pinche at Vicky's. While you're getting rid of your landlord, you might as well get rid of your boss, too. Throw all the bastards out of your life, and be free, Diego. It's time."

"But I won't have any money if I quit."

"Look, Diego, you have a nice way about you. I know about these things. I know about people and how they carry themselves. Everybody likes you, Diego, believe me."

"Everybody likes me," Diego wrote, "because I can't talk."

"No, Diego, people like you because you're intelligent, and because you're generous. Why do you think the people at the plaza ask you for cigarettes? The bastards don't know you're deaf. People ask you for cigarettes because they can tell you're the kind of person that will give them one. You'll find a job. Believe me, Dieguito, you'll find a good job, and that good-for-nothing you work for will never find another pendejo that will work for him like you have— and that's for sure. That rat you work for will kill you with that disease he carries. I mean it Dieguito, he doesn't deserve your loyalty." She grabbed his hands. "These hands belong to a worker— and that man doesn't deserve your hands, mi amor."

"Even if you're right," he wrote, "it's going to take some time to find another job. What will I do for money until then?"

"How much money have you saved?"

"Nothing. I had a little money put away, and I bought a new hat and some clothes—and I bought Mary a hat. I don't have anything left. Well, maybe a few dollars."

"You see what I mean? You've worked for ten years for that pinche and you haven't got a damn thing to show for it. Ten years, Diego, and you have shit—his shit, Diego, you're covered with it. Quit! It's time. Tell him to stick that blue bar up his ass. The only reason he gets any business is because of your cooking. Walk away, damnit. We can live just fine with the money I've saved. I can find a job easy, Diego. You'll find something, too, and we'll be set."

"I don't like the idea of living off you while I'm looking for a job," he wrote.

"Are your balls going to shrink?"

Diego burst out laughing. Luz threw her head up and clapped her hands.

"Is it a deal, my Diego?"

"It's a deal," Diego wrote. He took her hand and squeezed it. "MONDAY," he wrote in big letters, "I'M GOING TO SAY GOOD-BYE TO VICKY'S BAR."

 3

As the old woman walked through the streets of the dark and empty city, she suddenly felt strange movements at her feet. She looked down and noticed an owl pecking at her bare feet as if it were a hungry hen attacking kernels of dry corn. She kicked it away, and the owl disappeared into the darkness. She walked steadily forward and wondered about the owl. She should not have kicked it. She looked down at her foot and saw the owl had drawn blood. She bent down and wiped the blood away. The mark disappeared same as the owl. She walked faster; perhaps the owl would return. Suddenly, she felt feathers around her ankles. She looked down and saw three owls rubbing against her. She felt the beaks pecking at her feet. She stopped, kicked them away one by one. As she kicked the first one, it flew into the air and turned into a rose. The rose fell at her feet. She kicked away the second. It too, flew into the air, turned into a rose and fell at her feet. She took the third by the throat and began choking it. But as she squeezed, she realized she was cutting herself on the thorns of a wild rose. She wiped the blood on her face. It was dawn, and she looked for the sun to save her. She would be safe in the day. Just as the sun appeared, an army of owls flew out of the rising sun—flew closer and closer. They began landing on the streets of the city, millions of them, millions and millions of them. The old woman found herself walking through a sea of hooting owls. They made a path for her as she walked. As she looked down, she saw they were feeding on rose petals.

She felt unable to breathe. She wanted to scream for help. Doesn't anybody see? Can somebody help? She felt as if her heart were about to burst, the adrenaline flooding her fragile body. She looked down at her feet and realized the owls had pecked away her flesh. She stared at the bones of her feet.

Rose trembled in the bed as she opened her eyes. She took several breaths and made herself relax. She could not help but pull back the blanket and stare at her feet. They were all there, all the flesh, the same feet. She laughed at herself.

It was the third time the dream had come to her. Three times was two times too many. She had never had a recurring dream. "What's a dream, anyway," she said to herself, "it's the waking that counts." She concentrated on the dawn. The sun was on the rise. The darkness was disappearing. Early summer mornings in El Paso were cool, and Rose stared at the open window to her bedroom. "So much light," she said to herself. The weather was good for her bones, and for the first time in weeks, she was in no pain. "Rose, old girl," she said in a normal tone as if she was outside of herself, "your mind's getting as shot as your bones." She sat up, and lifted herself to the floor as if by doing so, she could leave the dream lying on the bed where she had been sleeping. But she knew exactly what the dream meant, what the dream would extract from her. She wondered why she was suddenly panicking at the thought of her own death. Perhaps there was panic before the final calm. She took in a deep breath. "But the bones don't hurt today, but the bones don't hurt." She walked to the closet and put on a white cotton dress Lizzie had bought for her. The cloth was as soft as her aging skin.

 4

Sunday afternoon Diego put the word out on the streets of El Segundo barrio that he was looking for Mundo. Diego waited for him on the steps that went nowhere. That evening he watched Mundo dance his way up the street.

"What's the word?" Mundo asked as he reached out to shake his hand. "You got some more private-eye work for me, ese?"

Diego shook his finger in the air, wrote down a few words, and stuck a note into Mundo's hands. "I'm going to quit my job tomorrow. I want you to be there when I do it. I'm going to give him this letter." He handed a neatly folded piece of paper to Mundo who began reading the perfect handwriting:

Dear Gonzalo,
I have always hated working for you. I don't like you—I never have. From the very beginning I could see that you were mean and cruel and awful, but I've never been able to figure out why. (I guess it doesn't matter, does it?) I've worked for you for almost ten years (ten years!), and you have never given me a vacation, and you've never treated me like a real human being, and you never even pretended to treat me with any kind of respect. I deserve some respect.

My friends have told me I was a pendejo for putting up with you, and do you know something? They were right. But as of today, I AM QUITTING. I don't think I owe you a two-week notice. I don't think I owe you anything. I have gathered witnesses that are willing to testify to the fact that I have been working for you for the last nine and a half years. I am reporting you to the I.R.S. and the Social Security Commission, and I am getting a lawyer to help prosecute you for breaking the law. I have no benefits, and I have not even paid a cent into Social Security because you paid me in cash so you wouldn't have to pay me minimum wage. I decided, in the name of justice, to make sure you get busted. None of this would have happened if I had ever seen a trace of human decency in you. I'm sorry it has to be this way, but I have the feeling if I just quit, you'd find another employee to step on. I'm going to make sure you never treat anybody like you've treated me ever again. I guess I'll see you in court. Maybe they'll put you behind bars. Who knows? Maybe they'll go easy on you.

Sincerely,
Juan Diego Ramirez

Mundo handed the letter back to Diego, thrust his fist up in the air and let out a yell. He picked Diego up and flung him around in circles, throwing him playfully back on the ground. He laughed and applauded, and did a dance up and down the steps that went nowhere. "Man, Mr. Diego, you should be writing for a newspaper or somethin'. You can do some smooth writing. That sonofabitch is gonna be mad as hell. It's perfect. I know what I'm sayin', Diego. It's the most perfect letter you ever wrote."

"You really think so?"

"Listen, you doin' yourself real proud. I don't read too much, you know, but I got a good eye. Look, I'll read it to you. Watch my lips real good, just watch." Diego handed the note back to him. He stood near the top of the steps, and began reading the letter aloud. As Diego looked up at him from a few steps below, he felt as though he were watching a play. He stared at Mundo's lips and tried to imagine what his own words sounded like. When he finished, Diego clapped his hands and laughed.

Mundo took a bow and snapped his fingers. He skipped down the steps. "You want to read it to him?" Diego wrote.

"Nah, Diego, what's wrong with you? That's not my job, man, that's *your* job. Just hand him the note and let the bastard get a good look at your handwriting. His teeth are gonna drop to the damn floor. That smile of his is gonna disappear off the face of the city—forever, man. It's gonna be great—it's gonna be so damn great! I hate that guy."

"Will you be there when I show it to him, just in case he gets violent or something?"

"Man, I wouldn't miss it, Diego. That good-for-nothin', spineless, dickless pig once had a friend of mine thrown in jail. If he even looks at you wrong, I'll jump him and tear a new asshole in him."

"Don't hit him, Mundo—promise me you won't hit him. I don't like that. Just keep an eye on him, that's all. I got another friend of mine who's going to be there. Her name's Luz, and she says she wouldn't miss seeing this for the world. Just get there around ten or so at Vicky's. I'm going in just like always, and he never comes in until later. Just be there around ten, that's all."

Mundo smiled as he read Diego's handwriting. "I'll be there, you bet. But who's this Luz that's gonna show?"

"She's an old friend. Remember, I told you all about her?"

"Oh yeah," he said, "that crazy maid that talks a lot and puts men down. I thought you said she was in Chicago?"

"She's back, and we're even going to be roommates. She's going to find us a place, and we're going to move in together."

"Man, Diego, you got yourself a sugar mama."

Diego laughed. "It's not like that. We're both tired of living alone, that's all. And besides that, it's cheaper. And if you ever need a place to stay, you can always come over to our place. It's going to be a real nice apartment—maybe even a house—not like I have now. It's going to be real nice. Just wait, you'll see, a kitchen and everything."

Monday, at ten o'clock, Luz and Mundo showed up at Vicky's, both of them wearing smiles. There were only a few customers lingering from a late breakfast. Diego sat them at a table right next to the bar. "Best seats in the house," he wrote.

Luz laughed and looked the place over.

"Luz," Diego wrote, "this is Mundo. He's my friend."

Luz lit a cigarette and looked Mundo over. She smiled politely.

"I hear you and Diego are gonna be living together."

Luz nodded, but did not attempt to make conversation with him. She disliked him on sight. He was too much like a lot of men she'd known—too much like her first husband.

"You got an extra cigarette, esa?"

Luz handed him a cigarette. "Don't call me 'esa,' " she said. "I don't like that. I'm old enough to be your mother. I got sons big enough to kick your ass, so just have a little respect."

She looked at Diego. "Since when have you started hanging around with gang members? Look at that tattoo—people like him wear those things like medals."

"He's a nice guy, Luz. Don't be rude."

She took the note and shook her head. "You really are a pendejo, my Diego. Just look at him." She looked directly into Mundo's eyes. "I know lots of pinches like this guy."

"Look, esa, I don't have to take any of your shit, got it? Diego here, he's all right—he saved my ass. We help each other out, just like you're supposed to do, got that? I don't want no trouble with his friends."

"Be nice, Luz," Diego wrote.

She made a face at his note. "My first husband was just like your friend here. He used to strut around the streets like he owned them. He left me with two sons when somebody blew him away."

"Look, esa, I'm not your pinche husband. Whatever that clown did to you, it's not my fault. I ain't got nothin' to do with it."

Diego brought them a cup of coffee. "It's on the house," he smiled.

Luz clapped her hands as she read his note. "Ay, Dieguito, you do have a sense of humor." She looked across the table and met Mundo's eyes. "I bet you use those black eyes to crawl into a lot of skirts."

Mundo smiled.

Luz smiled back at him. "I'm going to be nice to you. I don't like you, but I'll try and be nice to you for Diego."

"Look, esa," Mundo stared back, "I won't mess with you. I swear it."

"And don't call me 'esa.' My name is Luz."

He nodded. "Doña Luz." He laughed.

Luz looked around the room and puffed on her cigarette. She motioned to Diego and pointed at the bar a few feet away. "He's here, Dieguito."

Diego froze. He took a deep breath and felt his heart pounding. He thought it would leap from his chest and fly away like the pigeons at San Jacinto Plaza. "Maybe I should forget about it, and just walk out," he wrote. He put the note on the table.

"No, man," Mundo said. "Go up to him and flatten his ass." He looked at Luz. "Doña Luz and me, we'll be right here watching the whole thing. Show him what you got, Diego. Stay cool—real cool."

He looked over at his employer. "Ten years," he thought.

"Move, Diego," his boss said, "you still haven't mopped the floors." His eyes caught Luz's face—and he smiled at her. "He's getting a little lazy," he told her. His eyes looked her over carefully. He didn't notice Mundo sitting across from her. "You've never been in here before, have you?"

"No," she smiled at him, "but this place has a reputation. All my friends tell me that Diego is the best waiter in town—the best cook, too. If it wasn't for him, all your customers would leave—at least that's what I hear." She grinned at him and winked.

He smiled back at her.

Diego walked up to him and handed him the neatly folded note.

"What's this?" he asked. He opened the note and began reading it.

Diego, Mundo, and Luz watched him closely. His face turned red as he finished reading the note. He wadded it up in a fist. "You ungrateful pig!" he yelled. His contorted face wrinkled up with his anger. Diego's eyes opened wide, and he felt his heart pounding faster than a hummingbird's wings. He thought it was going to pound himself into powder. His boss grabbed a dirty, wet towel from the bar and threw it at Diego. Diego caught it as if he were intercepting a football and threw it back at him without thinking. His eyes opened wide as the wet towel hit his boss's chest. He felt as though he were somebody else; felt as if he was no longer the same man, the man who had worked in this dark place for ten years. His boss reached over the bar and grabbed him by the collar. "Nobody does me like that. I'm going to break both your fucking hands, and you'll never write another note again." Diego felt the breath pressing against his face like a hot iron.

Mundo leapt from his chair and threw a closed fist at Diego's boss. He stared up at Mundo, dazed, and fell back against the wall breaking the glasses behind him. He shook his head and wiped his bleeding lip, clenched his jaw and then raised his fist.

Luz got up from her chair and walked in front of him. "Look, you pinche, you swing that fist and you're a dead man." She stuck her chin out and pointed directly at his face. "You like the ladies, don't you? Well, you move one inch and you'll never make love to another woman again."

Diego's boss stared at the trio in front of him. He looked at Mundo, then Luz, then Diego—then looked toward the telephone.

"Don't even think about it," Luz said.

His faced turned white.

Luz winked at him. "You look like you could use a drink, Gonzalo. Your name's Gonzalo, isn't it?"

He nodded his head slowly.

Mundo looked over at Diego. "Pour the man a drink, Diego. On the house."

Diego walked over to the other side of the bar and poured his boss a drink. Luz and Mundo looked at each other and smiled while Mundo poured Gonzalo some tequila. Diego stopped, smiled, and took out three more glasses, and poured them all a drink. "This one's on me," he wrote. He took out a five-dollar bill and placed it on the bar. They raised their glasses, all of them except Gonzalo.

"Won't you have a drink with us?" Luz asked. "Have a drink with us, you pinche."

"Fuck you," he shouted.

"Ah man," Mundo said, "Doña Luz asked you real nice, Gonzalo. C'mon, have a drink. A little shot to settle your nerves."

Gonzalo raised his glass and they all drank. "I spit on all you bastards," he said. He looked at Diego. "I give you a job and this is what you do to me?"

Diego looked at his pad and wrote: "It takes more than three dollars an hour to buy someone's loyalty. My lawyer will be in touch." He smiled at Luz and Mundo then added to the note: "Rot— I hope you rot in this place." Luz and Mundo laughed as he put the finishing touches to his note. He shoved it in front of Gonzalo who tried to ignore it.

"Read it," Mundo ordered. "The man is trying to communicate with you."

Gonzalo stared at the note and read it.

"Read it aloud."

Diego watched his lips as he read it. He handed his apron to Gonzalo and stretched out his arms as if he were about to fly. He walked out from behind the bar on Luz's arm. They walked out of Vicky's windowless bar, and stepped out into the streets of the city. If I had a voice, Diego thought to himself, I would howl in the streets, I would howl *"I'm free, I'm free."*

 **5**

August 24, 1993

Leaving my body has become an addiction. I keep wanting to leave it forever. I ask myself if it isn't a death wish. I wonder. I used to feel desperate like this every time I fell in love with a man—and it never worked out. Why did I always need a man's approval so desperately? It's not that I ever let them know how I felt—not that it mattered. I was addicted to men until Salvador gave me his gift. Ever since that day, I've felt very free of them—and I don't really miss them. I used to look at them all the time, always staring at them wondering what they were like. Men and cigarettes—it was as if they went together. And both were bad for me. But they were such exhilarating habits. Funny thing about addictions, you fall completely in love with them—that's part of the problem.

But now this thing with leaving my body—it's scary. What am I supposed to do? I get up in the morning and all I can think of is leaving my body. I keep hoping it will grow old in time—but it hasn't grown old at all. It's like being a god or an angel—except that I'm not sure I believe in either of those things. I don't know what I believe in—I just know I can leave my body. And that I like traveling as if I were nothing but light. I used to think that the only ecstasy I'd ever know was the ecstasy I felt when I was with a man. I never thought I'd ever feel anything that approached joy. But this is joy. This is really joy.

403

And yet I've seen so much misery since I've arrived here. Maria Elena told me there was poverty here—I didn't know how much of it there'd be. Last week, I read in the newspaper about a bleeding icon in Juárez. A man held up a picture of the Sacred Heart of Jesus that had suddenly begun to bleed. A miracle, he said. The reporter had asked him why it was bleeding. "Because he feels our pain," the man had said. I wanted to see that man. I wanted to touch him. I wanted to read his mind and understand what he felt. The newspaper named the colonia where the man lived. I asked Nena what a colonia was. She told me it was a district—like The Castro or The Mission in San Francisco. That same afternoon, I left my body to find that man and his bleeding Sacred Heart. It's so easy to cross the border without a body. It should be this easy for everybody—that's what I thought. Why not? Why the hell not? Somehow, the place where the man lived was easy to find. The man lived in a colonia with no electricity and no running water. Already, they had built a shrine for the bleeding heart of Jesus. There was a line for miles, and all of the pilgrims were poor, all of them obviously from the same neighborhood. And there were groups of people dressed in different garbs dancing in front of the bleeding heart. A group of men had evidently butchered a hog and were cooking portions of it over an open fire. Vendors were selling food and brooms and rosaries. I was moved because there was an innocence about them that I simply do not understand. At the end of the twentieth century, some still believed. But it angered me because I wanted them to make a revolution. They lived so close to such wealth and had nothing. In this neighborhood alone there were thousands of them. I went home reluctantly. I told Maria Elena what I had seen, what I had done. "Take me there," she said, "I want to go." And later she added, "It's good that you take your body there, too."

And so we found ourselves in that neighborhood again. I felt odd and conspicuous. Maria Elena and I are both Mexicans by blood, and both of us speak the language. But kneeling among the pilgrims, I was nothing more than a gringa. I know nothing of Mexico—nothing of poverty. The poverty didn't scare Maria Elena—probably because she'd known it. It just doesn't scare her. She went there as a pilgrim. I went there as a tourist. Maria Elena and I, as alike as we are, sometimes reside in different worlds. She tells me I'm holy. I tell her I don't like that category of thinking. She smiles. I smile. Sometimes, all we can do is smile.

"You can't take off to Mexico just like that." There was a mother's tone in Maria Elena's voice. Eddie could taste the resentment on his tongue as he heard her response to his and Jake's plans to go to Casas Grandes. He was surprised at her response. He was even surprised at the taste at the base of his tongue.

"You're not speaking to little Jake, you know," Eddie said softly. He played with his coffee cup nervously. "I don't see a problem."

"Do you know where Casas Grandes is?"

"I looked on a map, damnit." The voice was no longer soft.

"And do you have your permit to travel in Mexico?"

"I didn't know we needed a permit."

"Eddie, they're a sovereign country—just like the U.S."

"You're being arrogant and snotty, wife."

"*You're* being arrogant and snotty. And don't call me 'wife.' I hate that." She picked up the baby who was wide awake and chewing on his hand. "Such a good baby," she said to him. The baby smiled, "Handsome boy, rey de mi vida."

Eddie listened to the lilt in her voice. Sometimes, he found her irritating. "We were having a discussion," he said. "I hate when you interrupt our conversations and pick him up. He's getting too big anyway." He bit his lip.

"Babies should be held," she said evenly, "and nobody ever gets too big to be held." She handed the baby to him. "Here, you hold him." She stepped back and looked at them. "Handsome men," she said. She smiled at her husband. "It's not that I'm against the idea of you and Jake going to Mexico—it's just that you don't know crap about traveling in a foreign country."

"Oh, and you're an expert on Mexico."

"At least I've been there. At least I know the language. I don't know everything—but I know something. Something, Eddie. This is the first time you've even been out of California—"

"So what? It's a big state."

"So what? So is Texas."

"Texas sucks," he wanted to say. "I know enough," he said slowly, not quite softly.

"Yeah, well I know how to get to Casas Grandes. I also know you need a permit to travel into Mexico. Do you, Eddie?"

"What's bugging you, Nena."

"What's bugging me is that you think you can go to Mexico at the drop of a hat—and you're right, you can. And here we are, planning to build a goddamn wall on the border to keep "them" out. Did you read that in the paper? Did you read that? 'Operation Keep Them Out'—"

"It isn't called 'Operation Keep Them Out'—"

"Well, it should be. That's what it is, isn't it?"

He shrugged his shoulders. "Why are we fighting about this, Nena? I agree with you. Jake agrees with you. You heard us discussing it last night. We're as disgusted as you are. So why are you mad at us?" The baby's peace seemed disturbed. At first, he made a few grunts, then broke out into a full cry. "See, you made him cry."

"He just needs to be changed. I know my son's grunts. Your turn to change him. And you didn't even ask me if I wanted to go?"

"Oh, so that's it," he said as he placed his son on the counter. He felt the diaper. "You're right—he does need to be changed. Hand me a diaper, will you?"

She walked into the utility room and returned with a clean diaper and some baby powder. "I want to go, too," she said. "You didn't even ask."

Eddie said nothing, pretending to concentrate totally on changing his son's diaper.

"Is it a brother thing?" she asked.

Eddie nodded. "Don't be mad. Please don't be mad."

"OK," she said, trying to soften her voice, "I'll try not to feel left out. I'll take you to get your permits this afternoon. That way you can drive straight through in the morning."

"You're a good sport," he said.

"I want my brother, too," she said. "And I haven't even started to search—"

"Nena, we've been here less than a month. We're not even finished working on the house."

"Starting Monday, I'm going to begin looking. He can't be far."

What if he's dead, she thought, what if he's moved? She took the newly changed baby in her arms and rocked him slowly. She looked up at Eddie. "You and Jake be careful, OK? Sometimes a cop wants a bribe—sometimes they stop you. Don't get holier than thou. Jake won't—but you will. Just give the man a ten—and drive, OK?"

"OK."

"And call me."

"We'll be back by the evening."

"Call me anyway."

"I left last night."

"Again?"

Lizzie nodded. "I just can't help myself. It comes so easily. And by the way, it's a hell of an easy way to get to know a new town."

"Yeah, I'll bet. Doesn't it scare you?"

"You always ask me that. And I keep telling you it isn't scary at all. It's exhilarating. I actually went into a bar last night."

"You what?"

"I went into a bar."

Maria Elena looked at her strangely.

"What's that look on your face."

"You leave your body to go into a bar?"

"Well, no. I left my body just to leave my body. It's like climbing the mountain because it's there."

"But to go to a bar?"

"What's the big deal?"

"Where was the bar?"

"In Juárez."

"What was the name of the bar?"

"The Kentucky Club."

"I know that place."

"You been there?"

"Yeah, I've been there. It used to be a joint where hotshots hung out in the forties. Elizabeth Edwards, what the hell were you doing there?"

"I don't know. I mean, I was sitting in my room trying to relax, and suddenly I could read Jake's mind just by thinking of him. I didn't want to know—I didn't want to eavesdrop, so I made myself think of something else. You know, it's like I feel that I'm going to find your brother one of these days. I'm going to see him and I'm going to know him. He was in my dream—I'd know him anywhere—and that woman, that older Mexican woman—I'm going to find her, too—I just know it."

"What are you going to do when you find them without a body?"

"Follow them. Find out where they live."

"What if you stay too long outside your body. Aren't you afraid your body will die?"

"I might die when I'm in it—then what would I do?"

"Don't be flippant, Lizzie."

Lizzie took out a cigarette from her purse and put it in her mouth. She smiled at Maria Elena.

"You have no willpower. I can't believe you're starting up again. It's you and Jake—you both have addictive personalities."

"Yeah, but we're fun. And can we skip the lectures?"

Maria Elena laughed without wanting to.

"So anyway," Lizzie said dramatically as she lit her cigarette, "I was lying on my bed and I felt, well, peaceful—that's the word. And I knew I was going to float away, and I wanted to, so I just went with it. It's like being with a man that you just can't resist. Which reminds me, I haven't been with a man for years."

"Years, Lizzie?"

"Well, yes—over a year, anyway. That's a long time. Which reminds me, did you know this town has a whopping streetwalking business."

"It always has. It's nice to know some things stay the same."

"And a lot of them aren't what they seem."

"What's that supposed to mean?"

"Transvestites."

"Oh, there weren't any in San Francisco?"

"Oh, it doesn't offend me. I'm just, well, surprised. I thought the border would be much straighter."

"No, not straighter, Lizzie, just more underground."

"So I got tired of following these guys around. And I figured your brother wouldn't be in a bar."

"So how'd you wind up at the Kentucky Club?"

"Well, I just wanted to cross the border—and once I was there, I didn't know where to go—so I liked the name of this place and I just went in."

"Too bad you didn't take your body along. You could have had a drink."

"Very funny. I don't drink in bars—just restaurants."

"Oh, a classy dame, huh? So, did you see any men you liked?"

"That's not why I went in there. You think I'd leave my body behind if I were scoping out men?"

"So what did you do in there?"

"Listened to people talk. It's a fantasy—and I can live it. It's amazing. I'm the fly on the wall everybody always wanted to be. I just listened to people talk. It's amazing how much bullshit is tossed around in conversation. And you know what?" She puffed out some smoke through her nose. "You know what I felt?"

Maria Elena stared at her and shrugged.

"Compassion," Lizzie said, underlining it with her voice. "I liked these people. I liked being one of them. And you know what else? I stopped a fight."

"You what?"

"You want to know how I did it?"

"Can you intervene like that?"

"Well, I did. These two guys—friends—they were talking, then all of a sudden one of them got mad, and the other got mad, too. Pretty soon they're yelling at each other, and the other guy threatens to kick his friend's ass from Juárez to Austin. And I thought to myself, oh great, here I am about to witness a barroom brawl. And then I thought, 'Lizzie do something.' So I just whispered in his ear and told him everything was fine and told him his friend was a good friend. I willed him to hear it. He put his fists down. And he seemed calmer. And pretty soon they're having another drink and laughing."

"You intervened. Is that moral?"

"How is it immoral, Nena?"

"Well, are you supposed to be doing things like that? I mean, you're not exactly a guardian angel—you're just this woman who leaves her body at home when she goes out at—" Maria Elena stopped in mid-sentence. "Well why not? How would you like to do me a favor, Lizzie?"

"Like what?"

"Will you do it or not?"

"Not until you tell me what it is."

"I'm your best friend in all the world."

"Cut to the chase, Maria Elena."

"How would you like to follow Jake and Eddie to Casas Grandes?"

"What?"

"Can you do it?"

"It's not a question of can I do it—it's a question of why should I do it."

"Because I'm worried. What if something happens to them? Who would it hurt? All you have to do is follow them there and follow them back—just to make sure they're safe." "I can't," Lizzie said softly. "It's just—"

Nena stared at her friend. "I know that look, Maria Elena. You have that I'm-really-hurt-and-offended expression on your face. Well wipe it off. I'm not sure I could pull it off. I've never been gone for more than a couple of hours. And even if I could, it's not right. They're big boys. There are things they have to do without you or me standing over them to make sure they don't get hurt. If they get hurt, you have to deal with it."

"Well, I'm sorry I asked."

"Don't be angry, Nena. Please don't be angry."

"Let me be angry," she said. "It won't last long." She left Lizzie to finish her cigarette in peace.

 **6**

Driving down Interstate 10, Jake took the Juárez exit. He took his eyes off the road for a moment and stared down at Concordia Cemetery, the dead disturbed now by a freeway the locals called the spaghetti bowl. As the freeway curbed around, Juárez was straight ahead. It was so easy to get there, just get in the car, take an exit—Mexico—so easy, he thought. Joaquin would have had something to say about this landscape—he would have railed on about something, he was sure of it. He remembered how, sick as he was in his last days, Joaquin had been obsessed with denouncing the only two countries he'd ever known, ever lived in. "I hate Mexico," he mumbled, "I hate the United States. I hate—"

"What?" Eddie asked.

"Nothing, I was just talking to myself." Jake put a cigarette in his mouth but did not light it. He put it back in his pocket. "It's funny to live in a town where the other half of it is in another country."

Eddie nodded pensively. "I can't get used to it—it's—"

"It's like living on the edge—"

"Maybe it's not such a bad thing."

"Sounds like something Joaquin would have said. You're like

him—in some ways, anyway. But you think too white." His voice trailed off as if he had run out of breath.

Eddie knew instinctively when his brother did not want to discuss certain subjects—it was in his voice, his body moved as if he were waving away a mosquito. He was curious as to why his brother had never had a white lover, and always those remarks about white men as if he wasn't one—or didn't want to be one. Perhaps it was a peculiar form of self-loathing, a self-loathing he knew something about. Perhaps they would talk about it someday, but it would have to be on his brother's terms. Eddie made a promise to himself that he would not let his older brother die without talking about these things, but today he could wait. After waiting so many years to find him again, Eddie could be patient. Today, he would respect his brother's silences. Jake was private by nature, he thought, or perhaps by necessity.

"When you stop to think about it," Jake said looking out the side window as he changed lanes, "we grew up on a border, too. I mean isn't San Diego on the border?"

"Yeah, but what the hell did we know, Jake? All we knew was La Jolla. What the hell did we know about Mexico, about any-thing—even about our own damn country? Besides, San Diego isn't literally on the border."

"Actually, I went to Tijuana a lot in high school."

"Yeah? What did you do there?"

"Get drunk mostly. Typical stupidities, I guess. I slept with a whore there once."

"Really? Man or woman?"

"Not a man."

Eddie looked at his brother curiously. "How was it?"

"Well, it was awful. It was one of those initiation rights between me and my jock buddies. She was nice to me—I remember that." His voice faded away from Eddie as though he were trying to fit together some of the pieces from that part of his life.

"Did you have good friends in high school?"

Jake snickered at Eddie's question. "Are you kidding? I hung out with morons. I always wondered why everybody wanted to be like them. The group I hung with, they used to pick on this one guy—

and I used to pick on him, too. Funny thing, was, I didn't get it. I didn't get why it was supposed to be fun picking on this guy. He was very smart. We made him cry once. We followed him down the hall shouting "Faggot! Faggot! Faggot!" I sort of had a crush on him, and there I was yelling with the rest of them." He shook his head. "And you know something? I think we jocks hated that guy because he didn't admire us, and so we decided to ruin him. Isn't that stupid, isn't that the stupidest thing you ever heard?"

The sun was rising.

Eddie watched his brother as he spoke, and said nothing.

"Didn't know I could talk so much, did you?" Jake said.

"I like it when you talk," Eddie said.

They eased into a comfortable silence as they drove toward the border. It was early, five-thirty in the morning, and as they quietly entered Juárcz, the Mexican border guard smiled and waved them through. "Even the smells are different," Jake said. "You ever notice that we erase smells in the United States?"

"We like things nice and sanitized."

"It's what I'm beginning to like about this place, Eddie, it's got rough edges. It's gritty. In La Jolla we used to ship out all our trash— we made it invisible. El Paso feels like a more honest place."

"Didn't know you felt that way."

"You think your big brother's just a good-lookin' airhead?"

Eddie laughed. "I don't think you're an airhead."

"You just think I'm too angry to think."

"That's not true. I just don't know you, that's all. It takes time."

Eddie looked at the map, and gave Jake directions toward the highway to Casas Grandes. Maria Elena had told them not to stray from her directions. "And come right back," she'd said. "You two gringos are bound to get yourselves into trouble. Don't act cocky. Try and be humble, and don't act as if you have a lot of money. Act ordinary." Eddie chuckled to himself.

"Whatcha laughing at?"

"Maria Elena. She told us to act ordinary."

"Aren't we ordinary?"

"Right. Just two ordinary men driving to Mexico to spread a young man's ashes in the desert."

Juárez was still quiet as they drove through the avenue that would turn into the freeway heading for Chihuahua. A lone cigarette vendor stood quietly at a corner as he smoked his own cigarette. As Jake stopped at the light, he signaled the man over. "Marlboro Lights," he said, and then held up two fingers. "¿Cuánto?" he asked. "Uno cincuenta," the man said as he handed Jake the two packs. Jake handed him two dollars and signaled for him to keep the change.

"I didn't know you knew Spanish," Eddie said.

"I don't really. I know how to ask how much, I know how to ask for a bathroom, and I know how to order a beer. And I know how to introduce myself. J taught me—but that's it. You?"

"Well, I listen to Nena and Lizzie carry on in Spanish and sometimes I can really follow them—then they take a right turn and I lose them." He studied the map. He looked over at his brother and laughed. "Sometimes I still can't believe I found you."

Jake nodded. "Can I smoke?"

"Only if you share."

"Didn't know you smoke."

"Every now and again. They're good sometimes."

"I could never be a part-time smoker—either I do or I don't—all or nothing. Guess I'm that way about a lot of things." He took the pack from his pocket and tossed it at his brother. He tossed him some matches. Eddie lit a cigarette for each of them and handed one to Jake.

"Air," Jake said.

"What?"

"That's what gets me through the day. Being able to breathe. I can still breathe. I like breathing."

"*I want you to stay.*" Eddie kept himself from uttering the words. His brother was nothing like his wife—he didn't want to know everything he was thinking. He took a drag from the cigarette he was smoking. "Can I ask you a question, Jake?"

"Yeah, sure."

"Are you sad?"

"I'm sad about J—yeah I'm sad. I've been sadder. In some ways

414

I'm happy, I guess. I'm not a happy man, Eddie—never have been. But the thing is, I'm not as sad as I used to be. I mean, I really like living with you and Nena and Lizzie. They're terrific, you know? And Rose—well, with Rose it's like a having a mother. You know, Joaquin had a lot of women friends—well, he had a lot of friends in general. Me, I never hung with women much. I wasn't interested in them—not their bodies, not their minds, not anything. J used to say it was because of the way Mom was. Who the hell knows? He liked Freud, J did—armchair intellectual—like you, Eddie. Anyway, I thought these women would drive me crazy, but they don't. They kind of make me happy. It feels real nice."

Eddie nodded.

Jake took his eyes off the road, and smiled at his brother. "Can I ask *you* a question?"

"Sure—shoot."

"What's it like to be straight?"

"It's the best." He broke out laughing. "Nothing like it."

"Be serious."

"It's a silly question. What if I asked you, 'What's it like to be gay?' What would you say?"

"I'd say it sucks. It really sucks, Eddie. I hated it for a long time. And then I either got used to it, or stopped noticing that I hated it or stopped noticing that I hated myself. The only thing I really liked about being gay was the sex. The sex was great. I've had some great sex, Eddie. Better than you've had, I bet."

"I'm not willing to concede that point. I am willing to concede the fact that I've had less sex than you. A lot less."

"Yeah, well, now it's killing me."

Eddie reached over and touched his brother on the shoulder. "Being straight isn't so great, you know?"

"Yeah, well you never had to defend your sexuality, did you? I'll bet you've walked a thousand sidewalks with Maria Elena next to you—and a thousand people looked at you and said 'What a lovely couple.' You think those people would've said the same thing about me and J? It sucks, Eddie. Straight people are so fucking superior." Eddie listened to the anger in his voice. It made him sad, and yet he knew his anger was what had helped him to survive. "You know, something, Eddie? I didn't have any straight friends—Joaquin had them—but I didn't. I couldn't. I was too angry."

"I'm sorry," Eddie mumbled, "it was a stupid thing for me to say—"

"I'm not mad at you, Eddie."

"Maybe a little mad—why not?"

"Well, we were raped together, weren't we? It's made you different—different than most men."

"Don't give me so much credit."

"I know what I see." His lips stayed perfectly still. "But I'll tell you something, Eddie, no straight guy ever messed with me. I lifted weights, I worked construction—the whole thing. I only got out of construction work because Joaquin put me through school. I had a friend I worked with, construction-worker type. He always wanted to know why I was with a Mexican. He was like a lot of guys I know—only hung with whites. Funny thing, Joaquin was one of the first people I ever met who even cared if I had a mind—him and Tom."

"The doctor?"

"Yeah. Anyway, it was my turn to put him through school—and then—well, he didn't live long enough to finish. Funny thing about Joaquin, he grew up with nothing—not a goddamn thing—and this guy was happy. I don't mean he didn't get angry—he got angry plenty. But it was a good anger—not like mine. I needed to be with someone who wasn't born cursing the fucking world. He never hated anybody comfortably. He never held grudges. He didn't hate himself."

"It's a family thing," Eddie said. "In our family, we were taught to hate ourselves."

Jake nodded, took a puff from his cigarette, and blew out the smoke through his nose.

Eddie watched him. "You should have been a movie star, you know that?"

Jake laughed. "Yeah, just like Rock Hudson." He sneered and took another puff from his cigarette. "You were one sad kid, Eddie. I always wanted to make you happy. You're not like that anymore."

Eddie put out his cigarette in the ashtray. "I got tired of being alone. I got tired of pushing people away. And one day, I saw this woman. She was sitting on a bench at UCLA and she was reading a book and laughing. There was something about her. She looked as if she didn't need anybody—I liked that. I went home and cried, just cried like some kid in junior high school. There was nothing in me but want and more want. I wasn't angry like you—just, well, just sad and pathetic. The next semester, I saw that woman again. She was in an English class, and a part of me knew her instantly— because she was as sad I was. When she wasn't laughing she looked lost. And somehow I just knew. And I married her." He laughed. "And damnit, that woman saved my ass." Eddie laughed, "Strange that we both wound up with Latino lovers from the other side of the tracks."

"Just a coincidence," Jake said as he lit another cigarette.

"Yeah," Eddie said, "just a coincidence." *But Mom would have hated it.*

"Of course, our side of the tracks was just grand, huh?"

"We didn't starve, Jake."

"We had fucked-up parents, Eddie."

"And now we have their money, Jake. A lot of people get to be poor *and* have fucked-up parents. A lot of people never have shit. Esperanza—she never had anything till Mom and Dad died."

"You're raising your voice, Eddie."

"Sorry. It's just that a lot of people never got the chances we got." Eddie stopped, "It's just that—hell—did either of us have to work as hard as Joaquin?"

Jake nodded, but he immediately decided to change the course of the conversation. He didn't want to fight with his younger brother. It wasn't worth it. "She was a nice lady, Esperanza was. Did she like us or did she feel sorry for us?"

"Both maybe."

"Did I ever tell you that I visited her after I got out of jail?"

"No. How come she didn't tell me?"

"I made her promise not to say anything to you. It would only make you sad. I wanted you to forget about me. They were never going to let me take you with me. Anyway, I just wanted to see

417

her. When I was growing up, she used to make me smile. She was the only person in that household that knew anything about touching. She was the only person I knew who ever said 'thank you' and meant it. Everyone else said it because they were trained to say it. When she thanked you for something, she looked right at you. Sometimes I felt as if her sense of gratitude might break something inside me. Not like Mom and Dad—they weren't touchers. I'm still amazed Mom and Dad had children. Amazing. They hated each other, you know?"

"But they understood each other."

Jake nodded.

"Were you surprised when Mom shot him, then pointed the gun at herself?"

"I don't know, Eddie. I remember sitting in a coffee shop staring at this guy. I tried to pretend I was reading the newspaper—and then I saw the headlines. I just ran out of that place as fast as I could. I tore up the newspaper—I remember doing that—and I remember crying. I didn't know why I was crying at the time, but I know now: I cried because I wasn't sad. My parents killed each other *and I wasn't sad*. And then I just got drunk. You know, I should be dead. After the way I've lived, I should have died a long time ago. How come you're so sober?"

Eddie shrugged his shoulders. "Who knows?"

"Maybe sad was your addiction."

"Not anymore, Jake." He rolled down his window and stuck his head out. He laughed. "I think I'll get a dog." He laughed again. "Did you know, Jake, that the only reason I survived our parents was because I carried the memory of your face in my body? Did you know that? Your memory, it was everything."

"I kept your picture," Jake said. "I had to look at you every day. St. Jonathan, that's what Joaquin used to call you. 'I have my santos,' he told me once, 'and you have St. Jonathan's picture.' On holy days, Joaquin used to light a candle in front of your picture, and he'd place a glass of wine next to the candle in case you decided to walk in the door." He smiled. "Joaquin was a funny guy. I guess I couldn't have you both—both is too much to ask." He took his eyes off the road for a moment, and looked at his younger brother. "What would you do if you lost her?"

"I would curse God and die."

"No you wouldn't."

"Yes, I would."

"You have a son."

Eddie nodded. "I would mourn forever, and my son would have to heal me."

"That's a big job for a little kid."

"He'd have to be strong because I couldn't be."

"You could be strong. Trust me."

They both seemed to drift into their own worlds where they could not follow each other, worlds where they needed to go alone. The silence between them was neither dark nor cold nor harsh, but soft as one of Maria Elena's candles burning through the night. Eddie remembered the earliest memory he had of his brother. It was his fourth birthday. He remembered a birthday cake and Esperanza and his brother and his parents singing. He remembered tearing open presents. He didn't remember very much else. Something must have happened because he remembered his brother picking him up and telling him everything would be OK. He remembered Jake helping him change into his pajamas, reading him a story, and kissing him good night. That was his first memory of anything. "You carried me," he whispered.

"Huh?"

"On my fourth birthday, you carried me to bed."

"Yeah," Jake said, "what in the hell made you remember that?"

"What happened?"

"Mom and Dad had had too much to drink. They started going at each other. I didn't want you to see it—so I carried you upstairs."

"And you read me a story."

"I always read you stories."

"I never thanked you."

"I never needed to be thanked." Jake lit another cigarette. He blew the smoke out through his nose, and watched his brother through his right eye. "When I die—"

"I don't want to talk about that, Jake."

"Eddie? Eddie, when I die, will you write something in your journal about me?"

Eddie stared straight at the road, and did not look at his brother.

"And will you show what you write to your son? Will you do that?"

Eddie nodded slowly, but did not speak.

"And will you tell him that I loved him, and that he gave me hope?"

"Yes," Eddie said, "I'll tell him."

Jake finished his cigarette without saying another word. Again they both settled into a familiar quiet, a quiet that was part of the way they spoke to each other. They had learned quickly that silence was their ally. Words, with them, had their limits. Limits they respected. They said little else until they arrived at the ruins of Casas Grandes.

Jake carried Joaquin's ashes in a small clay vase as he toured the ruins of Casas Grandes. He had never seen or been near anything like this, though Joaquin had tried to describe this place to him many times. "What happened to the people?" Jake had asked him. "No one knows," Joaquin had answered, "maybe a long drought, maybe a war, maybe a plague."

"There's no water here," he said, looking at Eddie.

"Once there was," Eddie answered.

The crumbling adobe was dry as Joaquin's ashes, and as Jake touched one of the walls, warm in the noonday sun, he felt as if the wall might swallow him. There was earth on his palm as he pulled his hand away. Somehow he understood perfectly why Joaquin loved this place. His skin had been almost the same color as the adobe walls of this ruined city. He looked at his palm and felt he was looking at Joaquin, Joaquin who had been so like this place: peaceful and dramatic and full of the past—and empty of it. He wondered what kind of civilization it had been—barbarous or just? Not that it mattered—they had not been spared. He thought of San Francisco, he thought of El Paso and he wondered if those cities, too, would one day become like this place, unpeopled and desolate and peaceful at last in their deadness. He laughed out loud remembering how Joaquin told him that the only radically democratic institution on earth was death. He thought of the first time he'd seen him. He had fought Joaquin's memory since his death. It was easier to forget, less painful. But today he wanted to grieve, and to pay his grief all the respect it was due. He wanted to kneel on the ground, but felt stupid since that kind of homage was not natural to him. Joaquin would've knelt. Jake could not. He could only think of doing it. Joaquin had been a man who understood the necessity of humility. Jacob had not been raised in an environment that understood the concept. He found himself howling to a sky that had never known how to listen. He felt his brother's hand on his shoulder. He knew Eddie's hand kept him from falling off the edge of the world. He knew, too, that his howls were not only for Joaquin, but for his life—for everything that had gone bad in it, for everything and everyone who had hurt him and left him with indelible marks so like these ruins he was standing on. He saw his father on top of him cutting him like a knife; he saw himself staring up at his brother's room the night his parents made him leave; he saw the jail where he'd lived for almost a year; he saw Joaquin dying in his arms. He saw himself yelling at a heron, "Fly! Fly!" He tossed Joaquin's ashes into the air, and saw the wind scatter them among the grains of sand. "Fly. Fly." His voice was cracked and tired. He wanted to be the dead heron. He wanted to be Joaquin's ashes. He wanted to be the ruins of Casas Grandes. He wanted to be anything but Jake, Jake who was over forty and was lost in the desert that was his life. "I want to die," he yelled, "I want, I want to—"

Eddie grabbed him and placed his hand over his mouth. "Never say that," Eddie whispered, "say only that you want to live." He let his brother cry for a long time. "Say it, Jake," he said, "say *I want to live.*"

"I want to live," Jake said. He said it for his brother, his brother who had become his scarred and stubborn heart.

 7

Luz FOUND a small, perfect house on Prospect Street in Sunset Heights. The place was old and in need of paint, but the walls were strong, and it was a real house with a porch and a backyard where Mexican primroses grew wild. "It has lots of windows," Luz told Diego, "and we'll always have plenty of sun. No dark houses."

Diego inspected the house for the tenth time that day. "I like it," he wrote, "it feels right. Everything is just right." He sat on an old couch in the living room and watched the light coming through the curtainless windows. He stared at the worn wooden floors and thought of his mother. He thought she would have liked this house. He lit a cigarette. Luz walked into the kitchen, poured herself a cup of coffee and sat across from Diego in an old chair.

"It's just perfect," Diego wrote.

"Not perfect, Dieguito."

"You don't like the house?"

"I'm not talking about the damned house, mi amor. The house is the best—the very best. The house just needs a few plants—I'm good with plants, I can make a dead plant come to life, Diego, but it's not the house I'm talking about. I'm talking about something else."

Diego looked at her, shrugged his shoulders and stuck his hands out.

"You really want to know?"

"You're going to tell me anyway." He showed her the note and laughed.

"We've been living together for two weeks and already you're accusing me of talking too much. I don't talk too much—well, only compared to you—I just like to communicate."

"I'm not accusing you. I was just playing—just a joke. Can't we joke? Tell me, what's not perfect? Tell me, I want to know."

She looked at him. "Do you believe in dreams?"

"I already told you, Luz. Didn't I tell you about my dreams and Mary and about my dreams with my mother in them, and how I remembered how my mother was killed in that car accident?"

"Yes, yes," she said, "you told me. Poor Mary. I know I never liked her, but I never wanted that to happen to her. Pendeja that she was, she couldn't help it. God forgive her for claiming she was the Virgin, but she didn't deserve to die like that. Do you think the pinche migra had something to do with her murder?"

Diego looked at her and shook his head. "No. And I don't think you think so either. The migra isn't responsible for everything, They're not criminals."

"Pendejo," she said, "of course they're criminals. You think because they wear a uniform they're not criminals?"

"OK," he wrote, "they're criminals."

"You think I'm a pendeja, Dieguito? You're agreeing with me just so I'll shut up. Don't start acting like a man just because we're living together."

"I AM A MAN," he wrote. He held up the note like a banner.

"You know what I mean, Diego. Don't start acting like Mundo. There's enough of those already. God knows they've burned half the women in this damned city with their smoldering eyes and their pinche attitudes. You don't need to start acting like that, Dieguito."

"What does Mundo have to do with dreams? Mundo doesn't believe in dreams."

"I knew it," she said. She clapped her hands with satisfaction.

"Men like that don't believe in anything but a woman's body." She looked at him carefully. "Do you really believe in dreams? Because if you don't, I'm not going to tell you about the ones I've been having. If you laugh at me, Dieguito, I'll send you back to work at Vicky's."

"I won't la·gh," Diego wrote. "You should know better than that. Don't insult me."

She nodded. "God is punishing me, my Diego. Ever since I've come back from Chicago, I've been having dreams. There's a man who comes to me. I'm always sitting at the bridge in my dream, and I'm watching the people just like we used to do on Saturdays. And the man comes up to me. I feel like I know him, and he just looks at me. His eyes are even softer than yours, Dieguito. He sticks out his hand like a beggar. I try to hand him money, and he won't take it. He throws the money into the river and then I feel like a whore. I wake up feeling bad, Diego. And all day, I think about it. Even this week, since going back to work, I think about it all the time. And I've finally figured it out. All of a sudden, I remembered something I'd forgotten. I'm such a pendeja, sometimes. The man who keeps coming to me will keep coming until I give him what he wants. He's not like most men—he's not looking for sex, and he's not looking for a meal either, and he's not looking for a job or for money. He doesn't have that look like that at all. His hunger is for something else. In the last dream something different happened. He turned the brown river to pure blue. It looked like the sky, my Diego, just like the morning sky. I swear it, it looked so real. And his open palm was right in front of me. And this morning it came to me—I remembered—just like you remembered about your mother. Dreams do that, Diego." She paused and drank from her cup of coffee. "It's good coffee," she said.

"Remembered what?" Diego wrote.

"I remembered about the time my first son was sick. I don't remember very much, only that he was just a baby and he had a fever and was very sick. He was burning up, so hot, Dieguito. I went to church and I told God that if he let my son live I would go on a pilgrimage to Cristo Rey. Well, Dieguito, pendeja that I am I forgot about my promise. My son got well, and I never paid God what I owed him. And now He wants me to pay up. I have to pay back what I owe."

"So what are you going to do?"

"I'm going to climb the mountain."

"Which mountain?"

"Pendejo! Which mountain do you think? Cristo Rey."

"If you wait until October, you can go on the annual pilgrimage. They go every year. The bishop goes, too. Sometimes even more than one bishop is there—I've never been, but I've read about it in the paper. Hundreds of people go, hundreds of pilgrims, and they have a Mass at the foot of the statue. We can go in October, Luz, and I'll go with you."

Luz read Diego's note and shook her head. "No, my Diego, God won't wait. He's waited long enough. Dreams have their way, and I can't wait that long. I have to go now—as soon as possible."

"But they say it's dangerous. It's much better to go with a lot of people. What if something happens to us?"

"You think God is going to let something happen to us if we're climbing his mountain to pray?"

"I don't think the robbers are going to ask God why we're there. I don't think they're going to ask us either."

"Look, Diego, what are you talking about? The robbers? What kind of books have you been reading? We don't have anything worth stealing, anyway. Don't be a pendejo."

"What if they kill us?"

Luz shook her head and laughed. "We'll take Mundo with us if that will make you feel better. It will be good for that guy to go on a pilgrimage. Maybe God will cure him."

"Of what?"

"Of everything, Dieguito. You told me yourself that you found him in a garbage can. You think he couldn't use some changes in his life? He can't live like that forever, mi amor. You want him to live like he does for the rest of his life?"

"If he wants to, why not? It's his life, Luz."

She shook her head in disgust at Diego's cleanly written words. "Why not? Diego, his life isn't as simple as it seems. My first husband lived exactly like Mundo—and he was found dead on the streets of Juárez—drunk and dead. You want that for Mundo?" She lit a cigarette. "Yes, I think Mundo should go with us."

"Can he bring his friends?"

"His friends will ruin everything. Those gang members, Dieguito, are not good for each other. When they're by themselves, they're almost human, but when they're with each other, they turn into animals—like packs of wolves looking for fights or women in heat. Animals, Diego, they act like animals around each other."

"I like them," Diego wrote. "They were great at Mary's funeral. You should have seen them, Luz, *and they didn't act like animals.*"

"Ay, Dieguito, you think everybody's nice, don't you? That's a real problem, don't you know?"

 **8**

WHEN SHE WENT to sleep that night, Lizzie told herself she would spend the next day walking the streets of the city using what Maria Elena referred to as her "God-given body." But as soon as she woke, she was overwhelmed by the smell of another world, rose petals attacking her senses. Instinctively she felt her mother's presence. She went directly to her mother's room and knocked softly before entering. Rose was sitting up on the bed. She looked old and tired and frightened. Lizzie sat on the bed without speaking and took her mother's hand. "Mama," she whispered, but her mother placed a finger to her lips. There were no words in her mother's thoughts, just a tiredness in her body that made Lizzie sad. Her mother squeezed her hand. "Whatever happens, Lizzie, you mustn't be afraid. Never be afraid—it's such a waste of time." She nodded at her daughter. "I'd like some time," she said. Lizzie kissed her and left the room. Her mother was beginning to embrace something beyond the reach of her arms. Lizzie walked back to her own room. Her mother's sense of calm filled her for a just a moment; it was enough to ease her. The smell of roses in the room grew fainter and fainter until the odor disappeared altogether. And again, she felt restless, unsatisfied, purposeless. Then suddenly she smiled knowing she would follow Jake and Eddie all the way to Casas Grandes. She tried to fight the urge to leave her body. "Smoke," she said, "smoke all day—stick to normal addictions." But the thought of leaving herself made her feel alive; a surge of adrenaline shot through her and she laughed out loud like a girl.

Outside, the sky was already more blue than black. She put on a robe and went to her window. The birds were beginning to sing. She wanted to be among them, to be surrounded by their songs. She thought of the tree where the sparrows sang, a place where she often went. She heard the front door open, and then shut. She knew Eddie and Jake were leaving for Casas Grandes. She closed her eyes and found herself among the birds. She felt as if she were experiencing the purest form of laughter. How could she choose a body over this? She stared back at her form standing at the window. Today, she wanted nothing to do with that repulsive lump of flesh called a woman—that woman was a prison. Today, she would be a bird. She would go to Mexico undetected. She would watch Jake and Eddie, she would make sure they would return to Maria Elena safely. Today, she would have a purpose. She would be more than a bird—she would be an angel, a protector. Lizzie heard a car start up as she floated down to the driveway where Jake was pulling away. She followed the car as it made its way toward the freeway. The sun was rising. Even the river, poor as any river she had ever seen, sparkled in the dawn.

Maria Elena did not see Lizzie in the house all morning. She looked for her everywhere: in the backyard, the ballroom that she and Jake were slowly turning into a greenhouse, everywhere, but there was no trace of her. She even knocked at her door, but hearing no answer, she assumed she had decided to sleep in. This body thing is making her tired, she thought. All morning, she had a funny feeling, but the baby and the garden she and Eddie had started in the backyard kept her busy. Rose called her in from the garden about noon. "Lunch is ready," she said.

"Oh Rose, you shouldn't make lunch." She looked at the old woman and noticed she looked pale and tired. "You have to rest more," she said trying not to sound too alarmed.

"There will be plenty of time for resting," she said softly.

428

Maria Elena grew even more alarmed at her tone, but smiled. She washed herself at the kitchen sink and smiled at the baby who was playing with his hands and feet. "Rose, have you seen Lizzie?"

"This morning. She visited me early."

"Oh. I haven't seen her all day. Maybe she stepped out—or maybe she went back to sleep." She sat down, but did not touch her food.

"She wouldn't have gone back to sleep," Rose said definitively.

"Why not?"

"Never could. Once she wakes up, she never goes back to sleep. She's always been that way. Up with the sun, that girl, no matter how late she stayed out. Never could nap either. That's why she could never work anything but day shifts at the hospital. If she had to work nights, she just plain didn't sleep."

"She must've stepped out then."

"Did you check her room?"

"I knocked."

"Did you go in?"

"No. There wasn't an answer."

"You sound worried."

"Well, not—" She stopped herself. "A little. She's been leaving her body a lot—don't you think?"

"Yes—not that she tells me—not that she needs to. A mother always knows."

Maria Elena looked down at her son who was enthralled with his own feet. "Will I know, too?"

"Oh, you'll know more than you want to know—it's not instinctual exactly—just something you acquire—like tired bones and wrinkles."

Maria Elena laughed. She looked at the sandwiches Rose had made for lunch. She took one and bit into it. "Good," she said, with her mouth half-full. She wasn't hungry. She swallowed. "I did something stupid," she said.

"Again?" Rose laughed.

"Don't tease me, Rose—I'm afraid Lizzie went and did what I asked her to do—I shouldn't have asked. She said she wouldn't— and she was right to say no. But now I think she's gone ahead and done it."

"What is it, Nena?"

"Well, Jake and Eddie were going to Casas Grandes today—it would have been Joaquin's birthday."

"Joaquin?"

"Jake's lover."

"Oh yes, how stupid—of course—it's my mind—"

"Your mind is fine, Rose."

She reached over and placed her hand on Maria Elena's face and held it there for a moment.

Maria Elena felt as if the hand against her cheek were disappearing, becoming something immaterial. Rose pulled her hand away—slowly. "Anyway," Maria Elena continued, "I just got overly worried, and I asked her to follow them—just to make sure they'd be OK. She said she'd never been gone from her body for more than a couple of hours—I shouldn't have asked. I could just kick myself. And now she's out there, and—"

"Now, don't go beating up on yourself over the things Lizzie decides to do and not do. She only does what she wants to do. She could never be controlled even as a child. Besides, we don't really know if—"

"Don't we?"

"We can check her room."

"Come with me, will you?"

Rose nodded. "She's probably in her room reading a book."

"Think so, Rose?"

Her silence betrayed her.

"We'll take the elevator."

"I can still manage the stairs, Nena."

"It's for me, Rose—the baby's getting heavy."

Rose was grateful to her for the small lie. The house was too big for her, the stairs too unforgiving on her bones.

When they reached Lizzie's room, Maria Elena took a deep breath, turned the glass knob, and pushed the door open. Lizzie's body was lying on the floor near the window. She took a deep breath and looked at Rose. *"Don't panic. Breathe. Calm, calm."* Rose shook and seemed to be on the verge of tears, "Is she dead?"

"No." Maria Elena said immediately.

"Call an ambulance."

"She's fine. She's just left."

"Left?"

"To Casas Grandes."

"Is she breathing?"

"It doesn't seem like it."

"She's dead then," Rose screamed.

Maria Elena kept her voice calm, deliberate. "Listen, Rose. Just listen. Does that look like a corpse?"

"What will we do?" Rose fought herself, tried to remain calm.

Maria Elena handed her the baby. "Hold him," she said, "He needs you." She walked over to Lizzie's body and touched it. She placed her head on the body's heart.

"Is she breathing?"

"No—but her body's still warm."

"What does that mean?"

"It means she's left."

"Will she come back?"

"Of course she'll come back." Maria Elena smiled at the old woman. She tried to hide any hint of fear.

"What should we do?"

"I'll move her to the bed."

"Let me hel—"

"I can manage Rose, really."

"I'm not an invalid," she said. The words came out harsher than she'd intended. Her bones were beginning to hurt again.

"A seventy-year-old woman has no business carrying a woman in her thirties. Besides you're holding the baby." Maria Elena's tone was almost severe.

Rose recognized that tone in Maria Elena's voice—she sometimes used it with her husband: It meant she wasn't going to negotiate. She watched the younger woman pick up her daughter awkwardly. As she carried her to the bed, they seemed to be doing a clumsy, awkward waltz.

"You're strong," Rose said. She envied her.

"Lizzie's small—very thin. Thank God for that, huh?" She laughed. She was succeeding in keeping Rose calm.

"Are you sure we shouldn't call for an ambulance?"

"When she comes, she won't be able to find her body—then what will she do?"

Rose nodded. "You're sure?"

"I'm sure," she said. Long ago she had learned to play the role of being someone else. *Lizzie, damnit, you'd better come back—come back this instant, do you hear?*

"OK, but I won't leave this room until she comes back."

"Then, I'll wait with you," Maria Elena said.

Rose wondered which of them was more stubborn. She liked this woman more and more. When she had first met her, she had thought her too nice, too fragile. She was glad she had misjudged her.

The two women said little all afternoon as they waited for some sign of Lizzie's arrival. Occasionally, Rose would take her daughter's hand and look at Maria Elena. "She doesn't belong out there," she would say. The words became a prayer, a litany, and Maria Elena would nod in agreement as she sat wordlessly, the nod itself becoming a kind of amen.

When the hot, slow sun finally fell into the earth, nothing in the room had changed except the baby's movements as he crawled around the room reaching for things. Nena left the room and brought back candles. She lit them. The room, already too hot from the long day, seemed to turn into a burning ember. The two women were soaked in sweat, but they suffered the effects of the heat patiently as if to suffer it was a ransom they were paying for the return of the woman they loved. Come back, Maria Elena thought, come back. We cannot live without you, cannot live without your voice. She was too afraid to utter a single word aloud, did not want to worry Rose with stupid and unnecessary words that could not possibly help. After sitting perfectly still for what seemed hours, Nena finally rose from her chair and stood.

Rose took her eyes off her daughter's unmoving body and looked toward Maria Elena. "I didn't want her, you know, not at first."

Maria Elena looked at her as if to urge her to keep talking. It was time to break the silence.

"I wanted her brother—that's who I wanted. My husband wouldn't let me keep him—but that boy, I wanted him. I wanted a boy. Funny how women sometimes want boys more than they want girls. Lizzie was a consolation prize. I sometimes thought she knew that—maybe that's why we were always fighting. She was hell to raise, you know? But she's kept me alive. Yes, she has. And she knows how to love. She matters—"

Maria Elena moved closer and closer to Rose as she talked. She placed her hand on her shoulder, but said nothing. The old woman's throat was dry. She stopped speaking.

"Rose, would you like some water?"

"Yes," she said, "I'm thirsty."

As Lizzie hovered over the house, she felt a great sadness. She wanted to wander the earth forever. She wanted to go back to Mexico and study the desert, its peoples, everything that inhabited it. She wanted to be a student of the world. Today, she had been out of her body for hour after hour after hour, and with each passing hour, she had begun to let go of the heaviness of being a body, a person, a human—the robes of flesh had become a heavy yoke. Perhaps she was becoming a spirit. Perhaps she was becoming perfect. She circled the house. Jake and Eddie were at the Bridge of the Americas in Juárez—stuck in traffic. Lizzie was free of all traffic. The thought occurred to her that she did not have to return. Nothing, no one could force her. She could abandon her bones and leave them to rot. She would not care. But as she hovered over the house, she suddenly became aware that it was completely dark except for a faint light coming from the window of her room. She moved closer to the room, and was surprised to see her body lying on her bed and Maria Elena and her mother keeping vigil over her body. She did not even have to try to read her mother's mind to know that she was exhausted with worry. *I don't want to go back, Mama. Tell her, Nena, tell her I no longer exist.* But Maria Elena, too, was wearing the same look as her mother, and she could hear her name being uttered, *Come back. Lizzie, come back.* The women's faces could not be resisted. She knew there was no going back into the night. She

433

would have to reenter her old self for the sake of the women that were keeping watch. She would have to return and think about what she was going to do about a body for which she no longer had any use, a body for which she no longer had any love. She felt a stranger to herself. She found it odd that she still felt such strong loyalty toward these women and the things they felt.

When Maria Elena returned with a glass of water in her hand, a hot breeze came in through the window. The candles flickered but did not go out. Maria Elena smiled. "Thank God. ¡Ay gracias a mi santo Dios. Gracias!" She handed Rose the glass of water and pointed at Lizzie. The body that had lain on the bed all the long, silent day, lain as still as death itself, suddenly moved. Rose drank from the water and stared at her daughter as she slowly sat up on the bed. She looked at Maria Elena. "I'm seeing things," she said.

"No," Maria Elena whispered.

Lizzie looked up at the two women in the room. "Will someone please tell me why we're using candles instead of lights. Have we gone back in time to a previous century?"

"Don't ever do that again—do you hear me, Lizzie." Maria Elena's voice was as hard as the walls of the old house.

"Jesus Christ, Nena—"

"Don't Jesus Christ me—you scared the hell out of us. We've been sitting here since noon wondering if you were ever going to come back to us—and don't you ever do that to us ever again. Are you—"

"Stop it, Nena, you're being hysterical. This was all your idea in the first place. I followed them to Casas Grandes and they're fine, by the way—in case you were wondering." She tugged on her earlobe searching for an earring, but found none. "And, in the second place, I don't need your permission, Nena."

Maria Elena glared at Lizzie. "Selfish, you're so selfish, you know that. You could have at least let us know . . ." Rose sat quietly in the background regaining her composure as the two women argued. Their voices filled her with relief. Their was nothing serious in their disagreement, and it would be settled in minutes. She wanted to

434

scream with joy. She had been so afraid of losing her daughter, as afraid as she had ever been of anything. Her dream returned to her, but she banished it from her thoughts. Today, there would be no death in this house. She nodded at the exchange in front of her. She wanted to laugh, but she had no wish to show either of the women in the room her sense of exhilaration. She wanted to go to her room and be alone, perhaps shout out into the warm summer night.

"Well," she said, interrupting Lizzie as words poured out of her like sweat, "I hope you're rested enough to cook dinner."

"Dinner, Mama?" Lizzie asked looking a little confused, "I'm in the middle of an argument."

"Well, argue as you hover over a stove. If you can hover over Casas Grandes, you can hover over a kitchen stove. I'm hungry and I'd like something more interesting than a salad and a piece of meat. Mexican. I'd like Mexican tonight." She rose from her chair. "I'm going to take a shower and change. Waste of a day, I'd say—a waste."

 **9**

A WEEK LATER, Mundo and the T-Birds drove up in their cars and honked in front of Luz and Diego's house at sunrise.

Diego and Luz came out of the house a few minutes later. Luz looked at their cars and shook her head at Diego. "Their cars are too flashy," she said. "They should be ashamed. They look like something that should be hanging on a Christmas tree." She wrinkled her forehead as if she were smelling something unpleasant.

"Don't you like the colors? I think they're beautiful," Diego wrote.

She shook her head. "And they shouldn't be honking their horns. Just because I can hear doesn't give them permission to honk in front of my house. Can't they knock on the front door—they have no manners. They have no class."

Mundo waved them over, his motions telling them it was time to get going. They got in the front seat of the canary yellow Chevy Mundo was driving. Three guys in the backseat tipped their hats toward Diego and Luz. Luz forced a smile, and Diego greeted them by pointing his chin toward them. He recognized El Guante and El Güero, but he didn't know the other guy.

They drove toward Sunland Park to the entrance of the road that led to Mount Cristo Rey.

"Did you bring the water?"

Mundo took his eyes off the road for an instant and looked at

Luz. "You bet, Doña Luz, I don't forget nothin'—I got a sharp mind. Anything that passes through my eyes and my ears stays up there forever."

"You should paint this car another color. People on the road are looking at us."

"Let them look, Doña Luz, that's why they got eyes. Anyway, it's not my car—if it was mine, I'd paint it cherry red."

"Red would be worse—it would make me feel like I was covered in blood."

Mundo kept driving and laughed. He took his eyes off the road to look at Diego. "Hey, Mr. Diego, guess what? I saw a sign on a window yesterday. There's a flower shop behind the jail that's looking for a delivery man. I think you should go on Monday and apply for the job."

"He doesn't know how to drive," Luz answered.

"I'll teach you how, Diego, no problem. There's nothing to it—I'll just get you one of those DMV books, and you can read it, and then you take the test. Nothing to it—and then you got yourself a job delivering flowers. It's in the bag."

"Keep your eyes on the road," Luz said. "You're going to kill us."

"Will you really teach me how to drive?" Diego wrote.

He placed the pad in front of Mundo.

"You're going to make him wreck the car," Luz said.

Mundo read the note and nodded. "Yeah, I'll teach you, and when you go in on Monday tell them you already know how to drive, but that you can't start work for a week. You gotta lie about it, see? One week, that's all we need."

"Stop talking and keep your eyes on the road," Luz said.

"Do you think I should lie like that?"

Luz read the note aloud to Mundo. "Don't read Diego's notes, anymore—I'll just tell you what he writes, damn it. Just drive." Mundo nodded.

"Monday, I'll go down and apply."

Luz read the note to Mundo.

Mundo nodded and laughed. "That job's gonna be all yours."

"I don't know, Dieguito," Luz interrupted. "It sounds like a wonderful job, but I worry about you driving around this city. The roads are full of lunatics—do you really think you can learn to drive?''

"Don't worry," Diego wrote, "it'll all work out. Mundo will teach me—you'll see."

Luz smiled to herself. She was glad Mundo was doing something for Diego. She decided to try and be nicer to him. Maybe that was part of his problem—not enough people had been nice to him.

When they arrived at the entrance to the road that went up the mountain, the company of pilgrims got out of the cars and stretched their legs. "These guys," Mundo said, pointing to El Kermit and Indio, "are going to stay with the cars. We can't let anybody mess with these babies. They'll keep watch down here while the rest of us go up." He looked up at the dirt path that led to the statue of Cristo Rey. "It's a long climb, Doña Luz, you think you can make it?"

"I'm getting old, but I'm a long way from dead, Mundo—I can make it. My legs are strong. And I don't want any talking while we're climbing; this is supposed to be something sacred, so tell your birds not to talk. Tell them to pray if they know how."

"They're not birds, esa, they're people, brothers—have some respect. These guys are doing you a favor, so try and act real nice."

"I told you not to call me 'esa.'"

"Don't fight," Diego wrote, "this is supposed to be something holy."

"Don't tell me about pilgrimages and what they're supposed to be, Dieguito, I know more about these things than you do. Just put your pad away and be silent—I don't want to see that pencil move until it's all over."

Diego placed his pad and pencil in his pocket reluctantly. For a moment they all stood in silence not knowing exactly what to do until Luz began climbing the mountain. They walked behind her on the path without attempting to talk. At first, they climbed at a steady pace, but the sun was beating down on them like a belt against the back, the rays as heavy as a belt buckle. They moved slower with each step. Luz prayed her rosary as they climbed. Diego watched her hands as they touched the beads and fixed his eyes on her rosary as it swayed back and forth, back and forth touching her skirt and then swinging up toward the statue, toward the sky. Diego thought of his mother and how she had paced with her rosary in their small house, her lips moving, begging for things he could only guess at. They climbed slowly, higher.

Luz finally had to stop and rest though something in the way she stopped said she was angry with her body for having to take a rest. She put her hand on her back and arched it tossing her head up to the hot, open air. Diego put Luz's bag down on the ground, and looked out at the desert. It was amazing to him that the chamizos and the mesquites were so green. A miracle, he thought, the pale green that refused to surrender its color to the sand that swallowed everything, made everything parched, made everything die begging, begging for cool, begging for water. How could this green exist?

Mundo handed Luz a cup of water from the jug he was carrying. He offered her a handkerchief to wipe the dust that had stuck to her sweating face. El Güero and El Guante wet their bandannas with water and tied them around their heads. El Güero lit a cigarette, and the look on his face said the nicotine was as good as water. Luz looked over at Mundo; he shook his head. El Güero took a deep drag and crushed his cigarette on the ground with his foot. After their first rest, they moved up the mountain—slower now— too hot to go fast. Diego felt his skin burning in the sun—burning like a match too close to the fingers. Luz took out the hat Diego had given her, the hat he had bought for Mary. She tied it to her head with the ribbons so the hot breeze wouldn't blow it off. Diego watched her. She looked young in the sun, the way she looked before she had gone to Chicago, the way she had looked when he had first met her. He thought that many men must have loved her when she was young.

Diego stared down at the dust his feet raised as he walked. The path was full of rocks and he could see where people had left small monuments as they had climbed. Some had written prayers, and others had simply written their names on crosses they'd stuck in the ground. All these people, he thought, publicly begging God for more than he would ever give them. He thought of asking for a voice.

As Diego looked up, he could see the outlines of people climbing down from the mountain up above him. Angels, he thought, angels coming to get them. But they were too heavy and too solid to be angels. He watched them get closer and closer, counted the small crowd of people—there were five of them. Diego wanted to ask these people who they were, why they were there in the middle of the day. As they passed him, he caught the eyes of one of the men. He smiled and nodded at him. He had dark eyes and a warm smile, and for a moment, strange as it was, he wanted to stop the man and examine his face, and examine the face of the woman whose hand he was holding and ask them questions about their lives, about the purpose of their pilgrimage. Four of them passed him slowly, the man who had looked into his eyes and the woman whom he clung to who was too tired to look up, her face glued to the movements of her feet. And with them, an old woman who seemed too white and too fragile to him to be climbing up and down mountains, and a younger woman with hair as white as the clouds who almost smiled at him when their eyes met as they passed. Following behind was a big man with blond hair who also looked into his eyes as he passed. Diego nodded at him. The man nodded back. The big man looked sad and tired and Diego wondered what he was carrying around. Whatever it was, he had the weight of it on his face. Perhaps, he thought to himself, these travelers were sent as mirrors. He turned around and watched them move farther and farther away from him. He wondered why he felt the urge to run after them. They were gringos, he thought, what were these gringos to him? What could they possibly be to a deaf Mexican? He turned around and faced the top of the mountain and began climbing again.

The eyes of one of the men looked familiar. Lizzie thought of Eddie's boyhood picture, how she had always felt it was familiar. She had the same feeling. She wondered why her ability to read minds was so capricious, why it came and went as it pleased, why it was something beyond her control. She had the urge to turn around and look straight into his face and ask him questions. She wondered—no, it could not possibly be Diego—not possible. She wanted it to be so, but it was not so. But why not ask? She turned around and watched the group climbing up the mountain. She decided to chase them down and ask the man if he was Diego. It could be, she thought, it could be. She looked down, and saw her mother stumble. "Mama!" she yelled. She ran down and helped her up. "Are you OK?"

The old woman laughed. "Oh, I'm so tired, Lizzie. But I'm not hurt, just too tired to walk."

"You shouldn't have come, Mama."

"I needed to come."

"It's so hard on your bones."

"I wanted to climb the mountain. I wanted to look down and see the desert. It was lovely, Lizzie."

"Mama, you're so stubborn."

"Help me," she said, "I can't make it without you."

Lizzie yelled Jake's name. She did it out of instinct. He climbed back up from where he was and saw how weak Rose looked. He became her cane the rest of the way down. Lizzie walked beside them, the young man's dark eyes forgotten for the moment. She was angry with herself for letting her mother climb a mountain in the light of this relentless and punishing sun.

Diego tried to look up and see the blueness of the sky but the sun made everything so bright that he had to turn away. Luz appeared tired to him, but she kept praying her rosary. Mundo kept his eyes on her, and Diego wondered what he was thinking, wondered what he saw when he was thinking, wondered what he saw when he looked at her. Did he see the same woman he did—or did he see someone completely different?

Luz stumbled on a rock and fell, almost in slow motion—but Diego couldn't keep her from falling. He saw his mother falling in front of a car. He shook his head as if to erase the memory from his head, wanting to make the part of the brain that remembered into a chalkboard he could wipe free when it was too full of words. He found himself reaching his hand up toward Luz to help her up. He could see her eyes in the shade of the hat's brim. She looked up at him and laughed. He helped her up, and she dusted herself off. Mundo came and offered her his arm.

She shook her head.

"Take my arm," he said. "It's not an easy climb. Don't be so stubborn."

She grabbed his arm and steadied herself. She didn't fall again. They walked ahead of Diego, and he smiled as he watched them climb ahead of him. Luz leaned on Mundo until they reached the very top of the mountain, the very foot of the statue. The T-Birds followed quietly behind.

Luz knelt in front of the statue and prayed. The T-Birds fell back and lit their cigarettes away from Diego and Mundo. Diego's eyes moved from Luz to the face of the statue, then to the huge out-stretched arms. He saw the giant hands and looked across the desert. He could see El Paso; he could see Juárez; he could see New Mexico. I can see the whole world, he thought, and it belongs to me.

He looked up at the statue again. Cristo Rey's face was kind, not at all like the hard stone that withstood the wind. Diego studied the eyes, the lips, the well-defined chin. The statue stood so still—stone—and yet almost flesh, almost soft, somehow alive. Diego tried to memorize every feature. He thought he saw the outstretched hands move and the fingers wave in the air. Diego rubbed his eyes, rubbed them to clear the mirage. Too much sun, he thought. The statue pointed his eyes at Diego. The lips moved: "I can tell you where the jewels are, Diego." Diego stared up at the inanimate statue and shook his head. He turned his head away.

"The lips moved," he told himself. "They really moved." He turned his back to the statue, afraid to look at it again.

"Diego," he heard the voice, "Diego, Carlota's jewels, I know where they are."

I can hear! he thought, I can hear! He shut his eyes. One more time, let me hear one more time. My God, just one more time.

Mundo stepped up to him and placed a hand on his shoulder.

442

"You OK, Diego?" He could see his lips moving but he couldn't hear him.

Diego nodded. I'm going crazy, he thought, I'm deaf, I can't hear anything. He looked at Mundo and then looked down toward the ground. *But I did hear.* Mundo looked at him. "You're making noises, you know? ¿Qué te pasa?"

Diego shrugged his shoulders.

"The treasure—it's at the peak of Pico del Aguila," the voice whispered. "Diego, Carlota's jewels, the Juárez Mountains, Pico del Aguila." Diego laughed at the whisper in his ears. He jumped up in the air and laughed.

Mundo tried to hold him down. Luz ran up beside them.

"Dig them up, Diego. You'll find them." He looked up at the sky, saw it bluer than he'd ever seen it. He faced the statue and stretched his arms toward it—laughing. He gave in to the laughter.

"So this is what it's like." He felt the tingle in his ears. "My God! I can hear!"

Luz grabbed his arm. "Dieguito, what's wrong—what are you trying to say?"

"Do you hear me, Diego?" He stared at the lips. "Do you hear me, Diego?"

Diego nodded and yelled. He jumped in the air and tried to hug the air in his arms.

Luz and Mundo looked at each other.

Diego placed his hands on his ears, tears running down his face, and opened his arms toward the statue, then hugged himself. He fell on his knees, closed his eyes and focused on the sound of the voice. He wanted to be sure to remember what it had sounded like—more beautiful than any picture he had ever seen. The voice was like the stained-glass windows of the cathedral, like the chrome on the T-Birds' cars; like the color of the sky. The voice was stronger than Mundo's handshake; softer than Mary's eyes. The voice was like the green in the leaves of the rain bush. He stayed on the ground a long time. He opened his eyes and rolled over in the dirt, laughing. Mundo and Luz stood over him, afraid.

"Dieguito," Luz asked, "what's happening to you? Are you all right?"

Diego watched her soundless lips and shrugged. The voice, he wanted to say, the voice. Didn't you hear?

"Did you faint, Dieguito? What are you trying to say?"

He took out his pad. "I Heard!"

"Too much sun, ese," Mundo said. He motioned El Güero to bring some water.

"I don't need water," Diego wrote.

"Look, Diego, it's hot." He wet a handkerchief and handed it to him. Diego took it and wiped the sweat off his face to make Mundo happy. He took the jug and drank some water.

"I'm not crazy," he wrote.

"Dieguito, no one is saying you're crazy. We've just got to get you out of this sun."

Diego looked at the stone platform the statue stood on. He climbed it and kissed the feet of Cristo Rey. He climbed back down and wrote: "We're going on another pilgrimage."

Luz read the note and wiped the sweat off his forehead.

Diego smiled at her. He pointed toward Pico del Aguila. "Over there," he wrote. "We're going to get the jewels." His hands trembled as he wrote.

Mundo handed him a cigarette.

"The statue talked to me," he wrote. "I heard! The statue talked to me!"

The T-Birds carried Diego down the mountain following Luz's instructions. She had decided it was best to carry him rather than let him walk on his own—and Mundo had agreed with her. He couldn't write anything while he was being carried so he stopped trying to explain anything to them. He shut his eyes and tried to calm himself. He thought of the voice, how good and calm and easy it had sounded. He felt the sun on his face, warm like the voice. Exhausted, he fell asleep.

When he woke up he was lying on the couch in the living room of his house. Mundo and Luz and the T-Birds were drinking beer and standing around him, all of them wearing looks of worry.

Diego sat up slowly. They all stared at him. He looked around for a pad and pen. He made a writing motion to Luz. She walked to the bookshelf and found a pad and handed it to him.

"I'm OK," he wrote, "so stop looking at me as if I were in a zoo."

"We're not looking at you like that, mi Diego, we were just a little worried. It was the sun. It was all my fault—I could have killed you taking you out in that heat. You're not used to it."

"It wasn't the sun," he wrote. "The statue talked to me."

Mundo handed him a beer. "Look, Diego, drink this."

"I don't need a beer," he wrote.

He looked at Luz. "Get him his cognac. He likes that stuff."

Luz nodded and went into the kitchen. She came back with a glass of cognac and handed it to Diego. Diego reluctantly took a drink. He looked up at the T-Birds who were watching him like he'd done something wrong. Mundo motioned them to leave, and Luz pointed them toward the backyard. Indio picked up the case of beer on the floor and they walked out of the room.

"I'm not crazy," he wrote. "Stop looking at me like I'm crazy. It wasn't the sun—the statue told me where to find Carlota's jewels."

"Dios mío, what have I done?" Luz said. She looked at Mundo. "He's beginning to sound like La Mary."

"Look, ese," Mundo said, "maybe it was like a dream, you know? Sometimes dreams seem real."

"I thought you didn't believe in dreams." Diego wrote.

"But some people do."

"It wasn't a dream. I know the difference between a dream and what's real."

"But the dreams in the sun are the worst kind, mi Diego." Luz tightened her lips. "I know about these things."

"Goddamnit!" he wrote. He tore the page from his pad and shoved it in Luz's face. He stared at both of them. He started writing furiously. "Look, I'm not a little kid. I don't need to be taken care of, got that? Mundo, when you go out and do whatever the hell you want out on the streets, does anybody stop you? If you want to get laid, you get laid; if you want to fight, you fight—and nobody tells you anything. You do whatever you want. And you, Luz, you've had husbands and children and lovers and you've flown on a plane and done just about everything. And nobody tells you anything either. And you're always telling me I'm a pendejo. I'm not a pendejo. I heard the statue. A deaf man knows when he hears something, damnit! I know what I heard. I know. I heard! You don't have to believe me but you can't steal it from me. If you see the sun, how do you know it's the sun? If you see the sky, how do you know it's the sky? How do you know you have hearts? You just know. And I know where Carlota's jewels are, and I'm going to dig them up. Neither one of you is going to stop me. Do you hear? Or are you deaf, too?'' He shoved the note in front of them and took a drink from his cognac.

10

In the desert the sky is wide. I feel small here, small and weak and wordless. In San Francisco the fog erased the sky—but here nothing can spare you from the sky or the sun that beats us like children who must submit. There is more than space and time that separates me from my past. A month. I have been here a month—and already the desert has swallowed the yellow hills of California. I cannot picture them. California is dead to me, and somehow I know the path of the return has been obliterated. There is no going back, and nothing to go back to.

We climbed Mount Cristo Rey today in all the heat to spread out Salvador's ashes. I've always wondered why the living follow out the prescriptions of the dead. Why do the dead have such power? Maria Elena says quite simply that the dead are not dead, that they are more alive than the living.

The climb up the mountain was hell and the sun felt as if it were hanging a foot above my head. The path was well-worn by pilgrims, and I wondered about the footprints all the way to the top. Maria Elena called what we did a pilgrimage. I didn't much feel like a pilgrim. Pilgrims believe. I sometimes think the only thing I really believe in is believers. I believe in Maria Elena. Is that enough? I trudged up the mountain right next to her. We talked about our girlhoods. One hundred degrees—and we're climbing a mountain and talking about our girlhoods. She talked a lot about Diego. She said she'd hated him because he was so helpless until she realized that she only thought he was helpless because he was deaf. But she only came to that conclusion sometime after she'd abandoned him. "After my mother's funeral, I just walked out," she said. When we grew quiet, she prayed a rosary in my ear. I listened to her whispered prayers as we climbed higher and higher. Looking down on the whole valley, I realized I was happy to be breathing, happy to have a nose and hair and sweaty skin. Despite all the rows of cardboard houses, the homes with bootlegged electricity that often destroyed entire neighborhoods in the night in flames, despite the pollution, despite the tamed and beaten river, the desert I was staring at was as sacred a thing as I had ever seen. Mama cried when she looked out over the desert. I didn't want her to go, she's so old and tired. She's going away, but I don't think she could go away without seeing the desert from the top of the mountain. She wanted to be there for the spreading of Salvador's ashes, the child she had wanted more than me. She asked me to forgive her, and I told her there was nothing to forgive. She fell on the way down. I thought she would die there. I picked her up and Jake helped her all the way down. She looked so small next to him.

Eddie and Jake talked a good deal the whole way. Eddie laughed a lot—but he always does. He's easily amused, and he seemed to be particularly amused by the hats we were wearing—that and the way the dust was clinging to our sweaty skin. He teased his wife. "I remember when you didn't let me see you without makeup." He laughed and wiped her face with his shirt. I love that man—for his kindness and for his laugh. Jake was very thoughtful most of the way up. He seems more vulnerable to me now. Ever since Casas Grandes, he seems a little more lost. I think he liked having Joaquin's ashes in his room. I think he hated to get rid of them, though when I asked him about it he said I was being ridiculous. "People aren't ashes," he said. "What I loved of him is long gone." Somehow, I don't think so. I told Jake he didn't have to come on another ash-spreading expedition. He said he'd been to several with Joaquin and that he didn't mind them, and that he had been wanting to see what the statue looked like up close.

When we reached the top of the mountain, Maria Elena insisted on a prayer. It made me sad I hadn't known my brother. The world we had been brought up in had made us strangers to each other and so we never belonged to each other. Sometimes I think the world conspires to keep us all separate from each other. We have to fight to belong to those we love—maybe that's all we can hope for. I tried not to hate my father for separating me and Salvador because I didn't want hate to be a part of the moment. I didn't want any hate on top of that mountain—all I wanted was Maria Elena and Jake and Eddie—and Salvador's ashes. When Nena finished the prayer, I flung his ashes in the hot wind. For an instant there was a gray cloud that came between me and the sun. And then the ashes spread like grains of sand. I placed the urn at the foot of Christ the King. No one said a word, and after we lingered for a while, it was time to go. It was getting hotter and hotter, and it seemed as though we were not welcome after we had completed our task. As I said his name, we started to climb down. His name has come to mean good-bye.

On the way down from the mountain, we passed a group of pilgrims. Maria Elena didn't notice them. She was looking straight down at her feet and fingering her rosary. There was a woman among them, and she seemed too old to be climbing a mountain in the hot sun. But a young man had her by the arm and was helping her climb. Our eyes met as I passed him. I have thought of his dark eyes all day. I remember them from somewhere. Who knows? I sometimes don't know anything anymore. I thought it might have been Diego, but I have come to the conclusion that I am a very bad seer.

About halfway down, Maria Elena had to sit down and rest. For an instant I knew what she was thinking: I think I'm pregnant again. I smiled at her, and I was certain she knew I had just read her thoughts. She walked right next to me the rest of the way down. She handed me a folded-up piece of paper. I started to open it, but she stopped me. "I woke up last night after dreaming some words. I wrote them down—I just wanted you to read them." I asked her why she wasn't giving the words to Eddie. "You don't understand," she said quietly. "The words in the dream were whispered to me." She stopped walking, then paused, "It was Rose's voice." I stuck the piece of paper in my pocket. This afternoon I read the words she'd dreamed, the words uttered to her in Mama's voice.

I am writing these words onto this page, and I am giving Nena back the words she gave me. We must never lose them. I know what they mean. So does Nena. I must try to at least stay in my body through Mama's final season.

I haven't left my body for a week and I feel as though I'm suffering from withdrawal. I sat out on the front porch this evening and smoked a cigarette with Jake and drank a glass of wine. We talked a long time about Joaquin, and I wound up talking to him about Salvador, and how it was so strange that I'd wound up with my twin brother's ashes. He's still a little sore with me for having followed him and Eddie to Casas Grandes. He wanted to know if I had eavesdropped on their conversation. I told him I hadn't, but I think he's still trying to decide if I'm telling the truth or not.

Eddie said it was a sneaky thing to do and he and Maria Elena got into an argument over the whole episode the minute they discovered what had happened. But during dinner, Eddie wound up laughing so hard over the whole ridiculous event that he fell off the chair. "Tomorrow, Paris!" he howled. Maria Elena and I weren't as amused. Mama went the opposite way. She wept openly that night, releasing all the tension of the day. "If you ever leave me while I'm still on this earth, Elizabeth Edwards, I swear I'll die cursing your name." She made me promise to "stay within my form." I didn't argue with her, though I am not at all sure I intend to keep my promise.

 **11**

At dawn on Sunday morning, a day after the Christ had
spoken to Diego, he and Luz and Mundo and the T-Birds began their
climb up the Juárez mountains. Diego led them, his feet dancing as
though a tune was playing in his body.

"It's a little steep," Mundo said.

"I thought you were a man. I thought you could take it," Diego
wrote. He stuck the note in Mundo's hand and kept climbing.

"This is harder than yesterday," Mundo said as they stopped to
drink some water. "There isn't any road here. At least yesterday
there was a road."

"Sometimes people make their own roads."

Luz read the note over his shoulder and laughed. "That's for damn
sure, Dieguito, but it doesn't mean their roads take them anywhere."

Diego shrugged his shoulders, drank some water, and kept climbing.

When they stopped again, Mundo said something to Luz, then
walked up to Diego. "Hey Diego, I don't think we're gonna make
it to the top."

"Quit complaining," Diego wrote. He was still angry with him
and Luz for not believing. They were just humoring him. He kept
climbing.

Luz held on to Mundo's shoulder. Diego looked back occasionally

451

to see if everyone was all right. The T-Birds were talking to each other, but Diego wasn't interested in what they were joking about. He could see them laugh, and he could see Mundo and Luz speaking to each other, but he just climbed higher not caring what they were saying to each other. They probably thought he was getting like Crazy Eddie.

When they reached the top of the steep mountain, they took a rest and smoked cigarettes. Diego pointed to the statue of Cristo Rey on the other side.

Luz nodded. "Diego, you're going to be very disappointed when we don't find anything up here. If we find anything at all, it will be Carlota's bones." She puffed on her cigarette. "But at least it's beautiful up here, Dieguito—just beautiful! I've lived here all my life, and I've never been up here. At least you brought me up here, Diego, but please don't cry if we don't find anything. I hate to see you cry."

Mundo watched Luz speak, then looked at Diego. He said nothing.

"Get the shovels," Diego wrote. He gave the note to Mundo. Mundo called the T-Birds over. Diego walked around the back of the mountain and found a level place along the steep slope. He stood on the place and nodded. Mundo handed him a shovel, and he began digging. Mundo and Indio joined him. El Güero shook his head and looked at Luz. El Guante smiled and shrugged his shoulders.

The dust stuck to the sweat on Diego's skin as he dug, and after an hour's work he was covered with dust and sweat. Mundo looked at him and laughed. "Look at yourself, ese." Diego laughed and kept digging.

After digging a hole about six feet deep, Mundo stopped. "Time for a break," he said. He climbed out of the hole and took a deep breath. Luz handed him a cup of water, and they both looked down at Diego who continued working. "Come and take a break—have a cigarette and some water. The sun's too goddamned hot. C'mon, take five." Diego wasn't watching him, just kept digging. Mundo tossed a light pebble at him, hitting him on the back of the head. Diego looked up. "Take five," he said. Diego climbed out and took a cigarette and some water from Luz.

"Look, Dieguito," she said, "enough, ya basta. You're tired. Two pilgrimages in a row is too much for anybody. There's nothing here, Diego, just a lot of brown sand."

He took a pad out of his back pocket and wiped off the dirt. "The statue didn't lie to me," he wrote.

"It was a dream, Dieguito. Dreams don't always mean what we think they mean."

"Doña Luz is right, Diego. We dug six feet and there ain't no jewels. That Carlota took them with her, got it? She didn't leave nothing for us."

Diego looked away from him.

Luz grabbed him by the shoulders and forced him to turn around. "It's only a story, mi Diego, just a small lie our grandmothers made up, that's all."

Diego pointed toward the statue and jumped back into the hole. He kept digging like a wild man. "Please," he prayed, "please." The tears and the sweat stung his eyes until he couldn't see.

He dug until he was drenched in sweat and dust. He stuck in the shovel with the whole force of his body, again and again, feeling his muscles ache. "Please," he prayed, "please." The shovel went in and out of the ground, in and out until, with one last forceful jab into the earth, Diego felt the shovel hit something hard, something more solid than sand. He dropped the shovel and began jumping up and down. He waved his hands in the air. Luz and Mundo and the T-Birds watched him as he looked up at them and pointed toward the end of the shovel.

Mundo jumped in and began digging with him until they slowly uncovered what appeared to be an old coffin. Diego said nothing, though his disappointment was obvious to Luz and to Mundo. "All this for a coffin," Diego wrote.

"There might be something in there," Luz said.

"Bones," Diego wrote, "some rotting bones."

"I say we open it," Mundo wrote.

"It's bad luck to disturb the dead," Diego wrote.

"We'll say a prayer," Luz said. "What have we got to lose?"

Mundo motioned his friends over. "Help me pull her up."

"We'll pull it out," El Guante said. "We can get it." The T-Birds helped Mundo and Diego out of the hole and lifted the box out into the open air.

No one said a word as the coffin was lifted out of its place. Luz made the sign of the cross. Indio, El Guante, El Güero, and the others stood around the coffin and stared at it. Mundo poked at it. He looked at Diego and Luz—then looked at the coffin. "You open it, Diego, you should finish what you started."

Diego's hands trembled—and for a moment he was unable to move. He placed his hands on the coffin and slowly opened the lid. He shut his eyes, waited, took a deep breath, and then opened it. He stared at the skeleton. So that's it, he thought, this is the treasure, a skeleton. He walked away from it. No one said a word. Diego looked across at the statue of Cristo Rey and threw his arms in the air. He wanted to curse the statue, to drag it down with his bare hands and break it until it became as fine as desert sand.

Mundo caught him by the arm. "It's OK," he said, "no big deal. Doesn't matter, ese. We found something, huh?"

Diego did not bother to look at his lips. He did not want to be consoled. Diego laughed, just laughed and laughed, tears running down his face. Luz and Mundo listened to the echo of his laughter as it swept across the valley.

12

MARIA ELENA SAT at her desk carefully studying the words she had written on a yellow legal pad:

> Juan Diego Ramirez. Your sister has come back to look for you. She misses you. Please come to her at 9000 West Yandell (Sunset Heights).

She crossed out "She misses you." It was much too public a sentiment to parade in a newspaper ad. As if anyone cared, she thought. She wondered if Diego still read newspapers. He had always been reading something, had always been lost in his books—like Eddie. In high school, Diego was the only one in the house that read the daily news, the only one in the household to understand there was a world bigger than their family.

Maria Elena stared at her note again. It contained all the necessary information. It was enough. She thought of the poem she had dreamed. She hadn't told Eddie about it. He would gloat. "You wrote a poem!" he would yell triumphantly. He would wear an I-told-you-so look on his face as if her conversion had been inevitable. But she had only written down what she dreamed, had only copied it—and she was only interested in the sentiment it carried. Eddie would be interested in the poem, the form, the words; she and Lizzie were interested in the dream, the voice that had whispered the poem to her. She would keep the poem a secret. She turned around and stared at him as he sat on the bed, his nose in a book. He looked up at her and smiled, then looked back into his book. She stared out the window at the garden they had started. The rows were neat but they had started too late—it would be a poor harvest. It would take a few years before the ground was fertile again. The twilight was calm, still, hot. Maria Elena brushed the sweat from her face. She wished for a breeze.

"What are you writing?"

"An ad for the newspaper."

"What are you selling?"

"I'm not selling anything, corazón."

"Oh, then you're looking for a new husband."

She turned around, and faced him. "The old one's running just fine."

"He sounds like a car."

"He snores like one."

"Sometimes, so does the wife."

"Maybe you should trade her in."

"I don't want to trade her in. She's running just fine."

"Too fine."

"What's that supposed to mean?" He had a curious look on his face.

"My body—it works too well."

"How can a body work too well?"

"I'm pregnant." She hadn't intended to tell him—not then anyway.

"What?" He threw the book in the air and let it fall on the floor. "Come here," he said.

She rose from the desk—the ad she had written still in her hand—and threw herself on the bed.

He kissed her.

"Eddie, do you love me?"

"You still have to ask?"

"You hate my prayers."

"Hate is a strong word." He held her tighter.

"You think prayers are silly—innocuous, at best."

"You think the same of literature."

"I never said that."

"I'm not an idiot."

She pulled away from his embrace and looked into his face. "So what are you going to do?"

"You're going to keep praying and I'm going to keep reading— and about every six months we'll give each other looks, yell at each other, you know, it'll go that way."

"You don't want the children baptized, do you?"

He was quiet for a moment. He bit his lip.

"Oh, I know what biting the lip means."

"We haven't even had the second one yet."

"She'll be here in no time."

"I hope it is a she," he said nodding. "We'll name her Elizabeth."

She nodded, "But you're changing the subject. I want them bap-tized, Eddie."

"If it makes you happy, amor."

"Why don't you just pat me on the head and send me out the door?"

"All I'm trying to do is compromise."

"Is that the best you can do?"

"Nena, I don't believe—and that's not new information. Yes, it's the best I can do."

She nodded. She tried to hide her disappointment.

"Don't be sad," he said. He placed his hand on her belly. "You don't want her to be sad, do you?"

She shook her head.

"Do you love me?" His voice was soft as the warm air in the room, as soft as the twilight.

She nodded.

"You want to make love to a godless man?"

"No," she said—then smiled. She clutched the note she was hold-ing.

He stared at her clenched fist.

"Can I read it?" She handed him the note. "Think it'll work?"

"Maybe."

"Did you try the phone book?"

"Of course."

"Why don't you try a detective?"

"Can we do it my way?"

"Stubborn." He slipped his hand under the T-shirt she was wearing. Her skin was damp. He kissed her neck.

"Eddie, can I ask you a question?"

"Can I stop you?"

She pushed his hand away. "You hate El Paso, don't you?"

"It's a strange place," he said.

"Meaning it's ugly."

"Yes. It's ugly."

"You wanted something nicer."

"I didn't say that, Nena. I'll make it home. California's gone now.
I'll never get it back." He brushed her hair back with his thumb.
"California used to be the future, didn't it?"

"I always thought the border was the future."

"You were right," he laughed, "ours anyway."

Lizzie looked up from rereading what she had just written in her
journal. She knew Jake was at the door wondering whether he
should knock or not. She rose from her bed, opened the door and
stared at him as he stood motionless. He stared at her, almost pleading.

"Are you lost?"

He started to turn away.

Lizzie pulled him into the room. He let himself go wherever she
led him. "You don't want to go," she said. She saw he was afraid,
saw he was shaking as if he had been out in the cold for a lifetime.
Not even the heat of the desert morning could warm him. She led
him to her bed. When he started to cry, she held him tight, though
she could not keep him from shaking.

"Sometimes," he said, "I'm falling. I dream I'm falling—and
there's nothing but an endless hole. I just want to hit the ground and
break—I just want to do anything except keep falling. Sometimes I
get night sweats. That's the way it begins."

She let him speak, he who was not used to speaking. "I'll miss
my body—just like I miss his."

"It's just a body," she wanted to say, but said nothing.

She lay down on the bed, and held him until he stopped crying, until he stopped shaking.

"I'm sorry," he finally said, "I don't know why I came to your room." He could not say he needed comforting.

"It doesn't matter why you came," she said.

He started to rise from the bed.

"You can stay," she said.

"I've never slept with a woman," he said.

"Well, now you can say you have."

Jake smiled. He fell asleep exhausted as he leaned into her.

As Lizzie held him, she remembered a dream she had once had, a dream she could not remember for a long time, a dream that had frightened her. She had not had a body, and she was in a church, and her mother had become Our Lady of Perpetual Sorrows. Jake had been in that dream—though she had not known him then. That dream had come to pass, only in the living of it. She had learned not to be afraid.

That night, in Lizzie's arms, Jake did not dream he was falling. He dreamed of the thunder and the rain, of the desert being gifted with water. He was standing alongside the bushes and the yucca, holding his nephew in his arms—and they were being washed by the downpour. He was as clean as his nephew. When he woke, he was surrounded by Lizzie's smell. He slipped away softly—and she did not wake. He laughed to himself. He couldn't remember the last time he'd slept in all his clothes. Thunder echoed through the room and he took in the smell of the falling rain; he held it in lungs. He walked to the window and stared out into the dawn. Peace was this moment—it was only this moment. He unlatched the screen; he stuck out his hand and felt the rain.

"I'll say one thing about this place, Nena—lots of drama in the sky." Maria Elena dug her head into Eddie's chest. "Ummmmm," she said.

"Is that a go back to sleep 'ummm'?"

"Just listen," she whispered. A bolt of lightning seemed to hit right outside their window. The loud crack of the thunder startled her. She jumped instinctively.

"Guess that woke you," he said. The rain pounded the ground like millions of nails being pounded into wood.

"God is busy today," she said.

"Did you pray for rain?" Eddie teased.

"As a matter of fact I did."

"So we can attribute what's going on outside to your evening prayers."

She laughed. "Well, I won't stop you. Whose turn is it to make the coffee?"

"Yours," he said.

"No fair—I'm pregnant."

"I forgot," he said as he kissed her. "It's cold," he said, and pulled her closer.

They listened to the rain for a long time. He was happy listening to the rain and feeling the warmth of his wife's skin. He wanted to tell her that he loved her, that he would always love her, that his life had been a long drought and that he would always be thirsty for her, thirsty and grateful. He was happy. *Who'd have thought that I'd wind up in El Paso listening to a morning thunderstorm? Who'd have thought I'd ever be happy?*

"Where are you?" Nena shook him gently.

"Just thinking. This place," he said, "it could be mine."

"Good," she said, "because we're not moving."

Maria Elena rose from their bed and went into the bathroom. Eddie watched her as she moved from the bed. He always liked watching her move about the room in the morning. When she disappeared into the bathroom, he looked toward the baby's crib. It felt odd not to have the baby with them. He fought the urge to go into Rose's room and get him. She had insisted on watching him for the night. "Do it for me," she'd said. "I don't always want to spend the night in an empty room. And he loves me, you know?" Eddie wondered if the baby was sensing the rain. He was such a strange and calm and intelligent child. *What a lucky man—what a lucky, lucky man.*

Maria Elena came back into the room. "I miss the baby," she said.
Eddie didn't seem to hear her.

"Where are you now?"

He stared up at her blankly.

She slapped him gently. "Are you there?"

"I was just thinking about Lizzie," he said.

"And?"

"I was just wondering if she was out and about in the rain."

"Sans her body, you mean?"

"Yeah—sans her body." He paused for a moment. "What do you think about all that, anyway?"

"You asked me that already."

"I can't remember what you said."

"You probably weren't listening."

"Of course I was listening—I just forgot. I can't remember everything. What'd you say?"

"I said I thought it was wonderful—strange but wonderful."

"And you have no problems that she just up and leaves her body anytime she wants?"

"Eddie, I either have to take her word for it—or I have to believe she's cracked. Does that woman look like a lunatic?"

"No."

"A liar, then?"

"No. But—"

"But what?"

"I don't know. I'm starting to worry about her."

"Oh, you think she needs help."

"Don't put words in my mouth, Nena. I don't think we need to ship her off to the funny farm—I just get a feeling."

"I'm listening."

"Well, she seems more distant, less emotionally engaged. She's not one to hold back—and yet lately she seems almost unreachable. It scares me. I don't know why—and you've noticed it, too. I can tell by the look on your face."

She stared into her hands, then started doing exercises with her fingers.

"You used to do that all the time when we first started dating."

She reached over and combed his hair with her fingers. "What are we going to do about Lizzie?" Her voice cracked. "We're losing her. Rose, too."

"Rose, too?"

"She's preparing herself."

"That's silly," he said.

"No. I know."

"How do you know?"

"She's just tired, Eddie. She wants to."

"You mean if I wanted, I could just lie down and die."

"Of course."

"That's crazy."

"People do it all the time—it's just that some people do it differently, and for different reasons. She's tired, and she's old, and she's in pain. She's had a life, you know? Who wants to live forever? And I can't say that I blame her. But Lizzie, Lizzie's another matter—these experiences, well, they've confused her." She scratched at the sheets with her fingernails as if to tear them. "We can't do anything, you know?"

"Tell her to come back."

"No."

"Why not? I'll tell her."

"No."

"Why not?"

"She has to make a choice."

"I don't believe this. I just don't believe it."

"Good, so it will be easy to disregard the whole matter."

Eddie threw himself off the bed. "When are things going to get simple around here?"

"You want simple, Eddie? When have things been simple? When you were a child, were things simple? We'll be parents for a second time, and we haven't even begun with the first—is that simple? Hell, Eddie, sometimes even our sex is complicated."

He laughed grudgingly—almost disgusted. "I'm going for a run."

"In the rain?"

"It's stopped."

She looked out at the clearing sky. "So it has."

He put on a pair of jogging shorts. He tied his running shoes and stared at them. "Will you talk to Lizzie?"

"She already knows what I think."

"Because she knows you or because she's stealing your thoughts."

"She doesn't have to steal them, Eddie."

"Right."

"You're mad."

"No, not really. It's just that I need to take a day off from the truth."

"Take a day then," she said. She stretched across the bed and kissed his back.

 **13**

BONES. DIEGO SAT at his desk tracing the word, letter by letter, with his finger. He pretended his fist was full of sand—he emptied it out onto the desk. He blew it away with a breath. He thought the statue of Christ the King had a sick sense of humor.

Luz and Mundo had tried to comfort him all week long, but he refused to hear anything at all on the subject of the treasure. "At least we found something," Luz said, "and we placed a cross to mark the grave—those things are very important, mi amor."

Diego nodded, but was unable to hide his disgust. He wondered why the treasure had been so important.

He had begun to dream of his mother, and his dreams had brought back the memory he had hid from himself. He remembered clearly now that his mother had jumped out in front of a car to save his life because he had not heard it coming, because he had not been paying attention. He had been taught to be careful, to always look because he could not hear. But he had stepped out into the street because he had been thinking about a story he had read—a story, a stupid story. The next thing he felt was a hand pushing him out of the way. Then his mother lying there crushed. He found it odd that he had forgotten how she had died. He had not been a child when it happened. He suspected now that his sister had left because she blamed him for her death. Her blame was not exactly misplaced,

464

he thought. He began to despair, to hate himself, and he no longer felt anything except the full force of the dullness of his life. Diego was caught in a body that could neither speak nor hear, and he hated it, hated his life as he had never hated it before.

Bones. He traced the word on his desk again. He decided that he would start a new suicide letter. This time, he would carry it out. This time, he would end the nonsense. Mundo had come by every day and taken him out into the country to teach him to drive. It had been easier than he had thought. To keep his mind off the coffin and the skeleton and the deceiving Christ, he studied the driver's manual late into the night. On the fourth day of his driving lessons, Mundo had taught him to parallel park. Mundo tried to make him laugh, but Diego refused to let himself be amused by anything. Since he had nothing else, he let the act of driving become everything. He learned to drive in six days. He had never found anything difficult to learn—except for speaking. He had refused to learn to speak at school because he did not want others to hear his voice. Why should they hear what he could not? But driving a car—that was easy. On Monday morning, Mundo took him to get his driver's license. He got a perfect score on the written. Mundo explained to the uniformed official that Diego was deaf. The DMV officer pointed when he wanted him to turn in a particular direction. He took his picture and was given a temporary license. There was only one restriction placed on his license: All vehicles he was to drive had to have outside mirrors. Diego looked at his temporary license. "That's all?" Diego wrote. "That's all,' Mundo nodded. Diego shrugged.

"Look, ese," Mundo said, shaking him, "you got to get yourself together. You got to stop thinking about that coffin. No one cares, man. Did you really think we were gonna get rich, ese? This is America, Diego, and most people don't get rich in America—got that? You been listening to the wrong people."

"It's not about being rich," Diego wrote. He didn't even want to try to explain his disappointment, couldn't even begin to write the words that said what it had felt like to hear that voice speak to him. To have waited so long to hear and then discover that the voice had been a lie. "You're right," he wrote. "It doesn't matter."

Mundo tossed him the keys. "You drive," he said, "you're legal now—and now you can apply for that job delivering flowers. I talked to the guy about you—told him all about you, ese." Mundo didn't tell Diego that he'd turned down the job offer himself because the guy was a do-gooder—the kind that was always trying to help fix other people's lives. "No," he told him, "I got a job—it's my friend that needs the job." He looked straight at Diego as he sat in the driver's seat. "The guy says to go in and make your application."

I won't get the job, Diego thought as he looked away from Mundo and turned the ignition, and if I do get it, it'll be because he feels sorry for me. I'm sick of people feeling sorry for me. Mundo directed him to the flower shop. They parked around the corner. "Just go in there," he said. "Put in your application, got it?"

"I don't want the job," Diego wrote.

"You gotta work, ese. You and Doña Luz, gotta make the rent. That tough old lady ain't gonna last forever—you need to work."

"You don't work," he said.

"I get by," he said. "I got some skills, bro."

"Teach them to me." he wrote.

"No, ese. I taught you how to drive—that's the only skill I wanna pass on to a guy like you."

"I'm not going in."

"I'll kick your ass all the way to the door," Mundo said. He grabbed Diego's pad away from him. "Just try it," he wrote. "If you hate it—then quit. Just try it."

Diego threw the keys on Mundo's lap, stole back his pad and pen, and slammed the car door. He stomped toward the flower shop hating the power Mundo and Luz had over him. He stared at the door to the flower shop. He read the sign: IF YOU DON'T KNOW WHAT TO SAY, THEN SAY IT WITH FLOWERS. He pushed open the door and walked inside.

Mundo stood at the door smoking a cigarette and watched Luz as she stood over the kitchen table rolling out tortillas, each one as perfect and round as the one before. One at a time she cooked them on a comál she had inherited from her mother, the smell of them filling the warm September air. She reminded him of his mother—

except his mother had been more frail and had not been strong enough to keep fighting. Diego sat at the table patiently cleaning beans. His mind was on his letter and on his sister. He thought his final letter would be one in which he would ask her for forgiveness. It was his fault they were orphans. If he killed himself and left the letter to her, the authorities would be forced to look for her. As he fingered each pinto bean, he tried to imagine her face.

Mundo flicked his cigarette into the backyard.

"We have ashtrays," Luz said, "act like a person."

"It don't hurt the ground, Doña Luz."

"It does hurt the ground—and who the hell do you think cleans them up? The maid?" She cackled at her own joke.

He liked her laugh. "Don't take a clean backyard so serious."

"That's what's wrong with you," she said as she handed him a tortilla right off the comál, "you don't take your life seriously. What do you do? You hang out with gang members, you drink beer, you get into fights, you take up space—you call that living?"

"You clean other people's houses—you call that living?"

She shot him a look. "I work," she said. She spread out her hands and pointed to each corner of the kitchen, "and because I work we have this house. You? What have you got—you haven't got a damn thing. You sleep at your mother's house?"

"Mostly," he said, his mouth full of her fresh tortilla.

"Well, what happens when she dies? How come you don't get a job?"

"I don't want no fuckin' job. I just want to take up space—I wanna take up lots of goddamned space."

She stared at the cut above his eye and shook her head. "One of these days you're gonna mess with the wrong guy, Mundo. You think you're a real badass gang member, but I see you. I know what you are. You're a lot of things I don't like, but you're not a killer, Mundo. But one day they're going to find your brown ass out on the street and it's going to be dead. Dios te bendiga." She buttered up another fresh tortilla and walked over to Diego and handed it to him. He looked up and took it. "Come out of that world of yours," she told him firmly.

He took a bite out of the tortilla and nodded.

"He's depressed," Mundo said.

"Ahhh, only gringos with money get depressed—they're the only ones who can afford to."

Mundo laughed. "No, Doña Luz, you got that wrong. See, when a woman dumps me—man I get real depressed—it ain't no gringo thing. I mean, I get so depressed I have to hit someone."

"That's not depression, menso. Depressed people don't go around hitting other people."

"How do you know?"

"I don't know," she said emphatically, "but I know one thing— if you'd keep your cosita in your pants, women wouldn't go around throwing you out on your cholo ass."

He polished off his tortilla. "Marriage ain't natural—"

"Don't give me that natural stuff—what the hell do you know about natural? People like you, you think streets and concrete and barrios are natural. A mesquite—now, that's natural."

Diego moved his clean pile of pinto beans with one swift movement of his arm; they fell into a pot he held like a pocket in a pool table. The sound of the beans in the empty pot made Luz lose her train of thought.

Diego looked up at her.

"What are you thinking about?" She asked.

He took out his note pad from his pocket. "When are you going to learn sign language?" he asked.

"I've learned all the languages I'm going to learn," she said. "We talk just fine."

"Did you ever stop to think that my hands get tired?" he wrote. He underlined tired.

"You still in a bad mood?" Mundo asked.

Diego shook his head. He looked down at his pad. "Did you know I've never made love to a woman?"

"Yeah," Mundo said, "I figured that one out long time ago."

"Is that it?" Luz asked. "Hell, Dieguito, sex—it's not important."

Diego stared at her as if his eyes were stone. "How many lovers have you had?"

Luz shook her head. "What difference does it make?"

"Ten?" he wrote, held it up and tossed the paper in the air. "Twelve?" he wrote, and again he flipped the page in the air. "Twenty?" He stared at both of them. "Don't tell me it doesn't matter. My body's just like yours."

"OK, amor," she said. "It was a stupid thing to say. Of course it matters."

"Look, ese, I know where you can get some action."

"Shut up, Mundo, don't be such an asshole," Luz said. "Diego's talking about something else. ¿Que no entiendes?"

"He's got to start somewhere." Mundo looked at Diego. "Look, ese, you gotta stop feeling bad. Feeling bad gets you where, ese? They're always makin' us feel bad. Feel bad cuz you ain't got a job, feel bad cuz you ain't no gringo, feel bad cuz your cars are too goddamned flashy, feel bad cuz you don't got no fuckin' flowers in your front yard or cuz you talk the way you talk."

"At least you can talk," Diego wrote.

"Yeah, ese, it's really taken me places, ese—gone real far." He moved his hand in the air as if it were a plane. "Look, ese, none of it matters. Everybody's gonna shit on you. The only thing you gotta remember is not to shit on yourself."

"Go to hell," Diego wrote.

"OK, don't listen," he said, "I'm outa here. I try to help a guy out by tellin' 'em what I know—and what the hell do I get?" He shoved open the door.

"Don't go," Luz said grabbing his arm. "You haven't eaten dinner. I made dinner."

He nodded and sat at the table. She was too much like his mother. He stared at the empty plate Luz put in front of him.

"Don't go to hell," Diego wrote. He placed the note on the plate.

Mundo took the note, wadded it up and threw it at Diego.

Diego blinked as it hit him in the face. They both blurted out laughing.

They're like brothers, Luz thought. She thought of her sons who had abandoned her. These two would do, she thought. She served them albóndigas and fideos. They all ate as if they were eating something rare, as if they were tasting this common, ordinary, peasant food for the first time. Diego and Mundo had three servings, and between them they ate nine tortillas. Even Luz kept up with them.

As Diego ate, the heaviness and disappointment of the coffin seemed to grow lighter. He had food. He was no longer alone. He had someone. They were good people, he thought, and they had a kind of fight he envied. They knew how to survive. He wanted to have what they had. If only he could get and hold the part of them that was tough enough to fight back. Maybe Mundo was right— maybe you needed some kind of fist to get you through life. He had always felt too fragile, as though he were about to come apart like a very thin piece of paper in a relentless wind. Maybe he would put off starting his suicide note. Maybe he would get the job at the flower shop. The man had been nice. Maybe, if he looked hard enough, he would find his sister and maybe she would look into his eyes and say, "I forgive you." Maybe was his new word for hope.

As Mundo pulled away from Luz and Diego's house that evening, he was happy. He liked coming over to visit them. Going to their house was like going home. Maybe Luz was right. Maybe he could change, maybe he could get a job and then Rosario would see that he was worth loving. Maybe there was a place for him in the world where he could be happy like he felt right now. But as he drove toward downtown, Mundo forgot about a job, about settling down, forgot about everything except the familiar pull of the bar. He hadn't been out to The Hollywood Cafe in over a week. But tonight the thought of a beer and a bar that smelled of a hundred years of cigarette smoke made his throat throb as if it were his heart. He loved the smell of bars, the sound of a cue stick against the ball, the voices of the people who knew there was nothing better in the world than a good place to have a drink. He pictured the cold bottle of beer against his lips, the taste of the cigarette in his mouth awash with beer. He stepped on the gas pedal—maybe tonight something would happen, something new, something that had never happened. That was the good thing about a bar—something new might always happen. He loved the thought of that something. Maybe he would run into El Guante who was grace at the pool table or maybe Rosario who was grace in bed—maybe she had forgiven him. Maybe she would take him back. Maybe, after a few beers and a few games of pool, she would take him in, take him to that place only she could take him. He thought of the way she smelled after they had made love. Maybe tonight, he would be making love again.

When he walked into the bar, the jukebox was playing *"Volver, Volver."* It was his mother's favorite song and he had always hated it. He thought it was a bad sign. It was quiet, just a quiet night, and he was disappointed that there were so few people in the bar—just a couple of guys standing around, most of whom he'd seen before.

Antonio, the bartender gave him a cool greeting. "Hey pájaro— no trouble, OK?"

Mundo shrugged. "I don't like trouble, gringo."

The bartender shook his finger and placed a bottle of Mundo's favorite beer on the counter. "Just no fights," he said, "that's all I'm sayin'. And I ain't no pinche gringo."

Mundo lifted up his glass and toasted him without saying a word. He looked around the room trying to see if he recognized anybody. An older man was selecting tunes at the jukebox. He was eyeing a woman young enough to be his daughter. Nothing special, he thought. The two guys shooting pool were younger than he was. Old enough to drink, but not old enough to know how to do much else. At a small table near the corner, a man in a pressed white shirt was lighting a cigarette for his girlfriend. Those two were always in here, he thought. His eyes moved slowly around the room. He finished his beer in four gulps. "Another," he said. Antonio placed another bottle in front of him. He stared at the two guys shooting pool. One of them missed his shot and the other one laughed. There was something familiar about the laugh. He looked closer at the young man, studied his face. He laughed again. Mundo ran the laughter through his memory trying to remember where he'd heard it. *I'm gonna cut you up—clean as a surgeon.* Mundo nodded. It was him. This was the something he loved about bars. He walked up to the man with the laugh, stared him straight in the face. "Remember me, ese?" he said.

The man stared at him. "Don't know you," he said.

"Yeah, you know me. One night you were gonna cut me up clean as a surgeon—remember that? Threw me in a fuckin' trash can, remember that? Thought I was dead, thought it was funny, huh, ese?" He grabbed the poolstick away from him and threw it on the floor. He looked at him, then fast as a gust of wind, he swung his fist. The man fell back on the pool table. From across the room he heard a voice yell, "Hey, T-Bird." He looked up, did not even see the face of the man who had called him not by his name but by the name of his gang. No face, just the gun. He heard the sharp sound almost as if it were the crack of a whip or the sound of his boyhood on the fourth of July. He felt the pain in his gut, then another pain. His heart. There was no time to think of the life he had lived, no time to curse it or be grateful for it, no time to ask forgiveness, to say good-bye, to understand any of the pieces, to thank Diego for taking him out of the trash, to make love just one more time to a woman, any woman, to finish a beer, no time. There was only the fact of a bullet and the fact of a body that was not made to withstand it. A bullet, simple in design, simple in the way it entered the body, broke the skin, the bone, the simplest of things. In the instant Mundo felt the dance of the simple bullet in his heart, he did not wear a look of terror, but of surprise. It was the look of a man who never believed he would die this way—in a bar—a bullet. Everything in his life had prepared him for this moment from the time he smoked his first cigarette, from the time he had taken his first drink at the age of ten, from the time that he had embraced the streets not as a place where cars drive but as a home, from the time his father had abandoned them, everything, everything he had ever done had led him to a bullet that had found a home in his heart, a bullet that killed faster, if less elegantly, than any conceivable virus. Everything, everything had prepared him for this, and yet he was not prepared.

14

ROSE WOKE AS the sun lifted itself over the heavy desert. She had always liked the morning light, and had wanted to see it one more time. She went to the window and looked out. She stared at the bluing sky and wondered if she was about to become a part of it. She unlatched the screen, pushed it open, and reached out to touch a limb from the tree. It was hard to make her body reach. Such a simple task. She stretched, grabbed at a leaf and tore it from the tree. She groaned in pain. Rose crushed the leaf in her hand and smelled it as though it were an herb. Her hand was wet and green from the leaf. She licked the bitter juice and the bits of leaf. Everything is water, she thought, even here. She felt faint and tired and cold, and even as the bitter taste of the leaf was in her mouth, Rose felt far away from herself, far away from the tree and the leaf. She willed herself toward the bed and fell into it. "Lizzie," she whispered, "I had the dream again." She seemed to flow back into the dream that had taken her over in the night, the same dream she had been having—but this time there was a river and she had begged the river to carry her away from the owls who threatened to mutilate her body. "Carry me!" she had yelled. "Carry me!" In the dream, the only reason she had not jumped was because she had felt her daughter's breath on her neck. It was a rope that had pulled her back. Rose had returned to the morning to cut the rope. She would miss her daughter, would miss uttering her name. But she would not miss her life, she was done with it. She would not miss remembering the events she had lived and relived too often. Perhaps she would meet Salvador and she would tell him that she had loved him, that she had been forced to give him up; she would ask his forgiveness. If there was nothing after death, then nothingness was painless. It did not matter—she was done with it, with all of it, with the regrets, with the loveless marriage, and even with the skies and the rains—all of it. "Lizzie," she repeated. Rose willed her daughter to walk into the room. She was not surprised when she walked through the door. "Are you a dream?"

"No, Mama," the woman whispered. The old woman was moved by the tone of her daughter's voice, a soft voice, compassionate and warm as the girlhood she had spent in her father's rose garden.

"Will you sit with me?"

The part of her that was a nurse knew it was useless to call a doctor. "Yes, Mama," she said, "I'll sit for as long as you like."

Jake knocked at Lizzie's room at dawn. She had asked to go with him on his morning walk, and he had reluctantly agreed. "Lizzie?" he whispered as loud as he could, "Lizzie?" Slept in, he thought. "C'mon, get your lazy legs out of bed." He knocked a little louder. He turned the knob and poked his head in. She was nowhere in the room. He walked down the hallway, and as he passed Rose's room, he noticed Lizzie sitting on her mother's bed through the open door. He wondered if he should enter, then decided to wait for her to notice him. She sat perfect and still. Finally, he decided to clear his throat to get her attention. She moved her gaze slowly toward the door.

"Is everything OK?" he whispered.

Lizzie motioned for him to come in. She reached for his hand as he came near her. "Tell Nena it's time," she said.

He stared down at Rose, her labored breathing filling the room. He thought of Joaquin's breathing, how it had sounded almost exactly like this awful sound, a voice tearing itself away from the very air that gave it life. He said nothing. He squeezed Lizzie's hand. "I'll tell her," he said.

"A candle would be nice," she said.

"Yes," he said softly. "You need to eat something," he added.

"Later."

He left the room and knocked on Eddie and Maria Elena's door. He heard Eddie's voice. "Yeah?"

"You awake?"

"That you, Jake?"

He could hear Maria Elena laughing through the door. "You can come in," she said. "We're decent—Little Jake needs you to hold him—he's cranky this morning."

He opened the door and stared at Eddie and Maria Elena hovering over their son. "So this is what heterosexuals do in the morning."

"Sometimes they actually have sex," Maria Elena laughed.

"They do?" Eddie asked. "How would we know?"

Maria Elena was about to make another joke but she was stopped by the look on Jake's face. Eddie wore the same look when something was bothering him. It occurred to her that he might be feeling sick and something in her panicked. She had gotten used to thinking of him as strong and healthy, and she realized as she looked at him that she might never be prepared for his dying. She sat there silently and waited for him to speak. She heard Eddie's voice: "What's up, Jake?"

He looked at Maria Elena. "Lizzie's in Rose's room—" He stopped in midsentence.

"And?" Eddie asked. "Is that significant?"

"I went looking for her because we were supposed to go out walking in the desert. She was just sitting there holding Rose's hand." He looked at Nena. "She said to tell you it was time. She said to tell you to bring a candle."

"Rose?" Maria Elena asked. She was prepared for that particular bit of news.

He nodded.

She handed the baby to Eddie who said nothing. She pointed to the candle that had burned in Joaquin's room the night he died. "Take that one to her," she said. "Tell her I'll be there in a minute."

Jake took the candle, stared at it, and walked out of the room.

"How did you know it was time for—" He stopped.

"You can say the word 'die,' amor."

"How did you know? What is it with you and Lizzie—what is it?"

"I had a dream, Eddie."

"What did you dream?"

"I dreamed words."

"Words?"

"Yes, words. Rose—she whispered them to me. I wrote them down." She went to her jewelry box and gave him the words in the dream.

He took the folded up piece of paper, opened it, and read it slowly. "It's a lovely poem," he said.

"I knew you'd say that."

"But that's not what you wanted to hear. You wanted me to tell you that the poem was about Rose's dying because it was whispered to you in a dream."

"Yes."

"That poem is life," he said emphatically, "it's not about death."

"You think death is the opposite of life?"

"Well, of course it is."

"What if death is just another country?"

"OK, what if it is another country? We can't go there, now can we? And frankly I'm not really anxious to get there." He looked at her sternly. "And you better not be anxious to get there either. When Rose dies, Lizzie won't be able to follow her to wherever the hell she's crossing. It's not like going to Juárez, you know? And when Jake dies, I won't be able to follow him into that other country—wherever the hell he'll be living. We'll just be exiled from each other again—and this time it will be permanent."

Maria Elena studied his angry face. She took his arm and squeezed it. He wadded up her poem in his fist.

"I don't know anything anymore," he said.

"That's OK," she said, "Has knowledge ever made us more

decent?" She smiled at him. "Lizzie needs me," she said. "I'm going to go sit with her."

"Shouldn't you call a doctor or something?"

"Rose doesn't want one."

"Did you dream that, too?"

"She told us."

"You mean in a normal conversation."

"Yes."

"Oh."

Jake sat at the kitchen table drinking a cup of coffee, reading the newspaper and holding his nephew in his arms, occasionally giving him a spoonful of oatmeal. "Hey Eddie, look at this, it's Maria Elena's ad in the newspaper."

He walked over from the sink where he was doing dishes and glanced over his brother's shoulder.

"Think it will do any good?"

"Well, she claims Diego used to be a newspaper freak."

"Can't she just go to the cops?"

"What a great idea," he said. "How come we didn't think of that?"

"Straight people have a hard time thinking."

"Very funny."

"Thank you."

Eddie laughed. He kissed the top of his brother's head. "I want you to stay forever."

Jake nodded. "I can't, you know."

"I know." Eddie walked back toward the sink and began drying the dishes. "Can I ask you a question?"

"Sure."

"Do you think about death all the time?"

"No. Just every day." He laughed.

"Seriously?"

"Sometimes, I don't think about dying—I can't. I'm still healthy. I feel fine. It's hard to believe I'll get sick because I have this thing in me. I'll believe it when I feel it. Lately, I've been waking up at night—and I can't sleep, and I'm afraid. Remember, when we were small and we used to wait and pray Dad wouldn't come in? It's like that. And I can't stop shaking."

"So what do you do?"

"I go to Lizzie."

"What?"

"She holds me. She doesn't make me talk. She just leaves her door open, and sometimes I cry and she doesn't make me turn the tears into words."

"Good," Eddie said. He continued drying the dishes while his brother continued reading the newspaper. He stared at his reflection in a plate. For no reason in particular he understood clearly that his life, and his brother's, had been nothing more than a narrow escape. For whatever reason, whether by chance, by coincidence, or by fate, they had been brought together again. Here we are, he thought, in this kitchen, my brother and me and my son. I am the luckiest of men. And I understand the meaning of what I have escaped. He wanted to thank someone for his life. He would light a candle to Saint Jude, the patron saint of impossible causes as a symbol of his gratitude. He made this promise to himself as he looked at his reflection in the plate he was drying.

Again, the three women were together in a room with a candle. Only this time, they were not waiting for a body to rise, but to fall away from the earth. The two younger women had sat all morning with the old woman who worked harder and harder for each breath she stole. The candle burned in the room, and often the younger women would stare, shifting their gaze from the old woman to the candle. The old woman's eyes had been shut all morning, but suddenly she opened them as if to look at the visible world one last time. "I want to taste some water," she said.

Lizzie poured her a glass and helped her drink it, a simple but difficult task.

"I tasted a leaf this morning," the old woman said softly. "It was as good as this water."

The women nodded.

"I want to tell you something, Lizzie. I want you to know. The body is a friend. Do you understand?"

"Yes, Mama, I understand."

"Good," the old woman said. "Then don't leave it until it's time." They were the last words she spoke. Rose's breathing filled the room for the rest of the day and the two women kept a vigil at her side. She had risen with the desert sun, and with its setting, she took her last breath. Her final day had been peaceful and she had died willingly. It was the kindest of deaths. The old woman had lived her life—it had been what it had been—nothing grand—just a life. But she had at least lived it in some comfort, and she had at least had her say, and she had at least died welcoming the great silence that lay before her as if it were a quiet sky full of stars. Elizabeth wept in the arms of her friend not because she raged against her mother's death, but because a daughter never welcomes the death of a good mother.

 **15**

ON THE DAY Mundo was buried at Concordia Cemetery—not far from Mary's grave—Diego received a letter in the mail informing him he had gotten the job at the flower shop. "I don't want the job," he wrote as he sat at the kitchen table. He flashed the note at Luz who was sitting quietly across from him smoking a cigarette.

"You want to die, too—is that it?" Luz asked and though Diego could not hear the anger in her voice, he could see it everywhere on her face.

"I'm too sad to work."

"I'm sad, too," she said, "so what? Dieguito, we have to keep on living. Did you see Mundo's mother at the funeral? She's dead, poor woman—given up, feels nothing. Couldn't you see that?"

"She's had a hard life." He slapped his pad on the table.

"So what? I've had a hard life. You've had a hard life. So what? We've got to keep living."

"Live to work?" he wrote.

"Yes. Live to work. Please, my Diego. This day is too sad. Flowers are a good thing. Tell them you'll take the job." She looked at him, carefully searching his face for a sign. "He wanted you to have the job," he added. "He taught you to drive. He did that for you—a good thing. Don't throw it away, my Diego."

480

Diego watched her as she took another drag from her cigarette. She looked worn and pale. Today, there was not much fight in her eyes, but there was still enough strength in her to keep despair from possessing her body. The look she wore made Diego forget about his own sense of despair. Besides her, Mundo had been his only friend. And before that, Mary. He was disgusted at the way they had died, not died—been killed. They had lived hoping—*and for what*? And his myth, the one he needed so desperately, the myth of Carlota's buried jewels, it had died along with everything else. He had never known how much power a legend could have and now it was as dead as Mundo and Mary, as dead as the houses in Sunset Heights that had once stood at the top of the stairs that went nowhere. But the aging woman in front of him was a wall that refused to crumble, a wall that had been spit on, written on, pissed and defecated on, and still the wall refused to crumble. That wall was all he had left. But even Luz needed comforting. He did not want to fight her, not today. "I'll take the job," he wrote.

"Good," she smiled.

"Will you quit one of your jobs?"

"Such nice handwriting."

He looked at her sternly.

"I don't know if I can, Diego."

"You work six days a week. At least quit your Saturday job— you don't like that lady anyway—and she never pays you extra for ironing. Let her iron her own damn clothes. If you don't quit at least one job, then I won't deliver flowers."

She laughed, then clapped her hands. "OK, my Diego, I'll quit my Saturday job."

"Good," he wrote.

That afternoon, he walked toward downtown to accept the offer of a job delivering flowers. On the way there, he stopped at the steps that went nowhere. He climbed them and looked out at the city around him. He thought it was a sad city. He gathered the trash with his fingers as if his hand were a rake. He told himself he'd come back with a trash bag and rake up the litter. Things didn't have to be so dirty.

The man he was replacing taught Diego everything he needed to know about the job. He gave him a map of the city, showed him how to look up addresses. Every day for two weeks, they delivered flowers and then drove around parts of the city, places he never knew existed. The city was bigger than he had imagined and he liked the fact that they were always so welcomed at the doors they knocked on. Luz had been right, it was a good job. Even the saddest of people smiled when they were handed flowers. The man who was training him warned him that not everyone welcomed flowers. "Once," he told him, "one lady threw a vase of roses at me. 'Tell the sonofabitch to shove them up his ass,' she said. Just be smart and be careful. If they don't want them, just take them back. You're just a delivery man. The people at the shop will handle everything else."

He liked the people who worked there because they laughed a lot. One of the women wrote him a note and showed it to him. "A man who doesn't talk," she had written. "I'm surprised a woman hasn't swept you up." She had stood by him as he read it and then laughed. He liked it that she could joke—at least she wasn't afraid of his deafness. The job was going to be just fine, he thought.

Diego was anxious to go on the rounds by himself. On Friday, at the end of his second week, he came to work and was told he would be on his own. He smiled at his boss and nodded. He showed him a card he had lettered to take along on his deliveries. I'M DEAF, it read, BUT I READ LIPS. The boss nodded. "Good idea," he said. "You'll do just fine." Diego loaded up the van for the morning's deliveries. Diego wrote down the addresses, studied his map, made some notes, and drove out into the streets of the city.

For some reason, he felt compelled to peek into some of the notes and read them. He felt as if he was a part of the messages that were being sent along with the flowers. He trembled a little when he read the first note: "Betsy, Happy Birthday you old bag of bones. Love, Tonya." Diego shrugged his shoulders. He wasn't at all sure he would like to be called an old bag of bones. He read a few more of the notes before finishing his morning deliveries. One of the notes was attached to a large plant and said: "Rachel, I know you'll miss him. I loved him, too. My thoughts are with you, Letty." He figured it was death, must be a death. He wondered who the "him" was, and wondered, too, about the women, what they were like. Maybe they weren't even friends. Maybe they were sisters. He wished he had more information. He enjoyed the morning deliveries, felt free because he was able to drive through the streets. His last delivery before heading back to the flower shop was a dozen yellow roses to a woman who worked on the fourteenth floor of a bank building. When he walked into the suite 1404, he showed the woman at the front desk the name on the card. He also flashed the card that informed her he was deaf. "I'll show you to her office," she said. He followed her down the hall and opened a door. He walked in, smiled at the woman, and held out the roses. Instead of taking the roses, she took the small envelope, opened it, and read the card. She said something to him, but her lips were difficult to read. He held the flowers in one hand, and showed her his card in the other. She nodded and said something else. He put down the flowers on her desk and wrote out on his pad: "Some people's lips are hard to read. I can't make out what you're saying." She smiled and nodded as she read his note.

"I don't want the flowers," she wrote on a piece of paper.

He nodded. "Don't you want to give them to someone?" he asked.

"If you could deliver the man who sent them to me, I'd make him eat them."

Diego laughed. "I understand," he wrote. He took the flowers and drove back to the flower shop. When he went home that afternoon, he was happy. He worked in the sun, he worked in the city and had contact with its people. He was grateful for the job, and he promised that he would go by the cathedral in the morning before work and light a candle in memory of Mundo. He would not forget his dead. When he got home, Luz was making dinner, and he read the paper at the table as she cooked. He looked up from the paper occassionally, and watched Luz hover over the stove.

"We need to buy a better kitchen table," she said. "Why don't you look in the ads to see if anyone's selling something reasonable?"

Diego turned to the ads and went through all of them. His eyes fell on the ad his sister had written. She was alive, she was back. He kept himself from trembling. He read it over and over. It was for him. He knew the address—it was the large white brick house on the corner of Yandell and Los Angeles. He had noticed that some people had moved into that house in early August. It had been run down and they had wasted no time in making it look friendly and welcoming. Before, he had always crossed the street when walking past it because he had thought it was haunted. But the people had given the house a new life and it seemed a happy place. Luz had mentioned that she had seen an old woman sitting on the front porch holding a baby—and that the woman had waved to her. If they were rich, he thought, at least they were friendly. *My sister, my sister lives in that house.*

"Is something the matter?"

Diego watched Luz move her lips. He shook his head. He did not want to tell Luz about his sister's ad. She would make him go. She would drag him over there, and make him face her immediately. But as he read and reread her ad, he realized he did not know if he wanted to go and see her. Lately, he had wanted her forgiveness, but he realized now that he was afraid to see her. After all this time, she had become a myth, a legend like Carlota's jewels. She was what he made her—but she was not real. What did he have to say to the real woman who was his sister? What if she would feel sorry for him? He did not want her to feel sorry for him—he wanted her to love him. The big white house was not far from where he and Luz lived. She was rich now. What did a rich woman want with a poor deaf man?

"What are you thinking, my Diego?"

"Nothing," he wrote, "my first day on my own tired me out."

"Eat," she said, "you have to eat."

He nodded. "I'll wash my hands," he wrote. He got up from the table, taking the section of the newspaper with the ads with him. He did not want Luz to see it. He placed it in his room. Luz never went in there.

That night, as he read in bed, he closed the book and stared at Maria Elena's ad. He cut it out and placed it in the book. Would she know him? He tried to imagine her life in that big house, he tried to imagine what a house like that looked like on the inside. Maybe she had married a gringo with lots of money, a gringo who did not want to have the poor inside his house. He would not go, he decided. She was dead to him, as dead as Mundo and Mary. He hoped she would place no more ads. If Luz saw it, she would make him go. He would not go. He would tell Luz it was too late for forgiving. What was a sister? He had grown accustomed to his exile. He belonged by not belonging. *I will not answer her ad.*

The next day, when he was sorting out his afternoon deliveries, Diego noticed his sister's address was on one of the cards. He moved the two dozen roses to the side and decided he would pretend to forget them. Maybe his boss or someone else would deliver them. He would not take them, he could not take them. It would be humiliating to deliver roses to his rich sister, who would feel sorry for him. Diego got in the van, but before he could drive away, his boss motioned for him to wait.

"You forgot these," he said.

There was no way out. Diego smiled and shrugged his shoulders.

"It's OK," his boss said. "Mistakes happen."

"I don't want to deliver these," Diego wrote.

"What?" his boss asked.

"It's just that those people are mean. I live around there—they act mean."

His boss read the note and nodded. "Well, that's none of our business, Diego. These flowers are paid for, and it's our job to get them there. They won't hurt you. You'll be fine."

Diego nodded and drove off. He was angry at his boss for having found him out. There was nothing to do except deliver the flowers. He would save that delivery for last, he thought. He would ring the doorbell and run away. Maybe the old lady would answer the door, and he would be spared from running into his sister.

At the end of the afternoon, only his sister's flowers remained. He stopped the van at the Circle K on Yandell and bought himself a soda. He lit a cigarette and smoked it. After he put out his cigarette, he decided to read the note that went with his sister's flowers. It was probably from her gringo husband. Who could it hurt? It was a very small transgression. He opened the envelope and read the card: "Maria Elena, You are water, you are rain. Te adoro, Eddie." He liked what the note said and he thought that maybe his sister had married a nice man. But what was that to him? He was surprised at his own anger. But he couldn't help but think of his sister, of her name—it was a good name. He wondered if she was happy, and wondered why she had written that ad and why she wanted to see him. Was his memory painful in her heart? He began feeling sad, but made himself stop thinking about her. It was no use. What was done was done. Luz had told him he had to stop regretting. "Forgive yourself," she said. "Why are you harder on yourself than God. Who do you think you are, anyway?" He smiled. *I will stop with all regrets. I am still young. Regrets will make me old.* He finished his soda and drove down the street to the big house. It was only a few blocks away. He would ring the doorbell, and if his sister answered, he would look down, hand them to her, and run away before she was able to see his face. He had the advantage in this game, he thought.

He pulled up in front of the house, carried the flowers carefully in his hands, remembering that his boss had told him that balance was everything when it came to the art of carrying flowers. He made himself stop shaking. He prayed Maria Elena would not answer the door. He concentrated on not dropping the flowers—it was his job to carry them—not drop them. Rather than reach for the doorbell with the flowers in his hands, he placed the flowers on the ledge to the front porch, made sure they would not fall, then reached for the bell. As soon as someone answered the door, he thought he would point to the flowers and run—yes, that is what he'd do. He waited for a long time, then decided to press the button again. After waiting a while longer, the door opened. His heart felt as if it would jump out of his body and free itself at last. He prepared to run. A young, pretty woman with white hair smiled at him. "Yes?" she said. "May I help you?" He was relieved. It was not her, he did not have to run, he could act normal, walk away, go home, eat his dinner with Luz, and live his life, a sisterless life he had grown accustomed to living. The woman looked at him carefully as though she was studying every pore on his face.

He pointed at the flowers on the ledge and smiled at her.

Lizzie looked and looked at the man's face again and again. She stared at him for a long time. I know this man, she thought. Where—where have I seen him? She trembled as she remembered a dream she had had before coming to El Paso. She remembered a face she had never seen, the face of a man, still young, a dark face with dark eyes and a look of ceaseless wonder, a look that was easy to read as a child's. And then she smiled.

Diego looked at her strangely. He shrugged his shoulders. He didn't feel like running anymore. This woman's face kept him frozen in place. He was not afraid in her presence, something about her was as calm as the late September air. He wanted to ask her what had happened to her hair, why she would not say anything, why she kept staring into his face, and why she was suddenly smiling. He looked down at his clothes to see if there was something on him. As he was staring at his shirt, he felt the woman's warm hand under his chin. She lifted it.

"Diego," she said.

He took out his pad and wrote. "How did you know my name? I don't know you."

"It came to me in a dream," she laughed. "Do you believe in dreams?"

Her lips were as easy to read as Luz's. "I have had too many dreams," he wrote.

She took him by the hand, "And will have many more," she said as she took him inside.

He looked back at the flowers.

"Leave them," she said. "We'll come back for them later."

When they stepped inside the house, Diego was overwhelmed at the size of it. He was suddenly afraid again. He knew this woman would be taking him to his sister. He stared back at the door. Why did this woman have this power, why was he letting her lead him? It was not too late—he could still run. He thought of his mother. He thought she would think him a coward—she who had been so brave. "Today is not a good day for running," he thought, "not a good day for raging at the past." He stared at this young woman with the old hair, not knowing what to do, what to feel, not wanting to run, not really wanting to do anything but be led by her. Diego saw her standing at the bottom of the stairs. She was yelling. He could not make out what she was shouting.

And then he saw Maria Elena coming down the stairs. In ten years she had changed very little. Her hair was still long and black, she was still small and thin. She wore a look that was at once warm and arrogant, a look he knew, a look he remembered. She stared at him from the top of the stairs. The white-haired woman held out her hand to her. "Come," she said. Diego could see her repeat the word. "Come." When she reached the bottom of stairs, she looked at Diego and began to tremble. Maria Elena placed her hands in front of her and signed: "Forgive me." She signed it again and again, signed it frantically as if she would not, could not stop until she received an answer. Diego walked closer and closer to her. He had even forgotten that she had learned to sign just to talk to him. In his anger, he had forgotten all the good things about his older sister. He took her hands and held them in his, though he could no longer see them. His eyes were full of a blinding water. They had been dry through Mundo's funeral, but now they were a river and he felt himself lost in it. He felt her arms tight around his neck. He felt her sobs in his body, sobs that were as good as any word he had ever desired to hear.

 **16**

LUZ WOKE AT SUNRISE. She walked down the stairs of the quiet house. It had been built as a place to dress up in, but now it looked more like a house to take off your shoes and walk barefoot. Maria Elena's tastes were simple—it was not a lady's house. Luz nodded approvingly as she stood in the kitchen. She put on a pot of coffee and wrote out a list of things to be done for the evening dinner. She had promised to make the best meal any of them had ever eaten—and she intended to keep her promise. She opened cabinets and took out every pot and pan she thought she might use. She looked over the spices and found there was nothing missing— everything she'd need was there: cinammon, dried chipotle, chile pasado, cominos, fresh garlic, oregano—even fresh cilantro. She smiled. Good spices in a kitchen brought good luck.

She sat down at the table and looked over her list, the taste of the fresh coffee hot and bitter in her mouth. Luz would send Jake to pick up two pounds of masa at the tortilleria. She had not made fresh corn tortillas a mano for a long time, but now that she was going to the trouble, she wanted the masa to be as fresh as possible. She had spent the previous two days making a big batch of mole for her enchiladas, and had taught Lizzie and Maria Elena how to make flan. "Mexican vanilla," she'd said firmly. "That's the secret— no other kind will do."

As she sipped her coffee, she let out a laugh. She was pleased with herself. "I'll make my tortilla soup," she thought. She laughed again. She looked around the kitchen. "Esta casa, no lo creo."

"Are you talking to yourself or to God?"

Luz looked up at Lizzie and laughed.

"It's too early to talk to God—he's still asleep."

"You should tell that to Maria Elena—she's already gone to morning Mass."

"Well, she's pregnant—women do crazy things when they're pregnant."

"I do crazy things without being pregnant."

"Oh, then you will be very fun when you get big."

Lizzie laughed. "I don't know if I ever want to be a mother."

"Ahhh," Luz nodded. "Well, it's good to be a mother—but there's enough of us already. And my sons, well, they threw me away. Maybe it's better you do something else. Only, don't ever get married. It's better to be a mother than to be a wife." Her arms waved in the air. Her palm hit the table emphatically as she said the word *wife*.

"What about lovers, then?" Lizzie asked.

"Lovers? Lovers are very good. Yes, take lovers." She moved away from the table as she spoke and poured Lizzie a cup of coffee. She placed it in front of her.

"I take sugar," she said.

"That's bad, Lizzie—drink it like God meant."

Lizzie smiled and took a drink from the cup. She nodded. "Did you have many lovers?"

"Not many. Enough."

"Enough?"

"Enough to know a lover is better than a husband. I had a husband, too, you know. He loved the bottle more than he loved me—and I was a fool because I loved him more than God. And my sons, they treated me like I worked for them."

"What happened to him—your husband?"

"They found him dead in the street. Trago, Lizzie, le gustaba tragar. Somebody stabbed him, but really it was the liquor."

"I'm sorry," Lizzie said.

490

"Oh don't be sorry—he had it coming. He was a thief. He finally stole from the wrong person and got caught. Sea por Dios." She crossed herself. "You die like you live."

"Yes," Lizzie said, "Yes. That's true." She understood clearly why Diego refused to abandon this woman when he moved into the house. The house was happier for her presence. Luz had immediately taken to enjoying her arguments with Eddie and Jake, and so far she had never lost one, and neither of the two brothers seemed to mind at all. Maria Elena had whispered that "the boys" had fallen in love with Luz because she reminded them of Esperanza—though Esperanza had been less pushy. She looked into Luz's face. "Would you like some help cooking tonight's dinner?"

Luz nodded. "But only you. Too many cooks in the kitchen—how do you say that gringo dicho?"

"Too many cooks spoil the broth."

"Yes—that one. Just you and me."

Lizzie laughed. She remembered having seen this woman in her dream; she had looked tired there. Now, she did not look so tired. She watched her as she walked over to the sink and began washing out the pots she had taken from the cabinets. She left the smell of lilac where she had been sitting. Lilac and cinnamon.

Diego sat at the head of the table as Luz brought in the last of the food she had spent the day cooking. The table was crowded with the colors of Luz's food, and the flowers Lizzie had brought in from the backyard. Luz had bought a new satin dress for the occasion, the deep green of the smooth fabric shining in the light of the candles that flickered at the table. The whole room smelled of spices and candles and chile.

"I'm so hungry," he signed to Maria Elena, who sat at his right.

She placed her hand on his cheek. "Me, too," she signed back, "the food looks incredible."

Diego tried not to stare at her, but he could not keep his eyes off of her. Maria Elena's skin looked as soft as the cotton dress she was wearing. She was lovelier now than she had been as a girl. Wrinkles were beginning to appear on her face—they gave her depth. He noticed Eddie taking her hand. "He holds it like a treasure," Diego thought. He decided that something about Eddie would always make him look like a boy—a boy whose heart was clear. Diego remembered the first time Eddie had shook his hand, and how strong and warm it was. He had hugged him, then kissed him on the forehead. That act had made Diego laugh. Eddie had laughed, too. He was a sincere man. It was easy to be around them, and he enjoyed watching the two of them exchange words.

As the soup was served, Diego warmed his hands over the steaming bowl. He squeezed a lime into the soup, then added cheese and cilantro. When he tasted it, he clapped his hands. He finished the soup slowly, each spoonful as good a thing as he ever put in his mouth—the taste of corn tortillas, the onions, the tomatoes, the garlic, the chicken overwhelming his hungry mouth. He noticed Jake and Lizzie, how they seemed to be so close—and yet not lovers. Jake used his hands a lot when he talked and Lizzie liked tugging at her earrings. She listened carefully. He thought they were very beautiful, and he caught himself wondering how many men had fallen in love with her. Maria Elena told him Lizzie's hair had turned white with terror and grief, but it was slowly turning back to its color.

He didn't feel like joining any of the conversations. He just wanted to sit and eat—and watch. He wanted to see the candlelight in the eyes of the people around him. Everything felt soft and dreamy and the thought occurred to him that nothing in the room was real. He shut his eyes and prayed everything would be the same when he opened them. Let this be real. When he opened his eyes again, Nena asked him what he was doing.

He shrugged.

"Do you feel OK, amor?" she asked.

Diego nodded and wrapped his hand around her arm. He continued watching the people at the table. He thought of his suicide note and how he would never work on it again, how it was something in his past. He thought of the coffin he had found in the mountains of Juárez and how he now knew what it meant. The future was death. He had seen the future in those bones, the unavoidable fact of the body, the human body that would inevitably return to the earth. He saw himself staring at the bones. There was so little time. But little as it was, it was time for living, time for belonging, time for falling out of love with his own exile. Luz and Eddie began arguing about something; she shook her finger at him. Eddie laughed and told her to behave. Already they were old friends. He could tell Luz liked him. She was happy in her green dress, proud of the dinner she had made, her labor. Luz looked young tonight. When they had all finished the soup, Jake picked up the bowls. He said something and everyone laughed, but Diego could not see his lips which were, even in the best of circumstances, difficult to read.

Maria Elena signed to him. "He said he was good at picking up plates—he used to be a waiter."

"Me, too," Diego signed. "I hated it. Luz helped me quit—and Mundo."

When Jake walked back into the room, he opened up a bottle of red wine and poured Diego's glass first. When he had finished going around the table, he raised his glass.

"To brothers and sisters," Eddie said. His lips so easy to read.

"To brothers and sisters," everyone repeated, their lips moving in unison. Diego felt something shoot through his body. When he saw Mary at the morgue, something had shot through him like hot water being injected into his veins. When Luz had left, when Mundo had been killed, he had felt this rush of heat in his body. Now, his blood was feeling something again. Only this time, he did not feel bad. He had never known this kind of warmth before. His deafness did not feel heavy tonight. Perhaps it would never feel heavy again. He smiled, raised his glass letting it tap against all the glasses in the room. For one long second, he thought he saw Mary and Mundo sitting at the table with them. He looked into all the eyes, smiled at all the faces. He drank.

17

IN THE LARGEST CEMETERY in Juárez, people were gathering at the gates. The vendors' carts were loaded down with cempasúchil, candied skeletons made of pure white sugar, and copal for burning on the graves and invoking the gods. It was a good day for buying flowers, a good day for burning incense. The November sky was clear and warm, the cloud of pollution blown away by a cool wind that had come in the night as fast and as sudden as the sword of St. Michael had come down on the devil. A circle of people hiding behind skull masks danced around a grave. A child licked a candied coffin as she watched the feet of the dancers.

Diego, Luz, and Maria Elena had risen early to visit the graves of their dead at Concordia Cemetery. Diego carried a hoe and a rake to clean the gravesites. Together, they went from grave to grave, from Mary's to Mundo's to Rose's. Diego raked the trash around each gravesite, intent and deliberate in his task. When Diego had finished raking, he pointed at a wall that encircled some nearby graves. "Chinese," he wrote on his pad and handed it to his sister. "Even in death," Maria Elena thought, "even in death, they separate them." She looked around the cemetery and noticed all the walled-

494

in sections. Walls and walls and walls. She laughed. She remembered what Luz had told Lizzie: "We die like we live."

After the work of cleaning, they placed flowers on the graves and knelt in respect for the dead. Luz prayed fervently for their souls. Maria Elena simply thanked her God for their lives. Diego tried to empty his heart of the anger he still felt at losing them. Today, he would not blame. Maria Elena smiled at the thought that went through her head: "I am in love with my rituals, in love with the people who created them, the people who handed them to me." No one attempted to speak. No one wept. They had not come here to mourn.

The house was empty for the afternoon. Everyone—Maria Elena, Diego, Jake, Eddie, Luz, and the baby—everyone had gone to the park because an autumn cool front had come in and the weather was perfect, the heat banished at last. "I'm not feeling well," Lizzie had told Maria Elena, though she had never felt better in her life. It was a small lie, she said to herself, everyone's entitled to a few small lies. When the residents of the house left, she walked slowly to her room, locked her door, looked out the window, and leapt out of her body as if she were a hungry leopard about to pounce on its prey. She felt as graceful as any animal, as any dancer, as graceful as her mother on her deathbed, graceful as Jake's heron in flight.

She traveled to Juárez to watch the people buy flowers for their dead. Hundreds and hundreds of people buying hundreds of bouquets of cempasúchil, the orange flowers as bright as summer desert sunsets. The burning copal filled her with something that almost resembled faith. She remembered the first time she'd smelled that incense—in a dream—in a dream she had once had, a dream where she had not had a body. She laughed into the air, and it did not matter that there was no sound. It was a laugh, a laugh that made her feel as bright as the flowers the people were bringing for their dead. *The next time I come here, it will be on foot.* She crossed back over the border—slowly, slowly—wanting to remember every single sight of the early November day. She found herself in front of her favorite tree—a tree where sparrows gathered for some unknown reason, hundreds and hundreds of them, sparrows who, having gathered, did nothing other than sing. They sing and sing, out of joy or sorrow, the reason not mattering since the beauty of the song was the same. There is so much to sing about, Lizzie thought. She entered the tree, the singing of the sparrows all around her. It was the music of the desert, she thought, a music she would miss. Lizzie had found this place when she had arrived, and it had given her comfort to be around the language of these birds. It had never mattered to her that she understood very little of what the birds were singing. The hearing of the song had been enough. She would miss coming here. In the distance she could see the statue of Mount Cristo Rey. Maria Elena had said it was a place of miracles, and so it was. She followed the path of the river for a while until she came to the place where some workers were at the beginning stages of building a stone wall. She stared at the working bodies of the men as they labored on the wall. She wondered why they were allowing themselves to be used like this, but she knew the answer. They needed to eat, needed to eat because their bodies demanded it of them. For the longest time Lizzie had not known whether she wanted to have a body or not. But now, a body was all she wanted. Her mother had been right: her body *was* her friend.

She willed herself to go back to her room, back to the house where she had found a place, a home. She rose from her bed, and walked out into the backyard. The ground beneath her feet was firm and solid and good. Lizzie sensed the cooling of the wind on her face. It was a lovely thing to have a face. The coolness was good. Winter was coming. Let it come, she thought. Winters were not so harsh in the desert, and she welcomed a change of seasons.

18

Maria Elena watched as her son picked himself off the floor and walked awkwardly toward her brother. He fell into Diego's arms, both of them laughing, neither of them able to hear the sounds they were capable of making. She kept herself from interfering in their games. Jacob Diego Marsh had instinctively been drawn to Diego from the first time she placed him in his arms. Her son would not grow up isolated and lost. He would never know the cruelty of his grandfathers, but she would speak of it to him to remind him that love—even among families—was something as rare as rain in the desert.

As Maria Elena watched her brother and her son explore each other's faces, she felt her husband's breath on her neck. He had been in the kitchen making dinner and his hands smelled of onions. "I'll set the table," he said. She nodded: "Be there in a minute." He kissed her cheek and walked back into the kitchen. She remembered the first time her little brother had reached out to touch her face. She had kissed his small hand, just as Diego was now kissing her son's little fingers. She felt the new life inside her. Lizzie and Luz had both agreed it would be a girl and she had decided on a name: Elizabeth Rose Ramirez Marsh. *I will teach her Spanish, Eddie will teach her English, and Diego will teach her to sign—and she will have no respect for borders.* Jacob Diego broke away from his uncle and made his way toward his mother. He grabbed her leg to keep himself standing up, then clutched it as if it were life itself.

 **19**

JAKE WALKED toward downtown in the early evening. He liked his roommates but he felt restless and impatient. As he walked down Yandell, he thought about Luz and how she was already making her mark on the house. That morning she had successfully convinced them to hire a maid. "It's honest work," she had argued, "and if you have money you can pay a good woman a decent salary. What the hell would I have done if no one had ever hired me? I would have starved to death—I would have been forced to work the maquilas—and they pay shit." Eddie had the good sense not to argue with her. "You hire her, then," he said. She'd clapped her hands and laughed. He liked the fight in her, understood her intelligent rage, knew instinctively how to read her moods. And Diego, Diego was kind and curious and had infinite patience. He looked a lot like Maria Elena and when he smiled he looked fragile and innocent, looked as though no one could ever touch or scar him. He had watched him the previous night as he held Jacob Diego in his arms. "I'm going to be his teacher," Diego had written on his pad. But he was becoming teacher to all of them, teaching all of them to speak his language—and sometimes the dining room was full of flying hands. Everyone but Luz was learning to sign because she claimed to be too old to be learning to make words with her hands. "And anyway, when I use my hands, you'll know exactly what I'm saying," she had said flatly. The house was happy and full and busy. Lizzie spent her evenings studying to take her state boards. Jake had noticed that her hair was returning to its natural color. He had mentioned it to her. She had smiled and said, "So it has." Maria Elena had started to show, and Eddie was writing down ideas on how best to spend their parents' money. Eddie had decided to open a good bookstore. He laughed as he remembered Maria Elena's response: "A bookstore? That's what you're going to do with thirty-eight million dollars? Keep working on the list, amor." Jake liked watching his brother and his wife. Their conversations kept him entertained. It was a good house, but tonight as he walked and thought of the people he lived with, he wished he could find a place for himself. It felt too much that he was just waiting to die. He wanted to stop waiting.

As Jake walked the streets of downtown he remembered the streets of another city. In San Francisco, he would go out just to walk—to look, to see, to watch the city breathe. As he walked down San Antonio Street, Jake realized he wasn't paying attention to anything but his own thoughts. I've lived a strange life, he thought, and still there is more. El Paso was beginning to fit like a favorite shirt; he liked the way it looked on him, wanted to wear it every day. He wanted desperately to find the thing in him that was killing him and rip it from his body with his bare hands. He wasn't sad, not tonight. All he wanted to do was live. He had never let himself belong to anything or anyone except Joaquin. But now he had a family. He belonged—and he wanted to belong. He was done with the business of separating himself from the world. He could feel himself smiling as he walked the warm pavements of the city. It was an ugly city, he thought—poor and ugly and polluted. Decay was everywhere on these streets. Jake thought of the ruins in Casas Grandes. That place, like his one, had been a city in the desert—and the desert had reclaimed it. He wondered if this city, too, was already turning to powder, to dust, to ash. This city could not erase desert, not the air-conditioned towers, not the layers of highway and concrete and asphalt, nothing could erase the fact of the desert. The desert would come back to reclaim what belonged to it, and El Paso would then and only then gain the knowledge of the walls at

Casas Grandes. But for now, the city kept the desert at bay like a cracked dam holding back the threatening water. For now, it was still a city. And what was a city, anyway, any city? It was just a cacophonous place he shared with a thousand other people, a thousand other people who fought with everyone else over the meanings of every word uttered in the meandering streets. Maybe the fight was all there was. Maybe that was why he instinctively liked Luz, because she enjoyed the hell out of the fight. Joaquin had been that way, too. Tom, too. He pulled out a cigarette and looked at his watch. It was early, the late afternoon sun making its way toward another place.

"Can I have one?"

He heard a tired voice and looked around the street. In the entry way to an abandoned building he had just passed, an unshaven figure sat wrapped in a dirty blanket.

"A cigarette," the voice said, "you got an extra one?"

"Sure," Jake said. He walked toward the figure and handed him a cigarette and a book of matches. He could see that the man was not very old—certainly no more than thirty. The man trembled as he lit a cigarette.

"It's good," the man said, "real good." His thin hands shook. He looked unhealthy and as worn out as an old dirt road. "So cold today," he said.

Jake nodded, though he was sweating even in his thin cotton T-shirt. "Are you OK?" Jake asked.

"Can't you read?" the man asked pointing at the sign at his feet.

Jake stared at the sign: SICK WITH AIDS. AIN'T NO QUEER—JUST AN ORDINARY JUNKIE. SPARE CHANGE WELCOME.

He was surprised the sign did not offend him. There was a time he would have hated that man—disease or no disease. There was a time when an anger would have swept over him, an anger so uncontrollable that it knew nothing but destruction. But today the sign did not make him angry. Jake simply read it as if the words had lost their power over him. "So did you make any money today?" He asked.

"Not much. Five bucks maybe. Don't matter. Today, I just can't make myself care 'bout nothin'."

500

"Where do you sleep?"

He pointed at the empty building. "Back door," he said.

Jake nodded. He placed a ten-dollar bill in the man's cigar box. The man nodded. "You rich or somethin'?"

"Yeah—I'm rich."

"Never cared none for rich folk."

"Me neither," Jake said flatly. He tried to make out the color of the man's eyes—somewhere between blue and green. "How come you tell people you got that disease?" he asked.

"It's in, man. People like to give to things that are in—get it?"

"You're not really sick with it, then?"

"Wish I wasn't. People don't touch me anyways—what's the difference?"

"Yeah. What's the difference?" Jake lit another cigarette and kept walking down the street. He tried not to think of what the man had written on his sign, I AIN'T NO QUEER . . . To their dying day they'll hate us, he thought. He took a deep drag from his cigarette. He walked the streets for an hour, the shadows getting longer and longer. He tried not to think of Rose and the hurt look on Lizzie's face as they buried her at the cemetery, tried not to think of Joaquin. Jake tried to think of something good. He thought of his nephew. He thought of Maria Elena and the baby she was carrying. He thought of Tom. He'd started a letter to him, but somehow had not managed to finish it because he did not know what to say to him.

Jake walked toward the Santa Fe Bridge. He gave the woman a quarter at the small station. It was like paying to see a movie, he thought—but here the price of admission was cheap. He slowly walked across into Mexico. At the top of the bridge he stared at the river below—the water hemmed in by the cement. It was a chained animal, an animal that had been kept tied up for so long that it had forgotten how to be itself—all it knew was this captivity. "Goddamn us all," he said. He looked back at El Paso, behind him now. From here, the tenements, the poverty of the barrio was invisible. From here, it looked almost pretty, but he had just been walking on some of those streets and he refused to think of it as pretty. He watched the vendors selling their goods to the cars making their way back to El Paso. They were children—most of them—children. Some of them no more than six years old. They ran and laughed and held up candy and crucifixes and colored cloths. He remembered that Joaquin had once told him that he would never know what it was like to be poor. His remark had made him angry, but as he watched the children, dirty and skinny from spending too much time trying to sell items that were not worthy of them, he realized the truth of what Joaquin had said. Jake had been without many things in his life—but he had never known what these children knew—and they did not even know they knew anything at all. He watched them play hide-and-seek between the cars, watched them playfully tag each other. Their games did nothing to comfort him. "The poor but happy children," he said to himself, then laughed. "Goddamn us to hell." Perhaps the death he carried within him was making him soft, but now, he didn't mind the softness. He didn't want to be hard anymore—it was too much work, a kind of work that he could no longer continue because, like the items the children sold, it was not worthy of him. There, at the bridge, Jake nodded. He remembered how Joaquin had died cursing the idea of borders. It was dementia, he had thought at the time, a man speaking nonsense, a man losing his mind. But there, at the bridge, he understood what borders were for: They were there to keep these children out. He remembered how he had once lectured Joaquin, "We can't feed everybody." And he remembered his stubborn answer: "Why the hell not, gringo? The Incas did it—what the hell's wrong with us that we can't?" Jake felt tears running down his face. He knew why the tears were there: He had lived so many years with a good man, and he had not fully understood the meaning of that good man's life.

Jake walked slowly into Juárez, turned around and walked back into the United States. Today, he did not have the stomach to play tourist. When he declared his citizenship to the gatekeeper, he was ashamed, but he knew it was not a bad thing to feel the shame. He headed back to Sunset Heights. He found himself back on San Antonio Street in front of the queer-hating junkie. *They will hate me with their dying breaths—but I—I do not have to hate them. I do not have to hate.* The man was now lying on the ground. "Hey," he said, "are you OK?"

"No, man, I ain't never gonna be OK again." His voice was distant and he trembled as he spoke.

"Are you cold?" Jake asked.

The man nodded, his head too heavy now for his body.

"You need some help getting inside this building?"

"I'm tired, man. I just want to sleep. I just want to fall asleep."

"I'll carry you," he said. He remembered the night when he'd carried Joaquin to the hospital and he remembered what he'd said. "Like water." He picked up the man who was small and frail and weighed no more than a hundred pounds. It was not a difficult thing to carry him. The man remained completely passive in Jake's arms, but he hung on to the sign he had made, clutched it in his hands as if it were life itself. Jake made his way slowly up the hill toward Sunset Heights from downtown, the man who smelled of old sweat and urine in his arms. People stared at them as he walked. Jake just smiled. When he reached the house, he rang the doorbell. Lizzie answered the door. "He's sick," he said.

Lizzie stared at his sign. "We can put him upstairs," she said, "In the ballroom." She took the sign out of his hand. "He'll need a bath first. I'll run the water. You want to help me bathe him?" she asked.

"Why not?" he answered.

Jake stared at the piece of paper on his desk. He didn't know how to begin the letter. The only thing he'd ever written was a diary addressed to his brother, and that had been easy to write because it had been only for himself. He had not even let Joaquin read it. But now he wanted to write a letter to Tom, wanted to tell him about his new life. He wanted someone who had known him when he was someone else, wanted someone to know that rage had not had the final say. Jake took a drink from his glass of wine. He placed the pen on the white stationery his brother had given him:

Dear Tom,
Today, I committed an act of kindness . . .

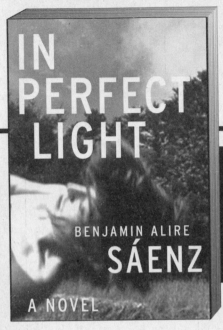